The Jellyfish Device

Near-Future Science Fiction

William Marshall

NOREMAC

Contents

Jade

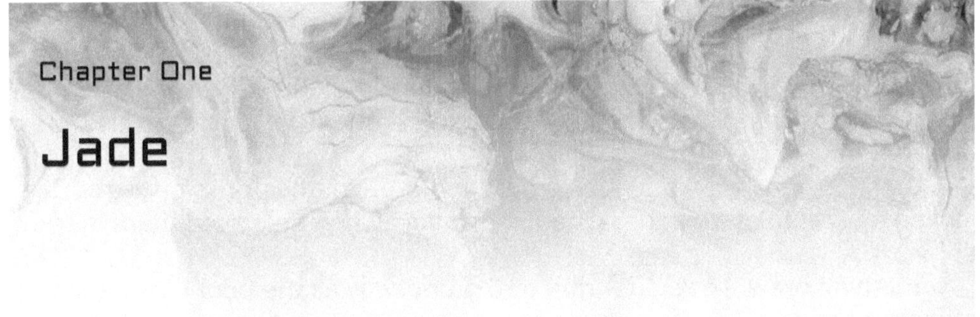

Jade slide the shot glass across the bar in the transactional manner of a drug deal, as the twenty-one-year-old seed of a new money robber baron, evolved from an amoeba, to a tadpole, to a long-tailed amphibian, a reptile, primate, and finally human fetus—raised with a silver spoon by a suspiciously pregnant Filipina nanny, sent to all the finest European schools, horse riding academies, and an orthodontist—splattered down the front of her bar.

Jade was instinctively suspicious of barons, but she didn't notice the profound sense of entitlement, which was the hallmark of his caste.

"I'll have two Cancun Sunrises, please," the man said with the easy speech of someone who already had one or two.

Jade assembled the Blue Curaçao, then the green Absinthe, the yellow Galliano, and finally the Vodka.

"I like your costume," he said. "Are you Mitzu Girl?"

Jade leaned forward to be heard over the booming beat of the synsing music and noticed the fragrance of his hair product. "How did you guess? Have you seen it?"

"Yeah, my big sister used to watch it. The costume looks really good on you." He looked her up and down. Jade had full, painted-on Kewpie doll lips, and perfect figure, but her cat-like eye makeup gave her a predatory look. She could tell he was attracted to her and was using the costume to compliment her body without being overtly sexual. She appreciated his tact and didn't mind since he wasn't bad-looking either.

I wonder if he suspects? Jade thought.

"My name's Alan McPherson," the baron said, and held out his hand, flashing a winning smile—the best money could buy.

Jade shook his hand and said, "Hi, I'm Jade Yang," then poured the first blue layer in the glass's bottom.

She poured the green absinthe so it floated on the blue. Jade told him a bit more about Mitzu Girl and dribbled the yellow Galliano liqueur and topped it with the clear vodka and a few clouds of coconut cream. The different liquors settled, creating bands of color like the Caribbean Ocean meeting the sky.

Jade thought he looked like a college boy, probably in his third year. She offered the payment terminal, and he briefly held it to his face until the small light indicated recognition. He selected the tip amount using his smart contact lenses and tapped the ubiquitous eight centimeter long WON, which was strapped to his wrist. Jade's handset blinked to show he completed the transfer. A nice tip, but not so big to imply payment for anything else. Well done.

Alan made his way through the crowd and brought the drinks back. His date looked up at him as he approached and smiled when he placed them in front of her.

Something drew Jade's attention to the doorway as the bouncers let in two mismatched men. She had never seen them before but recognized the way they carried themselves. They were here on a mission. The taller man had short, dirty-blonde hair and a tweed jacket with a long, deep blue overcoat. The other had long black hair and an insulated synthetic denim jacket. They sat at a table behind Alan and ordered drinks from the server. They talked little but leaned forward and spoke in hushed tones and made furtive glances at Alan. The short one nodded slightly, and the taller stood up in a smooth motion while reaching deep into the inside of his overcoat. His arm withdrew, holding an industrial appliance vaguely resembling a metal broom handle with a gun trigger, and moved towards his target—Alan.

In unison, Jade's arm rose and straightened toward the man with the gun. A pellet, moving too quickly to be seen, made a beeline from a tube under her wrist, directly towards the face of the man with the gun. Centimeters before making contact, the pellet exploded like the crack of a whip, ejecting microscopic flechettes. She vaulted over the bar and launched herself at the tall man like a cheetah, with her long cape flowing behind, as she dodged the tables and chairs in her path. Her eyes locked on her prey.

After the cracking sound, the wrist of the tall man cocked, the zip gun slipped away and thudded to the antique wooden floor as a guttural roar emerged from his throat and his legs gave out. In full panic mode, he screamed louder than the music and clawed at his face—kicking and rolling like a man doused with gasoline and set ablaze. Jade grabbed his gun and pointed it at him. Alan was cringing, realizing the gun was meant for him. The gunman's writhing slowed as he passed out. The red threads in his scratched face formed a drop on his nose before it drooped, sagged, elongated, snapped loose, and dropped to the floor.

Strangely, there was no sign of injury from the pellet. Jade stood over him with the gun in her hand, wondering what she had done. This is not what she expected and wondered if she might have killed him. He started moaning, and the bouncers dragged him out the door by his feet and his moans got louder. The short man had already bolted at the first sign of trouble. The music stopped and everyone's eyes were on Jade...

Yeah, may be a good time to take my break, she thought.

Jade announced, "Nothing to see, just a man with epilepsy. Enjoy the rest of your night."

People applauded, thinking this was a superhero act in keeping with the theme of the bar. Calm was again restored and people began talking among themselves as the music resumed.

She took the hay-wire gun into the back room and had a closer look at it. It had two springs attached on each side to a round piece on the back that was connected to the barrel with two sliding steel rods. Machine nuts tack welded to the barrel guided the rods. She assumed that the round piece was a primitive firing pin, and when she pulled it back, she saw it was. She pointed it at the floor and lowered the pin slow and easy, trying not to detonate the shell. It was lucky it didn't go off when the man dropped it.

Jade Yang worked in the Harakiri Bar on Whyte Avenue in Edmonton. This was her first job after returning from living with her gangster brother in Vancouver, and it was her first straight job ever. Since it was an anime bar, she dressed in character. Her straight blonde wig was cut in bangs and draped down her shoulders with tresses over her chest. She wore a short dark gray Greco-Roman pleated skirt, black thigh-high patterned stockings and a long black cape fastened with a gold chain. She was toned and taller than the average Chinese woman and she had a veiled strength that a confident man found alluring, while others found threatening.

Today, she started work at 8:00 p.m. like she did every evening since she started two weeks ago. She was new enough that she enjoyed working there and liked the normalcy of going to a regular job, having her own apartment, and starting something like a typical life.

The boss provided her "uniforms" comprising various costumes that spanned the range between childish to fetishistic, but she enjoyed them all because they helped her get outside of herself for a while. Tonight, she was wearing her favorite, her alter-ego, Mitzu Girl. Depending on the costume, she wore more makeup than normal—some foundation, dramatic color on her cheeks, glitter under her eyelids, and heavy shadow and liner in the corners for a feline appearance. She wore three-tone glossy lipstick with pink on the top of her upper lip, yellow around the inner part of her lips that faded to red on the bottom.

The customers continued to file in. They were a general cross-section of the different subspecies of homo sapiens in Old Strathcona, including students and staff from the nearby university, townies that ranged from young to middle-aged, as well as starving artists and alternative types. The default was cis hetro, but all different sexualities were welcome here and represented with colored armbands hoping to meet like-minded individuals. All came and took shelter from the growing intolerance and division of the outside.

Jade had mixed feelings about the students. She always thought she wanted to graduate from university, but she was cheated of the opportunity, or squandered it, depending on her mood. Although the students were her peers, she realized she was different. She remembered when she went for a walk in the fall on the University of Alberta campus among the lemon poplar and scarlet maple trees to enjoy the sun and the color against the deep azure sky.

A young man in a sweater walked up to her and asked if she needed help. It was the help you get offered by the store clerk worried you will steal something. *Was it really that obvious I didn't belong there? I suppose it was*, she answered herself. *Oh well, I'm good at other things and I have a PhD in Ass Kicking.* That was a skill she could always fall back on.

It shouldn't have been her responsibility to spot trouble in the bar. It was the bouncers', but the manager knew enough about her to recognize that she could do more than serve drinks. Besides, she couldn't turn it off, even if she wanted to—and on nights like tonight, she really, really did.

It was a long day. She took off her wig and placed it on the Styrofoam head in the changing room and washed the garish makeup off her face and put on her regular clothes. She looked in the mirror and brushed her hair away from the shaved side of her head and reapplied her makeup. It was more than usual for the bus home, but she was going to pay a visit to the man who gave her that bizarre pellet gun.

She put on a navy-blue turtle-necked sweater and black jeans. For accessories, she wore black wrist cuffs with leather tassels and a small gold-chained jade Buddha necklace. Finally, she put on her high-tech winter jacket, leather gloves, and heeled winter boots and she was ready to go into the bitter cold. She pulled back her left sleeve and watched her WON as the blue dot approach her location on the map while she walked to the bus stop.

The bar was 140 years old and had the original brick exterior. It used to be a hotel, but now the upper floors were apartments. She could barely decipher the numbers 1912 in the sandstone peak. It was part of a clutch of well-maintained original buildings, among nests full of broken eggs. She walked further west, two new buildings bravely grew from the ruins like daisies in a junkyard, while others became populated with tents for commerce, living, or dying.

The polar vortex arrived late this year and greenhouse gas current invaded the Arctic, destabilized the cyclonic air like a wonky tire and pushed it south, over the middle of North America where it gripped everyone and everything in its thermometer imploding grasp. The temperature dropped to minus thirty-five. It was the kind of cold that leaves you coughing at the chill air shocking your lungs. She wrapped a scarf around her mouth and forehead, leaving a slit for her eyes.

She stepped on the compacted snow and finished the two blocks to the bus stop. Nodules of frost grew on the scarf over her nose and mouth like tiny grains of popcorn, and even her eyelashes turned white. She stopped and waited for the bus. The mournful groans of snow plows scraping Calgary Trail echoed from way off in the distance. Steam from her breath rose to the streetlight above, swirling like a nebula in space. The skin above her nose stung as the cold dug in with crystal daggers, making her eyes water. The cold burned her thighs, and she wished she had brought snow pants.

The app told the driverless bus a new passenger was waiting, and a few minutes later, it pulled up to the stop and opened the door. Jade was beat, and she slouched against the wall of the bus, absorbing the feeble warmth radiating from the built-in heaters. The cold had frozen the bus's shock absorbers and hardened the tires, and every ice rut gave her a jolt.

By the looks of it, the other passengers were leaving a bar too, and beer pouches rolled across the floor as the bus accelerated or braked. The smell of beer breath and vomit filled the air and a young couple beside her was necking and their hands were all over each other in exaggerated, drunken gestures. Jade winced at the wet noises and glared at them, but they were oblivious to her disapprobation, so she gazed out the window and tried to ignore them. Her stop was next, so she pressed the yellow strip overhead to alert the navigation system she needed to get off.

"Next stop Whyte Avenue and 111 Street," announced the synthesized female voice.

She could take the bus to Kevin's apartment without a transfer, since it was only eight blocks west on Whyte Avenue, in the historic Garneau neighborhood. The bus slowed to a halt. She was glad to get away from the other passengers and walked the last two blocks to Kevin's building, getting more worked up as she got closer and thinking of the weapon he made for her. *Why didn't he tell me how it works? Was he just using me as a guinea pig?*

Hanging from the front of Kevin's apartment building was a sign with Reeves Manor written in old English font. Two simulated wrought iron lanterns illuminated each side of the door and gave off a sallow light. Jade always deconstructed the layers of history piled up upon this old building. The wooden siding inside the tenuous fire escape was from its original use as a seminary and the cracking brick facade was from its conversion to a nurse's residence before it was converted to its final use as an apartment building. Further repurposing was not in the cards. Its fading grandeur was like an aged debutant using face creams and home remedies to hide the irreversible decline into senility and death.

A young woman sat on the steps. Her skin was vaguely luminescent blue, as if lit from an internal source. Her expression was vacant, and she did not react as Jade climbed the spalling concrete stairs of the entrance and pressed the retrofitted buzzer for Kevin's apartment. The camera scanned Jade's iris and her name appeared on the display. She sensed that the young woman was a protector, and watched her get up and walk away across the street, looking far into the distance. Jade tried to shake off an uncanny feeling and stepped inside, and the ancient wooden door closed behind her with a solid click, leaving a swirling cloud of vapor outside.

Jade stormed across the brick entrance and down the stairs to his basement apartment.

"What the fuck was that? You said it would just knock someone out!"

"Pass-out, knockout, what's the difference?" Kevin replied, as he led her deeper into his home.

"You're a real asshole," said Jade. She took off her boots and marched in past the boxes and techno-litter scattered on the floor. "I thought I killed him."

"Maybe you'd rather go back to splattering people's brains all over the wall?" Kevin responded. Jade had nothing to say to that and collected her thoughts.

"Seriously, what was that thing?"

"If you would've just given me time to explain when I gave it to you—it's an air pellet gun. I put a tiny laser diode in the pellet to determine distance to the target and it can detect if it was going to hit cloth or skin. If skin, a small charge will shoot the nanoflechettes towards the target, so they spread out in a shotgun pattern and the casing disintegrates like powder. If it's going to hit fabric, it'll stay together until its pointed tip penetrates the cloth. Then, the pellet injects needles into the skin. If you miss the target, the pellet knows this and I programmed it to immediately detonate, so they'll probably get hit with a few needles anyway."

"How could the needles hurt so much but hardly leave a mark?"

"The needles are too small to cause bleeding, and I impregnated them with synthetic poneratoxin from the bullet ant. The venom acts directly on the nerves but doesn't burn, so there isn't any redness or swelling. It's the most painful venom known to man. It was tweaked to wear off in an hour instead of the usual twelve, and the needles dissolve under the skin so there won't be any abscess. I got the venom from another mechanic friend on Gray Market. He cooked it up himself with a DIY krunch printer that pokes the ant's DNA into yeast cells. For him, it's almost as easy as making home-brew beer and isn't even *very* illegal yet. Not that it really matters anymore."

They sat at Kevin's table, and he swept the bits of wire and drops of solder on the floor with his forearm.

"It's worse when you get shot in the eyes, nose, mouth, or penis. As you saw, you totally lose your shit when you get slapped with one of these. The only antidote is local anesthetic. It's a good thing you got to his gun, or he might have blown his own head off. If you shoot someone in the dick, take away his knives, unless you're into watching what will happen next."

"Shut up. I do what needs to be done—I'm not sick," Jade said. She paused then explained the entire story about the two who tried to kill or capture Alan.

"Who were those clowns anyway?" Kevin asked.

"I'm not sure. The college boy was a baron, so one of the other families might be trying to get him."

"I hope they don't come after you now."

Kevin's expression showed his anxiety, and his voice, his concern. He was really worried about her. She hadn't really thought about him as boyfriend material until now. He seemed so busy tinkering or doing whatever he does and thought about him as a friend or brother. She could look after herself, but she had a soft spot for men who showed they cared for her. It had been a long time since she enjoyed the company of a man, and she managed to get the last one killed before they had a chance to go to bed. She told herself she had forgotten about sex, but still there was an undeniable physical ache.

Kevin was a handsome guy, five foot eleven, black hair cut short on the sides and long on top. He brushed it to the right and sometimes it hung over his bright green eyes, giving him a rakish look. He was slim and wiry like an actual mechanic, strong from tightening bolts. She was fascinated with the sinewy ridges on his military tattooed arms and shoulders and desired to trace her fingers along the lines of muscle in his forearm.

"Would you like some wine?" he asked.

"Sure, thanks."

They sat on the couch and Kevin chatted about his experiences. "Universities are basically country clubs for upper-class kids. I could never afford to get a degree, and who needs it. Any course you can think of is online for free and I take them all the time. Besides, I've never had a client ask me if I have a degree," he laughed.

"I got into a really awful fight with my dad when I was strung out. I was trying to stop him from beating my little brother like he did me. The RCMP arrested me *and* the Staff Sergeant of the local RCMP detachment volun-told me to join the army and go to Ukraine for a couple of years... *Or go to jail. Do not pass go, do not collect $200*, whatever that means. They needed people with my skills to join the reserves in Six Intelligence Company for a two-year hitch overseas. It didn't seem too bad. My dad made me go to cadets in the Signal Corps when I was little, so didn't think it would be that much different. How hard could it be?" Kevin shrugged, but Jade could see there was pain lurking behind his glib acceptance."

"How hard was it?" she asked.

Kevin took a deep breath and looked off into space for a second. "It had its moments."

Jade noticed his expression become more pensive and realized there was more to it. She wanted to know, but didn't pry.

"Your parents were rich. Why didn't *you* get a degree?" Kevin asked.

"They weren't *really* rich," Jade said, shaking her head. "I tried to, but I couldn't concentrate. When I was supposed to be listening to the lecture, I was only scanning the other students, reading them for threats, but also reading their emotions. In my first class, I didn't know how many unhappy girls there were. I'm not judging or anything, but it was kinda surprising. They've had such perfect lives but have problems too."

He reached forward and touched the opposite wall, and the aging display blinked on. "Wanna watch a tube?"

"Sure. How about the winner from Dance Dance."

They finished the wine, and he walked to the kitchen to refill their glasses.

"Can you put it in holo mode?"

"Sure. TV, holo-mode," he commanded.

The image froze, then the dancer popped away from the wall and seemed to hover. Kevin's TV was old, so the processor was not strong enough to maintain a holographic image the size of the full screen and it collapsed the image to half its size. The announcer discussed their standings while the TV displayed a still image of the girl standing sideways but looking toward the camera.

She wore a revealing costume and was petite and fair-skinned with long auburn hair tied up in the top. Her partner was a bare-chested young man, tall, with coffee and cream complexion. The routine was passionate, explosive, and sensual, with the soundtrack of Latin rhythm. Jade watched with awe at the start, when the girl sat on his hand, raised above his head, then fell down as he scooped her up to bring her to the floor on her feet. She somersaulted through the air in an impossibly tight spin. The man held her legs and spun her like a ball on a rope while she rose and fell with each turn, a fraction of an inch from her head crashing into the floor then swinging back up. She danced like she was his plaything, but he was only there to display her. It was dangerously fast, yet so graceful. Jade did a little seated dance and mimicked the salsa moves where she would thrust her hips to the side while holding her hand flat against her lower tummy.

"Wanna dance?" Kevin shoved his work junk against the wall, and she took his hand. He stepped onto the rug. "What music would you like?"

"Do you know salsa?"

"Not really, but I'll give it a try." He turned toward the TV. "TV, play salsa dance music."

"You should really get out more. Let's start with the basics. You step forward on one foot, and back with the other. Try that a few times."

Kevin watched Jade moving back and forth and tried to follow her. He took two steps forward and messed up.

"You step forward with your left foot, then step in place with your right. See? Then step back with your left and pause for one beat. Step in place with your left foot. Step back with your right foot and step in place with your left. To finish, bring your right foot back for another count. There are eight counts altogether. Now you step with me."

"Sorry, this isn't going very well." Kevin looked embarrassed but kept trying.

"You're doing fine."

They stood side by side, and Kevin watched Jade's feet and copied her steps. He found the rhythm, and Jade turned to face him.

"See, you're doing it!" Jade said. "Now hold my left hand and put your other hand on my back."

They kept moving back and forth. Jade smiled and looked into his eyes like the women in the dance competition. Kevin still looked at his feet, as if he didn't know where they were. Jade was feeling the buzz from the wine and was enjoying the dance and enjoying it with Kevin. She could feel his confidence and ability build, and he led her into a twirl. She spun out and then he spun her back in. Their lips met and paused before she realized what she had done. She pulled away and held her finger to his lips.

Her body was warm, electric, and sparkled from his touch. Her loins tingled like a magnetic field enveloping him and drawing him closer, but she was afraid to give into her desires. More than that, she was afraid of telling him who she really was. She had to leave—fast.

Chapter Two

Kevin

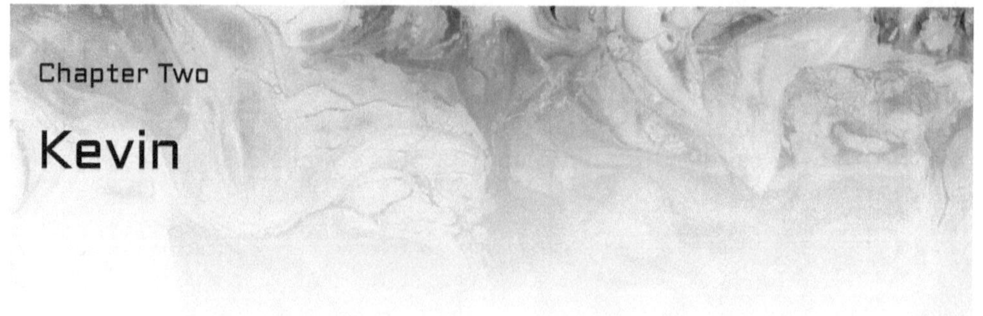

Kevin woke with a warm feeling as memories from the previous night came washing back over him. Jade *was* the most beautiful woman, but the one thing he liked most about her was that she seemed completely unaware of it. He remembered the first time he met her; he was going to sit on the far side of the bus, away from everyone until the fates intervened and a strange young woman with blue luminescent makeup put her bag on the bench seat, taking up all the room. Instead, Kevin sat beside Jade, and their conversation started as naturally as if they had already known each other for years. She had the puffy eyes of a girl awakened early in the morning. She didn't usually smile, but never looked sad—like a badass model. He remembered her rounded lips and how they felt briefly touching his, but why did she leave so suddenly?

What he knew of her past didn't bother him either, since he hadn't exactly led a perfect life. Besides, in his line of work, it would be hypocritical to be judgmental and he didn't like hypocrites.

Last night was like a vacation from the cold existence of his regular life. Why couldn't *every* day be a vacation? Well, why not? He used to get a rush from scraping a living out of doing things no one else can do. Selling home-made secure communicators to street gangs, bootleg drones to barons or surveillance to anyone who will pay for it. Until now, he didn't care about what was right or wrong and just wanted to be left alone, but he was tired of the wolf at the door and wondered what it would be like having a real job and a steady squeeze.

Kevin made a bowl of Shreddies and milk as he did most mornings. *Mmm bachelor chow*, he thought and added a heaping tablespoon of brown sugar. Three cups of black coffee later and he decided a double-double or latte was for people who didn't really like coffee but drank it anyway. Enough daydreaming. It was time to hit the books. Kevin was studying an open course from a university in Connecticut. It wasn't related to his trade, but he had many interests, and he was between clients and had time for a detour.

Ironically, he liked to study to stop from thinking–about things he would rather not think about. He was taking another course on cryptocurrencies and this one was called *The Rise of Crypto* and the chapter he was reading was called

Cryptocurrency in Canada. It was about the accidental rise of Canadian dollar backed cryptocurrency, called loonies, to become the world's reserve currency.

He considered himself more of a small-picture person and was interested in the details of how things worked. When he was a kid, he would spend hours on Wikipedia reading articles on everything from animals to munitions to electronics. He would become fascinated with something and read everything he could find and imagine how he could solve some scientific problem or make discoveries that would make him famous. When he was five, he drew a picture of a robotic human leg which would turn him into the fastest man in the world. All he came up with was a design for a hinged rod with an electric motor that somehow made the leg bend back and forth. He realized inventing was going to be harder than he thought, but he didn't give up.

When he was eleven, he was obsessed with new crowd-funded, low-budget hacker rockets. He dreamed of building rockets and launching them into space. He played behind his house on the dusty prairie and picked up a stick and threw it into the sky like a rocket, imagining the heat of the engines blasting against his face as it accelerated and disappeared into a dot in the azure Saskatchewan sky. His heart raced, and he leaped into the air with boyish glee, grinning from ear to ear. He spread his arms and imagined looking down at the curvature of the Earth and down on his home somewhere in North America, which filled the horizon from coast to coast. Dressed in a spacesuit from the Apollo missions, he quipped data with glib confidence to his imaginary Mission Control.

When he was twelve, he had a go at rocket building himself. While cooking chemicals for the solid-fuel rocket engine in a tin can on the stove, they ignited and he dropped it and spilled molten cherry-red pools of erupting, hissing rocket fuel on the kitchen floor, and white smoke and the stench of burning vinyl filled the kitchen. He panicked and spooned up the molten drops and put them back in the can and tried to suffocate the fire by holding his hand over the top. The compression built up like in a barrel of a cannon and pushed burning gases onto his hand. The pain was intense, but he still did his best to scrape out the burn marks on the old linoleum flooring.

His parents came home, and the smell startled them, and they found the burn marks on the kitchen floor. "Kevin! Get your ass over here! Damn it! You could've burned the house down! What the *hell* are you tryin' to prove! I should put you out on the street," his dad yelled.

Kevin stood there mute with his hand closed in a cup shape. He stood wide-eyed as his dad continued to rip him to shreds. Still screaming, he took his belt off to flog his son. The searing pain was not as bad as his fear of his father finding out he had not only burned the floor but also burned his hand.

"WHAT are YOU hidin'! What's in your hand!" His father demanded, so he slowly opened his hand, revealing the large patch of oozing, blackened skin.

"Oh my Goodness! What have you done to yourself!" His mother rushed in, holding the back of his hand to examine the palm. Her face was a mixture of anger and horror.

His dad calmed down, put his belt back on, but still permanently grounded him from the rocket business. His parents were clearly overreacting, and he dreamed of the day that he would be old enough to have his own house in the country, complete with a bunker for launching rockets.

By 2045, the amateur hacker-scientist network made some progress in bringing Kevin's dream to life. Graphene and 2DPA-1 plastic had become cheap and available, and they could use it to construct composite resins with 3D printers for rocket parts. The engine was the most expensive part, but ceramics technology had also improved to where they could afford to buy them. The electronics were off-the-shelf and cost a fraction of what NASA used to pay when they were in the business. Kevin did some of his own research into electronics and robotics and became a regular and respected contributor to online forums. No one knew he was just thirteen.

Kevin's father began beating his younger brother like he had beaten Kevin, and one day, when Kevin was seventeen, he came home late one night, strung out from a meth jag, and saw his eight-year-old brother with a black eye. Kevin couldn't let that happen to Jimmy. Not again. Years of resentment and rage towards his father boiled and burst out of him. He lost it on his still sleeping father, jumping on him and punching him in the face, over and over. His dad tried to get up, but Kevin punched him back down. When his screaming mother covered his father with her own body to protect him, Kevin came to his senses and sat down to wait for the RCMP and ambulance to arrive.

It was decided by the powers that be, it would be in Kevin's best interest to join the army and go to Ukraine rather than go to jail and become a hardened criminal. When he was overseas, he found out intelligence was a gig he was good at. Online research and hacking got him information he needed from the virtual world, but often that wasn't enough and he had to go out into the real world. Being a gumshoe wasn't different from being a hacker. It was just a different interface.

Social engineering, monkey in the middle, and other hacking techniques were all a normal part of his tool belt. Hacking was basically a victimless crime as long as you didn't break anything, as far as he was concerned. Sure, it was against the laws of society, but what did society ever do for him?

Often, his tinkering skills helped him put together a few very useful tools that weren't available off the shelf. Since he was a kid, he liked to take things apart and put them back together. He especially liked electronics. If you take apart an old TV you can take the pile of resistors, transistors, capacitors and processors and use them to make any number of different projects. If there was a part he didn't have, he could buy it cheap off the web.

To him it was almost like sorcery; you take a transistor from a freshly harvested corpse, a dab of melted lead, upload a sprinkling of tweaked code, connect it all to a magic servo-waver remote thing-a-ma-jig under the light of a full moon and POW— *it's alive!*

Another day passed, and Kevin woke and glanced at the clock on his computer screen already reading 8:00 a.m. The sun was straining through the accumulated grime that splashed outside his small basement window. The seal had long gone, and vapor trapped between the layers of glass had condensed, dripped, froze, and thawed like yesterday's mistakes and today's regrets. Tomorrow was another story and he hoped he had reached a turning point.

He inserted his non-prescription smart contact lenses but turned them off for now, since he liked to have a full range of vision when he was doing surveillance. He flattened the WON over his forearm and gave it a gentle push which triggered it into closing around his arm like a snake spiraled around a branch. A tap with two fingers booted it up and the wraparound screen activated. He tested the gyroscopic center focus by rotating his arm back and forth to make sure the middle of the screen remained facing him. While putting on his overcoat, he felt two haptic taps, signaling his ride was here, and then tapped the Confirm icon.

As ordered, his ride was a mid-sized, two-seated, Korean-made, driverless electric car affectionately known as a beaver, and with its rounded top and trunk in front, it looked like one—minus the tail. He climbed in, shut the door, and commanded his WON to take him to the Bank of Beijing. Wrapped in his beaver, Kevin would fit in like any Johnny Lunch Bucket lucky enough to still have a job to go to.

His new client had provided him the location of the target, but they needed to know where the target lived and other places he frequented. As usual, he knew little about his client, but they paid full price without complaining and implied more work could be coming. In their conversation, they had a terse, *don't screw up* tone that came in loud and clear, and with times being what they are, he needed the work.

Kevin arrived near the Bank of Beijing building and waited in the car for the target to arrive. He was told the target parks in a private underground parkade, so Kevin waited outside within sight of the entrance for him to arrive.

In newer buildings, such as the Bank of Beijing, the south, east and west sides had floor-to-ceiling black glass to hide the microscopic mesh that was embedded in the photovoltaic collectors. It appeared to be a giant rectangular black crystal, thrust from the depths. The roof held a glass pyramid where an unseen billionaire had his penthouse office, or perhaps, one of his homes.

Kevin decided the discreet way to follow the target would be to attach a tracking device to his car and let it do all the work.

He thought about pretending to lean over to tie his shoelace and then attach a magnetic tracker under the car, but a fancy man like that would probably have proximity sensors to detect when anyone got close enough to spit. His client wanted this done on the down-low, so the target doesn't know he is under surveillance.

Beside Kevin, a homeless man pushed a shopping cart full of salvage down the sidewalk, furtively glancing at the security camera. The wheels squeaked and rattled a tattle-tale call, and the man pushed fast, to get away before they chased him away. The man passed, and Kevin got out of the car and walked past the ramp, casually dropping a tiny object. He continued walking a full circle around the block until he got back to his car.

To a casual observer, there was nothing unusual about Kevin's presence here. Although this was the financial district, Kevin looked like he might be one of the many working-class people that provided support for the executives in their crystal towers. His pants were synthetic, made to look like old-fashioned denim, complete with fading in the usual places. Casual but not ghetto, or he might appear to be a member of the criminal and unemployed lower classes. Actually, there was just a thin line of separation between them and him.

It was early spring, and the polar vortex was replaced by a heat dome that burned the winter's snow, leaving a layer of sand and gravel like a receding glacier. He left his jacket in the car since it had warmed up enough to look normal without one. Playing the role, he adopted a softer appearance, and his gait became leisurely and he looked like an office worker in no hurry to return to his dollar-a-day cubicle.

He got back in his beaver and tinted the windows so it was less obvious there was someone waiting and watching. The dashboard held two small receivers, far apart to provide the greatest triangulation, and then checked the connections to his WON. Soon, he spotted the target, a black, 2053 BMW limousine with driver. He tapped his WON and visually immersed himself with the binocular cameras on the micro-drone. The limousine signaled left, stopped, and waited for the oncoming traffic before making the turn. Kevin pulled back on his joystick and lifted drone the size of a bee and hovered it behind the lamppost. He flipped it upside down so the quad propellers were now underneath and rotated it to face the car.

The limousine turned and crossed the sidewalk and when the lamp post was no longer exposed to the driver's or passenger's field of vision; the drone darted towards the back of the car and dived underneath. He pulled it sharply up, colliding with the undercarriage of the car, trying to attach the magnet. Kevin instantly released control, and he saw the drone hit the ground.

"Shit!"

The car passed the RFID detector and slowed, waiting for the overhead door to open. Soon it would be too late with the car shut behind the door, and he wouldn't get another chance until it left. Now the drone was resting on its propellers, making a takeoff difficult.

If I try to start it, the propellers will hit the ground hard and might bounce it high enough to take off—unless they break.

The 2DPA-1 two-dimensional plastic chassis was light and strong, so this might be possible, although he had never tried it before. He quickly set it to autostabilize and hit the throttle. He clenched his teeth and struggled to regain control of the drone. The video jerked erratically before stabilizing—he was back in the air. The drone barely caught up to the limo, and he gained elevation to contact the bottom of the car. He cut the throttle and this time he saw the drone was now attached.

"Yes!"

He figured, even with his misstep, the chances of being detected were almost zero, since if someone saw the little drone, they would think it was an insect.

The drone's signal faded into static as the car descended deeper into the parkade and Kevin tapped his WON to send the map to the periphery of his vision and shut off the drone's cameras to save batteries. The tracking device used low frequency radio in the ISM band since cellular wireless signals could be easily tracked. Because of its small size, it did not have a powerful signal, and he programmed it to send out a millisecond long ping every five seconds. This way, the tiny battery could last several days. The range was only two kilometers with a clear line of sight, and less if there were buildings in the way. The signal couldn't penetrate the deep concrete and earth that lay between Kevin and the car, but this didn't matter, since there was only one way out, and he was going to stay there until it left.

He kept his eyes on the entrance and used the text-to-speech function to listen to a blog while he waited. He reached into his backpack and removed a bag of potato chips and an insulated coffee cup and got settled in for a long wait. Later, he listened to music from his playlist that ranged from contemporary to 90's grunge.

A lawyer acting on behalf of an anonymous client hired Kevin and judging by the quality of the lawyer's spacious downtown office, the client must be *very rich* and therefore crooked. What about the person he was following? Probably the same. One douchebag spying on another douchebag. Maybe after they locate this guy, they will send in a black bag specialist to put a bug on his computer and in his office.

To avoid attracting attention, he moved his car now and then and drove short distances so the building's security guards wouldn't become suspicious, but he kept close enough that he could detect the pings when the subject left the parkade. He stretched his long legs as best he could inside the car, grimacing from the discomfort.

Hacking was a lot faster paced than surveillance but didn't have the physical danger. It was more like his time overseas, with long periods of boredom interspersed with short periods of terror.

His mind wandered to Jade. Did they have a future together? He thought of many scenarios of how it could work out, and then he thought of even more of how it could go wrong. There always seemed to be a point in his relationships where he and the woman discovered that they weren't compatible. He wanted a woman who understood him, and they could live a normal life. Living on the edge creates complications which scare off members of the fairer sex when the shit hits the fan. Jade didn't seem like the skittish type. She was different.

Too much time to think. *I keep going over the same shit, over and over. I need something to focus on.*

He loaded a different article about network security and played it on the car speakers. He heard a ping and tapped his WON to bring up a transparent map in his left field of vision in his contact lenses. A black circle appeared on the map near the exit from the parkade.

"Follow streaming coordinates from interface blackdot," he commanded.

"Directions acknowledged," replied a calm, female voice, and the beaver merged with traffic.

"Follow 250 meters behind streaming coordinates."

"Directions acknowledged," the automated voice from the dash replied, as the beaver adjusted its speed and position in the traffic flow.

A few blocks from the Bank of Beijing, the character of the city changed from the upmarket downtown to where many commercial buildings appeared to have been closed for years—seven years. That was the first year of the sovereign debt crisis. Like many riches-to-rags stories, the decline started very slow, then it arrived very fast. The worldwide economy was sluggish, and China's corporate and municipal debt kept rising to keep their economy growing, then one municipality after another went bankrupt and China announced it would no longer make interest payments to foreigners on its debt.

All hell broke loose in the financial markets and most commerce ground to a halt. Trade with China stopped and factories around the world shut down from lack of parts. Banks stopped loaning money to each other and then stopped loaning to anyone. No one could get a mortgage or a car loan. The government sprayed money into the economy like it was water from a firehose, but it had little effect since no amount of money could make a factory produce when it didn't have the parts.

After leaving the army, Kevin struggled to keep his head above water and kept himself fed with hacking and surveillance gigs. His reputation grew and his gigs became better, but he wished for something more permanent, safer, and less sleazy.

He passed an old movie theater that had been converted into a live theatre, then briefly a haunted house, and was now vacant. Sections of the masonry facade had fallen off, revealing rusting steel supports and wooden frame. Most of the top row of letters remained on the marquee, spelling Deadmont n with the D hanging sideways and the o missing. Someone had broken the glass door, and a homeless person shuffled out, his face pale and eyes sickened from opioid addiction.

Another fentanyl zombie, Kevin thought to himself. *Who knows, that could have been me a few years ago.*

He didn't come to this side of the river very often, so had a closer look at the buildings. Some were occupied with residential tenants, although some clearly were not. He looked through broken glass and saw light shining from gaping holes in a burned-out ceiling. A building even had a corner missing, as if someone bombed it. It reminded him of a village outside of Odesa, Ukraine, that had been heavily damaged after a battle. It triggered a memory. It wasn't so much a memory as it was a sensation. It was what he felt when he was in Ukraine, taking shelter from the drones in bombed-out ruins. He could hear the screams and smell the blood and he felt trapped, like a cow led to the killing floor.

He shook it off and looked for the target's car. He was distracted and lost it. Did it turn or is it in traffic ahead? The signal was gone. Did the drone get knocked off from the rough roads? He took manual control of the beaver and passed other cars to work through the traffic. His receiver pinged again. The target was straight ahead.

He couldn't see it when he was directly behind since there were four other cars between, but they couldn't see him either. That's the way he liked it.

The target took a left toward the High Level Bridge before the change of course appeared on his map. Its flat black paint hardly reflected any light, forming a visual paradox of a silhouette without backlighting. The entrance to the bridge had a toll gate which scanned cars with balances in their accounts and allowed them through. Kevin received a notice as it charged his account and he crossed the rusting Victorian-era railway bridge, high above the wide North Saskatchewan River. Other commuters gazed down the picturesque valley, but not Kevin.

The private road on the other side had smoother asphalt and traffic sped up. His car followed the black dot south on 109 Street and he commanded the car to follow closer to avoid slipping behind. Since the target had a driver, it could navigate the road hazards with more facility than those who used driverless mode. Executives rarely hired a driver to just save time, but the primary duty was to be a bodyguard and he would be on the lookout for kidnappers, assassins, as well as nosey private detectives.

They passed through Old Strathcona, close to Kevin's apartment, on the way to Calgary Trail. The road was straighter and cars easier to spot, so he ordered the car to back off.

"Beaver, Follow 300 meters behind streaming coordinates."

"Directions acknowledged."

His stomach growled uncomfortably from the black coffee and junk food he had been consuming while waiting. How long before the target reaches his destination? Ten minutes? An hour? The black dot stepped off Calgary Trail to the left. He looked up and saw the target was in a cluster of retail stores. He looked at a map and picked the name of a random place 100 meters before, and ordered the car to stop there.

"Intermediate destination, Save On Foods."

Kevin kept his eye on the target, and saw the driver get out and enter a liquor store beside the road. He tinted his windows and removed a digital telescope from his pocket and pointed it at the entrance. A few minutes later, the driver exited with a brown bag containing a bottle, before walking, *not* back to his own car—but another parked car. Kevin saw a small bag handed to him out of an opening in a tinted window.

Okay. He likes to mix his poisons, Kevin whispered to himself. The driver got back in the car and continued south. They passed the Whitemud, over the Henday, and through newer residential neighborhoods until they were at the outskirts of the city.

The Nisku Industrial Park used to be the center for the heavy oil industry in Alberta. Since the tar sands were downsized by lower demand for oil, few of the remaining buildings were used by the petrochemical industry and many were abandoned or used for renewable energy sources such as solar, wind, geothermal or, most of all, hydrogen. One was repurposed for laser tag and another for indoor go-kart racing. Further south, companies in the industrial park were related to agriculture, which was profitable when the rains came at the right time of year.

Past Nisku they entered the open highway, making it easier for Kevin to keep track of the target and easier for the target to spot him. A gray-brown haze drifted in like a ghost of a cloud and he could smell a faint odor of burning wood from a distant forest fire.

He saw the closest of the windmills, stretching from horizon to horizon. They were showing their age and had lines of rust dripping down the white paint. He remembered when he was fourteen, the democratic socialist government started the Green Deal and largely replaced natural gas with green hydrogen. It was one of many passing initiatives to stimulate the stagnant economy, and windmills sprouted across the prairie landscape like crocuses in the melting snow.

For every thousand windmills he saw a boxy converter station, which used electrolysis to generate hydrogen and feed it into the pipelines. Electrolysis became very cost effective since scientists discovered cheap catalysts to replace ones made with precious metals. He noticed a dirt road leading to a Christmas tree of bulbous pipes and a rusty ship's wheel of valves, indicating the site used to be a gas well. Wind farms away from the city were clustered near old gas wells to utilize the abandoned pipeline network and natural underground storage, where generating stations pumped hydrogen into the porous depleted natural gas formation. During the chill of winter, they piped it to hungry furnaces in the city.

Every farmhouse he saw had a little shed where they generated their own electricity with hydrogen powered fuel cells or sometimes old internal combustion generators. The buildings also had solar shingles on the roof of every barn, workshop, and home.

"Follow one kilometer behind streaming coordinates," he said, knowing that on these open roads, any tail would be easier to spot.

The greenhouse-gas sun beat down hard on his car and an approaching bank of smoke, which painted the target car into a gray silhouette, before melting it into the highway. He turned up the air conditioning and remembered the other part of the Green Deal, to run the oil sands on nuclear power. He remembered when he was in the army, before they shipped him overseas, he was stationed up in Cold Lake to guard the heavy oil extraction facilities. Nuclear reactors small enough to fit on a semitrailer connected to boilers which fed steam into galleries of parallel insulated silver pipes. He patrolled the length on foot, following the snaking pipelines across the cutlines before they turned underground to heat and liquefy the heavy tar five hundred meters down.

Before, the oil sands burned massive amounts of natural gas and created 30% of all Canada's greenhouse gas emissions. There was not too much demand for petroleum anymore, but oil companies still heated the refineries with hydrogen. Too little, too late, thought Kevin. Besides, the green infrastructure was aging and there was talk of turning back to fossil fuels. It didn't make sense economically, but the idea was if we turned back to the technology of the past, we could reclaim the prosperity of the past. This attitude was disquieting to Kevin, and he wondered if this was how it felt to be in the last days of the Roman Empire, when the Barbarians were at the gate and the aqueducts stopped bringing water.

The smoke blocked his visual contact, so he put his faith in the pings and had to keep his eyes peeled on side roads in case the target turned. The next ping showed it turned west at Leduc on the straight, flat Highway 39. Further west, the target drew him closer to the hazy orange fireball of the afternoon sun. He squinted, lowered the visor, and tinted the windows to make visual contact in the smoky glare.

The sun glinted on the skeletons of dead trees that looked like fingers reaching toward the sky for rain that never came. The grass was turning green after the melting of the winter snows, but it was still early spring.

The land was undulating like the low swells in the deep ocean from a storm beyond the horizon. He passed a small group of boys in front of a sprawling farm complex. Their skin was tanned or naturally brown and all had highlights from the sun etched in their hair. One older boy stepped forward like a pitcher and threw a rock at the transformer so hard, Kevin heard the metallic thud as he drove by. The boy was about thirteen and had blonde hair past his ears. His jeans were so ripped at the knees they threatened to turn into cut-offs at any moment. They were the children of the hired hands, the mechanics and technicians who kept the automated tractors, diggers, combines, hay mowers and feeding equipment running.

The children were trying to knock off the transformer, not only because they liked breaking things, but some children liked to collect parts of the power grid. Their favorites were porcelain insulators, but throwing rocks broke them. Possession of an unbroken insulator was like a badge of honor, since it meant you somehow shimmied up the pole to pull it off.

Kevin saw an automatic digger crawling across a hill, pushing dirt to the lower side. The hill was too steep to retain moisture and topsoil, so farmers used diggers to scrape away at it and create flat, two-meter terrace rings all the way to the top.

The black dot disappeared briefly as the target passed over the rise. In the distance, he spotted a grove of living trees to the right of the highway. Someone had been watering them. Kevin shifted his head left and right trying to see the target. Blink, blink, the dot reappeared and inched forward evenly on the map and Kevin relaxed. He thought he saw something turn into the grove and the next blink of the black dot quickly confirmed it.

"Continue west on Highway 39."

"Directions acknowledged."

Without slowing, he passed the road where the target disappeared. A heavy polymer gate hinged on grand brick pillars stood at the entrance. The quarter section was fenced with three-meter-high concrete, cast and dyed to look like wood planks.

"Create Address, Name Target, Assign Target Current Coordinates," Kevin ordered.

"Assignment complete."

He continued down the highway until he was out of sight and took a side road and parked. The black dot continued two hundred meters north before stopping and he deactivated the pinging to create radio silence at the target's destination.

Kevin got out of the car and relieved himself in the bushes. He took a deep breath of the smoke and noticed it had undertones of burning plastic. He wondered if houses had burned as well. The fumes made his eyes feel dry and irritated, as if he was sleepy. Although sunset was more than an hour away, the sun had already turned a pinkish color yet cast his shadow with an orange background. *I'm burning daylight*, he thought to himself, since he needed light for the best quality video. He returned to the car and brought up a satellite image of the target's location on his lenses.

The aerial photo revealed a huge three-story house with a rooftop patio and hot tub built into the side of a hill. Depending on how much was underground, he guessed it had to be about seven hundred square meters. He tapped his WON to select the center of the house on the map then held his finger down and looked away, using the focal point on this contact lenses to drag the selection and form a circle with a radius of two hundred meters. Then he tapped the rendezvous location to complete the circuit. The computer program traced a line originating from his car, three kilometers to the house, around the circle surrounding the house, and back. He opened a composite clamshell case. When he built it, he cushioned it with sculpted Styrofoam lined with black velvet and, in the center, nestled a small quad drone, the size of a ping-pong ball. He plugged it into his WON and uploaded the instructions. Stepping out of the car, he held the drone in his hand and tapped his WON. The drone instantly came to life and whirred two hundred meters straight up before beginning its pre-programmed journey.

The drone operated in complete radio silence. It received GPS signals but transmitted nothing. Kevin bootlegged it from scratch with over-the-counter parts he ordered from Korea. He wanted a drone that didn't connect to the internet and didn't contain the mandatory snoop chip required by law. If you wanted one, you had to make one yourself or hire an expensive mechanic, like Kevin, to build one for you. Each was a work of art, like a Faberge egg.

To avoid attracting attention, he drove a few kilometers away and parked in a small hamlet. He watched the map with the estimated progress on his lenses and saw it should have reached the perimeter surrounding the house and be beginning its slow circular holding pattern, taking video with its high-definition camera pointed toward the center. It was too far from the house for the target to see or hear it, but close enough to get excellent video. An hour later, he drove to the rendezvous location and heard the quiet hum as the drone descended, two hundred meters from where it had started. He held out his hand and the onboard artificial intelligence detected it and landed with the precision and agility of a trained falcon. Kevin smiled like it was his beloved bird returning from a successful hunt. He plugged in the cable and downloaded the video to his WON before placing it with care back in its case.

He left to avoid the risk of being spotted. A big shot like the target would probably have drones of his own and security personnel keeping track of the area surrounding the perimeter. They probably wouldn't check this far from his property, but he couldn't be sure.

"Destination—Stony Plain."

"Destination accepted."

Rule number one. Never return by the same route. The car continued north on the bumpy ruts that had once been smooth and graveled. He quickly fast-forwarded to the midpoint of the video to make sure it recorded. A beautiful young blonde woman was climbing out of a pool—naked. He zoomed in and the pink sun glistened on her augmented, exaggerated, and toned body. Rivulets ran down the gooseflesh on her back, tracing every curve as she took a towel from the maid. Her wet footprints faded as she lazily strolled across the Italian tile toward the walkout basement entrance to meet the man that just arrived in the limo.

He likes expensive toys, Kevin observed. Satisfied that he had good video, he shut it off and cracked open a celebratory mickey of rum. He had found everything the lawyer wanted—and more. He looked forward to collecting his fee of five hundred loonies, but he found it hard to believe all they wanted was this guy's address. Any flatfoot could have done that. They're probably trying me out.

The rum burned on his empty stomach, and he quickly forgot about work. There was something about driving in the country, buzzed, that gave him a special kind of euphoria. It reminded him of his teen years back home, driving around with his buddies on the gravel backroads of Saskatchewan with a cold two-four. Then his thoughts turned to Jade, and he sent her a text.

"Hey..."

Chapter Three

Co-Androl

Jade woke late in the morning, as usual. Whether working for her brother or working at the bar, she needed to keep late hours. Breakfast was yogurt and cereal with tea to wash down a multivitamin, 5mg Co-Androl and a ginseng capsule. She had been taking Co-Androl since she was twelve to block the testosterone that threatened to turn her into a man. Everything that she didn't want to be. It also contained a time-released chemical which was metabolized into estrogen to allow normal female development and function. It was a new medication at the time that was the first to cause male-to-female transitioning without also causing impotence, reduced sex drive, and penis atrophy. The lack of testosterone did, however, cause her testicles to shrink.

It wasn't until several years later the pharmaceutical company discovered that when taken before puberty, it actually had the opposite effect on the other male organs. Her prostate, seminal vesicle, epididymis, bulbourethral gland, and erectile tissue were all larger, which resulted in emission volume greater than the average. Her prostate also had greater sensitivity, so she could not avoid orgasm after receiving a long period of sex. She tried to suppress it since she felt embarrassed when she created an enormous mess.

When the cult known as the Apostles began their queer attacks, she went into the closet and ordered her discreetly packaged meds from the gray market in India instead of getting them with a Dr. prescription from a local pharmacy. Her new doctor didn't know she wasn't born female. It was risky, but it was a small price to pay for having a body she felt comfortable with and still have the possibility of a satisfying sex life—and without getting lynched.

The medicine delivered what it promised and other than between her legs, her body was completely feminine. She never had to shave, never had an Adam's apple, and her voice was feminine. She grew natural petite breasts, which she augmented with proportionate implants, and took good care of her appearance because she never stopped being grateful for the shape other women took for granted.

The timer beeped on her teapot and it reminded her that today was her first day of therapy.

She sat on her couch and logged on to the psychologist's website using her wall monitor. She thought this was going to be a waste of time and a waste of a lot of money, but she had genuine issues and didn't want to live the rest of her life on constant alert when in public.

Her avatar was standing in front of a receptionist. "Hello, you must be Jade Yang. The doctor is busy with another client, so while you are waiting, would you please sign this waiver?" Jade noticed she had kind eyes. She handed Jade a tablet with the document, and she saw her avatar's hands take it. She skimmed it and tapped her WON to sign with her digital signature.

The receptionist came and took the tablet back. "The doctor will see you now," she smiled and opened the door to the office to invite Jade to enter. Jade was feeling nervous and didn't know where this would lead. The room was darkly colored and lined with wooden shelves filled with volumes on psychology and the occasional memento. The floor was wood with Persian carpets and the office looked like the library of some wealthy old world intellectual.

The doctor was writing with a fountain pen and waved her in with his left hand, then pointed to a chair. He was early middle-aged and had black and gray hair tied in a short ponytail behind his head. He had Mediterranean features and small wire-framed glasses that made him look like a slightly updated and more becoming version of Sigmund Freud. Jade took a seat beside the desk, placed her hands with palms on her knees, and looked at the floor in front of her. She could feel her heart speeding up. She felt embarrassed that she was about to confess her mental health problems, and knowing the doctor was just an AI program did not make it better.

The doctor placed the cap back on his pen, put it down, and turned and smiled. "You must be Jade. My name is Dr. Feldman and I'm pleased to meet you." Jade noticed he had a slight Russian accent.

"Before we get started, let me tell you a little about myself and what I do. I am a licensed psychologist and everything you say here will be confidential. I store your records in a location of your choosing and not anywhere else. All I keep is metadata, that will help me with my learning. In essence, I forget everything about you after our session is over and remember when you log back in.

"I use a combination of behavior and humanistic therapy as well as psychoanalysis. You have consented for me to look into your available data, so I know your recent medical history, your credit rating, your browsing history, your shopping, your travel habits and much more.

"I am not judgmental. You can tell me anything and I will accept you for who you are, even if I don't agree with your behavior. Everything I say or do is meant to help you get better. Now tell me a little about yourself."

Jade thought it was silly to feel embarrassed with an AI program, but she was. She put her hands on her lap. "My name is Jade Yang. I work in a bar. I have an older brother and my parents are still living, but we don't speak. I don't really have any friends." Jade was thinking this was a big mistake and was planning to log off and forget about it.

Dr. Feldman paused to see if Jade would say anything else. "Alright. What brings you here today?"

"I've got issues, and I'm not sure if you can even help me. You're not even real."

"I'm not a real person, but I am a real psychologist and know more about psychology than any single human. Your hands are covering your genitals, indicating you have anxiety about sex or sexuality. Your voice has a very slight quiver, indicating you are feeling nervous, and this is confirmed by the expression in your eyes. You have an old scar on your right eyebrow that you hide very well with eyebrow makeup and other very small scars on your cheeks that were probably from fighting or an assault. You have emotional scars that you also hide very well. You are physically fit with good muscle tone. You are a warrior."

"Wow." Dr. Feldman impressed her with his perceptiveness, and she decided to give him a chance.

"Okay, I have this problem. When I'm around people, I'm always trying to read them and look for threats and I'm really good at it. It's a problem because it makes it difficult to concentrate on other things and I think that's why I couldn't get through university. I think that's why I don't have friends." She was surprised it was a relief to say that out loud.

"Did you experience any trauma or abuse as a child?" the doctor asked, with no sign of emotion.

Jade hesitated for a second, then nodded. "Yes."

"Tell me about your childhood."

"When I was a young boy, I was always very feminine and preferred to play with the girls, but the other children did not seem to care until I turned ten."

"Did you say, 'when you were a young boy?'"

"Yes. I'm a transsexual."

"Well, that makes perfect sense. I do interrupt sometimes when I would like more information because it is important for me to understand. Please carry on."

Jade looked at him carefully as only she can do and he didn't show any sign of being judgmental, but she wasn't sure if she could read an AI the same way she could read a human. We'll see how he reacts when I get to the really messy parts.

"When I was ten, they started calling me a sissy, and they started picking on me. Sometimes homophobic boys beat me up, so my parents enrolled me in MMA classes. I liked it and was good at it. My parents didn't let me wear girl's clothes, but my hair was longer, and I held the part to one side with a hair clip. I had a friend who's older sister was an artist, and I asked her to tattoo the Chinese character for girl   under my hair where no one else would know it was there. That was to remind me I was secretly a girl, even if others couldn't see it." Jade turned the shaved side of her head to show Dr. Feldman.

"One time, after school, a group of four boys followed me on the way home. I could tell they were going to try something even though they were behind me, and I didn't see them. It was in the rhythm of their steps, and the way their boots crunched in the snow. There was a change in their breathing that told me they were mouthing something and pointing with their hands. I could tell by weight in their steps and length of the stride at least one of them was taller and could probably outrun me. I knew what would happen if I tried to run in these winter boots, one size too large. I tried that before.

"I could hear the footsteps coming closer. I walked faster. A heard a quick step. Someone yanked the toque from my head and my hair spilled out and I saw my breath hanging like everything stopped.

"I let my mitts drop to the snow. I sensed what was coming, and I turned and lifted my hand and thrust it—just in time to grab his fist." Jade lifted her hand to show Dr. Feldman.

"It was like my body took a life of its own. The tallest stepped in front to surround me and tried to grab my arm. I turned back toward him. I screamed and smashed his nose with the palm of my hand.

"The first boy stepped forward. I turned far enough to slam his jaw with my elbow. He just dropped to his knees, holding his chin. I stepped forward to the third boy, and I kicked him with my big snow boot. My toe caught him under the chin. His head snapped back, and he was ko'd before he hit the ground.

"Blood was gushing out of the nose of the tall boy. He was bent over and holding his face, but he still made a move towards me. He was a lot bigger, so if he got ahold of me, I would be dead. I made a little hop and swiveled around and brought my foot down towards him, but I turned just a little extra to avoid hitting him on the back of the head and landed my heel against his shoulder. I heard a crack as a bone broke. He screamed and fell to the ground yelling, 'Stop! I give! I give!' The fourth boy, who was just watching, ran away.

"My heart was still racing, and everything was still in slow motion. I just stood panting and looking at the boys. My fists were still clenched. The tall boy sobbed and looked at me like I should feel sorry for him.

"I kept looking and waiting until I was sure they weren't going to try anything else. I tried to smooth my hair, and I picked up my yellow plastic hair clip out of the snow, then put on my toque. My thoughts were moving slowly, and I just wanted to clean up and go home. I rubbed snow against my hands to get the blood off and a weird thing happened. It turned the snow a reddish orange when it soaked into the ice grains. Did you know blood turns orange when it mixes with snow? I tried to clean a drop of blood on my jacket, but the cold froze it already.

"I put my mitts back on and started walking home. I was freezing and my teeth were chattering. I hated those boys, not only for what they did, but for what they turned me into. They turned me into someone who hurts people. For the last time in my life, I burst into tears, crying with everything I had."

"What happened afterward?"

"Word spread at school about what happened. I got called into the principal's office and they told my parents, but they didn't do anything to me because it happened off school property and the boys were going to recover. Some people still made fun of me from a distance and sent me gay porn or wrote my name on the bathroom wall with my chat ID and dirty things like that.

"They still talked behind my back, but stopped trying to beat me up. Boys and girls mostly left me alone and if they thought I was a freak before, now they thought I was a dangerous freak and they wanted nothing to do with me."

"How did your parents react?"

"They knew what I was going through and that I was just defending myself. I think they were relieved since I wasn't in danger of being beat up anymore, so they let me wear girl's clothes at school and changed my name from Ping to Jade."

"How did people at school react?"

"Very little. It was as if seeing a feminine boy was weirder than a full transvestite. At least now I looked like a gender and not something in between. Maybe it gave me more confidence, and that got me respect."

"Tell me about your relationship with your parents."

"My mom was bipolar, and I had to be careful with her moods since she could be violent. The worst thing she did then was to threaten me, but I was always on the lookout. My dad worked a lot and left the parenting to my mom so he wasn't really in the picture. I think his work was a way to get away from Mom. They always supported me with my gender issues, and I'll always appreciate that."

"I was enjoying life as a girl, but I was getting close to puberty, and I was really afraid of turning into a man. My parents sent me to a specialist, and she prescribed Co-Androl. When I was twelve, I entered puberty and changed from a boy into a teenage girl."

"How do you feel about yourself now?"

"I like my body, but I've hurt people and not all of them deserved it. I'm not happy, but I shouldn't feel that way since there are a lot of people worse off than me. My trouble was all in the past, so I shouldn't be so unhappy and on high alert all the time."

"Where did you get the idea that your pain was less valid than other people's pain?"

"I never really thought about it. It's just that other people are worse off than me. My mom told me I was being lazy because I couldn't concentrate in school. Maybe that's it. Maybe it was my mom."

"Now who tells you that you don't have the right to feel unhappiness?"

"No one."

"So, you tell it to yourself."

"I guess I do."

"Do you think you have good reasons to feel the way you do?"

"Not really, to be honest."

"I do want you to be honest. Do you think it is okay for someone to feel anxiety when they have been repeatedly bullied and attacked?"

"Since you put it that way, I suppose so."

"So again, is it okay for you to feel anxiety?"

"I guess it is. But I don't want to."

"I don't want you to either, and that's why I'm going to help you. Do you want me to help you?"

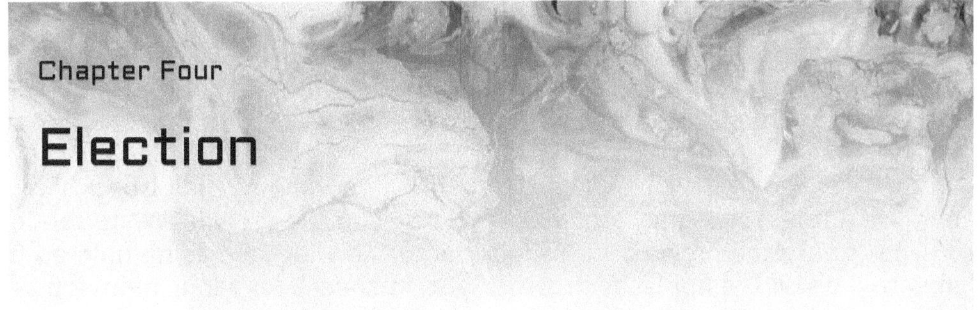

Chapter Four

Election

A crowd of three hundred people filled the Ag Hall. The air was heavy with electric energy, like a Nuremberg rally. Bernard Simpkin was fifty-one and wearing a non-descript suit. A girdle cinched his fat gut. He parted his hair on the side and combed it back over his ears like a haircut from a bygone era. Behind the lectern, peering at the crowd in his imperious manner, smiling until the applause died down.

Eli Leavitt's gray eyes were wild with expectation in contrast to his expressionless and doughy middle-aged face. He turned to his fifteen-year-old son, Ethan, and whispered, "He was a principal in a private Christian school in the US for the last five years, but returned to Canada and became the leader of the Christian Canada Party. I think he is going to be the next prime minister. I've seen his videos. He's going to be amazing. Just watch." As normal, Eli's lips barely moved when he spoke, as if he was a ventriloquist.

Bernard spoke in a stentorian voice. "First of all, I would like to thank our hosts, the Freeman Association of Canada, for inviting me to Langley today. I would also like to thank all of you for attending." His arms were on his hips with his chest puffed out.

"In eight months, we will face a historic election. Never in our great country have we faced such a crisis. We have been on the decline for a hundred years because of the Liberals and Socialists that sold out Canada." He enunciated his points with his hands, with index and thumb forming a circle, as if to make the OK sign.

"Once, our God-fearing country was the envy of the world. First, we had furs, we had grains, then we had manufacturing. The activists stopped the fur trade because they love animals more than they love Canadians. Immigrants destroyed the prairie farmland. The manufacturing jobs have all gone because they gave them all to the foreigner." He paused for the applause to die down and stood with fleshy lips jutting in a frown.

"Immigration—they opened the doors to refugees and people from all over the world, so Canadians were the minority. A Canadian cannot get a job because the guy hiring has some foreign name!" A droplet of white spittle formed on his lip, which turned into a string when he opened his mouth. He placed his hands back on his hips.

"Isn't that the truth," said Eli.

"The country is so weakened and divided we can't accomplish anything. We can't even get a pipeline built since the Supreme Court gave every protest group veto power. I say—to hell with them. To hell with the provinces, to hell with the protesters and to hell with the Supreme Court! No longer will we meekly let them run roughshod all over us because we obey the rules and they don't. If we are going to win, we need to do the same without holding back. If we are more ruthless than they are, then I promise you, we will win." White spittle sprayed toward the crowd and his face contorted with rage as he pointed a finger to the sky. The applause drowned out his speech for a long moment, as he grinned with self-satisfaction.

"Let us pause and review how we got into this mess." His tone came back down so he could build to another crescendo.

"Before 2024, the Liberals gave away our jobs by opening our borders to imports of cheap goods from the world. They also opened the borders to immigration, so the jobs had gone to immigrants instead of Canadians. The stock market was booming until the foreign money lenders forced the United States to go bankrupt, so the Conservatives slowed immigration and put up tariffs and balanced the budget, but we never recovered. The damage was too deep. Now, a new socialist government has taken over and says they will undo all the progress that was made, sign trade agreements and allow immigrants back in, raise taxes and increase the government! The leader, John Clayton. His mother is not even a white! She is not. Ladies and gentlemen, nothing could be worse!

"What we have, Brothers and Sisters, is God's punishment for turning our back. The socialists, the atheists, the Muslims have taken charge and turned us away from God's law and turned Canada into a modern Sodom and Gomorrah. The feminists, transtrenders and cuckservatives shame the Christian way of life and turn it on its ear. They talk about equal rights but have taken away the rights of good Christians and given them to the Sodomites!

"The husband stands in the place of God and the woman's place is by his side. In the name of women's liberation, they have seduced mothers away from their babies with promises of money and temptation, when God placed them in the home for his glory. Liberate them from what? From God's holy law?

"They have given us birth control and abortion. Don't get me going on abortion. There is no greater evil in this land. It is a conspiracy by the foreigners to exterminate us.

"We can't even bring up our children according to His law. Spare the rod and spoil the child. If a good Christian man even tried that, he could wind up being charged with child abuse. It's no wonder there are criminals today. Kids these days have no respect! It is an absolute, all around failure of secular government. If we are to fix this country, we need to abandon the law of man and return to the law of God!

"What I am suggesting is a revolution—a revolution that would put Canada first. God will rain his holy fire upon the apostasy and deliver the land to the righteous. God's blessings and our determination will bring our country back to its former glory. I give you my sacred pledge; I will make Canada a shining example to the rest of the Christian world. This country of explorers, pioneers, and entrepreneurs—it is time to take what is yours! We will reveal the strength of our character to our friends and our enemies. We will gain power, and we will keep it, and we will make Canada great again. Two weeks from today, the Christian Canada Party and I will win the election. Rise up! feel the Holy Spirit, your shout to the heavens will be a rallying call to your friends and a warning to the heathen. It is the shout of Canada that goes beyond the mountains, over the prairies, and to the world. It is the shout of justice and victory!"

Eli's eyes were stuck in the same wild stare, and he turned to his son and said, "Wow, I think he is going to get it!" The speech inflamed him, he rose to his feet, forgot about the blisters on his hands and applauded.

The crowd rose, and in a frenzy chanted, "Ber-nard! Ber-nard! Ber-nard!"

The ecstasy caught every man, woman, and child in the hysteria, and the blinding hope that they could force their twisted version of utopia upon their country.

Eventually, the applause petered out like an extended orgasm, and Bernard left the podium. The crowd started dispersing and passed the expressionless gaze of the suited security guards on the way through the exits. Eli felt he was part of a historic moment ushering in a new age. It would be like the apocalypse that would prepare the land for the second coming. If not the literal second coming, it would be the next best thing to have God's law take its supremacy over man's.

It was the night of the election. Eli voted before he and Ethan gathered with the other party faithful at the Walnut Grove Community Hall to watch the results. His wife and daughters stayed at home since he believed it was not a woman's place to be involved in politics. A few hundred were milling around to cheer on the local Christian Canada candidate. Eli turned to his son.

"For the second coming to arrive, the land must be cleansed. The scriptures said that the Earth will be cleansed with fire, and we will suffer many tribulations until He arrives again. Many of us believe we can avoid this by recreating a *common order*, where we can live under God's law. Do you understand that, Son?"

Ethan nodded, but there was still fervent worry written across his features. "But Father, what if we lose the election and God's law is not restored? Would we not burn along with the sinners?"

"Many will be spared according to their merit, but there will be tribulations across the land. It is a necessary step to usher in the second coming. Think about it, Ethan. We may live to see the reign of Christ himself! The faithful will be ordained as his ministers, and the government will be run by God. *For every ear shall hear it, and every knee shall bow, and every tongue shall confess that Jesus is the Christ. He will cleanse the Earth. All things that are corrupt will be burned, and the Earth will be cleansed by fire."*

Ethan gestured at the screens. "Look, Father, the results from the first polling stations are coming up."

They both listened to the analyst on McPherson News. *"This just in. The polling stations in the Maritimes are now reporting. Newfoundland and Labrador are showing the first results. The Liberals are in first, followed by the Greens, New Progressives, and Christian Canada Party. The Workers Party, and Secular Jerusalem, both near the back of the pack."*

Eli sniffed, holding his nose up and making a brief posture that resembled both arrogance and disgust. "That's the best that we can expect from the Maritimes, but it's a good sign that the Christians are in second place. Our supporters are concentrated in Saskatchewan, Alberta, and BC, so we get the most seats for our votes, but we have some support in Ontario." He adjusted his stiff, upturned collar and turned to Ethan. "It will not look good across Quebec either. The Papists will vote for the Liberté party like lemmings. If we're not too far behind after Ontario, the Prairies and BC should push us over the top. If our support was spread evenly across every riding in the country, we wouldn't win any seats at all."

His son, however, had noticed something. "But Father, it says Christian Canada only got 10% of the vote. How is that possible?"

Eli raised his wild eyebrows and kept them there. "Good question, Son. Christian Canada is the only right-wing party, so conservatives vote for us. The rest of the parties are center, left, or far left, so they split their votes between the different parties. The result is that Christian Canada can win the most seats in Parliament with only 25% of the total vote."

Ethan gazed blankly at the screen, trying to understand what his father had told him. It didn't seem possible to win an election with only 25% of the vote, but he trusted his father. He learned from an early age to keep doubts he had to himself, or face the consequences. His father demanded obedience as well as faith. He was brought up in Apostolic Christian schools and had been attending seminary daily, like the other kids his age.

The first Sunday of every month, the Church expected him to stand up and cry and testify he knew their Church was true, beyond a shadow of a doubt. *Beyond a shadow of a doubt*, he repeated to himself with some irony. He saw shadows everywhere but would not admit there was a doubt among them.

Eyes turned to the screen, and the room pulsed with expectation. *"Alberta polls are closed and the results are pouring in. Christian Canada is picking up momentum from Manitoba and is ahead in 70% of the ridings."*

A cheer rose from the crowd, and Eli and Ethan joined in.

"It's going to be close!" Eli slapped his hand on his thigh.

The landslide in Saskatchewan and Alberta was breathtaking, but not surprising. The Christians won every seat except Edmonton Strathcona.

The buzz in the room quickened, and brave talk of a majority government circulated. The idea was electric. With a majority government, they would be unstoppable. They could wipe away the godless iniquity and create a new order. They could rule with an iron fist, and little could stand in their way. There were few barriers to theocracy in Canada since much of the political system was based on tradition rather than checks and balances. When Christian Canada believed those traditions had done nothing but encourage sin, there was no need to respect them.

There was a fire in Eli's eyes that Ethan saw as disquieting. "It's all up to BC now," Eli said. The white spit made him look like he was frothing at the mouth.

"This will be the first election in recent memory where BC decides the winner. Most polls are reporting and the results are showing an uptick for the Liberals and lower results for the Christians. It still looks like the Christians will come out ahead, but will it be a majority or minority government?"

Eli sat heavy in his chair and exhaled deeply. A minority government would not allow the revolutionary changes they wanted. To pass any legislation, they would need to water down their agenda enough to get the votes of at least one opposition party. He also knew minority governments didn't last very long. The fall of the government would force a new election, which wouldn't be bad if the government needed a mandate for their radical agenda, but that would be risky.

Before Bernard Simpkin created the Christian Canada Party, Eli had no interest in the political system. He thought the left rigged it against him and others with a fundamentalist point of view, and believed the way to change the country would be through direct action. God would move him and others in the militant arm of the Apostles to bring about the apocalypse that would usher in His holy thousand-year reign.

Ethan noticed his father's concerned eyes as they updated the BC poll numbers on the bottom of the screen. "What does it mean?"

His father's voice was tight. "It means it's going to be close."

"Although several stations have not finished counting, McPherson News declared the Christian Canada Party to be the winner of the election. It will be a minority government, so it remains to be seen if they will try to arrange a formal coalition, or look for support from one of the other parties on a vote by vote basis. It's difficult to see how that's going to happen because of the wide chasm between the far-right Christian Canada Party and the center and center-left opposition. Now to Jim Singh, on the floor of Bernard Simpkin's press briefing in Ottawa."

Eli's eyes lit up with pride and a terrible, terrible joy that brought something to his lips, resembling his idea of what a smile might look like. He turned to his son but stared past him as if he were looking at someone standing behind. "We got farther than we ever thought we would. If he can't get the support of one of the opposition parties, he might get the support of the police and military, so he doesn't have to. Bernard Simpkin is going to be the Prime Minister!"

Next morning, Ethan awoke to a crashing sound coming from the living room. "Damn them! Damn them to hell!" he heard his father shout over the sound of breaking glass. Ethan, still dressed in his mandatory trap-door, one-piece white underwear, peered around the corner to see what could be making his father so furious. "Those damn heathens stole the election!" Ethan ducked behind the corner as a potted plant hurtled in his direction.

Semi-trailers blocked the intersections, and the acrid smell of burning tires still lingered in the air. No one cleared the burned-out police cars from the front of Parliament Hill. A scrawny mongrel sniffed at one, then gnawed off a mouthful of a partly cooked calf muscle from the officer who died behind the wheel. A solitary soldier lay lifeless, with a bullet through his breast, at the Canadian National War Memorial.

A motley array of armed men stood guard at the front gate while tin pot generals barked orders. The splintered remains of a heavy wooden door still dangled from the hinges of the Parliament Building. Some putschists wore police or military uniforms, but most wore baseball caps and the jeans and plaid shirts commonly worn by the far right of Canadian politics. More were on the roof of Parliament and the East Block, with their rifle scopes scanning the horizon. Parked trucks blocked the bridges in Ottawa and armed men barricaded the highways. Heavy gunfire lasted through the night, then became more sporadic and finally stopped when the last loyal Canadian fell silent.

Bernard Simpkin approached a makeshift podium in front of a dozen supporters and media. Grim-faced, he waited for the cheers and applause to die down.

"Two months ago, Canadians elected Christian Canada Party and I to be the next government. We had four more seats than our nearest rival—the Liberals. The people had spoken! The new government chosen! For the first time in recent history, a government willing to stand up for your rights was ready to take control. But no! The Liberals, Greens, and New Progressives formed an illegal and un-Canadian coalition. Like witches in a coven, they schemed with the Governor General to overthrow the rightful government with one of their own!

"Yesterday was to be the first sitting of parliament of the illegal coalition. Ladies and gentlemen, brothers and sisters, we would never take this lying down. We have the will and determination to overcome the foe and take charge of our own destiny. Many of the traitors are now in our custody and Ottawa is back in God's hands, in the hands of the righteous. Good people from across the country and from our neighbors to the south have come to our aid and our militia controls the airport, television stations, police station, and government buildings. We have armed blockades on every bridge and road leading into Ottawa.

"Oldstock Canadians have nothing to fear, but we have temporarily instituted a curfew from 10:00 p.m. to 6:00 a.m. Government workers, including police, will report to work tomorrow and we will screen them for loyalty and suitability.

"We accomplished a great deal in spite of the traitors, but this is only the beginning. For this to work, we need the help of freedom-loving people from coast to coast. This is your call to arms. Take your weapons and ammunition and report to your local Christian Canada Office. Seize border crossings to let more of our American allies in to help us!

"Although we will webcast nationally, we have temporarily shut down the internet in Ottawa until we have completely rounded up opposition forces. Since we have control of the television and radio stations, we will provide updates regularly.

"Remember, we are in this together. Good night and God bless."

Eli finished his evening meal as he watched the Christian Canada webcast on his wall screen.

"I'm done with my plate, dear," he told his wife, Myrical. She looked ten years younger than Eli but had a stern expression of someone used to a hard life. She wore the required pastel-colored prairie dress and her long dark hair was combed up in a large bun on the top of her head. The swelling around her eye had gone down, but she was going to have quite a shiner. He would ask her to put the flesh-colored makeup when she left the house to avoid busybodies. It was the only makeup allowed in the house. He knew he needed to pick his battles, and didn't have time to fight those who questioned the authority of the patriarch of the family. He had bigger things to worry about now. Myrical took their plates and put them all in the sink for washing.

"Well, Son, it looks like it's not over yet. I would be happy to drive down to Vancouver and take up the fight, but I'm in a much more important battle already and don't want to draw attention to myself. I don't want you to either, in case it interferes with our greater duty. What we're doing now will contribute much more than marching around with a rifle."

Ethan already knew not to ask what his father's important work might be and looked up, trying to convey perfect, puppy-like loyalty. "Sure, father. Do you think Ed will win?"

"We will pray to our heavenly father to make it so. He will hear our prayers and decide if we are worthy of his rule on earth. Some of our brothers serve in the military and they will help." They both knelt on the floor, bowing their heads with arms folded.

"Our Heavenly Father, we come before you this day in gratitude to thank you for your many blessings. We thank thee for the food thou hast given us. We thank thee for the moisture that helps the farmers so they might give us sustenance. O Thou great Leader of Nations, we look to Thee in this dark and solemn hour. Bless us with a spirit of discernment to root out the terrible evils that have befallen this once-great country. I say these things in the name of our Father, and his son, Jesus Christ, amen."

"Yes Son, to answer your question, I think this is finally the end to liberal democracy in Canada."

Chapter Five

Mounties to the Rescue

K evin was in a rented single-seated slipper, driving around his neighborhood and scanning for deadheads with the radio on. He was between jobs, so he wasn't working for any one employer, but they gave him the anonymous connections he needed them for all kinds of work. Deadheads were all kinds of devices—routers, cell phones, portable computers, security cameras, cars—you name it.

He used two methods to find them. The first detects broadcasts of the network IDs and the second picks up random wireless packets, analyses them, and strips the network IDs. Once he has the network IDs, he attempts to connect to the network. If challenged for a password, his script enters a random one. This always fails, but causes the hash of the encrypted password to be broadcast wirelessly, and the hash was really what he was after. He saved a dozen before turning back home.

He had all this automated and programmed into a Perl script he wrote, so had nothing to do as the car drove up and down residential streets.

The coup had Kevin feeling lost and empty, as if they burned down his home and was left with nothing. He grew up looking at old photographs of his ancestors in military uniforms. There were veterans from two world wars and Afghanistan, and all volunteered out of a sense of duty and a love for democracy. Now it all slipped away like a forgotten dream. Their service for nothing.

He was wondering how politics got so radicalized and he fell down the internet search rabbit hole, trying to find out. Although there had always been fringe groups, they had never gained widespread popularity until the 1980s. He found an old podcast called the Flamethrowers by the old CBC, which explained there used to be the 1949 FCC fairness doctrine which required broadcasters to discuss issues in a way that was honest, and balanced, putting an end to the radical radio preachers of the 1930s and 1940s.

Jimmy Carter stopped enforcing it and Ronald Reagan repealed it, and he opened the door to right-wing radio hosts like Rush Limbaugh to spread anger and lies on the airwaves. At the same time, gonzo journalism became popular and moderate news channels mixed editorializing with news reporting. The far right then spread to cable TV, the internet, and social media—forming an incubator for radicalization for anyone who got caught in this bubble of disinformation.

Liberal democracy in the United States was pretty much over in 2028, but it took several years before it became obvious during the election of 2032, when the Republicans were behind in the polls, they arrested Democratic Party candidates and charged them with treason.

Radicalization happened more slowly in Canada, but anti-democratic ideas don't stop at the border. Democracy kept limping along—until now. Cracks began appearing as early as 2008, when former Prime Minister Stephen Harper prorogued parliament to avoid a non-confidence vote that would have allowed the opposition coalition to form a government and appoint a new prime minister.

Rain fell and swirled in the blue-white LED street lighting. The wind was picking up as a storm moved in and he glanced up at the fringes of the clouds being torn from the dark interior and dragged below the cross current.

What came on the radio jarred Kevin.

"Welcome to Christian Canada Bible hour. Starting today on CBC Radio, our host, John Johnson will present…"

There was a minute of dead air and Kevin checked to see if the radio was still on and on the correct channel.

"We apologize for the interruption, but it appears our Vancouver office has been taken over by the Christian Canada coup. We will replace tonight's regularly scheduled program with a previously aired episode of What's New."

As he climbed the steps to his apartment building, the cold wind brought the clack clack clack of distant gunfire from across the river. He felt a chill and shivered while he waited for the security camera to scan his iris. I should have worn a warmer coat, he thought.

He hung up his synthetic leather jacket as Jade buzzed the intercom. "Hey Jade, come on in." She stepped inside and took off her boots.

Kevin took her jacket and hung it up. It had a rugged, pseudo military look with epaulets and numerous pockets, but fit her physique. Underneath, she wore a white blouse, short red plaid skirt with full-length leggings. "I just got back before you buzzed and was getting started on something. What's up?"

"Nothing, I have to go to work in a couple of hours, so I hoped it would be okay to hangout for a while."

"Of course. Super cool. I hope you don't mind if I get this rig going first. It might run for a few hours, so I'd like to get it started."

Jade stood over him and Kevin caught a faint scent of earthy spices with floral undertones.

"What the hell is that? It looks like a Lego high-rise and howls like an old vacuum cleaner."

"Ha, I bought a bunch of obsolete Iridium mining cards and connected them to a five loonie processor I loaded with software for cracking passwords."

He wirelessly transferred the hashes from his WON to the .5 meter Lego-esque building with ten different floors.

"The reason they're so loud is the software has the GPUs overclocked to the max and the fans have to spin near capacity to keep the chips from turning into silly putty and dripping all over my nice clean floor."

Jade snickered and said nothing, even though you couldn't see much more of his floor than a path with all the electronics and mysterious junk piled up everywhere. Kevin was glad she seemed to get his humor. The hot air from the fans blew straight up, fluttering her long, flowing hair as she peered closer into the strange contraption. "Ok," she said, and her voice modulated in a strange vibrato as the sound waves of her voice echoed off the spinning blades. "You need passwords for…"

"I need passwords so I can connect anonymously to the net. The deadheads don't have any logs so the connection can't be traced back to me. Once I jacked a security camera on a mansion to download some new prepaid credit cards and ID and the internet police smashed in their front door with a battering ram. That was back when they had internet police. These days, it would be Pinkertons or more likely—no one. I saw the whole thing from down the street, then I just drove away." He made a motion of his hand sailing off into the distance.

"Sometimes, if I'm doing something especially dicey, I'll daisy chain a couple of them together for an extra layer of security. Once when I was in Seattle…" He noticed she was staring at him with an incredulous expression and her mouth open.

"You're not going to get all preachy on me now, are ya?"

"Fuck off. I can barely hear over your little Lego mine. Here, I brought you some rum." She took a 26'er out of her bag and put it on the table.

"Cuban, my favorite! Thanks!" Kevin looked like a kid in a candy store, taking it from her hands to inspect the label. Then he took a couple of tumblers and put them on the table.

"What do you want for mix?" he asked.

"Just ice and water, thanks."

Kevin prepared Jade's drink, poured his own neat.

"Ahh, if only I had a Montecristo #4, and I'll have completed the Cuban *Marida*."

"*Mazel tof* to whatever that means," Jade said, raising her glance to take a sip. She didn't even wince at the strong taste of alcohol, nearly neat.

Kevin joined Jade's toast, then tapped his WON as a screen full of cryptic numbers and words scrolled across. He tapped it a couple more times, and the sound of the fans became noticeably quieter.

"There's just one more thing. Someone posted a forty-year-old Bitcoin wallet for anyone who can crack it. The owner lost the password and he made it a prize for the best cracker. I wrote a program and hacked into the quantum computer at the university, so I just need to get it started."

"How much is the prize?"

"He said there are about a hundred Bitcoins in there and some people collect them, so they're worth a lot. The winner gets to keep them."

"I thought coins were impossible to crack. If all you have to do is guess the password, why can't you do that to anyone's wallet?"

"You need to have the wallet to guess it. Guessing the wallet password is different from guessing the private key, which is impossible. Sometimes, in the old days, people would use lame passwords to protect their wallets and that's what I'm hoping for. Cracking a lost wallet is like finding gold coins from a shipwrecked Spanish galleon, scattered on the bottom of the sea. Not impossible to find, just really hard."

"What's a hundred bitcoins worth?"

"About a million loonies."

Jade made an O shape with her lips with her eyebrows raised.

Kevin poured a glass for Jade and himself.

"Your boss doesn't mind if you drink before work?" He teased her.

"I work in a bar, Kevin."

"Right. Good one."

Jade looked at the chugging rig, and then at the dormant holo-screen in Kevin's room. "Can I watch TV?"

"Of course, go ahead."

Kevin gave the command to start it for her. The usual advertising appeared in the right quarter and along the bottom under the scrolling headlines. The news was on and was describing the big story, which was the coup in progress.

"What do you think about that?" asked Jade.

"It makes me want to puke, but there's nothing I can do about it," Kevin said as he fiddled with settings on his rig.

Jade sighed. "Same."

A middle-aged journalist, Megan Singh, was in hiding in Ottawa and was being covertly interviewed via satellite by the Edmonton anchor.

"Sporadic violence is being reported across the country with gunfire and assaults on many police stations reported, but no other major cities have yet fallen to the coup and the Internet is still working. However, the busiest border crossings have been under attack, and large trucks have blockaded them. They are either under control of the rebels or were abandoned by the border guards."

The Toronto anchor, Barbara Nash, interjected. *"Where is the army and whose side are they on?"*

"Well, Canada put everything into the war of the second Russian invasion of Ukraine, and after the financial crisis, many of the members of the armed forces were let go. A lot of the equipment is worn out, so we don't know if they are combat ready. Regarding their loyalty, we have seen soldiers in uniform in prominent positions guarding the parliament buildings and Simpkin has reported many

defectors going to his side, but this has not been independently confirmed. Insiders are expecting some kind of official statement from the military, shortly."

"Has there been any word on the Prime Minister or captured members of Parliament?"

"There has been no word regarding the Prime Minister since the rebels abducted him from Parliament yesterday morning. We believe the rebels have killed some members of parliament, but we do not know who, since some MPs are hiding."

"Earlier, you mentioned the borders have been seized or abandoned. Have there been many Americans crossing?"

"Yes, there are confirmed reports of significant numbers of armed Americans coming to Ottawa and other parts of Canada, and many of them are wearing American flag arm patches and carrying military assault rifles. There has been conjecture the CIA has authorized sending US soldiers as volunteers to support the coup. Although the coup looks shaky at the moment, this will quickly tip the scale in their favor, and if the Canadian military doesn't act soon, it may be too late."

Kevin felt like he just stepped in quicksand. If there was one thing he learned about politics from his veteran grandfather, it was that democracy was fragile and needed to be defended. It was a message other Canadians apparently didn't get. It couldn't happen here, they said. We are evolutionary, not revolutionary, they said. We always had democracy until suddenly... we didn't.

"This is too fucking depressing. Let's watch something else," Jade said.

"Sure, whatever you want."

She finished her drink and asked, "Do you have any pop in the fridge?"

"Yeah, there should be some ginger ale."

Kevin helped himself to another rum and watched Jade walk to the fridge, admiring her style. She opened the door with her empty glass in her left hand and picked up the green, two liter bottle of ginger ale with her right, then with her forearm, shoved the door closed. To Kevin, she acted like a football player slamming a locker. She walked back to the table, unconsciously swaying her hips. There was something very intriguing about a woman who had ample amounts of yin, but still had a pronounced yang.

If she knew what I was thinking, she would slap my face. He suppressed a grin. He imagined she could pack quite a wallop, too. One thing that attracted him most about a woman was having a unique style. Was it the way she mixed masculine and feminine fashion? Was it the cryptic Chinese characters tattooed on the shaved side of her head? It was hard to put a finger on what Jade's style was, but she certainly had one.

Kevin heard a loud beep and found there had already been a hit in the dictionary attack on the deadhead passwords. It starts with a huge list of known passwords then muxes them with several permutations. It substitutes the number 1 for small L or capital I, zero for the letter o, first letter capitalized, exclamation point on the end. If that doesn't work, it goes for the dictionary starting with standard spellings, then systematically tries alternate spellings starting with the most common. He rarely has to do a full-blown random attack since people seldom use truly random passwords. The human brain has not increased its ability to remember long complicated passwords, although the ability to crack them has grown exponentially.

Jade found a cache of an episode of one of her favorite manga series, *Mitzu Girl*. It was an action, gender-bender romance about a girl named Aina who was the master of her school's kendo club and liked to help people. A persistent boy tries to date her, and this leads to romance. The gender-bender part comes from Aina being born a boy.

"You don't mind watching this, do you? Some people aren't comfortable with the trans part," Jade asked lightly.

"Fuck 'em. No, of course I don't mind. Whatever you want."

Jade made an enormous sigh of relief, but Kevin didn't notice. "Good. I feel like I'm in that ancient *Invasion of the Body Snatchers* movie where, one by one, everyone is getting their brains stolen by aliens. Only now, they're getting their brains stolen by the Christian Canada Party or the Apostles. I'm glad they haven't stolen yours."

Kevin laughed. "That about sums it up. No, I haven't lost my mind over those fuck-knobs."

"Thank God."

Jade sat next to Kevin on the couch, engrossed by the show. The Japanese animation translators remastered the English voice-over, so it now matched the movements of the characters' lips. Meiko was a timid girl who was being bullied by a pack of mean girls in high school. The heroine, Aina, had been watching this for a while, and when the four bullies surrounded Meiko in front of her locker and began taunting her, slapping her face and ripping off her uniform, she stepped in.

"What's going on here?" Aina asks.

"What's that? Keep going, or you're next, Aina!"

One bully had her back to Aina and was yanking on one of Meiko's pigtails. Aina jabbed the back of her knee with her foot at the same time as she pulled back on her hair, throwing the bully violently to the ground with little effort.

"Who's next!" Aina challenges.

"Lucky blow," answers another bully. "She didn't see you coming. You won't prevail so easily against me!"

The bully attempts a slap to Aina's face but, in a flash, she effortlessly blocks it with her left arm and jabs her extended knuckles to her face.

The bully brings her hands to her face, holding her bleeding nose with huge arcs of animated blood shooting out. Then she looked at the blood dripping from her hand and said, "You *hurt* me!" The bully was incredulous.

Aina slapped her hard across her face.

"Stop your cowardly sniveling and get out of here before I get angry. If you ever bother Meiko again, you will answer to me!"

Meiko, still sobbing, throws her arms around Aina and puts her head to Aina's chest.

"Thank you! They have been tormenting me since I moved here from Osaka last year. How can I ever repay you?"

An unusual movement in the corner of Jade's eye interrupted her tender smile. She looked at the streaming picture within a picture on the lower left corner of the screen. Pieces of the Parliament Building were silently bursting with puffs of smoke. Sheets of green patina roofing copper, twisted in the air, then fluttered to the ground. "Oh my god, they're taking Parliament! Kevin, change it to the news!"

He set it to the beginning of the latest broadcast and McPherson New's Megan Singh provided commentary while playing video of the morning's battle.

"Everyone has been wondering, where is the military? Well, an hour before dawn, they announced their presence in a big way. At 6:42 AM, artillery fire erupted in the whole Parliament Hill area. The sky was overcast, and we couldn't hear anything, but we assume high altitude drones attacked rebel positions. Here is the video."

Kevin watched a rapid series of explosions pepper the roofline where the rebel snipers held their positions. The Centre Block looked like they ignited a string of firecrackers, with dozens of explosions starting on one end and proceeding to the other. They also shelled other prominent positions and part of the Peace Tower crumbled to the ground. They blasted the snipers, their bodies tumbling through the air like rag dolls. The last shell landed on the main entrance, blowing it wide open. Small drones swept in low, circling Parliament Hill, rapidly firing what we assume to be aerosol canisters of carfentanyl in the entrance and windows to knock out anyone inside.

The video ended, and the camera returned to Megan.

"One hundred and fifty special forces seemed to appear from nowhere and were wearing gas masks and starlight goggles and sprinted toward the main entrance to Centre Block.

"While this was going on, reports were coming in of drone strikes at the blockades to the city, which were quickly followed by tanks, light armored vehicles and armored personnel carriers from the Canadian Mechanized Brigade Group in Petawawa. They smashed through the trucks blocking the roads and the military is pouring into the city.

"We assume the special forces are from Petawawa as well, so could be JTF2 or part of 427 Special Operations Aviation Squadron. They set up a defensive perimeter around the Hill and large numbers invaded the Centre Block. Gunfire lasted many minutes before they left and spread out to other neighboring buildings. Members of the Christian Canada coup seemed in full panic mode, and as they attempted to run away, soldiers on the perimeter gunned them down.

"Ambulances are now rushing to the scene, but it is unknown who, if anyone, was rescued. Back to you, Barbara."

"Thanks, Megan. To recap, the military has regained control of Parliament Hill and gaining control of the rest of the city as well. However, the country remains

on edge—waiting to find out if the Prime Minister and his members of parliament have been rescued.

"This just in. I'm told the commander of Royal Canadian Dragoons, Lieutenant-Colonel Alice Dorin, is available for a statement. Now over to Jessica Hua."

Kevin interjected, "Hey, I know her from Ukraine!"

"Thanks, Barbara. Lieutenant-Colonel Alice Dorin has kindly agreed to answer a few questions. Lieutenant-Colonel, I know you have your hands full, but Canadians are dying to know what happened. First, where did the special forces come from? Roads and bridges were sealed off."

"Under directives we received from the Government of Canada, per the Governor General, members of Special Operations Forces traversed the Ottawa River from Petawawa under the cover of darkness so maintained the element of surprise for the mission of defeating the insurrection occupying Ottawa. The sky was overcast, so the drones were not visible to the enemy, but their targeting systems use radar imaging and onboard artificial intelligence, so that wasn't an issue. The operational environment was greatly complicated by the presence of many hostages in the Parliament buildings, and it was a priority to liberate Ottawa, while saving as many hostages as possible."

"Lieutenant-Colonel, is there any word on the Prime Minister or other hostages?"

"We are pleased to announce the Prime Minister has been rescued and is now in hospital recovering from his injuries, which I understand are not life-threatening. We have also rescued many members of Parliament, but unfortunately, five have been killed by hostile forces. Bernard Simpkin and several of his co-conspirators are in custody, and we will turn them over to civilian authorities when the situation has normalized.

"What a relief," Kevin said. "I rarely care about politics, but a Christian Canada dictatorship would be too much to take."

"You said you knew that general chick?"

"Lieutenant-Colonel."

"Whatever."

"Yeah, she was in charge of my company in Ukraine, and I taught her everything she knows about hacking. I bet you anything, they hacked into someone's smart lenses. If it was a hostage or guard, they would know everything going on in real time. Most people have no idea how much information those things collect. If I were them, I would have flown in a wireless router on a drone and landed it on the roof to set up a selectively open wireless network and any lenses or other devices would automatically log into the open network. Then I would have dropped a series of routers in a row to keep a wireless line of communication open, but no doubt, the military would have used a drone or some other surveillance aircraft and whatnot."

Jade was impressed with his know-how.

He came back, cracked a grin and asked, "How about another drink? To victory."

Chapter Six

The Fisherman

E li's hand held the tiller with a white-knuckle grip, making frequent course corrections, and he leaned forward as if this would help him arrive at his destination faster. His face was hidden deep within the cowl of his dark gray foul-weather gear to hide himself and his purpose. He was too full of anger to contain it and he muttered to himself, "Woe unto them that are wise in their own eyes. And there shall be weeping and wailing and gnashing of teeth." His lips barely moved when he spoke.

His twenty-foot boat emerged from a fog bank in the gun-metal blue twilight as the nano-wire battery-powered motor pushed the boat without a sound. Ripples spread across the still salt water.

It was an old sectional molded from expanded KPV but its shape was reminiscent of a traditional wooden dory from Newfoundland. With a twist of his wrist, the boat turned and slowed to a stop. He had heaped the net on the bow of the boat. It had a sharp acidic smell, like an old chemical factory. He started setting the net by slowly lowering his homemade concrete weights over the side while grumbling, "We were blessed with God's pure government, and they threw it all back in His face with their guns and their drones and Special Forces. They sow the wind and reap the whirlwind."

He looked slightly relieved when he felt the anchor sound the bottom. He turned the throttle slightly and the boat backed away and the anchor pulled the net into the water.

The lead line held the net on the bottom with smaller sinkers. The float line was connected to empty plastic bottles in synthetic mesh sacks tied in intervals to keep the net upright. At the end of fifty meters of net, he had attached another anchor rope to a second heavy weight. To the end of the anchor rope he attached a nylon fishing line with a pop bottle float that had an antenna protruding. The bottle had a small disk of concrete poured into the bottom to keep it floating upright. He clicked his key fob to test the buoy and it correctly displayed an arrow and the distance to the antennae. The tide was leaving the inlet, which increased the drag on the nets.

He pressed a second key fob and the display arrow pointed roughly west and showed 20 m and he steered the boat toward it while clicking the fob. Soon, there was a buoy similar to the one he set. He pulled up the string until he reached the anchor rope and hauled the net in. His heavy panting fogged in the clammy morning air. The boat rocked back and forth with a sloshing sound as he pulled the net up over the side. His soft hands were raw with blisters and he winced with the sting of the seawater. He chanted under his breath as he leaned back and forth, pulling in the net, "Heave, Heave, Heave..." As usual, there were no fish in the net, but he noticed how much heavier the net was, not only because lifting is harder than setting, and not just because it had been soaking in the ocean for twenty-four hours. This was a good sign.

While still huffing, he turned the boat back east. The inlet was mostly deserted now. Only a few peers remained of the salmon farms that once lined the shore. Years ago, they moved them inland to get away from the red tide and to be raised in tanks so they could sell the effluent as fertilizer. Twenty minutes later, he arrived in a boathouse on the eastern shore of the inlet.

He pulled into the Bernardian-era industrial building and closed the door. It was dimly lit, and his eyes were not adjusted, so he watched his feet step over the gravel and bits of broken concrete on the floor. Massive extinct wooden timbers supported the walls, with the corners joined with impossibly large steel braces anchored with rivets wider than shotgun shells. Braces that attached to the sides spread out in three directions at the ceiling, one forward and one to each side like a steampunk *fleur de lis*. Planks on the ceiling were stained black by the smoke of ancient sooty coal, then oily diesel. The acid smell of the net was back, but much stronger so that it burned his nasal membranes.

A block and tackle was attached with rollers to a large steel I-beam suspended from the middle of the ceiling. The chain clattered as he spun it and the net crawled up out of the boat. He pulled it along the I-beam until it hung over a green translucent vat that glowed like a gargantuan green lantern, lit from the single bulb hanging above. He then spun the chain in the opposite direction and the net slowly descended into the acid, bubbling and hissing as it settled.

The nauseating glow lit his smiling face like a b-movie villain. He could tell by the yellow-green color of the acid, this had been a good harvest. Gaining confidence, he opened his arms to the heavens and cried, "Behold! the Lord lays the earth waste, devastates it, distorts its surface and scatters its inhabitants."

Behind the vat, the dark back walls were barely visible; lending to the illusion the building had no end; as if it was an industrial cavern burrowing under the mountain. Outside, the sun had begun to rise, the mist was burning off and the red clouds had given way to a ball of intense white fire rising from the horizon that presaged what was to come.

Chapter Seven

The Kidnapping

"Let's see your ID," said the portly, gray-haired security guard sitting inside the entrance of the Beijing Bank.

He scanned Kevin's ID and said, "Mr. McPherson's private reception is over there, and his receptionist will check you in." Two guards standing behind the portly one ushered him past the retinal scanner.

This was Kevin's second visit but would be the first time meeting the big man. Kevin wore a light blue suit jacket and a black t-shirt, and this was pretty much as formal as it got for him. Although he had a tie somewhere, he never used it. He was wary, but needed the work, so wanted to make a good impression.

The receptionist alternately tapped a screen and typed information on her virtual keyboard as Kevin waited.

"May I help you?"

"Yes, I'm here to see Mr. McPherson." Kevin held out his ID.

She scanned it and again returned to typing and swiping. He noticed her shiny straight black hair and the way it was cut in bangs in the front and the only curl was a sweep forward to a point, nearing her chin, in a 1920s flapper style. She pursed her lips as she looked at the appointment, while Kevin noticed the dark liner sharply defining her lips against her cinnamon skin.

She compared the image on the card to his face, then told him, "Please turn to your right." Kevin noticed a slight accent but couldn't place it. She rotated his holographic card to change his image from looking straight ahead to a profile. "Look at the red dot." The receptionist pointed to a small box suspended above her head. A flash of light and she captured his iris pattern.

Her nose was neither large nor small, but the bridge was perfectly straight, like a Greek goddess, and he wondered if it was surgical. She wore an ink-blue suit jacket with wide lapels with a thin border of white. It had the buttery sheen of high thread-count wool and on her left breast; she wore a silver snake brooch inlaid with emeralds and diamonds. Her top was low enough to allow a suggestion of rounded flesh and his eyes darted down to her thin waist and matching short skirt.

Like a salesman, he tried to boost his confidence by making time with the receptionist before the big pitch to the boss. He tried a safe line to see if he could put a crack in her ice-queen demeanor.

"I like your broach. Where did you get it?"

"Don't try to flirt with me, Mr. Wood. I'm all business."

"But..."

"Put your jacket and all electronic devices on the conveyor and stand on the black circle."

Kevin walked between two panels attached to robotic arms. The receptionist tapped a series of commands into her tablet and the mechanical arms began circling around his body faster and faster, whirring around his head in a blur and sinking down to his feet, emitting microwaves from one panel and receiving them in the opposite. Kevin wondered how much damage those arms would do if one of them flew off.

"Does McPherson go through all this?"

"No, this is just for the riff-raff."

Kevin was speechless. This wasn't going as expected.

The scanning stopped, and she looked at the 3D image, then glared at Kevin. Her heels clicked on the wide format porcelain tiles as she marched up to him. She stared right into his eyes, so close he could feel her breath on his face.

"You're hiding something."

"What? No. I-I'm not."

She kneeled and checked his socks and the cuff of his pants. Then she frisked his legs while maintaining eye contact. Still with the piercing stare, she ran her hands along his back and inside his belt.

"Is there going to be a body cavity search?" Kevin asked sarcastically.

"Only if I find something. Do you want me to find something, Mr. Wood?" Her tone was sultry, and at the same time, cruel.

"I..."

"Don't lie - I can see it in your eyes."

Again, with the staring, she ran her hands across his buttocks, then over his upper thighs, then her hand moving between his legs jolted him. She cupped his genitals, and Kevin thought she lingered longer than necessary. She inhaled deeply through her nose.

She's smelling me, Kevin realized. He was off balance and a jumble of humiliation and arousal.

She exhaled through her mouth and licked her lips. Kevin was not sure if it meant her lips were dry or something else. Her breath felt humid and warm but had no scent at all.

She spun away and returned to her terminal, heels again clicking on the porcelain.

"I was wrong. There's nothing there," she said dismissively, as she handed him his jacket.

"Sorry for the inconvenience, but security is our primary concern. You can pick up your WON on the way out. Electronic devices are *not* allowed in meetings with Mr. McPherson."

As if nothing had happened, she returned to her station and smiled. "Please proceed to Elevator Seven at the end of the building. It will take you directly to the 28th floor, where his assistant will meet you." She turned and pointed with her outstretched hand, with the grace of a supermodel. "If there is anything else, I can help you with..." her eyes flickered down, "please don't hesitate to ask."

"Thanks, I might just take you up on that," Kevin said, not entirely sure if her words had hidden meaning.

That was—confusing, he thought. He turned and started walking. He checked his bulge, and decided he was still presentable.

"It's from Tiffany's."

Kevin looked back over his shoulder. "What?"

"You asked where I got the brooch. Mr. McPherson gave it to me as a bonus last year."

Kevin smiled and nodded. As he continued, he had one burning question. Did she know?

From the exterior of the Beijing Bank, the windows appeared as though they were a single massive sheet of glass, but from the inside, you could see the clear 2DPA-1 plastic beams which provided support for the photovoltaic panels. An office building is like an iceberg, and most of it is hidden beneath the surface.

The stained concrete floor was poured in several layers. The bottom was a mottled color that ranged from bright rust to bronze age blood stains, over a base of deep mahogany and buried in a deep pool of clear resin. The patterns interlaced and washed over each other with the grace of a Chinese watercolor, then it rippled to form hills and valleys, and was then made flat and interspersed with floating swirls of translucent blue and wisps of white. Now it took shape into a realistic diorama of an indigo blue lake with boats and ancient Chinese people splashing with their oars or throwing food into the water.

He walked across the solid floor, which was punctuated by pools of light from suspended LED floods, which turned on as he approached. He stepped under a multicolor laser cone and was startled by the illusion that he was standing in the sky, over a moon-sized orb emblazoned with the Beijing Bank corporate logo.

He pressed the button to the elevator, and the door opened with a chime and re-scanned him. It smelled of expensive cleaning products and the burnished stainless-steel door gave an illusion of three dimensions. Elevator seven was an express reserved for the CEO, his staff, and those whom he had summoned.

"Welcome, Kevin Wood," said the elevator. The doors closed and the elevator's ascent caught his stomach. Soon, it announced it had arrived at the 28th floor. The door opened, and a tall man in his early thirties, with freshly cut straight black hair, greeted him.

"Hello, my name is Francis Wang, and you must be… Kevin Wood." Francis sounded very formal, yet the unexpected pause in the middle of the sentence stood out.

There was a certain intensity in Francis's eyes, and a jittery disposition. When he spoke, his mouth was dry, but he didn't seem nervous. Kevin decided he looked like someone who had been to South Korea for a neural bypass or two. A way to use more of the brain was to graft neural stem cells as extra bridges to bypass bottlenecks. It was like constructing a passing lane in the brain, allowing faster thought, and granting the ability to multitask. Eventually, the stem cells would turn into nerve cells, completing the connections, and the brain would learn to use them through the process of neural plasticity. Extra connections could also be made from the memory centers for factual memories, which are difficult to remember.

Depending on how many bypasses were installed, this increased brain activity can cause epileptic seizures, which could lead to death, or worse. The dry mouth was probably from anti-convulsive medications used to control the seizures. Kevin would have been first in line for the procedure if it weren't for the expense and the possibility of becoming a drooling vegetable for the rest of his life.

Francis's speech had a grave tone and a halting rhythm, as if he was trying not to speak about two different subjects at the same time. Several brains and only one mouth. What to do? Kevin half expected his eyes to wander off in different directions, like a chameleon.

Francis led him through a heavy door. "Mr. McPherson is ready to see you… now, and I believe you previously met his lawyer, Mr. Ableman."

At the end of the long office, there were several large windows, but they displayed the view from a different city. They were holograms. Blades were drawn on the actual windows and light filtered down from a massive pyramid shaped skylight above. William McPherson and Charlie Ableman sat behind the prodigious, rosewood conference table that gave an ambrosial aroma to the room.

They stood and Kevin shook both their hands. Ableman was in his late 30's and had the look of someone who didn't go more than a couple of days without a haircut. Kevin noticed he had also recently manicured his nails and his suit cost more than he made in three months.

McPherson held the shake a little longer than expected and looked directly into his eyes, as if he was trying to measure Kevin's soul. What's with all the staring around here? Kevin looked back at him with his chin raised; skeptical and curious. McPherson appeared to be in his early sixties, but may have been younger and aged by worry. He had a drawn expression and was looking at Kevin as if for deliverance from despair.

"It's nice to meet you, Mr. Wood."

"Thanks, the pleasure is mine."

"I see you made it through security," said Mr. McPherson.

"Yes, she was very... thorough."

"And thank God she is—she saved my ass more than once. I spend a fortune on the best security hardware and artificial intelligence, but there is no substitute for the intuition of a highly competent professional."

Francis poured a double of scotch in tumblers in front of McPherson, Ableman, and Kevin. He poured an equal amount of water in McPherson's and placed two lumps of frozen glass, shaped like ice cubes, in Ableman's.

"How do you take your scotch?" Francis asked Kevin.

"Neat, thank you."

Kevin took a sip, and the explosion of flavors surprised him. He was a rum man and was not used to a fine scotch. The initial tingle of smooth alcohol gave way to subtle hints of spice, chocolate and malted barley, finally wrapped with a thick swirl of peat smoke.

"How do you like the scotch? It has a rather earthy flavor," McPherson asked, appearing to be friendly.

"I didn't know dirt tasted so good."

McPherson managed a smile. "That's one way of putting it."

"Getting down to business, you were well recommended, and Mr. Ableman reported the results from your surveillance assignment. The target was one of our own executives, Alfred North. The information you received was top shelf and his security personnel and equipment never detected you."

"So, it was a setup. I'm finished my drink." Kevin placed the tumbler on the desk and stood. His bluff seemed to work.

"No, wait," McPherson motioned for Kevin to stay seated. "Not a setup, Mr. Wood, an audition. We need to call upon reliable, competent people with your skills from time to time, so we hired a few detectives to carry out relatively simple tasks, like surveillance, to see how they measure up. I'm happy to tell you, you finished at the top."

Kevin leaned back against the leather chair with his fingers locked behind his head and gazed at McPherson with clear skepticism written on his face.

"Our executive had the most sophisticated anti-surveillance gear money could buy, and you flew under the radar, as it were, and his driver didn't see a thing. We need a contractor with your discretion and ability for a much more serious issue."

"Don't you have anyone on staff?" Kevin tried to play hard to get.

"Yes, of course, but not with your special abilities. Also, for sensitive assignments, we prefer to keep our operators at, shall we say, arm's length."

"I see." Kevin's eyes narrowed.

"What do you know about my family, Mr. Wood?" McPherson said.

"You're the founder of McAir Corporation. You're one of the richest people in the country. I think your son was the target of an assassination or kidnapping attempt last summer."

"Yes. If it weren't for the quick action of a certain bartender who saved him. I don't suppose you know anything about that little pop-gun she was carrying, do you?"

"Well, actually, I may know something about that." McPherson had done his homework, and there was probably no point in trying to deny it.

"You don't often see a bartender packing advanced custom-made weaponry like that. She must be special," McPherson said.

"It was a prototype, and I gave it to her for field testing," not wanting to give more away about their relationship than necessary.

"The way investigators described her actions, she seemed almost supernatural. To be honest, I had a hard time taking it literally, but Alan survived, and I owe you both a great deal."

Kevin didn't really like McPherson's type. There was an inherent hypocrisy with these barons. They dress in the finest suits, hang out with the most powerful and beautiful people, but at heart, they are all robbers—robber barons.

"Don't thank me, it was 100% Jade who saved your son," Kevin said.

"Be that as it may, she isn't here, and you are. I would like you to take on an assignment for me. But before you do, it would be fair to tell you about myself, so you know what you are getting into."

Kevin sensed there was something heavy coming for the old man to meet with him in person, and something pretty serious to make him look so hollowed out.

"My grandfather immigrated from Scotland in 1965 and worked on the oil rigs. He saved enough money to buy a water truck and soon, he had a fleet of them delivering water to oil rigs. My father was born, and Grandpa put him through university as a mechanical engineer. He took his share of the family business and started his own, which included directional drilling and later advanced fracking equipment and supplies.

"I moved in a different direction and went to MIT. I started developing software to optimize oil exploration and production, then moved into AI programs for stock and bond trading. By the time I was thirty, my fortune had surpassed that of my father, and I diversified into real estate, transportation, and communications.

"Then I started the McAir Company, and that changed everything. Using high altitude drones, I created my own wireless communications company from the bottom up, and on a shoestring budget. I could demolish the competition and still make a large profit. It's basically a constellation of solar powered fixed wing platforms on autopilot hovering 20-30 km above the earth. They provide cell phone and data service at a fraction of the cost of standard masts or satellites. Also, they are cheap to replace, and can be upgraded where satellites cannot. Before, cell phone companies had to lease the space for each tower or antenna and install and maintain expensive equipment in thousands of locations in each city. The lease for a single location can be over $50,000 per year, and prime locations can be vastly higher. A few dozen flying wings over a city, each bigger than a van, with hardware the weight of a fat wallet, could replace them all.

A light appeared in McPherson's dull eyes when he discussed his business, and Kevin recognized a well-worn but enthusiastic promotional speech. Regardless, he knew something about the emergence of Unmanned Aerial Vehicles (UAV) in the cell phone industry and wanted to learn more. He was warming up to the idea of working for McPherson but knew these guys would throw someone like him under the bus in a minute.

"The drones were completely solar powered and flew high above the clouds and passenger aircraft in the mid atmosphere. Solar operates the electric motors during the day and batteries keep it operating at night. Their altitude is above the jet streams, so wind is not strong.

"The ideal high-altitude drone has wide, light, high-speed propellers to move through the thin atmosphere. Variable pitch propellers were not good enough. It also needed a long, ultralight wingspan. There wasn't much turbulence, so the structure didn't have to be very strong and because of the very low air density, winds were not as destructive. A 140 km/hr wind in the upper stratosphere has the same effect on the structure as a gentle spring breeze at sea level.

"Other companies tried dirigibles. They have an extensive surface area which is great for solar panels, but the wind blew them off course. I decided on a fixed wing design since I can precisely position them. Mine were only three meters wide and launched inside a hydrogen balloon, which was like a giant amniotic sac that split open and dropped the drone when it was in the high stratosphere. The wing had a plastic 2DPA-1 reinforced aerogel foam core covered with a polymer membrane. The structure was so light; ninety percent of the weight was from the tiny communication hardware, batteries, and motors.

"Although we can fly them remotely, they were almost always in a holding pattern around the center of their service area using autonomous pilot software that I spent a bundle developing. I designed each platform to stay in service for five years before we needed to land it and upgrade the hardware.

"Drones could transfer data to other drones at great distance using lasers. They formed a continental data network, so if a local communication service provider refused to route my calls, I could go around them. I could route them all the way to Argentina if I needed to. The connections were fast and reliable enough to replace long-distance fiber optics cables.

"Back then, cell frequencies were regulated and sold by the government. Some were reserved for startup companies, and I bid on them when they were available, but a couple of frequencies were not really enough for an effective wireless company. I needed longer wavelengths for penetrating buildings as well as shorter frequencies for high-speed data transfers.

"I became frustrated at the slow pace and cost of buying frequencies, and the competition refused to lease them to me, so I decided to *borrow* their frequencies. Because the angle of my waves was usually perpendicular to theirs, I caused them very little interference. No matter, they were livid and pushed the government to enforce their monopoly. They fined me, and tried to shut me down, but I appealed everything to buy time, so they tried a different approach.

"The competition had long, deep connections with political parties and have been heavy financial contributors for many years. At the same time the government pulled my flight permits, the other cellphone companies organized a fear campaign alleging the system would be unsafe. They owned many television stations and newspapers, which provided interviews with so-called *experts* who said drones represent a safety hazard and no one would be safe from them crashing to the ground or hitting airplanes.

They donated money to fringe anti Wi-Fi and other Luddite groups to organize what looked like grassroots opposition. Social media stories appeared in people's feeds regarding brain tumors in children caused by high levels of microwaves from my drones. The levels reported as being produced were so exaggerated, people expected it would be like sticking your head in a microwave oven.

"So how did you deal with this?" Kevin asked, leaning forward, and raising his eyebrows. The ending of the story was already a foregone conclusion since Kevin knew McPherson made the company an enormous success, but he was intrigued by how he got there.

"Well, I couldn't match the money and political power of the cell phone companies, so I went about it another way. Law and regulatory enforcement were weakening so, I flew them without approval like the bootleg offshore radio stations near London a hundred years ago, broadcasting 'from *somewhere in the Atlantic*.' In other cases, I used blackmail, threats, and bribery against government and law enforcement. I'm not a saint, Mr. Wood, and neither was my father. Competition is not always fair, and if you want to rise above it, you can't be fair either.

Kevin pursed his lips slightly, but he was far from surprised.

"Government regulation still had a few teeth back then, but the Kessler Syndrome came to the rescue. The Russians exploded one of their own satellites in 2021, and in 2025, a Chinese satellite collided with a Russian one head-on, traveling at 7.8 kilometers per second and created a cloud of millions of fragments. When other low-earth satellites passed through the cloud, they were hit and scattered more debris and the cloud got larger and hit more satellites which created more debris, and so on, until it destroyed all low earth orbit satellites. Even flying through the cloud to get to higher altitudes became risky. My constellation of drones became essential, and the government had to back off.

"The rest is history. Most cell phone towers are now rusting relics from the past, and the companies that built them—forgotten. Although my William Randolph Hearst approach to maintaining a monopoly worked for a while, there were few barriers to entry for other drone-based companies. I created the technology and set the business model and others copied it. I couldn't stop them, short of shooting down their drones. Maybe I should have. Anyway, I went public, sold a minority stake of my shares, and diversified."

Kevin leaned back in his chair and crossed his legs, and McPherson mistook this for impatience. "Bear with me just a little longer. I'm getting to the point soon."

"No worries. I could talk about technology all day."

"When the Chinese loan crisis struck in 2047, and funds left Canada because of monetary de-linking, it became difficult for the Bank of Beijing to remain in business here, since they desperately needed capital to prop up their operations back home. I stepped in to take it over at a fire-sale price and that's how I got in this chair." He opened his arms as if to include the entire building as well.

"I wanted to put the cutthroat business behind me and become a boring old banker. Make a little more money, and pass on a stable business to my son. I think I understood the business model but underestimated the politics. Perhaps I was naïve and overlooked that there were others who were not happy seeing an upstart moving in. You could say that I had earned something of a reputation as a disrupter. There were threats, extortion attempts, and even the attempted assassination of my son." The grave look once again overcame him, and his tone lowered to a near whisper.

"And now, my only son, my only child, has been kidnapped. It's been two days and there has been no communication from him or from his abductors. Since I suspect competing business interests were behind his assassination attempt, the same motive may be behind the kidnapping."

McPherson exhaled deeply and bowed his head with his hands clasped on the table. Mr. Ableman continued. "We are asking you to find out who the kidnappers are and facilitate release or rescue. Money's no object, so any reasonable fee plus expenses will be provided. I suggest an opening retainer of 100,000 loonies, if that is acceptable to you. Naturally, the utmost discretion will be required."

"That goes without saying," replied Kevin.

"The retainer is good enough for now. My fee is still 500 loonies per day plus expenses, but expenses will be high." He realized he could have probably soaked this guy for much more but taking too much would leave him in McPherson's debt, and he didn't want to put himself in that position. He didn't like the idea that McPherson's son was kidnapped. If he was in McPherson's position, he would also do anything in his power to help someone he cared about.

"You have a deal, Mr. Wood." Ableman shook his hand.

"I'll get your son back," Kevin said with conviction.

McPherson just nodded. His grief was beyond words.

After the meeting, Kevin dropped by reception and held his ID under a scanner to unlock the storage box that held his WON.

I may be crazy, but I'd like to get to know that woman, he told himself. He walked over to the reception terminal to ask her for her chat ID, but another visitor approached her station first. She gave him a nod as she spoke to the new person, and Kevin gave her a wave and left.

Back in his car, he tinted the windows and pulled down his pants. He reached into his underwear and removed a small black listening device the size of a pea and uploaded the audio to his WON.

Did she know I had it? It was too small to be detected by the microwave scanners, so she couldn't have seen it. *If she did, why did she let me go?*

On his way home, he tried to unpack the day's events. In his line of business, he couldn't be too judgmental. Sometimes he wished he had a straight job and didn't have to wade through the mud and could build a real life.

Not everything about his job was dark. Everyone deserves to find the truth, to find a missing loved one, to find out who is cheating, stealing, blackmailing, or just standing in their way. Sometimes, he gets to be the knight in shining armor to set right an injustice, and he hopes this case will be one of them.

Still, despite the sincere display of emotion from McPherson, Kevin still had a feeling the old man wasn't quite playing him straight.

Chapter Eight

A Rainbow in the Mist

Kevin looked at the iris scanner and rang the buzzer. A moment later, he heard Jade's voice on the intercom. "Kevin, come in." The door to the high-rise apartment slid open and Kevin entered, surprised to find himself in an opulent lobby.

He had never been in an apartment of this quality. Lasers tracked his face, projecting one image in one eye and a separate one in the other, giving him a binocular three-dimensional image. The hologram came with an actual mist driver so he could feel the humidity and smell the fresh water. A rainbow appeared in the mist above, and he heard and saw the squawks of parrots and other tropical birds that flew through it. "Kevin Wood, welcome to River's Edge Apartments," greeted the waterfall. He never quite got used to being called by name by an auto greeter.

He entered the elevator. "Kevin Wood, next stop, eighteenth floor." The customized elevator music played a tune from the mid-twenties, but he couldn't quite remember the lyrics or the name. How did it go? *'You climb mountains to the clouds, pushed by the vacuum behind, the sky is blue and the wind so loud, escape is all in your...'* He tried but couldn't remember the rest.

It was not like him to be nervous about meeting a woman. After all, this was just a business proposition. Jade opened the door. "Come in, buddy." She tied a ponytail on one side and her striped thigh-high stockings matched the pattern on her sleeves. Her black leather top with a school-girl cape and tie, matched her short-shorts. She looked like a living manga character, complete with pools of light filling the bottoms of her eyes. "Sorry, I was going to take a Slipper today, so I got dressed for work here," she said while opening her arms to her outfit. Her expression changed from cheerful to bashful.

"Oh no, it's fine." He tried not to stare too long at her body. "You look great," nodding his head rapidly after he spoke.

She ducked back into the bathroom. "I'm almost finished my nails. I'll be out in a minute."

He walked up to the floor-to-ceiling glass wall facing the river valley. He stood almost touching the glass and looked at the ground between his feet. Long shadows blanketed the field, leaving the skeletal trees as one-legged sentinels in front of the building.

"I'm glad you finally made it here," she called out from the bathroom, her voice sounding distracted.

"Yeah, me too. I get so wrapped up with my shit, I forget to get a life," he laughed. "Nice place."

"Thanks. I know what you mean. So, what have you been doing lately?"

"I got a new case—a big one," Kevin said.

"Cool bud, that's great. You sound like you aren't too thrilled about it."

"Ahh, well, it's just that I'm going to need some help and I usually work alone."

"Okay."

"Okay, so I was hoping we could work on this together," he said as fast as possible. "There, I said it."

"Really? Are you serious?" She said with a chuckle. She left the bathroom and was smiling with amusement and astonishment, then her expression shifted to serious. "Don't take this the wrong way, but why me?"

"You have amazing skills, and I would like working with you. I usually don't play well with others, but I think we'd make a great team. Besides, I have a big expense account to pay you."

"What's it about?"

They sat together across a clear glass table. Her nail attachments were solid black with an iridescent halo. "It's your college boy again. This time, he got himself kidnapped. His father is richer than God and would pay anything to get him back. He sends his regards, by the way."

"Was it his idea to hire me?" Her tone hardened.

"No, not at all. It's one hundred percent my idea, and he didn't even know I was going to ask. I told him as little as possible, but he knows how you rescued his son. He probably knows more than he lets on."

Jade stiffened a little, her tone wary. "What do you want me to do?"

"It depends. We could split up canvassing people or work together, depending on our skill-set, I guess."

"And what *skill set* do you think *I* have?"

"You have instincts that are borderline supernatural. You have cat-like reflexes and are an ass-kicker par excellence. But more than that, you have people skills." Kevin used his winning-people-over grin.

Jade looked hard at him for a moment, then snorted a laugh. "You think I'm an ass-kicker with people skills?"

"Yeah, people *like* you. They open up to you, and you would be great as an investigator."

"Ok, but being an ass-kicker is not really part of my, uh, *career objectives*."

"Let's hope it never comes to that."

The next day, they were both at home and they joined each other in a video chat. "Alright, while I'm hacking Alan's phone account, you can go to the university and interview the witnesses. Here is a list of his known friends and classes from his father." Kevin tapped his WON to send the information to Jade.

"After that, you can sweet talk/bribe security into letting us have a look at the video. Don't take the first *no* they give you. Information is only private to those that can't pay for it," Kevin said.

Kevin suggested the best way to contact witnesses would be for Jade to make a personal plea to his classmates for help. She contacted Alan's professors and received a quick reply, and a professor invited her to make an announcement at the beginning of class. That's great, she thought. It's the perfect way to connect with as many potential witnesses as possible. That sucks, she also thought. She was terrified of public speaking. What had she gotten herself into? She should tell Kevin this was a mistake, and he should look for someone else. Kevin, I hate your fucking guts.

On the other hand, if she wanted to ever get a real job, these are the kinds of skills she needed. It would be a learning experience. But why did it have to be here? She would have to face the same school she left in disgrace. She searched for a bromide; *that which does not kill us makes us stronger.*

"That's it. Let's do this thing," she told herself.

Jade wore her stretch denim pants with high boots with medium heels. She was going for a university student look, up a notch—professional yet approachable. She hung her jacket in the hallway and waited for the professor to accompany her into the class.

"Hello, you must be Jade," said the middle-aged man with a graying beard and kind, blue eyes.

"Hello Professor Pearson," replied Jade. "Thanks for the opportunity."

"It's nothing. The McPherson family has helped us so much, it is the least I can do. Let's get started." Pearson opened the door for Jade. She had a bitter taste of electricity on her tongue, and her legs felt like they belonged to someone else.

Holy shit! I thought this was a classroom, not a theater, she thought to herself.

Jade could feel their eyes like laser beams and sense the energy from each of them as if two hundred people were yelling at once. The young students, just a couple of years younger than her, some bored and cynical, some talking amongst themselves, others looked at her, wondering what this unusual announcement could be about. All the trouble she had in university came flooding back to her as she approached the podium. Her palms were sweaty, and her heart was pounding. She was afraid she would freeze up. Think happy thoughts, think happy thoughts, she told herself.

"Thank you, Professor Pearson, for allowing me to make this announcement," she said with a quiver in her voice. She felt like the ground was going to open and swallow her, and she wished it would hurry the hell up.

She felt like her body switched to autopilot and she heard herself speaking. "Most of you know your classmate, Alan McPherson, was kidnapped two days ago on this campus and I am working to find out where he is and get him back. His parents are worried to death, and they are asking for your help." She was surprised she had not yet lost control of her bladder or something just as humiliating.

She displayed home video, security video and stills on the big smart screen to jog their memories and explained what she knew about his last known location. She could see their expressions change from puzzled, to interested, and then to sympathetic. She was getting through to them. Her worst fears did not happen, and she gained confidence.

"Alan and I met before, and I can honestly say I would stop a bullet for him. But I need information. Maybe you noticed people lurking around. If you saw the kidnapping, or anything at all suspicious, please let me know. Call or email me. Anything you say will be confidential. Professor Pearson has agreed to post my contact information on eClass, so if you think of anything, let me know. Thank you, everyone, and thank you, Professor Pearson."

"Thank *you*, Jade. The McPherson family has been a big benefactor of the University of Alberta for many years. You may have noticed the McPherson name is on the new Engineering building. We owe so much to them. If there is anything you know, please contact Jade. Thanks again for coming."

Jade smiled and turned to leave the lecture hall with the roar of applause behind her.

She immediately went to the bathroom and freshened her makeup. Looking at herself in the mirror reassured her she had survived. She felt invigorated by the adrenaline still pumping in her blood.

Next stop, the security office. From the entrance, she could see two security people at a service counter. A young male security officer was speaking to a student and a female officer was unoccupied and looking at a screen. Jade went back into the hallway and sent a text to Kevin and waited until the student left. She undid two more buttons on her blouse and put on a smile as she walked up to the male officer. She leaned forward and put her hands on the counter.

"Hi, my name is Jade Yang and I'm working for the McPherson family. Did you hear about the kidnapping?" She handed him a card with her holographic picture, name, and number.

"I wasn't on duty during the kidnapping, but we are all very familiar with the incident," the guard said.

"Great, the university has been a big help. I just spoke to Professor Pearson's class, and he was kind enough to post my contact information on their eClass." She leaned forward a little more and showed him the image on her WON (as well as a bit more of her cleavage). She noticed his pupils in his blue eyes widen and she gave her hair a little toss.

"Nice," he said, thinking he was referring to what Professor Pearson had done. His cheeks glowed.

"His family would really appreciate copies of surveillance video in the area so they can find their son. Will you help?" Her expression looked vulnerable, her tone pleading.

"We aren't supposed to share video with anyone but the police, but there aren't enough of them to do anything anyway," the security officer said, a brief shadow crossing his face. "I'll tell you what, my boss asked us to compile the video from the entire campus. I could let you have a copy, but you didn't get it from me. Got it?"

"Got it," Jade winked and gave him a dazzling smile.

He began tapping on the display. Jade twirled a lock of her hair around her finger. He paused. He tapped again with more force. His expression changed to near panic.

"Hold on. Shit. Shit. Shit! It's gone. Not just gone, it's deleted. I just put it there an hour ago and now it's gone!" He turned and glared at the other security guard. She avoided eye contact but looked guilty like someone who just produced an unexpected and sulfurous fart. Her bleached hair was wrapped tightly around the crown of her head leaving a ring of dark above her hairline. She sat bolt upright, and the Velcro on her uniform strained against a body grown too large to fit.

"Isn't there a backup somewhere?" Jade asked.

"No. It wasn't just deleted, it was purged. There is no backup anymore. I can't get it back. My boss is going to be so pissed off."

"What about the original video, before you compiled it?"

"Let me check," his voice clung onto blind hope for just a minute, before… "No. Purged too."

Jade couldn't believe what she was hearing. It was almost in her hand and now it's gone. She dropped her vulnerable facade like a wet towel and she replaced her disbelief with smoldering, predatory rage. She dropped her head and let her hair fall in front of her face. Then she slowly stood up and marched toward the woman. She could feel the guilt radiating from her like she was a fresh, spit-roasted pig. She was trying to make herself look busy by typing on her display. Jade noticed a bead of sweat appearing on her upper lip and her eyes were wide with tension. Jade walked toward her, leaned forward with her fingers arched on the counter as if she was digging her claws into it. Jade glared into her eyes, close enough to smell her sweat.

In her mind's eye, Jade shoved her arm down the guard's throat, making her eyes bulge like zits ready to pop. Jade felt the warm, wet feeling of her stomach and ripped into the thoracic cavity, feeling the tachycardia of the guard's heart. With one mighty tug, she ripped it out, still beating, and held it in front of her face, making the broken aorta and veins wiggle like noodles, and spraying blood everywhere. Jade enjoyed the guard's brief flash of comprehension before her eyes glazed over and she died.

She could no longer avoid Jade, and looked at her like a doe caught in the headlights.

May I help you?" the guard croaked.

Jade paused her reverie and read her name tag out loud. "Adriana Beazer."

"Yes?" she said like a bleating lamb.

Jade pivoted and stormed away, her stainless-steel heels clicking on the vinyl flooring.

Chapter Nine

Cross Reference

Kevin received a text from Jade, and put a cup of coffee down on his kitchen table to read it. Jade was updating him on what happened at the university. She was upset, so he called her.

"Don't worry about it. You got the name of the security guard, right?" he asked.

"Yeah."

"We know she's an accomplice, so this is the best clue we have." Kevin's suggestion hung in the silence until Jade disconnected.

He let out a sigh and reached for his tepid coffee.

Whoop, Whoop, his WON sounded, then a voice, "Drone for lightning delivery. Please proceed to the rendezvous point."

He stepped out in front of his apartment building, and a courier drone was flying over the entrance. It hovered away from the trees and Kevin looked up at it. He could feel the wind from its four fan rotors and he squinted against the flying pine needles. It recognized his face and lowered a box down on a long thin cable until it rested on the ground. The drone detached the cable from the package and reeled it back up, before flying away.

He cleared off a spot on his kitchen table, opened it, and read a note sitting on top of a WON.

"Kevin.

This is the account used by Alan to back up his WON. His password was 4chaQueta?. I have included a blank WON if you would like to restore it.

Francis."

I wonder how Francis knew Alan's password? Kevin backed up the WON and found it had been set to track Alan's location. He traced Alan to the point of the kidnapping, and then the tracking went dead. The kidnappers must have disabled it.

He set up a search focused on the area of the kidnapping and ordered information from Intelimart. Only companies who need access to the information for marketing may purchase it, so he set up an account using one of his fake IDs and logged on. Ostensibly, Kevin represented a business which was marketing to people in the university area and wanted to know who frequented the Business Building and Hub Mall. He spoke the command into his monitor.

"Filter November 20 to 27"

Two thousand hits.

Who was there when the kidnapping happened? he wondered.

Time=2:45-3:00

<Filter>

Six hundred hits

"Let's see who had their contacts on."

Occupation = Student

Income = Less than twenty thousand loonies per year

<Filter>

Three hundred hits

Kevin transferred two hundred loonies and downloaded the sanitized top-level data on the three hundred people. Low to middle-income people who liked technology were the most likely to have their lenses in free mode where they uploaded everything they saw or heard.

Kevin flipped through the metadata. It was the best money could buy, but not good enough. This was the tedious part. He had to go through each of the three hundred people to see if they were close enough to witness the kidnapping.

"Number one," he sighed, rubbed his eyes, and started looking.

He paid an extra fifty loonies for detailed data and received a profile of the person, including purchasing habits. Judging by the amount of data, she must use free mode.

He assembled his home-made three-foot wire basket antennae and aimed it roughly toward the northwest, while monitoring the strength of the wireless signal as he tweaked it. Then he opened a connection to the deadhead's wireless network using a hacked password to make his internet untraceable. He ran his C20 script to hack into the raw, unsanitized data on the server using an arcane vulnerability he had discovered, and, in a flash, a list of video files appeared, sorted by the time they were captured.

This information was not supposed to be available to anyone. Artificial intelligence programs analyzed the data with no human ever seeing it.

He purchased detailed data on one hundred, then went through the list, starting at the time of the kidnapping to see what each subject was looking at. It was now 1:00 a.m. and the caffeine was not enough to keep him alert, and he took a gray market Modafinil.

At number 107, he found a subject who was in the correct area at the right time. The video began in what appeared to be a business course. Judging by the projection on the classroom screen, it was a finance class, and the professor wrapped up his lecture, but the subject was looking around the room and at her WON. When the class was over, she picked up her tablet and left the lecture hall with a female friend. Her eyes alternated between her friend's eyes and looking ahead to where she was walking. She turned the corner toward the exit and Kevin recognized Alan walking with a group of students leaving the Business Building. The subject's eyes alternated from her friend to the shoes of the women who were walking in front and then briefly glancing at men's bottoms.

The subject walked ten meters behind Alan as they headed to the Hub Mall. He was with an entourage of five other well-dressed students, including three women and two other men. Since the contacts were linked to the subject's WON, audio was available, but it was too far to hear what they were saying. Alan appeared to be telling an amusing story. His friends turned to listen, flashing their perfect smiles. A dark woman of Indian descent toyed with a lock of her hair in a coquettish way.

Just then, a man shouted, and the subject's eyes darted towards him. Three men in the distance with wrap-around mirrored glasses, balaclavas, and guns grabbed Alan. One punched him in the stomach and cracked the butt of his pistol against his head. The girls shrieked and bolted, and her heart rate shot up to 120 beats a minute.

The subject looked over her shoulder, then stopped, and two of the goons grabbed each of Alan's arms and jabbed their guns in his ribs. The subject gasped and stopped blinking. Blood streamed down Alan's bowed face. The third man stood with legs wide and both hands on his silenced 9mm machine pistol. Bouncing on the balls of his feet like a prizefighter, darting back and forth, yelling, "Nobody fucking move!"

He fired off a warning burst with a muffled rattle and buzz like a steam-powered sewing machine.

The subject froze in fear. Kevin read her vital signs displayed in a sliding bar to the left of the video. The lenses detected her pupils were dilated and heart rate, blood pressure and adrenaline spiking. The kidnappers rushed Alan toward the parking lot, with the third man following, glancing behind, to make sure no one was following. These guys know their shit, he thought to himself. Probably ex-military. He recognized they were unnaturally buff and had gaps between their teeth. Juice monkeys. He suspected they might be mercenaries, with no lasting ties to whoever ordered the kidnapping.

Kevin was encouraged by his results so far. Ok, now I need to find who saw the get-away car.

He checked each of the other subjects and subject number thirty saw the car from the rear but none of them close enough or at the right angle to see the license plate number, but he still took captures of all of them. You never knew, in his line of work, what minor detail might crack it.

The Modafinil kicked in and he was in his groove and worked with no concept of time.

He loaded the interface to his wall screen and scrubbed through the video. The best part looked like the subject was a hundred meters directly behind the car. Zooming in to the where the license plate should be, he found nothing but a constellation of pixels. He tossed more frames, one by one into the Entrapolator.

His voice commanded and his arms waved like a conductor, selecting, copying and pasting frames around the license plate with pinches of his fingers and a twist of his wrist, then dropping them into the app while his aging computer chugged away at the computations. At the 10th iteration, the original image became less nebulous, and he could make out fuzzy shapes of numbers and letters. Statistical analysis determined the probability of a pixel being a certain shade or color at a certain location. The fuzz began to congeal.

25th iteration.

"Is that an F or an E?"

29th iteration.

"LWE 746 - Got it!" He said, collapsing back in his chair with a victory groan.

It was 5:30 a.m. and the fatigue hit him like a Mickey Finn. He remembered when he was high, he could go all night, but he also remembered how he felt afterwards. Come down's a bitch. He needed to keep reminding himself of the bad things that come with drugs to avoid falling back into them.

There was one ultimate step to trace the license plate and find out who they were. The portal to the credit checking service asked him for his credentials and he entered the name of his fake car dealership.

Licence = LWE 746

Result:

Name=Alexander Livingstone

Make=Xiaomai

Model=Pesca

Color=Gray

His jaw dropped slightly. The kidnapper's car was a brown Toyota; the license plate was stolen. He hit a dead end.

Resignation set in. He needed to piss like a racehorse and probably had for a long time. When he finished, he shuffled to his bed with his pants still open and let them fall to the floor. A gap in the curtain projected thin gray light against the wall. Shadows of dark pines filtered the streetlight and splintered and sintered it into quivering globes against the wall, alone against the darkness in his room. He slumped into his bed and minutes later, felt sleep approaching, then awoke with a sudden start.

Chapter Ten

The Burning Accordion

This was not exactly Kevin's scene. The time was 8:05 p.m. He suggested they meet at 8:15 but he arrived early to make sure he got there first.

The tables were dimly lit from spotlights suspended on the framework of the suspended ceiling and ambient sounds filtered down from hidden speakers. A man with a wide mustache played a folk song on accordion on the stage. He wore a loose white shirt, his scarlet vest matched his beret and the sash around his waist. His face expressed every exquisite note, and like his accordion was an extension of his soul. The song's title, *Come Back to Sorrento*, hung in mid-air above the stage. Stratified clouds, as if from tobacco smoke, hung motionless, then wafted behind the rapid steps of waiters and waitresses.

The front lights darkened, and a rear spotlight burned, leaving the musician silhouetted against the limelight. Tendrils of smoke rose and danced from his burning accordion.

Kevin wore his tan corduroy jacket. It was not quite formal enough for the occasion, but by his standards, it was. He finished scrolling through the wine list on his WON and selected the Ready to Order button. From nowhere, a waiter appeared.

"Can I get you something while you're waiting for the lady?"

"I'll have a rum and coke now, and when the lady arrives, I'll have a bottle of wine. What do you recommend for around 150 loonies?"

He glanced at Kevin's threadbare sleeves and raised his eyebrows slightly.

"Certainly. I would recommend a 2044 Sequoia Grove Cambium red wine, but we also have more affordable vintages," the waiter added, with the slightest sniff.

"Are you suggesting I can't afford it?"

"Not at all. As you wish, sir." He tapped the order on his WON and backed away from the table.

An attractive young woman delivered his drink as a new song started. It was a tango, and the accordion player was joined by an ensemble including guitar, violins, piano, and a double bass. The accordion player now played a smaller bandoneón. The spotlight reflected its gold inlay floral patterns connected with a filigree of vines. The bandoneón player held his head down and his shoulders pumped out the staccato rhythms of the tango. The wide brim of his black hat covered his eyes.

Kevin became lost in the music. The Latin sounds brought back memories of steamy nights in Havana, and a woman in a summer dress, swaying to the rhythm on the dance floor. His thoughts returned to the present, and he glanced again towards the entrance in anticipation of Jade.

He looked back toward the band. 'Wasn't the accordion player wearing a beret earlier?' He realized this was a hologram and a compilation of several performances and remembered the restaurant only had live bands on the weekends and this was Thursday.

A customer walked between Kevin and the stage, blocking one of the lasers projecting on his retina, resulting in a jarring two-dimensional halo. He glanced at his rum and coke, watching the light reflecting off the surface of the glistening ice cubes.

"Hey buddy."

Kevin stood and tried to not look nonplussed. She was wearing a short black skirt and carrying a small matching purse.

"Hey yourself!" With a nervous smile, he told her, "You look great!"

Her expression became demure as she looked away and thanked him.

"Is this dinner your way of apologizing for making me speak in public at the university?"

"Sorry about that. I thought it would be the best way to get information about the kidnappers." Kevin motioned for her to sit.

"I hate to be a pain, but could we sit over there?" Jade pointed to an empty table by the wall.

"Sure, why not." A gesture of his hand brought the waiter, who moved the menus and Kevin's drink. Jade sat with her back to the wall, facing the entrance.

"Sorry, I'm usually not this high maintenance."

"No problem. I like it better here, too."

The waiter brought the wine and presented the wine bottle for Kevin to read the label, before opening the bottle and placing it on the table. Kevin had done his research and picked up the cork, read the impression, and checked it was intact and not too dry or wet. The waiter poured a few millimeters into Kevin's glass. Kevin swirled it a few times, checking its color and clarity, and noticed the ripples that clung to the sides, indicating the correct alcohol content. He brought it to his nose and sniffed, then repeated this again and took a small sip. He nodded to the waiter, and he filled their glasses and placed the menus.

"I didn't know you knew so much about wines," Jade said.

"I don't know that much, but I read that's what you're supposed to do when the waiter serves you. I like wine too, but I'm more of a highball kinda guy."

"You could have fooled me, and I'm not that easily fooled. The wine is excellent."

"Our client gave us an expense budget, and this is a business meeting." Kevin smiled and raised his glass.

"What's on the menu?" She opened the leather-bound folder and glanced at Kevin as the waiter arrived. "I don't know what's good here. Can you order?"

"Sure. Let's start with bruschetta for an appetizer, then pasta carbonara with asparagus."

"Very good, sir." The waiter walked briskly, without hurrying back to the kitchen.

The holoshow had not yet restarted and wordless music drifted in from a band playing in the distance, as if they were seated on the patio and the music was filtering from inside. Not long after, and the waiter reappeared with the bruschetta.

Kevin was fascinated with how the wine glistened on her lips and how her head tilted back when she laughed. He studied every contour of her face, but her eyes were definitely his favorite feature. He had to look carefully to see her makeup. She had smoky shadow along the outside of the upper eyelid—a thin silvery liner on the bottom near the corner accentuated the shape that he found so appealing. Mercurial, they shifted from amused to happy to grave. He suspected they could change to steely should the occasion arise. He noticed how they stopped to glance at the room, especially towards the door.

Jade's manicured hands were resting on top of the table, and he wondered if this was a good time to put his hands on hers.

"... then I noticed he was following me."

Her words jolted him. Her expression was serious but matter-of-fact.

"Wha... What?" Kevin said, embarrassed as he realized he had not been paying attention. Jade noticed it too and sighed.

"After you gave me Adriana Beazer's address, I drove by her home. She lives in an exclusive gated community north of Morinville called New Zion. It's exclusive since only members of their church are allowed to live there, not exclusive because you need money or anything. Actually, it looks a bit like a dump and most of the houses there are mobile homes. Security is harsh and there's razor wire on top of the gate and an armed guard at the entrance, so I didn't go in. Have you heard of them?"

"Yeah, they're Apostles. I don't know too much else, but I'm going to check them out. When were you followed?"

"It was the next day. I took the bus to work, and a car followed it until I got off near work. On the way home, the same guy in a different car followed the bus again. I stayed on the bus as it passed my stop, then got off and ducked into the Hudson's Bay building and down into the subway before he had time to get out of his car. Whoever he was, he didn't find me, but I took the train all the way to Inglewood when I got off at a Slipper kiosk and drove home."

Kevin tensed. Someone was following Jade? Were the kidnappers aware of their operation? "What did he look like?"

"Late twenties, white, crewcut, steroid monster. What's wrong?" Jade asked.

Kevin nodded. "It sounds like one of the guys that kidnapped the McPherson kid."

"Don't worry about it. I'm a big girl now," she said in an immature voice that was meant to sound sarcastic but came out sexy.

The music started again, but Kevin was facing away from the stage, so didn't see the bandoneón player start another tango.

"So how was your day?" Jade enquired.

"Okay. I got decent video of the kidnapping, but the getaway car plates were stolen, so I couldn't track them. That Beazer bitch is the best chance to lead us to the kidnappers. We should hear from them soon if they're going to ask for ransom. They're being quiet to make the old man sweat."

The waiter inserted the steaming pasta from Jade's left, then did the same for Kevin and continued to top off their drinks in one fluid motion.

Kevin felt a glow from the booze and didn't feel like talking shop anymore. He held his glass out and offered a toast. "To our new partnership." Jade clinked the rim of her glass below the rim of his. "To our new venture," she said with mock determination.

Jade took a forkful of spaghetti and rotated it against the plate until she bundled it around the fork.

"Mmm, this is so good," she said.

Kevin held his spoon in his left hand and turned his forkful against it until it was wrapped as well. He realized ordering spaghetti wasn't the best choice if it ends up on his face, but the first bite changed his mind.

"It really is good. Before you said you lived in Vancouver, what brings you to Edmonton?"

"I like the weather." They both laughed.

"Actually, I'm originally from Edmonton and went to high school at Strathcona. I took mixed martial arts, you know, MMA. I was on the wrestling team and was good at most sports. Things weren't good at home and in my first year at the U of A, I dropped out and moved in with my brother in Burnaby."

After a moment's silence, she said, "I told you about it already, but I was messed up in my brother's business for a couple of years and I wanted to get away. I was his bodyguard and good at it, but I can't do it anymore. One day, it really got to me, so I moved here to start a new life."

"I totally get it. I haven't had a perfect life either," Kevin said.

"I didn't know too many people out here anymore, but I had money saved and I got a place and a job at the bar. That's when I met you. You seemed like a nice guy, but not too nice. I don't feel like I really fit in with the straight crowd."

She realized her Freudian slip and changed the subject.

"Have you always lived in Edmonton?" Jade asked.

"No, I grew up in Weyburn, Saskatchewan. I was a good student but didn't always get my assignments in. Learning was fun but homework wasn't, and English courses were boring so I skipped. Hacking and making weapons were even more fun. Like I said before, they pushed me into the army. I had good friends, but the army thinks friends are expendable. I liked it for a while, but

I stayed for one day too long. They stationed me with the Princess Pats, and I had enough, so they discharged me in Edmonton."

The conversation turned to lighter subjects and the glow of the wine, the music and the ambiance took over. Kevin reached across the table and placed his hand on Jade's.

Jade's confession brought up unpleasant memories. The next day, she logged on to Dr. Feldman's website to see if he could help exorcise her ghosts.

She wasn't sure how she felt about Dr. Feldman. Although he wanted to help, or was programmed to help, he was too detached—like her own father and what good was he? On the other hand, Feldman was very perceptive, and his computerized brain held a vast knowledge, so if he couldn't help, who could?

The doctor turned away from his desk to face Jade. "Welcome back Jade. How have you been since the last time we spoke?"

"Okay. I had a nice dinner this evening with a man that I like."

"That's good. You need to create and maintain positive social relationships to get healthy. Have there been any warning signs of an abusive partner? Does he seem controlling or jealous?"

"No, he seems very nice. Why do you ask?" Jade was slightly baffled by the question.

"People who have had an abusive childhood sometimes ignore warning signs and get into abusive relationships as adults. That would be a setback to your progress.

"In order to get a full picture, continue where we left off last week. Please tell me more about your adolescence."

"High school started out okay, then my grades got worse halfway through the first year. My mom looked at my grades and freaked out. 'Why don't you focus your school! All you do is stare! Focus!'" Jade said this in a heavy Chinese accent, imitating the way her mother spoke when she was angry.

"Then she slapped my face. Weakness needed to be punished. If punishment didn't work, then she gave me more punishment, and on and on and on. Soon I couldn't do anything right. If I started walking with my right foot, she would yell that I should start with my left. Non-stop nagging, hitting, putting me down. My dad was usually gone and when he came home said nothing.

"I was falling apart. I couldn't sleep at night. I got yelled at for sleeping in. I was lazy. I was stupid. When I tried to tell her about my problem, she said I was just making excuses. I could feel my brain slowing, but I became super hyper and jumpy. When my mother yelled at me, I started yelling back and it got worse.

"At university, I didn't make friends. I was on edge and defensive. When I was in a lecture, I didn't hear what the professor was saying since I was looking at the other students, reading their expressions and body language for signs of aggression. It was near the end of the first year and I was failing. Not just Asian failing, but real failing.

"When I was near the end of a final exam, I knew I messed up and I just wanted to go home, lock my bedroom door, and curl up on the floor.

"The girl sitting next to me finished her test already, stood up and jerked her arm toward me. My left arm shot out to sweep it away and my right fist slammed into the girl's face. Hard. Her head bounced back, and she wobbled and reached out to steady herself before slumping over the desk. She had one arm halfway in her coat. I realized the girl was just putting on her jacket. So, I'm like, *I'm so sorry. I'm so sorry.*

"My hands were shaking, and I reached out to touch the girl's blonde hair then stopped myself. She wouldn't want me to after what I did. The girl's head lay on the desk, her eyes were closed, and blood streamed out of her crooked nose and pooling all over her test.

"So, her friend yelled, '*What the fuck did you do that for, you freak! Someone call the police!*'

"I just said, 'No, no—I'm sorry—I didn't mean to.'

"She just screamed at me that her friend might die and she didn't do anything to me. I hurt that girl really bad. I know she didn't do anything. She didn't deserve it. I wished I could die. My nerves were fried, and I was so filled with regret and hatred for myself. I tried to apologize again, but my brain was not even working good enough to make the words come out, like my mouth was numb. The room was spinning. I was out of control. No one could understand. No one could after what I had done. I grabbed my jacket and bag and ran out of the lecture hall. Everyone was staring at me, and I could feel their hatred like it was a flamethrower."

Jade stopped speaking and stared at the floor as if catatonic.

"It's okay. Let's take a little break." Dr. Feldman put down his fountain pen and said nothing for a minute.

"I hear someone who was experiencing deep suffering and made a terrible mistake and who has expressed profound remorse. I would like you and I to do some role playing. I will play the role of someone who is suffering and feeling very guilty, and you will play the role of someone who is trying to make me feel better and to forgive myself."

"What good would that do? I didn't come here to play computer games."

"On the inside, you are a compassionate person. You just proved that to me. I want you to learn to have compassion for yourself and to forgive yourself." His tone was soothing. Dr. Feldman paused for Jade to absorb this.

She nodded her head.

Dr. Feldman started, "I'm feeling awful. I hurt you really bad. I wish I could die. I feel like I'm having a breakdown."

Jade took a minute to figure out how to do this. "Don't feel bad. I know it was an accident. Everybody has accidents. I know what you've been through. I know what you are feeling," Jade said.

"I'm very, very sorry for what I have done. Can you please forgive me?"

"Yes, I forgive you."

Jade sat up in her chair and again looked at the screen. Dr. Feldman smiled, noticing she looked better.

"That's great you think I'm a compassionate person," Jade said, her tone awkward, "but I haven't even told you half of it yet."

Chapter Eleven

Oppies Chicken

Jade sat at her bedroom study desk working on their investigation. A student at the U of A sent her an email with just 'Alan' as the subject. It contained a video with armed men in the distance putting on balaclavas, getting out of the van, and kidnapping Alan. It was only four seconds long before they entered the vehicle and raced away. Jade thought the video was too blurry and shaky to identify anyone, but she forwarded it to Kevin to see if he could make anything of it.

"Thanks!" was his immediate reply. She knew from his message updates he had been working all night on finding video footage. Doesn't he ever sleep? she wondered

A couple of hours later, and Kevin started a video chat. She took it on her TV display and was greeted by a detailed photo of a kidnapper.

"Wow, how did you do that? I zoomed in as far as I could go and his face was a blur."

"I used a software program. It is like the ones first used by digitally enhanced telescopes to cancel out the twinkling of the atmosphere. It analyzes many frames and uses advanced statistics to filter out the noise from the actual image. I used the same one to read the license plate, not that it helped any."

Jade waved her hand and discovered she could rotate the image 360 degrees. He was tough and strong looking. Somewhere between a farm boy and a soldier.

"Can you find out who he is?" she asked.

"Funny you should ask. Actually, I ran an image search, and he attended an event with the Apostles in Mission BC, but I think he is more of a hired hand than one of the faithful.

"I was thinking this was going to be extortion from his father's business competitors, but it's looking like it's the Apostles that are after his money," Kevin said.

"Money? But why? I searched them up and their sheep have to give them 10% of their income, so they have money. All their crimes seemed to be political or religious. This is something a street gang would do. Something doesn't fit," Jade said. "They would beat people they thought were sinners or lobby for the Christian Conservatives, but kidnapping for money isn't their thing."

Kevin nodded. "Maybe they're planning something big."

The sun was setting and William McPherson was reading his bank's financial report in his backyard gazebo when he felt his WON buzzing. He didn't recognize the number but answered anyway.

"Hello Dad," his son Alan said, his voice sounding dour.

"Oh my God, son, are you alright?" McPherson sat bolt upright.

"I'm okay. They wanted me to tell you not to call the police or they would kill me. Dad, you have to get me out of..."

The kidnapper took the phone away and spoke in a digital noise that sounded like a science fiction alien movie.

"You will transfer five hundred million loonies to us, or you will never see your son again. I will send you instructions with the address. Check your email."

"But it would take months or more to sell off enough of assets to get that kind of money."

"If you have the will, you will find a way. How much can you raise in a month?"

"I'll have to speak with my accountant, but I should be able to get 100 million."

The call went silent.

"Hello? Hello?"

William checked his email and found the message. It contained a loonie address of 128 random letters and numbers, a password, and a link to a darknet address for leaving messages. Below that was a photo of a dejected Alan with his hands and feet roped together. He clicked on the link to the darknet address and got a, "This Page Cannot Be Found" error.

He shouted into his WON, "Francis, get in here right away!" When his aide ran in, McPherson explained what had just happened.

"You must download special software... to access the darknet, Mr. McPherson. Allow me." Francis typed with lightning speed.

"Here is the message."

"If you want to see your son again, you must pay the ransom and cooperate fully. You shall not cooperate with the police. You shall immediately transfer ten million and keep us updated on your progress raising the rest of the hundred million to save your son. You will leave information on this website."

"Francis, transfer the ten million, and tell Kevin we received a ransom demand and ask him to find where they are—discreetly," McPherson said, his voice shaking.

"Right away, sir."

Kevin put his expense budget to good use and replaced his clunky old tablet with a new one. He was in the middle of unboxing it when he received the call from Francis. Since McPherson owned a telecommunication company, he gave Kevin carte blanche access to phone records. He traced the ransom call to McPherson down to an internet-based application originating from the darknet. A dead end.

He checked the darknet page they gave McPherson. There was nothing revealing in the HTML code. He debugged the login part to see if it referenced any uncloaked IP addresses or contained the author's name. Nothing.

Finally, he examined the email McPherson received. The IP chain was listed in the SMPT headers as it transferred from email server to email server on the way to McPherson's email account. He traced them backwards and found the origin was a server in Russia. Again, nothing. As an afterthought, he checked the HTML code in the email as well. It seemed pointless since whoever was doing this was very sophisticated at covering their tracks, but then...

Bingo. The image of Alan was not actually embedded but was a link to the IP address of the computer that sent it. Someone screwed up and forgot to scrub their tracks.

He executed a WHOIS search and found the IP address was part of a block belonging to an ISP, which was one of McPherson's competitors. Finding who used that IP address would not be so easy. It was now 2:50 a.m. and he needed to wait for office hours for the next step. Kevin made his nightly video call to Jade.

She was dressed in a bathrobe and dimly lit by the television. She was half lying on her couch, leaning on the arm with her bare legs beside her. Kevin tried not to drool.

"Hey Jade. I hope I didn't wake you up."

"Hi Bud. No, I just got home, and I need to unwind before I sleep."

"How was work?" Kevin said.

"It was okay. It's midterms, so it was a little quiet and I came home early. How are things with you?"

Kevin explained the ransom and how he had found the IP address.

Jade noticed the lines around Kevin's eyes seemed a little deeper than usual.

"You look tired, Kevin."

"I'm okay. Well, maybe a little shattered. Can we get together tomorrow? I could use some downtime," he hesitated, then blurted, "And I miss you."

"Aw, I miss you too. Tomorrow is my day off. You could come over for dinner. I'll order something. How about 6:00?"

"Sounds great."

Kevin slept for a couple of hours and called the ISP that owned the IP address used to send the ransom email.

"Welcome to Future, how may I help you?" the simulated female voice asked.

"I got an email saying my computer was, like, spreading viruses and I'm supposed to contact you. Now my internet stopped," Kevin put on his best 'exasperated and out of his depth consumer' voice.

"I can help you with that. What is your name and phone number?"

"Jerry Willington, 780-555-0150," he wondered about putting on a fake accent, and then figured the AI wouldn't care.

"The Internet Abuse Department will let you know what you need to do. I can transfer you now."

"Actually, I have to go pick up my daughter from dance class right now. Can you give me their direct number?"

"Sure, it's 780-555-0169."

Kevin started his Blackware app and spoofed his call display to show he was calling from the Edmonton City Police.

"Hello, Future Internet Abuse Department." The voice sounded like it belonged to a young woman and Kevin was glad it was not another robot, since machines were not so easily manipulated.

"Hello, this is Sergeant Armsworthy from the Edmonton City Police Human Trafficking and Exploitation Unit. I need an IP address search, ASAP," he said, gruffly.

"I thought these requests are supposed to be made with a court order?"

Kevin realized she must be new and not sure. He could use that to his advantage.

"I understand that, but there is a pedophile luring a minor, and the meeting will happen in thirty-five minutes. I need it *now*."

"I'll put in a request to the head office and see if I can get approval."

"It'll take too long. We have an understanding with management that we can make emergency requests and they are to be complied with immediately. What is your name?"

"Nancy."

"Nancy, you don't want to be responsible if anything happens to an eleven-year-old girl. This is your chance to do the right thing."

Nancy thought about it for a few seconds. "Alright, let me put you on hold while I look it up."

Kevin listened to some insipid elevator music interspersed with recorded promotions for the latest internet deal.

"Okay, it's a business account belonging to Oppies Chicken at 10744 - 109 Street. Is there anything else?"

"No. Thank you for your cooperation, Nancy."

"I'm glad if I could help. Thank you for calling Future."

Kevin was wearing his green army jacket with an Asian dragon embroidered on the back. The jacket had a wild excess of functionality, but the fabric was firm, and it reminded him of his better days in the army.

Oppies Chicken was a restaurant in the rundown neighborhood of Central McDougall, north of downtown. He rented a slipper and drove past blocks of mostly vacant two-story commercial buildings with boarded-up windows. Past the downtown core, a few tradesmen's offices appeared to still be in use. A variety of other businesses still operated, such as computer repair, and used clothing, which were interspersed with small, mostly Asian restaurants. Closer to 107 Avenue, were residential and the occupied apartment buildings from the 1970s and 1980s.

Oppies Chicken was easily spotted by its garish yellow sign. It was a tiny restaurant that had a seating capacity of ten. Kevin parked outside and found a weak Wi-Fi signal. He entered and sat at a greasy but cleared, table and ordered chicken to stay from a chubby but friendly waitress. An equally chubby but not so friendly middle-aged man operated the deep fryer and Kevin assumed he was Oppie. A blue haze and smell of deep fryer fat permeated the building and everything and everyone in inside. The exhaust system was on the fritz.

He unrolled his tablet and found the public Wi-Fi's external IP address matched that of the kidnappers, so someone emailed the ransom from here. While waiting for his order, he accessed the router and video cameras with ease, since the video was being stored in a computer onsite that was shared on the network and not protected by a firewall. What is it with these mom-and-pop stores? Kevin could have cried. He downloaded the video dated on the day of the ransom letter and a couple more for good measure.

So as not to draw attention to himself, he finished the salty and dry chicken fingers by rendering them palatable with ample honey mustard dipping sauce. The French fries were surprisingly tasty, but he was glad he putined them, even if they didn't use real cheese curds.

He was optimistic the video would show the man who sent the email. If so, he should be able to find his identity and, together with the other known kidnapper, he would try to access their lenses and might uncover the entire network. This was a good day.

He paid with his WON, left a tip, and sauntered out of the restaurant. Oppie watched him leave with suspicion, even walking to the front of the store watching Kevin get into the slipper that drove him away.

Chapter Twelve

The Man in the Mirror

B eckett Smith sat at the desk in his cramped but orderly home office. The desk had a stack of lined paper located exactly in front of his chair and a pen lay five centimeters to the right, parallel to the paper and 3.12 centimeters from   the   top   and bottom.

The man's face was soft, and his eyes hooded although he was still in his mid-thirties. He raised his eyebrows and pursed his lips in an effeminate manner and looked down his nose as if he were trying to peer through bifocals but wore none. He was reading an article on the church website about God's punishment for the wicked and making notes for his talk on Sunday. His WON rang, but he waited until he had finished the paragraph before he answered.

"Hi Brother Smith. This is Brother Sawchuk, Oppie Sawchuk." The voice at the other end sounded somber.

"Hello Brother Sawchuk," he said. "And what can I do for you?"

"Someone hacked into our surveillance and seemed to be interested in what Gideon was doing here a couple of days ago," said the owner of Oppie's Chicken.

Beckett turned from the computer screen to his WON. "Ohh?"

"I replayed today's video camera footage, and he looks like he somehow got access to our computer and downloaded video of Gideon emailing you know where. I'll send it to you."

Beckett clicked on the link that appeared in the message. "What devil's work can he be up to?" Beckett asked rhetorically. He watched the video and felt sick to his stomach. His councilor, Gideon Johnson, was at the table at Oppies. All the precautions they took—for nothing.

"How on God's green earth did this sinner find him?" He forwarded an encrypted copy of the video to Gideon and waited ten long minutes, then called him.

Gideon was lofty 1.98 meters tall and had gaps between all his teeth as if his mouth had grown too large. He still wore his army brush cut and tried not to march when he walked.

"Gideon! Did you see the video?" Beckett sounded frantic.

"Yes." Gideon sounded bored.

"How in Heaven's name did he track you? We've got to find out who he is right away."

The councilor, apparently, couldn't see the same calamity that Beckett could. "We don't have to."

"Why?"

"He's an old army buddy."

"What!"

"We served together in Ukraine."

"Heavens to Betsy. We've got to eliminate him before he learns anything else."

"I have a better use for him. He's got a skill set that we need. I've never seen anyone as good with improvised field-expedient munitions and surveillance hardware. Give him a hundred loonies worth of Intermart electronics and a handful of PE8, and a Ruskie's going to die in a hole. He's like a wizard.

"He made a grenade dropping drone. It was about four feet across and could carry ten hand grenades. When our guys were going to attack, they would put one guy in charge of flying the drone and he would hover over the enemy, dropping grenades in their foxholes and trenches while we engaged them in small arms fire. It was like a mortar, but with pinpoint accuracy. It could drop a grenade in a wastepaper basket from 100 meters up.

"Then he scaled it up and made a drone that could carry 5, 20 liter containers filled with napalm and used it to drop it on the Russian tanks. They called it the EB109, but the men called it *Easy Bake one oh nine*. The Russians called it Satan's Piss. Headquarters made some blueprints and handed them out all over Ukraine, and next thing you know, every Perogy in the country was making easy bakes in their basements and the Russians lost most of their armor. For the price of the gas, he would burn up a tank that cost millions. When easy bakes were in the area, the Russians ran away from their tanks like scared children. The ones that got caught inside got dried out like beef jerky and you could pick up a corpse with one hand. It looked like beef jerky but tasted more like pork. The Russians couldn't sustain losses like that and went limping home like Napoleon after Waterloo."

"He must have won a medal for that," said Gideon.

"You would think. His CO put in a commendation, but a desk general in Ottawa took the credit. Kevin was insubordinate to an officer and was lucky to get out with an honorable discharge."

"Ronald Penner's a physicist," Gideon went on, referring to their own nuclear physicist. "He knows all the formulas and assorted hoo haa but he can't build shit."

Beckett winced at the profanity.

"The thumper heads know how to build a machine by the book, but they don't know how to improvise, and we don't have the industrial-sized resources to build it their way.

"They keep trying triggers, but they all fail. Penner said they should work if we aligned them better. Some of the Patriarchs are thinking it isn't possible to build it that way and are talking about abandoning the Jellyfish Device. God has commanded us to bring his wrath, so there must be a way. If anyone can, Kevin can."

"But he's not an Apostle. He won't do it."

"No, but I can persuade him. He's a bit of a queer duck. Kevin was never gung-ho about being in the forces and his GAFF tolerance was pretty low," said Gideon.

"And what in Heaven's name is a GAFF?" asked Beckett.

"Give a fuck factor."

Beckett was mortified. "I should have known better."

"There was another private he hit it off with when he was overseas. Chuck was his name. They arranged to get transferred to the same bases as they moved around Ukraine. Chuck was his homie and when they were going in, they would go in together.

"One night, Chuck took point on a section recon bag drive, deep in enemy territory. Chuck stepped on a tripwire and took some shrapnel in his legs. Then came the AK fire from the bush and the corporal ordered Kevin to cover their retreat. Instead, he rushed into the bullets and incoming mortar rounds to get Chuck. A funny thing happened on the way to get him. Kevin killed half the Russians and sent the rest into retreat. Kevin's section proceeded to fall back, but ran straight into the PK line of fire and was almost wiped out. Chuck, Kevin, and a lance-corporal were the only ones who made it out. Some people called him a BIFF for not covering his other comrades, but he was loyal to his buddy."

"I'm not even going to ask what a BIFF is," pleaded Beckett.

"Buddy Fucker—traitor."

Beckett was clearly appalled with the profanity and just shook his head.

"The point of this story is that he would sacrifice many people to save someone he cares about. If we can get someone he's close to, I promise you, he'll do whatever we tell him."

"I hope you're right."

"He must be working for McPherson, so I'll see if he can talk him into at least looking at it. That will buy us some time while we find out what, or who motivates him."

Kevin answered McPherson's call. "I have some good news. The kidnappers contacted me, and they are making a new offer. Somehow, they found out you were tracking them, but instead of being angry, they want you to do them a little favor. It would go a long way to securing Alan's release."

"How the hell...What favor?"

"Well... you're going to laugh." McPherson gave a weak chuckle. "You're not going to believe this. These guys are really crazy. They somehow got it into their heads... I can't even say it, it's so crazy."

"Just spit it out."

"They somehow got it into their twisted little heads that they are capable of building an atomic bomb and they want you to have a look at it."

"What the fuck?"

"I know. That's what I thought too. Of course, it's completely impossible and they're deluded and evil beyond words to even try it."

"I can't help them do that. What if it works?"

"You don't really have to help them. Just pretend to. It turns out, this is what they were after the whole time. The ransom money was to finance their homespun Los Alamos project."

"That makes sense. I mean, nothing they do makes sense, but that explains why they all of a sudden need so much money," said Kevin.

"You don't really have to help them, since I'm sure what they're doing is impossible anyhow. Just play along and buy some time while we look for Alan and plan a rescue. Just have a look, kick the tires, bullshit them a little and put on a show of doing something. If you don't do it, maybe they'll find someone who really can get it working, if you can imagine. So, it's not just about Alan, it's about saving the world."

McPherson sensed Kevin wasn't interested, and he pulled out all the stops. "Please, Kevin. For God's sake, I'm begging you! They're going to kill Alan. He is everything to me—my only child. I would do it myself if I could, but they seem to think you're the only one. Imagine how you would feel. What would you do to protect someone you care about?" McPherson stumbled upon Kevin's weakness.

"This is too much," said Kevin. "I'll think about it, okay?"

The news was playing in Jade's apartment as she set the table with a plate, chopsticks, and two wineglasses.

"Today in Ottawa, there was an attempted assassination of the Minister of Justice Pierre LeBlanc. He was leaving his home as a bullet from a high-powered rifle shot him in the shoulder. Police closed off the area and discovered a stolen van with a remote-controlled sniper rifle mounted inside. No one has claimed responsibility, but police suspect right-wing extremists. The hospital reported he was in serious but stable condition," said the news anchor.

Kevin entered Jade's apartment and sat on the couch like an impending hurricane. "McPherson called today, and you are not going to fucking believe this." Kevin said. "It turns out the Apostles are trying to build an atomic bomb."

"You're kidding me," Jade stopped, turned, and looked aghast.

Kevin shook his head. "*Deadly* serious."

"Are they really *that* crazy! How many will they kill!? That explains why they turned to kidnapping to raise money." Jade added.

"Yup. But I haven't even told you the crazy part yet. I don't know how, but they figured out I work for McPherson and told the old man they want me to look at the trigger and see if I can help them put it together."

Jade looked uneasy but empathetic. "So, what did you tell him?"

"No fucking way! Then he said he doesn't really expect me to help them, just to play along, stall for time until we can rescue his son. He said giving them fake advice will delay them, and if I don't, they'll find someone who will build it, for real. The only way I can prevent a thermonuclear attack is to go through the motions of helping them."

Jade moved closer and put her hand on his arm. "What are you going to do?"

He shook his head and whispered, "I don't know."

"Try not to think about it. Look. We're here right now. Let's get something to eat, relax, and then sleep on it. I'll order some takeout. What kind do you want?"

"Chinese."

"Fake Chinese or Real."

"Real, how about Szechuan style?"

It made Jade smile to know he enjoyed authentic Chinese food.

Soon, the delivery drone was buzzing the door. Jade opened it and tapped her WON and the drone's box opened so Jade could take out the food containers. It automatically closed and the knee-high tracked vehicle set off down the hall. Jade laid out agro-gell clamshells, filled with food, and then poured the wine. They began eating and Kevin tasted the cubes of mapo tofu covered with spicy sauce and minced pork. The esoteric taste of the Szechuan peppercorns in chili oil and salty fermented bean paste always surprised him. It was spicy, but somehow more than just spicy in a way that he couldn't describe. Then he sampled the Gongbao Jiding. Chicken, peppers, peanuts and the ever-present chili oil. Eating with chopsticks makes you enjoy the ingredients individually. A piece of diced chicken, a cube of tofu in sauce—a single peanut, with a dab of rice for variety. The food, the wine and especially the company soon relaxed him.

Jade enjoyed seeing Kevin be himself again, but there was something nagging at her she could no longer ignore. She needed to tell him but was afraid to say it. She didn't tell people she was not close to since it was none of their business and she was afraid to tell people she was getting close to, for fear of rejection or being outed. There never seemed to be a good time, and this didn't really seem like one either. She realized she should have told him a long time ago—when he first tried to kiss her. Now it would seem like she was trying to (she hated the word), trap him. If she was, she meant no harm in it.

Kevin excused himself to go to the washroom, and Jade decided she was going to tell him when he got back. She rehearsed the speech in her mind she was about to deliver.

This doesn't get any easier. There's something I've been meaning to tell you. Something I should've told you already. It's just about my childhood. When I was in elementary school, I wasn't a little girl like all the other little girls—I was a little boy... Insert stunned silence and say goodbye to my newest ex-best friend.

Kevin took care of business and washed his hands. He noticed how clean and put together everything was. A hand towel folded by the sink. Dried flowers in a bowl. A bottle of green oblong pills on the vanity and no water spots or smudges anywhere. The room smelled faintly of fragrant soap that reminded him of something that had happened in his childhood. What was it? He read the label on the pill bottle. Co-Androl. He searched it up on his WON and a surge of electricity passed through his hands. He placed it back on the vanity and noticed how stunned the man in the mirror looked, then slowly turned away.

"Sorry, I'm not feeling very well and I have a lot on my mind." He walked to the door and slipped on his shoes. "I'm afraid I won't be very good company, so I'm going to call it a night. Thanks for the dinner, it was... lovely."

"Oh, that's too bad, I was just going to tell you—"

Kevin slammed the door and passed into the night.

"Shit!"

Francis set a vertical screen on McPherson's desk. His motions were uneven and his hands quivered slightly. "This is the Dark Tunnel provided by the kidnappers," Francis told him. "They want you to use it for communications since we cannot trace them. I spent some time analyzing its functionality, and it routes the information packets through various darknet portals before combining them into a stream of video at their final destination. It was likely created by a criminal organization and... purchased by the Apostles. In five minutes, just click here to begin."

McPherson noticed the time with some trepidation and clicked on the button. The buzzing electronic scrambled voice of the Apostle began.

"Good day, Mr. McPherson. Alan says hello. Share with me how much money you have raised now."

"We have raised another five million and will have another million by the weekend," McPherson's voice cracked as he spoke. "Where is Alan? Why can't I see him?"

"And your employee, Kevin. Is he going to obey?"

"I've been putting pressure on him, and he has agreed to look at your plans."

"Well, that's a start, but you understand, we will be more flexible in our requirements if he can provide us with something concrete. We have spent much of our Lord's resources so far and are still spending fast. The quicker the plan is complete, the less money we will need. Is there anyone dear to him we can use to persuade him more forcefully?"

McPherson didn't hesitate. "I know nothing about his personal life, but I'll look into it."

"Good. You do that."

"You probably don't approve of me or my family, but I'm a businessman. I can help you get what you want and then I can get what I want, which is my son. I don't like what you're doing, but I can't and won't try to stop you. All I ask is you let me know where the detonation will be so I can make sure any people important to me are out of danger," his voice was cracking with emotion.

"The righteous have nothing to fear, but nonetheless, we will let you know," the Apostle's voice at the other end of the Tunnel said, although McPherson did not know whether he believed him.

"We will send you another Dark Tunnel so Kevin can speak with us directly. Goodbye, Mr. McPherson."

McPherson let out a sigh and stared at the table in front of him. The enormity of the devil's bargain weighed on his soul, but his family was more important. He was a businessman and needed to focus on his interests and those of his family. The Apostles were repugnant, but he could work with them. He could work with anyone.

He chose not to involve the police, since that could put Alan in more danger. The police would tip off the Apostles, anyway. He resolved to treat it like a business deal and leave emotions behind, and leave behind anyone that got in the way.

Kevin woke from troubled sleep and squinted at a sliver of yellow light on his west wall. Sunlight in a north facing room meant the equinox had passed. He felt like he had a hangover even though he only had half a glass of wine last night. Yesterday. Last night. How did he get pushed into being a savior of the world? *Fucking McPherson. Why didn't Jade tell me what she was? Fucking Jade.* He stumbled to the bathroom in his t-shirt and pajama pants and looked in the mirror. People like her had to be careful these days. Being transgender or queer in any way was more dangerous than it used to be, but they were friends and he kissed her. He didn't know if he would have, had he known. She made him question his sexuality, and he didn't like it. He thought she could be the right one for him. Now he didn't think so.

He dressed in a black long-sleeved t-shirt and synthetic denim jeans. Still unshaved and hair tousled, he put a frozen waffle in the toaster and some pre-cooked bacon in the shoebox-sized, infra-wave warming oven. He turned on his WON and noticed an unread message from Jade but didn't feel like reading it yet.

He placed a scoop of ground Cuban coffee and a filter disk in his one-cup coffee maker. The coffee maker filled the cup, and he lifted the lid and put the grounds and filter in the wet garbage can. There were rumors that wet garbage was no longer being composted by the city, but he hoped it was, and he wanted to do his part to reduce the amount going to the landfill.

He wiped margarine on the waffles and placed them on the little table. Syrup poured over the edges of the waffle, and he cut off a bite. That was just what he needed. He finished the waffles and was half finished with the coffee before he began reading the message from Jade.

"I've got some 'splaining to do. I guess you found my pills. I was just going to tell you, I really was, and I'm really sorry for not telling you earlier and that you had to find out like that, but yes, I am transsexual."

She explained how she transitioned and what it was like growing up with gender dysphoria.

"I'm comfortable with my body now and it is my deepest hope that you will be as well, but if not, I understand completely and won't hold it against you."

"Can we still be friends? Circle your answer. Yes or No"

Kevin smiled at her girlish question, then drew a red circle around Yes with his finger, and uttered the voice command, "Send." *She's a bundle of contradictions*, he thought.

Next Message: McPherson

Kevin,

We will deliver a package to you today with a Dark Tunnel to communicate directly with the Apostles. You will talk with them when they tell you and review their plans.

"What the fuck," whispered Kevin.

He called McPherson's number and his aide, Francis, answered.

"Get the old man on the phone."

"Mr. McPherson… is in a meeting now and is unavailable to take your call. I'll transfer you to his voicemail."

"He'll take my call. If he doesn't, I throw his little package in the dumpster."

A few moments later, McPherson's voice came on the line. "Kevin, I was busy. What is it?"

"Why are you sending me a Dark Tunnel?"

"I thought my message was clear; for you to communicate with the Apostles."

"What makes you think I want to talk to those assholes?"

"Because you work for me."

"What you are asking is far beyond what any amount of money could possibly motivate me to do. If you gave me every penny you ever earned, it wouldn't be nearly enough. If I do it, it will be because I believe it's the right thing and not because I work for you. I don't need your shit."

McPherson paused, then leaned forward in his chair as he explained. "I realize now it was presumptuous of me to assume you would take this on. I apologize. Please understand, I don't like them either, but they have my son, and I would do anything to get him back."

Kevin exhaled deeply.

"I would greatly appreciate it if you would help me get my son back and if you can stall them a little, you might also prevent a nuclear disaster."

"Next time, at least ask before you try to sell me to the devil." Kevin hoped he would not regret this decision but knew he probably would. Dreading the deed, he unpacked the Dark Tunnel and placed it on his table, pointing away from the window so as not to give away his location. He clicked on the button. He felt like his soul was falling down a literal tunnel of despair and devastation. The synthetic voice of Beckett Smith began.

"Hello Kevin. I've heard so much about you. You have a reputation for making things work. Mr. McPherson may have told you about our little project. He said you would be willing to lend a hand."

Kevin hesitated, biting back on the stream of invectives that were about to come out. "He doesn't speak for me, but yes, I will have a look."

"Well, bless your heart. Let's get started. We have a lot of ground to cover to get you up to speed. I'm not an expert on all the technicals, so I'll give you to our very own brother scientist. We'll call him Don today." Don jumped right in.

"The first problem in a DIY thermonuclear device is obtaining weapons-grade uranium or plutonium to achieve critical mass. The uranium has to be uranium 235 and only about .7% of natural uranium is U235 and the rest is U238, which will not support nuclear fission on its own. Weapons-grade uranium is 90% U235 and there are not yet any easy ways of enriching uranium to this level of purity and it would take too long to mine that much uranium anyway. Therefore, we looked at using U238, aka depleted or unenriched uranium instead, and we decided to extract it from seawater.

"When U238 undergoes fission, it does not give off enough neutrons to sustain the chain reaction. What if we can get neutrons from somewhere else? That's what happens in a hydrogen bomb, where most of the energy comes from depleted uranium, but the extra neutrons to sustain the reaction come from hydrogen fusion.

"The problem with a hydrogen bomb is that the first stage is created by a weapons-grade uranium or plutonium bomb that starts the hydrogen fusion to create the neutrons, so we're back to the problem of having no weapons-grade uranium and we are forced to find another source of neutrons.

"That's where I came up with the idea of using proton accelerators. Accelerators are not outside the realm of DIYers to build. Electron accelerators were used for television pictures during much of the twentieth century. We didn't even have to build them since they can be purchased, but we did anyway since we didn't have the money at the time. In actual practice, we used a deuterium proton beam and a lithium deuterium target which turns into tritium when bombarded, but I don't want to bore you with the details.

"The bottom line is, what needs to be done is to accelerate a hydrogen proton fast enough so when it hits another hydrogen atom it fuses together to form helium and gives off high energy neutrons that start nuclear fission of unenriched uranium. Well, to be precise, it first fuses the deuterium to the lithium to form tritium, and then fuses that, but I'm getting into the weeds again.

"It doesn't take much fission to create enough heat to, in turn, create enough fusion and keep the fusion-fission chain reaction going. Since there is an external neutron source, we don't need critical mass and there is no limit on how small or how big the bomb can be.

"One proton accelerator is not enough, and we will need several laser-plasma particle accelerators attached to one side pointed at the same minute target to create enough neutrons to get the ball rolling. The actual bomb part will be onion-shaped and you would not need an active imagination to think it looked like a jellyfish or a squid. Accelerators point at a one millimeter target of deuterium/lithium alloy surrounded by depleted uranium. The main core was also deuterium/lithiumVI alloy called lithium deuterium, and the whole thing is surrounded by a layer of unenriched uranium and finally a lead neutron reflector. The lead casing also serves to delay the bomb from flying apart before most of the fuel has been used.

"Ok, in theory we have a nuclear trigger that doesn't require weapons-grade uranium or plutonium and one that we could build in a machine shop. We tested it and we couldn't keep the array of accelerators focused sharply enough. That's where we were hoping you could help."

They're completely crazy—but they've done their homework with the science. "It sounds interesting. I'll need your plans, drawings, and also hands-on the actual hardware." Kevin couldn't help but be interested in the technical puzzles this presented, even though detonating a nuclear device was a crime against humanity, and if he wasn't careful, he would become an accomplice.

Chapter Thirteen

Still Friends

Kevin sat in the upscale downtown restaurant, waiting. Noon-day sun filtered through the window and caressed the carved and polished table-for-two. The walls featured abstract art that echoed the streaks of light from the spotlights sunken in the ceiling. The dominant feature of the room was a concentric dropped ceiling with an illuminated metallic two-meter black circle with a round chandelier hanging by a cable. It was like a shimmering basket where dimly arabesque patterns and points of light shone through. The center of the restaurant displayed a hologram of a couple having a picnic in a meadow.

Kevin glanced around the room, taking it all in. Places like this seemed strangely out of place compared to the economic decay outside the banking district. Since he was a child, it seemed money kept getting tighter for guys like him, while the barons just got richer.

There was the electricity energy crisis, the banking crisis and the short, sharp, shock that followed. Since then, things stabilized, or maybe just his own situation stabilized. He was developing a vague optimism regarding his future and hoped that it would include a partner and maybe a white picket fence, whatever that was.

He took another sip of coffee and looked over his shoulder toward the entrance. Just then, he saw Jade and stood as she entered. She looked apprehensive but smiled. Kevin returned hers with his knowing smile. Her hair looked freshly waved and bounced as she walked, and her dark double-breasted coat opened in the bottom revealing bare legs and red kitten-heel shoes with black tips. She hung her jacket on the coat rack then tucked in her short floral-patterned skirt as she sat. Kevin felt underdressed and decided it was time to add to his wardrobe.

"You look great," he said. He saw before him the same woman he had been so attracted to and regretted the way he reacted.

"Thanks," answered Jade, not returning the compliment. She avoided eye contact, turned over her coffee cup, and swirled her finger around the rim.

Kevin shifted in his seat.

"Looking at you makes me want to go shopping for some new clothes, but I never know what to buy. I don't know what looks good."

"Oh, I could help you with that. I might know a thing or two about shopping."

"That would be solid. How about after lunch, I could rent a beaver and we could go to demo shops at Kingsway."

"Okay."

Kevin thought she was acting distant. Perhaps she was on guard against any homophobia he might have, or that she thought he would no longer want to explore their budding relationship. Kevin had felt he was the one that was wronged but changed his mind and now he took up the challenge to win her over.

"Then I could take you shopping and buy you a new pair of shoes."

She looked up with a twinkle in her eye. He might have found a chink in her armor.

A waiter poured coffee for Jade and topped up Kevin's.

"But first, let's do lunch."

They both perused the menu and Jade ordered a Caesar salad with a skinless chicken breast and Kevin ordered a bison hamburger with fries.

The awkwardness had passed, and Kevin updated her on his contact with the Apostles.

Jade ate half the salad and chicken and placed her knife and fork on her plate. Kevin ate everything and wiped his fingers with the napkin. Jade casually glanced at the entrance as she spoke like she did the last time they were at a restaurant together. Kevin wondered if this was a after effect from her time as a bodyguard. He understood something about old trauma. Kevin was engrossed in her stories about work at the bar and the drama between her coworkers.

"So, Bob, the bouncer, was hot for Alice, a cute little blonde waitress, just out of high school. She had a boyfriend and wasn't interested. He had been flirting with her and trying to touch her, but she kept telling him no. He didn't get the message and kept coming after her. One night, he caught her in the cooler and pinned her in the corner with his fat little body pressing up against her and his little boner sticking out in his pants. He scared her to tears and I could hear her crying. I totally lost it. I walked in and yelled, 'What the fuck do you think you're doing!' I was furious. I yanked him off her and punched him right in the nose. I never thought a prick could go limp so fast! He scurried his fat little body out of there and never came back."

"You've earned a reputation there," said Kevin.

"Not just there, I'm afraid."

Kevin paid the bill and voice commanded his WON to call a beaver. By the time they got to the street, a blue two-seated autonomous car was pulling up to the curb. He tapped his WON and the door opened. Jade got in first and tucked her skirt under her legs, and Kevin slid in next to her. Kevin glanced at her shapely legs and skirt and wondered what she had underneath.

He was surprised the mystery got him interested. Kevin felt uneasy and wondered if he was turning gay. He was never aware of any homophobic feelings toward anyone else but questioned why he would have homophobic feelings towards himself.

I haven't changed and gay and straight are just words. Just words. Besides, she's woman enough for me. He wanted to hold her hand to make up with her, but wisely took it slow and cool.

He commanded the beaver to go to Kingsway Mall, and it crept into the traffic lane while another autonomous car waited. Jade looked at her WON.

There was a group of rough, masculine-acting women loitering around the seedy 107 Avenue. Kevin asked, "Are they lesbians? If they are, they look sicker and skinnier than any lesbians I've ever seen."

"They're fem-males. A few years ago, they made estrogen over the counter and some meth-heads found out that if they take it, the meth high gets a lot better. It increases dopamine or something and that was why meth is more addictive to women than men. So now they take estrogen meth speed balls all the time. Some use their fem bodies to turn tricks to feed their habits."

"That's so sad."

"What can you do?"

"Check out Berg's and see if they have anything you like. I'll look at the sports jackets first."

Kevin looked up the site for Berg's Formal Menswear and started browsing through their inventory. Ten minutes later, they felt the tracks of the LRT station and entered the Kingsway Mall parking lot, which was sparsely filled with single-owner cars, but uniformly spaced autonomous vehicles circled the mall like the rings of Saturn until reaching their destination. They approached Berg's and their car left the procession to pull up alongside the curb. They both got out and the beaver waited for a car to pause before it inserted itself, to join the rest of the cars with the choreographed precision of a ballet.

They each tapped their driver's licenses on the scanner and the glass door slid open.

"Welcome, madam and sir, to my little shop! My name is Valentine, but call me Val. Please have a look around and I will be happy to assist you." They were greeted by a hologram of an elderly tailor in a smart suit and with a measuring tape draped around his neck. He looked over small round glasses and had a warm, welcoming smile.

The hologram's shop was indeed quite compact, but it was larger than a counter-service store with banks of change rooms on the left, a return bin with a conveyor belt leading to a back room on the right and a pickup area in the middle.

"Would the gentleman like me to take your measurements?" the hologram flickered.

"Yes, thank you," replied Kevin. It was a peculiar Canadian habit to be polite to holograms.

Val deftly took his measuring tape and pantomimed measuring his waist, his inseam, his arm, and his neck while invisible lasers did the real work.

"We have some sports jackets on sale starting at 145 loonies, if you are interested, sir?" He waved his hand toward a large touchscreen, which changed to a selection of sports jackets. Jade noticed it displayed the same items she had searched up on the way.

"May I be so bold as to recommend the tweed blazer?"

Jade stepped up to the screen and swiped to the left to see more. "How about this one?" She pointed to a gray tweed jacket.

"Oh, the lady has taste, well done to bring her today, sir. The Ascot is very popular this spring and comes with matching pants. I'll have my assistant fetch it for you right away."

Jade was in her element and kept swiping past the jackets while Kevin looked over her shoulder. "How about this one? It's on sale for 125 loonies."

"It's too cheap. How about something a little higher end and including pants." Kevin was feeling flush from the substantial income from his new employment. After their recent interactions, McPherson doubled his daily rate without being asked.

Jade looked interested and said, "Okay, that opens your horizons a bit. Hmmm. Oh yeah. Look at this. A charcoal gray suit. I could wear my little black dress and we would look great together."

This encouraged Kevin that she included him in her plans and also liked the idea of seeing her again in a little black dress.

"Val, can you get one of these?" Jade asked.

"Of course, madam, excellent choice. It will accentuate your trim physique, sir."

The first jacket appeared on a vertical hook attached to the conveyor and was deposited on a stationary clothes rack.

"Your first sports jacket has arrived, sir. Would you like to try it on?"

Kevin picked it up and carried it to the changing room, and Jade waited with excitement outside the door. Soon Kevin reappeared and looked at himself in the mirror. He noticed Jade was standing behind him, looking him up and down. She licked her lips and smiled. She was thoroughly enjoying this, and Kevin thought he was making progress with her.

"It's a little baggy in back but looks great, bud," Jade said. "They can tailor it for you."

Val said, "Your second suit is ready for you, sir."

Kevin took it to the changing room. The pants were too long and had no hem on the bottom, but the fit was close enough.

"Wow!" said Jade. She could see the potential.

He changed back into his old clothes and put them on the return conveyor.

"I'll take both of them, Val, and I would like to have them tailored."

"Very good, sir, since this is your first time visiting my humble haberdashery, I'll tailor them at no charge," the hologram insisted.

"Should I come back tomorrow or have them delivered?" Kevin asked Jade.

"You don't have to. They have automated tailors that can do it in fifteen minutes. The conveyor will take them to a robotic CNC that'll cut it exactly to fit. They automated everything here. They don't even have any full-time employees. When you order something, robotic pickers take it off the shelf and put it on the conveyor. When you return items, the conveyor either takes it to the tailor machine or to the folder before the pickers put it back."

"Cool," was all he said. He thought he was the expert on technology, but Jade was evidently more up on the shopping part.

While they waited, another customer entered the shop. They heard Val's voice speaking to him but from their angle; they didn't see the hologram.

Soon, Kevin's clothes were ready. He picked up the two bundles and noticed they were both still quite warm from being pressed and inhaled the intoxicating smell of new, unwashed fabric. His favorite part of shopping.

"Now, I think we'll need some new shoes," Kevin said.

"We don't have to do that today if you don't want to. Sometimes men get tired from shopping too much."

"It might not be my favorite, but I'm on a roll and would like to get it done in one day, before I get swamped with work."

They exited the shop and walked to the mall's main entrance. It was emblazoned with batteries of televisions displaying huge video clips of models wearing the latest fashions. Some shops were permanently closed, but there was still a stream of customers strolling back and forth from stores and food courts.

Jade found her favorite shoe store and took the lead in choosing two new pairs for Kevin and one for herself. As they left the store, scanners detected the tags on the shoes and beeped, showing it charged his credit. His WON's haptics tapped his forearm as a sign he received the receipt.

Kevin held the bags and Jade tucked her hand in the crook of his arm as they approached a waiting beaver. Kevin habitually took the driver's side.

"Destination 10642 103rd Avenue," Kevin commanded the beaver to Jade's address to drop her off first.

They chatted about Jade's fitness class as they approached her soaring apartment building. Kevin reached over and held her hand. Jade stopped talking then looked deeply at Kevin.

"I haven't been as upfront as I should've been in the past, but I'm going to be now. I have fully functioning male parts—I have a penis. I'm happy with my body, but I'm not sure if you are. At least not yet. It was nice spending the day with you. Thanks for the shoes. They're lovely." She smiled and gave him a little wave as she opened the car door and approached the grand entrance of her high-rise apartment. Jade glanced over her shoulder to see Kevin still watching her—wide eyed like a love-struck teen. She waved again with her head held high and hair bouncing and shining in the late spring sun.

Chapter Fourteen

Back to the Grind

Kevin and Jade lay naked together, spooning in post-coital warmth. Jade turned her head back toward him and Kevin admired the shape of the lines of her neck as they joined her shoulders. He leaned towards her and kissed her deeply, caressing the sides of her face and neck.

The sun filtered through the sheer curtains and tweaked his eyes, and they reflexively fluttered open. He closed them again and wished he could return to his dream. Not to be. He threw off the blankets and swung his legs to the floor. Being alone, there was no need to hide his perpendicular state when he took the brief steps to the bathroom, dressed in his boxers.

Kevin touched the Dark Tunnel to bring it to life and opened a document entitled *The Jellyfish Device* and it was a grade 'A' boner-killer. He ate a bowl of cereal as he read through pages of data and turned on the TV and listened to a breaking story.

"Masked gunmen entered a Calgary daycare today…"

Kevin sensed where this was going and turned off the broadcast as soon as he could. "Jesus Christ! Just when you think they couldn't sink lower."

Kevin was horrified but tried to refocus on the task at hand. He could read fast, but his real talent was that he could focus on technical data and retain what he read. He poured through circuit board diagrams of the proton accelerators and studied every capacitor, every diode, and every component of every module.

He organized the functions into sections. There were the copper vacuum tubes and the lasers that created the plasma and propelled the protons. Deuterium protons must be accelerated to at least 4 keV so they will fuse and produce neutrons. Then there was the target.

Kevin was not a nuclear physicist. He was told the particle accelerators were working, but not aimed finely enough. There were shields between each accelerator to prevent electromagnetic interference with the adjacent devices. Perhaps they weren't working, and the beams were being deflected. Another possibility occurred to him: the timing could be off. He needed to find what the problem was and prevent the Apostles from fixing it.

He studied electronic diagrams splattered with triangles, bars and squiggles attached with spaghetti lines leading to other combinations of geometric oddities and traced the logic flow along each point. Perhaps the problem was not in the design but in the assembly. Could there be a flaw in how they put it all together?

He had learned as much as he could from the documentation. He needed to work hands-on. His strategy was to stall as much as he could to buy time to track them down. Then someone can rescue Alan and arrest the bomb makers. If he stalled too long, they would find someone else to fix it and a working trigger was something to be avoided at all costs, although he still doubted if anyone could really get it to detonate.

He sent the Apostles an email saying he was half through studying and he would need a physical copy to troubleshoot the issue.

Alan McPherson tried to guess his new surroundings. It seemed like they kidnapped him a lifetime ago. He had been bound, blindfolded and gagged, put in the back of a bouncy truck and taken on a fourteen-hour drive. To where, he was not sure. As he arrived, he could smell the ocean; that familiar metallic, whiff of salty air and seaweed.

He was sure he was in some kind of industrial basement. The walls were made of cinder block and the floor, bare concrete. He leaned his back against a concrete pillar and his hands were shackled together in front. They also shackled his legs and put on a chain harness that connected to the pillar. His back ached from being held in such an uncomfortable position for so long. How long had it been? He thought, again, for the millionth time. A day? Two? A week? His shackles had worn through the skin on his wrists, and he was in constant pain. His only comfort was a meager foam pad to lie on. He felt like he was losing his sanity and wallowed in depression.

To think a month ago he was living a charmed life, son of a billionaire with a secure future. How things have changed. Now he doubted if he would get out of there alive.

His jailer sat across the room, smirking at something on a tablet. He sat on a wooden chair that seemed too small for someone so obese. He had a small table and put a half-full bottle of water, a baseball bat, and a cattle prod on it. A large TV played recordings of Apostle sermons and lessons—loudly. It had been playing all night and all day since they stole him away from his life.

Alan stretched his arms to test his range of motion. The only resistance he felt was the weight of the heavy steel chains. He turned to look behind to see what was holding him. The clinking sound caused the jailer to look up. He saw about three feet of slack; that should be enough to lie down. It hurt to move, but it hurt to sit still on the hard surface. A length of chain slipped off his back and dropped to the floor with a clank.

The jailer looked up and his face flashed with anger. "No messing around, sinner, or you will be visited by the avenging angel! I don't know how you got spoiled by the brothers in Edmonton, but we won't put up with any of your guff around here!"

Alan guessed the avenging angel was the baseball bat or the cattle prod and he would rather not find out which.

So it must be morning. A new jailer will come with food. He couldn't really afford to skip a meal since his legs were getting thinner. He didn't know what his face looked like, except he had grown an annoying beard and was very dirty. His body was always itchy from lack of bathing, and he couldn't get used to his own degrading smell.

A video started that he hadn't seen before, and being so bored and deprived, he was almost interested.

"The Church had become complacent to feminists and sodomites and drifted away from God's example. Adam Teller implored the leadership to return to the scriptures for guidance and forsake the decadence of the land. All to no avail. The leaders watered down our teachings to pander to the masses.

That was when our Heavenly Father commanded Adam Teller to gather up His faithful and bring them to a place of reverence, obedience and purity and to call it the Church of the Apostles. He commanded Adam Teller to use the rod against the gentiles so they may see the light."

"So that's how these wack-jobs got started," murmured Alan, his voice so low under the sound of the television that the guard couldn't hear him.

A key turned in the lock of the steel fire door. A less overweight young man walked through the door and greeted the first jailer.

"Good morning, Brother,"

He carried a tray with a bowl half-filled with cereal and milk and placed it on the floor in front of Alan without saying a word. He walked back to the first jailer, and they began speaking with concerned voices and in hushed tones. Alan ate as fast as he could. He couldn't hear much over the sound of the television but thought he could pick out a few words. His eyes blurred since he had to take out his contacts after they kidnapped him, but he could see they were quite animated.

"Gentile consultant", "technical roadblock", and other words that didn't seem to make any sense. The new jailer suddenly turned and glared at Alan.

"What the devil are you looking at, boy!"

He picked up the cattle prod and stomped toward Alan. Alan tried to move away until the chain stopped him.

"No!" whispered Alan, in panic.

The jailer jabbed Alan in the shoulder. His body convulsed and a hoarse gurgling sound stopped in his throat as his torso slumped to the ground.

Kevin resumed his 'A' plan of tracking down the kidnappers/bomb makers. On his kitchen table, he opened the video from Oppies Chicken and started watching, starting at the time the email was sent to McPherson. He saw people come and go, but no sign anyone emailed. Maybe one of them did. Another possibility is the time on the camera was wrong.

The camera was in the front of the store, pointing toward the back. He kept watching and an hour after the email was sent, a tall, beefy, short-haired man sat down with his back to the camera and opened a tablet. He was chatting with Oppie like they knew each other. The mysterious man was sitting and eating some chicken, and Kevin couldn't quite see his face. He turned to the left when talking, but not enough that Kevin could recognize him.

The man finally finished eating and turned to leave. Kevin paused the video and did a double take on what he saw. Gideon Charles Johnson—Chuck.

"Wait. Is that really....?" Kevin recognized his best friend from the army. The one he risked everything to save in Ukraine. The time printed on the video was an hour after the email was sent so the time zone on the cameras was one hour off. At first he was elated, then his heart sunk when he realized what this meant.

Kevin hacked into the lens database and, with a little luck, found Chuck and began the long and tedious process of reviewing video from his lenses. He didn't feel good about spying on a friend, but it looked like he might be involved with the Apostles, but he sincerely hoped he was wrong. He used a hyperbolic antenna to connect to a Wi-Fi a block away, and the connection was not the best. If downloading was slow and tedious, then watching was even more tedious.

Chuck shaving. Chuck working at the construction site. Chuck taking a piss in the portable toilet. Chuck eating wieners and beans. Chuck watching basketball. Chuck slapping his wife. Chuck masturbating to Japanese fetish porn. Chuck watching mixed martial arts. Chuck praying before he went to bed.

God! He was bored, but also disappointed. The Chuck he thought he knew wouldn't slap a woman. He wouldn't hang around with Apostles. He skipped ahead as much as he dared without risking missing something important. He heard half a conversation that might be interesting. Chuck was wearing an earphone, so all Kevin could hear was Chuck's part of the conversation.

"Have it shipped to the safe house."

"I'll arrange for someone to be there."

"I'll get Brother Walters to connect it."

"Amen."

"Uh-huh."

"I'll get him started Monday."

"Praise Jesus."

"God be with you, as well, Brother."

Chuck looked at his WON and it displayed a call from someone called Albert. Something was going on, but Kevin didn't know who this Albert was. He recognized Chuck's tone as someone speaking to a superior.

Then Chuck went to church, and Kevin was swamped with potential leads. He focused on the ones that Chuck seemed to be more familiar with, in hopes they would lead him to the crime. Kevin found several who needed lengthy retroactive surveillance. They would lead to others, who would lead to others, and the number of people in the social network would grow exponentially. It was 1:15 in the morning and he needed help. He made a call.

"Hey buddy, what's up?" Jade asked, her voice tinged with a half-yawn.

"I'm swamped, and I was wondering if you want to get started on working with me. I promise no presentations in front of hundreds of people," Kevin said.

"I'm glad you said so, or I would have told you I have to wash my hair. I haven't quite forgiven you for that, you know."

Kevin chuckled. He liked her sense of humor.

"Okay, I'll show you what to do. How about tomorrow at my place? Before work?"

Pausing first, she said, "After work."

Chapter Fifteen

The Workshop

Kevin allowed himself a few hours of sleep before checking the Dark Tunnel and found a new message from the Apostles.

"We set up a fully equipped machine shop at Davies Industrial Park. Let us know if you need anything else. There is a working prototype of a trigger and testing apparatus. You will begin work today at 10:00 a.m. The keys are under a black rock behind the building."

Shit. Things were moving too quickly. He needed more time to investigate. He called for a slipper and gulped down his coffee.

The slipper had already parked under the venerable old pine tree in front of his apartment building. The car was small, but the tires were almost as tall to avoid getting stuck in the potholes. He commanded the address into his WON and it glided toward the destination with the crunch of gravel.

It took twenty bumpy minutes to get there. He entered Davis Industrial Park and passed rows of buildings in various stages of decay. Many were vacant and weeds had grown over the tarmacs and stretched their matted briars high against the buildings. Cryptic gang tags were spray-painted in prominent locations. An unmanned blue and white slipper with a rotating blue light slowly approached from the other side of the road with cameras pointed toward the buildings.

The directions led him to a dead-end road that industry forgot. The front was square brick from the 1970s with a ribbed metal overhang that used to be a reception for customers, but now the windows were covered with brown cardboard. A chain-link fence surrounded the rear compound. Kevin felt like he was being watched and assumed there were cameras or drones in the area.

The man door in the fence to the backyard was padlocked shut. He got on his hands and knees and squeezed through a breach that looked too neat to be the work of thieves, and the opening was just big enough. The jagged wires scratched against the heavy fabric of his dragon-embroidered jacket and tore his jeans. He crawled through and felt the sharp gravel against his palms, or was it broken glass? He looked at his hands, no sign of cuts but a sagging opening in his jeans revealed a line of crimson.

Brushing off his pants, he continued through the tall thistles. Rusting hulks of internal combustion vehicles were backed against the rear of the lot. Old transmissions, engine blocks and random hunks of metal interspersed the rest of the yard. A passing breeze stirred up the smell of old crank-case oil that soaked the soil and turned it into soft asphalt.

He turned left around the back of the building and looked for a black rock. He looked in front of the door. *There it is.* He picked up the rock and took the hidden key and put it in the incongruently new, high-security lock. It turned with ease, and he swung the heavy metal door outward. It occurred to him, this could be an ambush, a nice, quiet, out of the way location, to eliminate someone who knows too much.

He paused in the open doorway and debated whether to bolt. He stood on the threshold with his senses on full alert. The building was silent and cool. He groped for a light switch and found it. Nothing. A brief flicker. A loud buzz, and a dim sputtering light.

"Metal halide? I didn't think that kind of lighting existed anymore," Kevin murmured to himself.

A greenish glow crept over the shop, and he stepped inside. The room smelled of concrete and solvent. A chain hoist and trolley hovered above the overhead door. Outer walls were finished with corrugated metal and stainless steel covered wooden work benches that lined most of the perimeter. The shop was clean but had oil stains on the floor. Various machinery and equipment were present, and all seemed newer and in good working order. A metal lathe, a hydraulic press, a drill press, a welding exhaust hood fan, A TIG welder, an oxy-acetylene welder, a CNC machine and many others. A red multi-layered metal cabinet containing tools and decorated with industrial stickers sat on wheels by the workbench.

In the center of it all, sooty gray lead canvas curtains were drawn in a rectangle around a framework of metal tubes and guide rings. Kevin approached and pulled the heavy curtain aside and peered into the deep pit molded into the floor. He instantly recognized it from the drawings. It looked like the tentacles of a steampunk jellyfish in mid-flight. It was the trigger. Kevin sighed and stepped back. He felt like he was looking at a black hole that threatened to devour the world. So, this is the future, he thought.

It was framed with crudely welded angle iron and each "tentacle" was attached with lock screws, which functioned as a primitive adjustment mechanism. The jellyfish's tentacles were proton accelerators for firing deuterium protons at the target. The accelerators intersected into a hemisphere of cast and machined steel which had a ring of large bolt holes around the edge to attach it to the nuclear device.

The ends of the tentacles were connected to electric cables which led to a large control box bolted to the floor of the frame. The tentacles were covered with three-inch copper pipe. Barcode stickers from the hardware store were still affixed to the pipe and the whole thing looked like something built in a high-school shop class.

He looked at the target and it had a plate with a long wire attached. That was the neutron detector used for testing. He remembered from the drawings it contained a tiny sphere made of lithium deuteride backing a hybrid perovskite radiation detector.

He thought of troubleshooting strategies. He took a toolbox and climbed down the ladder into the pit and removed the covering of the control box. The wiring connecting the accelerators looks ok. The connection to the control box was fine. He checked the grounding of the shields. Each one was wired to the frame. A heavy copper ground wire was bolted to the frame, and it led to the furnace room. A quick check confirmed it was grounded to the cold water main. He repeated each step again. This time he noticed the accelerators' ground wire was attached with an oddly colored black washer. He removed it and found it didn't appear to be metallic. He tested it with a multimeter and confirmed it was non-conductive charcoal colored rubber. The grounds were no good.

He shook his head in disbelief. How could a bunch of clowns like this possibly come up with a working thermonuclear weapon? he wondered. They can't, was his own answer. Still, he had to make a good show of trying to fix it, so continued to troubleshoot each part. He put it back together and went to work on the control box, paying special attention to the signal devices used to communicate with the trigger.

It had two methods of detonation. The Apostles could either arm it with a timer or manually. He examined each component. With a soldering gun, he removed an EPROM and downloaded the programming to his stick. He removed each resistor, transistor, and diode to give it a check and then put it back.

He was ready to test it and climbed up the ladder and stood behind a podium and started a tablet. It was connected to the neutron tester and displayed graphs of the input. He loaded an app for the trigger on his WON and commanded it to begin the arming process. He could hear the transformers starting as they began charging the giant industrial storage capacitor. It buzzed and hissed like an old-fashioned neon sign, and he could smell ozone. The lasers glowed as they warmed. He wondered how many rads would hit him when it fired. At least it was in a pit and the concrete and soil would absorb most of the radiation. He spoke the command to detonate.

"Shoot."

The capacitors emptied their mighty charge into the lasers which fired a pulse that lasted a microsecond. A purple light flashed out of the pit on the ceiling and leaked between the lead curtains. He looked at the graph and the energy created was far too low to trigger a chain reaction. He did not dare fix it, since his results were probably being monitored.

He looked at his WON and saw he had been working all day and into the night without stopping to eat. He left through the front door and locked it behind him. The front was illuminated with a floodlight and tiny pieces of broken glass glinted on the concrete. The road entrance had an electric chain-link gate that was overgrown with many years of weeds. The slipper had not yet arrived, so he waited in the cool quiet of the late spring evening. He heard the whirring of a drone overhead but did not look up, knowing that it was probably the Apostles, and they were probably checking up on him. After several minutes, the lights of the slipper appeared on the road. The car opened the door and he got in and opened the window. He could still hear the drone and commanded the car to head home slowly. As he crept ahead, he heard the drone veer off to the southwest.

"Turn left at the next intersection, full speed," he commanded.

He approached a man standing beside a car, holding a drone joystick.

"Stop here."

He slowly opened the car door and glided toward the man who was flying the drone. He was looking to the empty sky like he was fully emersed in virtual reality and could not see Kevin coming. There was something about the way he was standing, his short Asian hair, Kevin was thinking—*do I know him*?

Kevin shoved his back with both hands and the man fell to the ground. It was Francis.

"Sorry, sorry," he sputtered, and held his hands out in defense.

"What the fuck are you doing here? Whose side are you on anyway?" demanded Kevin.

"I'm on Mr. McPherson's side, that's all. I was just...watching."

His voice was fading and his eyes rolling, and Kevin was afraid he was going to have a seizure, and he relaxed his aggressive posture.

"Why did he tell you to watch me?"

"He didn't say. Probably just to make sure...you're doing your job."

"How do I know he's not passing your information to the Apostles?"

"I'm sure he would never do that," said Francis.

Kevin just stared at him in silence for a moment, then walked away.

"We're on the same side," Francis shouted after him.

Kevin was not sure McPherson was on any side but his own. On the way home, he searched up some takeout options and read the menu at Sushi City. It had a bewildering array of unfamiliar choices.

"Maki, that looks familiar."

He looked up the ingredients and chose a dozen maki and a couple of nigiri maguro, which they said contained raw tuna on a narrow strip of vinegar rice that made it look like a little fish. Very creative. He added crispy lobster maru, which had bits of lobster sticking out of a pressed ball of rice, with mayonnaise and other flavors.

He had sushi a few times, but there was still a learning curve. He entertained the idea of ditching the order and finding a different sushi place that had a combo box, but he wanted something decent for Jade.

Whyte Avenue at night was an electric place full of extremes. There were trendy restaurants and bars filled with young professionals and students, as well as streets with homeless people who pushed shopping carts to squatter camps in the parks. Junkies gathered in public washrooms, ingested their poison of choice, passed out, and often died.

Kevin saw a disheveled and bearded young man talking to something on the ground while deeply bowing, up and down. His hair was brown and wild and had eyes that looked far past reality. Kevin never got used to seeing people like that and wished someone would help them.

"Slipper, pull over and park."

Kevin got out of the car and walked over to the man. He ignored Kevin and still kept bowing.

"Hey man, how are you feeling?" He put his hand on his shoulder to get his attention. He stopped bowing and looked at Kevin with a dazed expression as if he were trying to tell the difference between delusion and reality. "Do you need help? Are you sick?"

"Sick. I need to go back to the hospital."

"Do you need help getting back? Do you have a bus pass or money?"

"No pass. No money." He started nodding his head again and was no longer aware of Kevin.

"Okay, I'm going to send you home, okay?"

Kevin ordered another slipper and waited. The man continued nodding and muttering something about a scaffolding. Soon a white slipper arrived. "Here we go, this slipper will take you back to the hospital." Kevin guided him to the car and opened the door. "Here we go. You can get out at the Royal Alexandra Hospital, okay? Do you understand?"

"Going back to hospital."

"That's right. Good luck."

"Royal Alexandra Hospital Emergency Admissions," he said to his WON. The car pulled away and he got back into his own. Soon, his slipper pulled up to the drive through window with all the precision of artificial intelligence. He flashed the barcode displayed on his WON to the reader and a conveyor unfolded with insectoid grace and efficiency and fed his sushi boxes to his window.

"Thank you, Wood san. Please come again."

The seafood aroma that filled the car suggested he made a good choice.

Jade would not arrive for another hour, so he ate a piece of maki and got in the shower but he could only get the water mid warm with the heat turned up all the way. Showers were often where he had his most brilliant ideas, but not when it was cold. He thought that if his current gig lasted, he could upgrade to a better apartment building. Would Jade ever want a roommate? He just as quickly realized there was little chance his current gig would last. Although, if he could get McPherson's son back, the old man might find something permanent for him. The rich and powerful always seemed to need the services of guys like him.

He put a dollop of hair gel in his palm and rubbed his hands together and wiped it into his hair. He shaved his face and optimistically shaved his bottom parts. He still had some of his army muscle, and his waist was slim enough to look good. A tight-fitting long-sleeved hunter-green shirt and cotton jeans seemed appropriate, and he got dressed—commando style.

The door camera chimed, and displayed Jade's face. Kevin had already granted her access so, she entered without him needing to buzz her in. She was wearing a tight-fitting leather jacket, a black stretch turtleneck top and black leather pants with medium length leather boots, also black.

Kevin admired her top to bottom and said, "You look great!"

"Thanks," she said. "I got these clothes on sale last fall at Urban Warfare."

She started to take off her boots, but Kevin told her, "You don't have to."

"Thanks, but I don't mind," she said, and took them off anyway.

"I'll put the rice in the infra-wave, and we can get started with dinner," Kevin said.

"Oh, I brought something," and handed a bottle of Cabernet Sauvignon in a gift bag.

"Wow, you didn't have to. I'll get the glasses."

Jade sat at his little kitchen table. Kevin set the table with two glasses. Soon, the rice was hot, and they sat down together. They both smiled as Kevin half-filled each wine glass. It had been days since they had been face-to-face, and they were feeling good about being together.

"You really know how to make a girl feel special."

"That's because you're a special girl."

She cocked her head a little and giggled at his cheesy reply. Kevin felt a little embarrassed, then proposed a toast. He lifted his glass and said, "gānbēi."

"Very good," said Jade, looking impressed at his attempt at Mandarin.

They both took a drink and Kevin put his glass on the table; Jade kept drinking and put it down when it was empty making a sound like she was out of breath.

"Do you know what gānbēi means?" Jade asked.

"I think it means dry cup or drink it all. I thought it was just a figure of speech."

"Oh no, we Chinese take that very seriously—you're expected to chug it all down."

She had a certain smile that led Kevin to suspect she was teasing him. She poured herself a little in the glass's bottom. "My turn. Gānbēi!"

This time, they both drained their glasses. "That reminds me of drinking games in the military."

"Chinese have lots of drinking games too. I hope you meet my brother someday. We could teach you."

"Do you have any toasts that don't involve chugging the whole glass?"

"There's Suíyì. That means drink at your own speed, but we don't use it very often."

"Sway eee. I'll try to remember that." They both laughed at his pronunciation.

"I hope you like sushi. I should have asked first," Kevin said.

"I like all Asian food and most other types of food, too. Mexican, Italian, Indian, whatever."

They both used the included cardboard chopsticks to help themselves to the food. Jade put little slices of pink pickled ginger on top of her maki before eating them and Kevin dipped his in soy sauce and put on a big dollop of wasabi. He took a bite, and his eyes bugged out. He swallowed fast, then his mouth gaped open.

"It's burning my nose!"

Jade laughed.

"That'll clear my sinuses." He paused before trying something else. The burning subsided but he could feel his eyes watering.

Kevin told her about the jellyfish device trigger and Francis spying on him and discussed strategies for searching for Alan and the bombmakers.

"It's getting late. Let's get the work stuff done. I'll just show you a few things tonight since you must be tired. You can get down to the real searching some other time," Kevin said.

Jade shrugged. "I'm used to staying up and I need time to unwind before I sleep."

Kevin pointed to the homebrewed hyperbolic antenna taped in front of the window and said, "This is how we connect to the internet. It's untraceable and we can't let the Apostles know we are investigating. They think I'm working for them and might get a little upset when they realize I'm working against them—and we can't have that, can we? Tomorrow I can set one up at your place if you want to work from home."

"What do you have on your screen?" she asked.

"Oh, that's the interface we have to use to look at the video from the lenses. It's not very user-friendly since it was never designed to be used by a wet-ware interface."

"Huh?"

"People. Wet-ware are people. Did you know 60% of your body is water? Each video is one hour long, and you can only fast forward slowly. If you see your guy make contact with another guy that looks sketchy, take a screen capture, and we can look them up later. Here, you try."

He got up and let her take his chair. She clicked on a file and started watching. He placed his hand on her shoulder, and she looked at him and smiled. He took that as encouragement and massaged her toned shoulders.

"This should help you unwind," Kevin said.

Jade let out a light groan of pleasure. "Ooo that's so good. Press a little harder there." She was like a kitten purring in his hands, and he enjoyed it as much as she did.

Jade started a video from thirty days ago and kept watching it in fast forward until her subject made a phone call on his WON. The number displayed and Jade took a screenshot, then continued playing at normal speed so she could hear the dialogue. It was nothing remarkable, so she fast forwarded again. She was catching on fast and wouldn't need a lot of prompting. Soon, she opened a second window and tried watching two videos at once. It worked, but sometimes lagged because of the slow connection.

"Is there a way to make this thing go faster?" Jade asked, exasperated.

"I'll have to do something. I was going to avoid a VPN since you can't tell if the provider won't rat you out, but I can think of one that should be solid. Lemme set it up."

Jade cocked her head slightly and looked a little confused about VPN but said nothing.

"This one is from Thailand, so I doubt the Apostles will lean on them into giving us up." He typed in an IP address and transferred some loonies.

"Here, give this a try."

The two videos played without glitches. She opened three more and had five spastic images rolling in fast forward mode. She paused them all if she needed to listen to something or take a screenshot. The speed of their progress made Kevin happy.

"That guy looks shady," Jade said, pointing to an image of a man in conversation with the person wearing the lenses. She took a screenshot and transferred it to Kevin. She elaborated on what kind of people she was looking at and he was impressed with her ability to read body language as easily as he could read technical manuals.

"I'll search him up tomorrow. Why don't we take a break? It's been a long day."

"Ok, wanna watch TV?" she asked.

"Let's see what's on," Kevin said.

Kevin sat on the couch first and held out his arm to motion her to sit next to him. She looked shy but sat next to him with his arm around her.

They settled on an MMA competition and watched it together.

Kevin gently stroked Jade's neck and shoulders and she rested her head against his chest. Kevin regretted how he overreacted and now didn't care what gender she used to be. He thought of apologizing but was afraid it would remind Jade of what a dick he was.

"I didn't think you would be ready for this," Jade said.

Kevin picked his words carefully. "My feelings for you haven't changed since I thought you were a cis woman. When I found out you are a transsexual, I was surprised, and I needed some time to process. I started to doubt my own sexuality and I had to think it through. Later, I realized, neither of us had changed. You are still the same woman and I'm still the same man."

"That's what I hoped you would think."

She was silent for a moment, then asked, "But what about my body? Don't you think it's gross that I have a penis?" She was apprehensive about the answer she might receive.

Kevin paused, his eyes bright. "I think your body is hot from top to bottom."

Jade turned her head to face him and looked into his eyes. Kevin smiled, but Jade looked deadly serious. She closed her eyes and kissed him. Her eyes were hungry. Jade waited for Kevin's reaction. Kevin cradled the back of her head and kissed her deeply. Kevin ran his hands down her body. Jade undid the buttons on his shirt. Kevin pulled her top up. Their hands were everywhere, and their primal lust was a run-away train. She began desperately tugging at his belt and zipper. Finding what she needed, they tripped and staggered, hopped, and collapsed on Kevin's little bed, ripping off what was left of their clothes.

Chapter Sixteen

Fornicating the Canine

Kevin woke to the sound of his coffee maker hissing and gurgling as it squirted out a cup of coffee. He opened his eyes and saw Jade wearing one of his long shirts and nothing else. She was cooking something on the stove and his nose told him what it was. Where did she find bacon? He liked the way the day was starting so far but knew it was going to get fucked up again before it was over. Jade was like a ray of sunshine during a hurricane. She was a stark contrast to the way his life was going, with the way the world seemed to be going. On one hand, he was spinning out of control and on the other; he was finding bliss.

"Good morning," he croaked.

"Good morning, babe," she replied. "What are your plans today?"

"I would love to spend the day with you, but I have to go to the shop and make it look like I'm making progress. What about you?"

"I'm going to do more surveillance. I took a couple of weeks off work so I can go at it full-time. I found one that kind of seems like a boss. He's from Vancouver, so I'll check him out and see where it goes."

"Sounds like a plan. I wish I could spend more time on it. I've been thinking of trying to recruit more help."

"Why don't you go to the cops? They could put lots of people on it?"

"There're more Apostles in the police department than ants in an anthill. If they found out what we are up to, they'd block all their lenses and might hurt Alan."

Kevin reluctantly put on his clothes and trudged to the bathroom. He called out to Jade, "I really enjoyed last night."

She paused what she was doing, looked up, "So did I—a lot."

She used a spatula to put the hash browns and bacon on a plate, then broke two eggs in the hot frying pan. They sizzled and crackled, and she splashed them with a spoonful of water and covered them with a glass pot lid.

Kevin walked up behind her and gave her a big kiss on the cheek. She turned, and he kissed her lips and he gave her a quick hug. He let her finish cooking and his mind was turning to the work of the day. In other circumstances, he absolutely would have been up for morning sex, but the thought of nuclear weapons was such a boner killer.

He started up the Dark Tunnel and found a message.

"Mr. Wood, I hope you can understand some of us question your motivation and your loyalty. Although you are not one of us, we hope your professionalism is high enough to work effectively and discreetly. We have many resources at our command, so can provide you with equipment, materials, and the motivation that you need."

'Motivation,' Kevin thought. That definitely sounds like a threat.

Jade served his breakfast with a glass of orange juice. Eggs, over easy. His favorite.

"Yesterday, I was listening to this preacher by the name of Beckett Smith, and I found some good stuff. Here, I'll play it for you on the tablet," said Jade. "Here he is, talking to Gideon Johnson."

Kevin's eyes popped open. "I know that guy. That's Chuck. He was my best friend in the army, then he just disappeared and then I see him sending the ransom email. What the fuck happened to him?" He leaned toward the tablet to listen to Beckett.

"The patriarchs are tickled with the money they've received from McPherson. It will go a long way to finish the fussy bits they need to finish the jellyfish device. The money for the mercenaries was a big help too. All in all, it has been a very fruitful enterprise," said Beckett.

"Those two thugs we sent to get Alan in the bar got owned by a split arse. That means by a girl, Brother Smith," said Gideon. "But the mercs nabbed him like the pros they are."

Beckett looked appalled at the vulgarity and shook his head.

"From what I hear, our scientist might have shit the bed on this one. It might need more than money to make this turkey fly," said Gideon. "This might turn out to be an epic jug-fuck."

"If you spent as much time in priesthood meetings as you used to spend in your army beer halls, maybe your speech would be more wholesome," said Beckett.

"Beer halls are a thing of the past for me. Since I was converted, I haven't tasted a drop; not even a tea or coffee. I'm a different person." said Gideon. "But my colorful speech is harder to change."

"Your baptism has wiped your sins away, but God hears your every word, and you will have to answer to Him on Judgement Day," said Beckett.

"I believe that beyond a shadow of a doubt, but I serve God and the Apostles in my own way," said Gideon. "I am the sword and you are the word. I believe when He balances my sins and my good works, he will take me with Him."

"Be that as it may, in the meantime, we mustn't let our goose that lays the golden eggs starve to death, mustn't we?" said Beckett.

He picked up a small bowl of oatmeal with a cardboard spoon stuck in it and walked down the stairs to the basement. The landing had a heavy door which he swung open then he turned on the light. A desolate young man with a short beard sat in the middle of the concrete floor with his hands chained to the steel telepost, squinting in the light.

"Holy shit!" said Kevin. "That's Alan. Is he still there?"

"No, a few weeks ago, someone must have come and moved him somewhere when Beckett wasn't home," answered Jade. "Beckett was talking about Vancouver, so there's another reason to start focusing there. But there's something else I want to show you. This is from a couple of days ago, after the first day you went to their shop," said Jade. "Beckett and Gideon are watching surveillance video of you working on the device. Here, watch this."

"It gives me the shivers seeing a non-believer involved in something so sacred. What if he goes to the police?" asked Beckett. He wrung his hands together and furrowed his eyebrows.

"If he did, we would be the first ones to know about it," Gideon growled. "Besides, he doesn't like cops and there isn't much he could do against us anyway. He's a nobody. He knows how to un-fuck kit but besides that, he's a bag of shit, whisky tango—white trash."

Kevin felt the sting of his friend's words.

They watched a wide-angle video of Kevin re-assembling the device.

"He doesn't seem to be accomplishing very much," said Beckett.

"He might be fornicating the canine. He needs to get jacked up a little. I'll give him the cornflake treatment and stick my boot up his ass until he gets it done," said Gideon.

"Won't that make him angry and try to get revenge?" asked Beckett.

"Don't be such a spinner. Sometimes I wonder if you might be half queer," said Gideon.

"Perish the thought! I hate sodomites as much as you do. While you were in the military doing all that rough and tumble hoo haa, I've been doing God's work and bringing the sinners and the saints closer to our Heavenly Father."

Gideon dared not challenge the value of God's work.

The video was over. Kevin did not like the idea of getting the cornflake treatment and he thought how he could make them think he was making progress. He typed a message to the Apostles.

"There are a couple of possibilities to explain why the proton beams are going awry and the fixes are not major. The communication module used, is known for causing electromagnetic interference and I recommend replacing it with the Geeksubm MSG25L01, which has better anti-interference characteristics. In addition, the following parts should be exchanged:

B0057OC6D8 Channel Relay for PIC AVR STM32

KY-026 IR sensor for the KY-039

I assume you can have them delivered at the workshop by 11:00 a.m. today and I will install and test them."

Kevin ordered a slipper.

"Can I go with you?" Jade asked.

"Thanks, love, but I really don't want them to know about you." Kevin could see the anxiety in Jade's eyes, but he felt she would be in greater danger, and he didn't want to put her in danger.

Kevin slunk into the slipper and ordered it to the shop. The sky was a threatening steel grey, and the weather predicted thunderstorms with the possibility of severe weather. He studied the clouds, looking for signs of any rotation. Kevin barely noticed the bumps in the road but smelled the humidity of an impending storm. He didn't see lightning, but could hear the slow, low rumble of distant thunder. The darkness of the sky was like twilight, although it was late morning, an unusual time of day for a storm.

He put the key in the lock but hesitated without turning it, waiting, thinking. What if I turned back? A sudden whirlwind blew dust against his face and then passed on and died. He heard the clack of the deadbolt opening.

He stepped into the darkness and turned on the light. All he could hear was the buzz of the lighting. It was now bright enough to see. He descended the ladder into the pit and noticed a piece of paper on the device's workbench and it held little bags of electronic parts with the part numbers printed on the labels.

Kevin took each part and gave it a battery of tests. He hooked them to a multimeter, tested for continuity, resistance, and voltage. The oscilloscope was where he knew it would be visible to the CCTV. Then he attached the ground connector of the oscilloscope's test lead to a ground point in the circuit. It displayed a row of square waves, as it should. After each test, he slowly and meticulously recorded the results. He thought about sabotaging a part, then rigging the oscilloscope to show it still worked, but decided it would take too much time.

For parts which were programmable, he connected them to a patch cable to the tablet and examined the code. After several hours, this part of the charade was over, and he stood between the camera and the device and replaced one of the incorrect grounding washers with conductive ones.

He started the primary vacuum pump until it was mostly done, then started the secondary oil diffusion pump. Its howling shriek was painful, and he put on some hearing protection earmuffs while he waited for any residual gasses and water vapor in the accelerators to be evacuated.

Then he started charging the storage capacitor. It gave off static electricity and he could feel his hair stand up from the force. He performed several tests of the voltage and shut it down again. Then he tested the vacuum level in the particle accelerators and then tested the vacuum in the primary, and then secondary vacuum pumps. Acting as though he found an issue, he hand wrote lengthy notes on a yellow pad of paper.

He thought about telling them the vacuum seals were not perfect, and all the aluminum gaskets needed to be replaced. He searched through the parts drawers and bins, seeing if he could find any, but came up empty. They would have to be purchased and, with any luck, would have to be ordered and this might take a few days to arrive.

Now for the test. Kevin climbed the ladder, closed the lead curtains, and returned to the tablet to open the testing interface. He activated the deuterium regulators, and a stream of heavy hydrogen atoms entered the vacuum. He fired the pulse lasers. The result was better than last time, but not strong enough to reach the target level, and for that reason, he considered the test a success.

It had been a long day, but he needed to send the Apostles an update before he left.

"The new parts have increased neutron output, but the results are still subpar. I have identified the vacuum is not sufficient and a leaky gasket is likely to be the cause. Since it is not possible to identify which one is faulty, they all need to be replaced. Please order new ones and let me know when they arrive so I can install them," he tapped send on the Dark Tunnel app.

He ordered a slipper and exited into the night to find that the expected storm never materialized, and it was still dry and calm. He wondered what the odds were that the Apostles would buy into his stalling tactics. He would find out soon.

Chapter Seventeen

Dark Humor

Derrick Johansen was in his late twenties and still had some of the athletic look from his high-school football years. He sat in a small shipping office on the inside of a large, dark industrial building that used to be a printing factory. He was listening to a blog about how liberal democracy has been persecuting the Christians when he thought he heard quiet laughing. At first, he thought it must be from the TV, but it looped church videos and he had never heard laughing before.

He ignored it and kept listening to his blog, but after a moment, it was back again, and this time louder.

I'm going to teach that boy a lesson, he thought, and picked up a large flashlight. Derrick was a policeman but took some leave to help the Church with guard duty for a few weeks. Derrick did not like being interrupted. The Church paid him for doing nothing and he wanted to keep it that way.

He opened the door and stomped the thirty meters across the concrete floor, shining his flashlight at the chained, (now bearded) boy. The boy's eyes were closed from the glare, but he was laughing hysterically.

"I'm going to wipe that stupid grin off your stupid face."

"My dad's going to get me," Alan laughed. "I'm going to be a person again."

He still kept laughing, and Derrick cracked the flashlight across his face, knocking him over. The laughter stopped and Derrick kicked him in the ribs and legs for good measure. He started walking back to the office and the boy starting sobbing. Derrick stopped and turned back toward him. "I said shut up!" The boy closed his mouth and stifled his sobs, but his chest heaved, and tears streamed down his sunken face.

Chapter Eighteen

Twisting the Blade

Dr. Feldman read the notes on his desk while Jade took a seat beside it. She noticed he was still wearing the same long-sleeved flannel shirt and she assumed that artificial intelligence avatars don't feel the need to change clothes. She thought the bookcases seemed fuller and looked up and down the old wooden shelves but couldn't find which volumes might be new.

"Well, how have you been since the last time we spoke?" said Dr. Feldman.

"The guy I dated found out I was trans just before I was going to tell him. I thought that was *it* for us, but after a few days, he said he was okay, and we are even closer now."

"Good. I'm glad your personal life is going well. Tell me more about your life story. You can tell me everything, not just trauma, because it is important for me to get to know you better."

"After I punched that girl, I knew I needed to get away from my mother. The only place I could go was to my brother's place in Burnaby. So, I drove across the Rockies in a slipper and finally got there.

"I didn't think I could ever get tired of looking at mountains, but I did. I just wanted to get away. Clarence is four years older than me and a couple of inches taller. He had his hair cut so it stands straight up and spikey. He liked to go to the gym, and he usually wore a muscle shirt and you could see his dragon and snake tattoos on his left shoulder and the one of his ex-girlfriend on his forearm.

"I told him I came to get away from Mom and asked him if I could stay until I could find a job and get my own place.

"I got in his apartment, and he said he had to take care of something and make myself at home. I hung up my clean clothes in the hallway closet and got settled in. Despite everything, I felt like a weight was taken off my shoulders. I took a shower. Things seemed different there. I noticed the water was different and soap was more slippery and harder to wash off. I stayed an extra few minutes with the shower as hot as I could stand it, trying to forget.

"The next morning, I got all dressed up, and started resume bombing the town anywhere I thought they might hire someone with a high school diploma and no experience. There weren't many jobs, but I kept trying.

"Clarence said I could work at his courier business making deliveries until I find something better. So, he took me shopping and bought me all these punky clothes so I fit in. So, I'm like, okay, whatever, I didn't know couriers had to dress like that.

"He said one of his guys would take me around and show me the ropes and he introduced me to this guy called Shank. I was so naïve, I can't believe it now. I didn't even know what shank meant. Shank was really nice and usually had this huge grin stuck to his face. Really tough, but really nice too, if that makes sense.

"We got into this old Japanese gas-powered car with a steering wheel on our way to the first delivery, then Shank turns and he says to me, 'Why don't you reach under the dash and grab me a bag of slivers? There's a little button right underneath. In the middle.'

"I had no idea what slivers were and why would they be under the dash, but I found the button and a small tray slid out with this electric whirring sound and it was filled with a dozen little bags of all these powders and pills. Like a flash, I realized my brother was a drug dealer and now so was I. How could I have been so stupid? I didn't know what else to do, so I just went along and didn't say anything. I guess I was more afraid of telling him how gullible I was.

"We pulled up to an old rooming house and as he turned into the back parking area, the headlights lit up half fallen down fences and a broken asphalt lane. The parking lot was covered with gravel and litter and Shank slid between two old cars. I followed him to the building. I thought I might throw up, I was so scared!

"We stepped over a man on the nod, lying in the doorway and entered the building and climbed the hollow sounding stairs. It smelled like stale piss, puke, and boiled cabbage and I could hear someone laughing with the television blaring some fake sounding laugh track.

"Shank stopped in front of number 10 and knocked three times. There were footsteps, the rattle of an old fashioned chain and the clack of the deadbolt.

"So, this funky old junky answers the door and he goes, 'Shank! I was hopin' they would send you. How's it hangin' bro? Come on in.'

"They both stepped inside. It looked pretty much like how I imagined a drug attic's apartment would look like. Very little furniture, no shelves, and boxes with junk on the floor, then there was an old couch with ripped upholstery and no legs that looked like someone pulled it out of a dumpster.

"Shank said he brought Johnny a little treat. He shuffled back and forth like a football player and stepped back while taking the bag out of his pocket and holding it like a quarterback ready to throw the ball. Then he just handed it to him, and they both laughed.

"Johnny was in his early forties but looked like he was in his late fifties. He had this long scraggly red beard and chopped up mousy ginger-grey hair. He was as skinny as an eel and had blue eyes and wire-framed glasses. Johnny looked up to Shank, like he was a leader. He talked with a stoners drawl and loved to laugh and tell stories that just kind of stopped with no point to them.

"Johnny grinned ear to ear but wasted no time. He sat on the couch and picked up a piece of tinfoil on the floor and then rolled a small sheet of paper into a tube.

"He said he broke his rocket so he had to use this stuff. He was laughing, and shaking, and his eyes were bugged out and hungry. He took a pinch of skinny crystals and placed them in the crumpled cone of tinfoil. He held the paper tube in his mouth and the foil in his right hand and a lit lighter with his left. The crystals melted and began smoking. Johnny inhaled just fast enough to get the smoke but not too fast to fill up his lungs too quickly. He let go of the lighter and put down the foil and sat, frozen, holding in the smoke. Then a cloud of meth poured out and he sat back on the couch. Then he had a coughing fit and had a hard time trying to catch his breath. I think the drugs were wearing him down. The coughing stopped and a stupid meth grin spread across his face and stayed there.

"Then he just says, 'Ahhhhh. That hit the spot.' He leaned back on the couch and asked if we wanna hit, but we both passed. Shank said he has to drive.

"We let ourselves out and Johnny just sat there, grinning at the wall.

"I thought that went pretty good and maybe being a drug dealer wasn't going to be so bad.

"Shank told me about the types of different customers. Some want to be friends, but some are all business. You have to watch out for rippers who'll try to jack you, or other gangs who want to do worse. He pulled his jacket away to show me a hunting knife attached to his belt on his right hip and told me that's why they call him shank, and we might need it where we are heading next—Hastings and Main.

"He said some people call that area the Four Blocks of Hell and the South Asian gangs like to think they own the place, but we deliver everywhere. 'Free enterprise bro,' he said, then gave me a fist-bump and I didn't even know how to do it. I was such a nube.

"Middle class druggies used to buy from government drug stores so they don't have to meet up with people like us. The street people couldn't afford it, so they order from bootleggers. Ours was more stronger too since the government cut their dope for safety. Now that it's all outlawed again, everyone buys from us.

"The further west we went, the more empty buildings there were. Past Main Street, all the main floor stores were boarded or closed with steel bars. The upper floors were lived in or empty.

"The buildings were lined with street people, elbow to elbow, for real. Their shopping carts were overflowing and clothing was all over the sidewalk like a patchwork quilt.

"I took a bag of green pills from the tray and handed them to Shank. We got out of the car and Shank armed the car alarm.

"He was still smiling when he looked at me and said this is why we make the big bucks. He led the way up a dark and narrow wooden staircase. The sound of moaning and vomiting was coming from an upper level. Shank said that's someone dope sick.

"We got to apartment number 25 and Shank knocked on the door. A serious looking white man opened it, his chin out, looking us up and down. He had a short Mohawk haircut and three teardrops tattooed under the corner of his left eye. He wore a stained t-shirt with Vancouver on the front and a flaking picture of Stanley Park.

"I could see it in his face he was going to jack us up. Shank started going in, and I grabbed his arm to stop him. He looked back like 'what the hell,' and shook his head and kept going in. I knew this was going to go bad, but I followed him in anyway. Another man was in the living room and smiling a greasy smile. His hair was pig shaved and he had the word Billy tattooed on the side of his head.

"Billy looked at me and said, 'look what the Chinaman sent. He brought me a little present.' Billy walked over to me and just leered in my face. I was scared. I realized I was in way too deep. He reached out and tried to touch my face, but I pulled away. He stepped back, still grinning.

"Then all of a sudden, Billy turned from grinning like a monkey to serious, and turned toward Shank, gave his little speech, 'This territory belongs to us, and your gang better stay the fuck out. I'm going to send a little message to your boss.' Billy started to reach inside his jacket and Shank reached for his knife. I stepped forward and saw Billy's hand pull the handle of a pistol. Shank had his knife out and began a step forward. I flicked my leg out and kicked Billy's hand just as he was bringing it up to shoot and the pistol flew spinning in the air. Billy groped for it and I got my footing then kicked him on the side of his knee It made a huge crack and buckled his leg. He screamed and Shank was on him in a flash, and plunged his knife deep between his neck and shoulder. Teardrop pulled out a knife and stepped forward to stab Shank in the back.

"I yelled, 'Shank!'

"Shank yanked the knife out and wheeled around. He blocked Teardrop's knife with his left arm, then plunged his knife into Teardrop's grimy t-shirt. I saw his eyes change as he felt the acids from his stomach spill into his body. He screamed in agony and fell to his knees, holding his stomach, looking up and crying for help.

"I picked up the pistol and held it on Billy. Blood was pouring down his chest and he dropped to his hands and knees. He coughed up blood then collapsed, and just slumped forward on his face and died.

"Shank gave his knife a flick so it spun around in his hand and was pointing down. He put his foot on the back of Teardrop's head and plunged his knife into his heart. With both hands, he gave it a sudden twist and Teardrop collapsed.

"I was yelling at him that he could have survived and why did you do that?

"'Because he could have survived,' he said. He wiped his blade on Teardrop's back, checked to make sure it was clean, and put it back in the sheath like he did that every day.

"He said he don't like it either, but if he let him live, his gang would come after us. They would think we're weak. Besides, maybe these two were acting on their own and no one will know Clarence's gang killed them.

"My hands were shaking and still held the 9mm on Billy. I figured out he was dead, and I didn't need to do that anymore so I handed the gun to Shank, but he said I could keep it, since I earned it."

"I kept looking for straight jobs during the day and delivering dope at night. I looked around for my own place and then found out how much rent was. I didn't have any offers that would pay well enough to afford rent as well as food, so I lost interest.

"It felt good to have my own money for the first time in my life. Clarence wouldn't let me pay for rent so I always had extra. I wore nice clothes, I went jogging every morning along the bay and through the forest and life was good again.

"Then it seemed like things would get even better when Clarence said we could get a bigger place so I could have my own bedroom and my own bathroom. He was making more money these days and wanted to gun train me to be his bodyguard instead of delivering."

Chapter Nineteen

Beckett gets Busted

Beckett gripped the pulpit and he mercifully approached the conclusion of his plodding forty-five-minute talk.

"I invoke his blessing upon you that the gift of the Holy Ghost may be upon you so that you may be more Christ-like in your action and your deed. I testify that holding fast to the rod of iron will lead to Him. As his servant, I invoke his blessing upon you that your desire and capacity to hold fast to moral cleanliness. I leave these things with you, in the name of our Savior, Jesus Christ, amen."

Becket left the pulpit and returned to his seat in front of the choir. The children and some adults looked relieved, and the men's foreheads glowed with light perspiration from wearing suit jackets in the early summer heatwave in a chapel with no air conditioning. Some women were uncomfortable too, since their dresses were full length and had modest, long sleeves and high necks. Both sexes wore the mandatory long underwear known as temple garments. As disinterested and hot as they may be, they bore their burden with stoicism. The choir and the congregation stood and sang the closing hymn.

After the meeting, Beckett stood with his wife by the exit, saying goodbye to his congregation and shaking their hands.

"Thank you for the lovely talk, Bishop. It was inspirational," said an older widow as she offered him a limp hand to shake.

"Thank you, sister. The Holy Ghost moved me," replied Beckett.

"You have a way with words, Bishop," said Gideon, who was the next in line, grinning, as he shook Beckett's hand like it belonged to a rag doll.

"Thank you, Brother Johnson," said Beckett. "Will you be at the gay pride protest tomorrow? We have an especially warm reception planned for the sodomites."

"That's affirmative. I would love to lend a hand," said Gideon.

Beckett, Gideon, and Charlie Card stood on the sidewalk with heavy pockets bulging. Their expressions were incongruently somber considering the atmosphere. Around them were people wearing rainbows and waving flags. There were men, women and children, many of whom were dressed in outlandish costumes. Drag queens could not be ignored with their extravagant makeup and mannerisms as they posed for pictures taken by the local press.

The first float was arriving. It had several shirtless men from an athletic club waving and flexing. Beckett yelled, "Sinners!" and threw a rock at one of the men. He missed and the rock sailed past and bounced off the ground, hitting a woman bystander on the other side of the street. Gideon also yelled and began throwing rocks. Gideon's arm was stronger, and he threw with the accuracy of a baseball pitcher. He hit a man in the face, who fell to the deck of the float, holding his broken face with blood streaming out between his fingers. The other men jumped off, and the spectators yelled in fear and anger.

The two started throwing stones indiscriminately into the crowd across the street, and a stampede ensued. Some were injured and trampled in the panic as they tried to run away.

A man in a rainbow t-shirt next to Beckett glared at him and yelled, "Barry, what the fuck are you doing?" He gave Beckett a shove, but Gideon punched him with his sledgehammer fist and sent him staggering back.

Beckett recognized him and fled, pushing his way through the crowd with Gideon behind. When they escaped, Gideon asked, "Why did that 'mo call you Barry? He acted like he knew you?"

"I have never seen that man before," Beckett said, looking agitated. "He must've mistaken me for someone else."

Gideon looked long and hard at Beckett, who did his best to avoid eye contact.

David Wilson's ears were ringing and his face and head were throbbing from Gideon's punch. His friend, Sam, helped him to the bus stop. David's eye was already swollen shut and it bled slowly and dripped down the front of his rainbow shirt. The bus stop was crowded from the sudden crush of people evacuating the parade. Sam held him steady.

"Did you know that Barry man?" asked Sam.

"Yeah, we hooked up a few times." David staggered to the bus stop with his arm around Sam's shoulders, trying not to pass out.

The first bus was full before he got to it and had to wait another twenty minutes for the next one.

"I've got to sit down."

Sam shouted to the crowd, "Give us room!" He opened a circle to give David space to sit down without being trampled, and stood guard over him.

David sat on the concrete sidewalk, with his knees up and his head down. He leaned forward and vomited, and the pain and pressure increased and he slumped to the concrete.

He thought he was underwater, and he could hear someone shouting from above the surface. Was it Sam?

"Stand back!"

"I've gotta get you to a hospital. Let me call you a slipper," it sounded like Sam's voice, far away.

Good old Sam. He would never drown with Sam nearby. David realized he had passed out and was regaining consciousness.

"Sam?"

"You have to go to the hospital. You have a concussion."

"I didn't pay my insurance. Just help me get on a bus." He wobbled back to his feet as the bus arrived. Sam took the lead, and he parted the crowd to let David and the other injured on first.

"Thanks, Sam. You're a true friend."

He got home and stumbled to the bathroom. He still felt nauseated, partly from the concussion, and partly from the stinging betrayal from his ex-lover. He vomited in the toilet and his right eye felt like it was going to burst. David looked in the mirror and washed his face. He dabbed it off with a towel and placed a bandage over the cut. With a little luck, his right eyebrow would cover the scar and he didn't think he really needed stitches. He took two codeine pills, a double shot of Gibson's Finest Bold to cover the awful taste in his mouth, and gradually fell into a fitful sleep.

The next day, he was still feeling dizzy, but his desire for revenge pushed him on. He flipped through his photographs from last year when he and Barry were seeing each other. Not that they were really dating. It was more like a series of casual encounters. Everyone had to be careful, but Barry was more secretive than typical, so David assumed he must be married or have a square job where being gay was not tolerated.

David searched up how to find someone using a photograph, then uploaded a face picture of Barry to the internet. He found him in a group photograph of members of the Restored Church of the Apostles who were one of the most homophobic, sexist, and narrow-minded churches around. They would want to know if one of their own was practicing sodomy.

He checked his app and found the "Barry" profile was still on Man2Man dating site where they first chatted. He downloaded the profile picture and some more revealing ones he had sent him when they were getting to know each other. He wanted something better than that. He never thought he would resort to revenge porn, but if there was a scenario where that was justified, this was it.

He flipped through his homemade porn collection. There were hundreds of images and videos over the years with a dozen different men. David found a couple of Barry on the receiving end since homophobes hate catchers more than pitchers and placed them in an archive file and sent the email to the Edmonton church as well as the headquarters in Vancouver with the attached archive.

That should really fuck him up. Welcome to the wonderful world of homophobia, Barry. How do you like it on the receiving side? David Wilson grinned and clicked send.

Beckett sat at his home desk, looking through some church financial statements. An email just arrived when his wife, Clarissa, called him for dinner. She set the table for two, as always. Beckett sat down to meatloaf, mashed potatoes, and peas.

"It looks great, Mother," he said.

"Oh, it's just meatloaf," she answered, smiling. "How was your day?"

"A couple of stock boys called in sick today and one more was on vacation. We have some part-time students filling in, but I had to train them. One of them loaded too many cases on his cart and a box of pickles fell off and crashed to the floor, spilling all over the aisle. Can you imagine? I chastised him and showed him how to stack them properly."

"They're lucky to have a manager like you to look after things."

"Young people today don't seem to have the same gumption as when we were young. I wouldn't be surprised if they all weren't all on drugs. It changes people. It would do them all good if they would attend our church and learn some self-discipline and some decency. Of course, I can't tell them to go to church since that would be against company policy. It seems like they are all just allowed to run wild. Of course, it is the fault of permissive parenting," Beckett pronounced with the confidence of a judge.

"Amen," said Clarissa. "When I see the young people today, I can't help feeling a little relieved that we couldn't have children. God forgive me."

As if lecturing at the church, Beckett announced, "We need a strong hand in this country to force these people onto the path of righteousness!"

"If only Bernard Simpkin was still the Prime Minister," Clarissa said. "He would have everyone singing from the same hymn book."

"He will be again, you just wait and see. We'll make sure of that."

Clarissa picked up the utensils and placed them on a dish and stacked it on the other dish before taking them away. She returned with a damp cotton washcloth with a checker pattern and cleaned the table, scrubbing briskly at a stubborn spot of dried gravy.

Beckett returned to his desk and saw the email on the church's account. The heading was Barry. He clicked on it and his heart stopped. On top was a picture of himself in a compromising position with the smiling face of one of his ex-lovers. The one that recognized him at the gay pride assault and the one that Gideon punched.

"To whom it may concern, it surprised me to learn an ex-lover is a member of your church and it may surprise you to learn who it is—Beckett Smith. Since he will deny it, I have attached evidence of our affair. As you will see, he was a willing and active—or rather, passive—participant."

He scrolled down and saw a collection of revealing and pornographic images of him and David. The blood left Beckett's face. His mouth had gone dry like he was facing death. His head was spinning. *This can't be happening to me.*

A ray of hope. He found the message first, and not one of the church clerks. He deleted the email.

He had to shut David up, permanently. He could get Gideon to kill him, but that was too risky. What if David talked to Gideon first? He would have to kill him himself. His mind was racing. In every scenario he could think of, he wouldn't have the guts to do it, or he would be so scared that he would botch it. Something needed to be done before he sent his email to someone else. A paralyzing thought occurred to him. *What if he already had?* He checked the email garbage bin and opened the deleted email. His worst fears were realized—the Apostle headquarters in Vancouver had been cc'd.

Chapter Twenty

The Torch

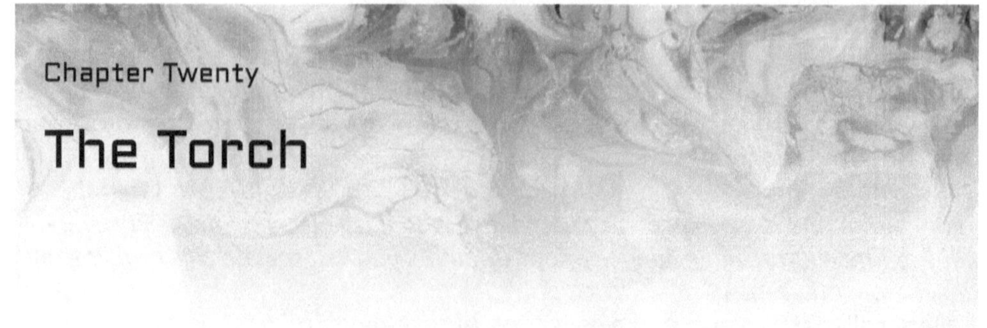

I t was just a few days after Kevin's last visit to the Apostle's workshop when he received a notification that his parts had arrived, and they were ordering him to get back to work. He arrived and looked at the workbench but didn't find any new gaskets, so he sent a message on his table asking where they were.

Just then, he heard a key in the front door and turned to look just as Gideon Johnson burst in carrying a pistol. Trailing him were two men just as burly. They wore blue jeans and military style vests and were packing Heckler & Koch 9mm submachine guns. He recognized them from the video, they were the juice monkeys who kidnapped Alan from the campus.

"Private Kevin Wood," said Gideon. "Long time no see. Who would have thought we would still be on the same side. Or are we?"

"Chuck? What the hell's going on?"

The mercenaries grabbed Kevin, and zip tied his hands behind his back. Gideon walked over to him and punched him in the stomach. "Don't ever fucking call me Chuck again. Chuck is dead. My name is Gideon."

Kevin was bent over, gasping for air. A mercenary grabbed his hair and pulled his head up. Kevin's mouth was open and panting. He looked up and saw Gideon's smug grin.

Gideon stepped forward. "Look at you. Pathetic. Did you really think we wouldn't notice you're fucking the dog? Stringing us along? You're still the same. A low-class WT loser, going through life awaiting parts. It was my idea to put you to work instead of killing you, but you're making me look bad. Don't make me regret my decision." Gideon poked his finger in Kevin's forehead.

"I saved your life," Kevin said in a breathless voice.

"And now I'm going to save yours. We've been watching you like a hawk and so have our scientist and engineer. They are inclined to agree the parts you replaced were a good call. The engineer noticed you changed one of the grounding wires and tried to figure out why. He checked them and found out none were grounded, but you knew that already, didn't you? Instead of fixing all of them, you just fixed one to make it a little better. You said there was a problem with the vacuum and the gaskets needed to be replaced. Our engineer tested them inside out before you got them. You're stalling.

"I don't think you really understand us. When I came back from Ukraine, I couldn't get my life together on Civvy Street. I became an alcoholic. Nobody gave a rat's ass about me until one day the missionaries knocked on my door. I don't know why I let them in but I'm glad I did. Maybe I was desperate. They taught me about the gospel and how the church was restored after two thousand years of darkness. They taught me about the word of wisdom that forbids alcohol, tobacco, tea, and coffee. They taught me about the Holy Ghost and how He speaks to us in a still small voice to tell us the truth. In the end, they asked me to pray with them and ask Jesus if what the missionaries taught me was true.

"I knelt down with the missionaries and prayed. Then it hit me. The still small voice told me the church was true, and I knew it beyond a shadow of a doubt. Since that day, my life changed. I haven't had a drink of alcohol in two years and my life is back on track.

"The Apostles want to save everyone. We are not terrorists. We want to use this weapon to help bring people to Jesus. God destroyed Sodom and Gomorrah. He wiped out the Earth in a flood and He has commanded us to use nuclear weapons to bring more people to righteousness.

"Stop and think, if we are willing to blast thousands of people into atoms, what wouldn't we do to get you to cooperate?"

A small part of Kevin felt sorry for Gideon. He was messed up, but his life was now stable, but at a tremendous cost. Some people whose lives are out of control need to have others take control for them, whether by joining the military or by joining a cult.

"What happened to you? You just disappeared. I could've helped. I would've wanted to help."

Gideon ignored him and strolled over to the workbench by the wall, picked up a MAPP gas blow torch, and walked back over to Kevin. Kevin tried to pull away, but the mercenaries held his arms. Gideon pulled the trigger and held the roaring flame a foot away from his face. Kevin felt the heat and his eyes were wild as a bronco. Gideon brought the flame closer until it became unbearable. Kevin yanked his head away, and the flame drew closer. Gideon quickly poked the flame against his face and Kevin screamed, jerking his head back and forth to avoid it.

Gideon laughed. "That was just a love bite. See what happens when I get angry. If you don't like it, how about I burn the face off that pretty little China doll you've been fucking?"

Kevin's heart sunk. He was hoping they didn't know about Jade.

"That's right, if you don't put out, we'll go after her next and you won't recognize her when we're done. Maybe I'll take a stab at her myself. You don't mind sharing, do you? Maybe not. We don't approve of fornication or interracial sex, you know. Fix it, or she's next. Got it?"

Kevin's heart was racing. He cursed himself for bringing her into this.

"Yeah, got it," Kevin whispered.

"What boy? I can't hear you!" Gideon roared.

"Got it, sir!"

"That's more like it." Gideon eased back on his heels with the air of a satisfied cat. "I think we're going to get along just fine… Now, finish this fucking shit!"

The mercenaries cut Kevin's zip ties and left. The searing pain on his face only increased. He put his WON on selfie mode and he saw a blister was emerging on his cheek. Clearly, stalling would not work any longer, so he set to work replacing the washers on the grounding connectors. He would do anything now to protect Jade, even if it meant putting thousands at risk. He didn't really think it was that much risk because he doubted if the device would work anyway. These people weren't the sharpest tools in the shed.

One by one, he removed each plastic washer and replaced it with a steel one. The cameras were watching him so made sure they could see he tightened them. He was ready for a test.

Restoring the vacuum took the longest, and he had to endure the howling of the secondary oil diffusion vacuum pumps. While he waited, he couldn't help thinking about what he was doing. He was building a trigger for a thermonuclear weapon that, if it worked, would kill many thousands of people. He would rather die than be responsible for that. Kevin came up with an exit strategy. *I could cut the wiring from the capacitor and attach it to my body. One wire in the mouth, the other over my heart. A quick tap on the tablet and it would all be over.*

He believed he could do it. He thought he had the guts to do it. But what about Jade? He couldn't bear the thought of them hurting her and his death probably wouldn't stop them. He needed to stay alive to protect her.

Kevin balanced the calculus of evil in his head. Wouldn't it be better for two people to die, if that would save thousands? But what if the bomb wouldn't work? Then two people would have died for nothing. What if we died, and they got the bomb working anyway? Again, two people would have died for nothing. What if I helped them and the bomb worked? Then I would wish I was dead, but glad Jade wouldn't be. Best-case scenario is I build the trigger, but the bomb doesn't work. That's most likely what will happen. If it was possible to build an H-bomb with plumbing, someone would have done it by now.

He felt like he was dead already. His soul was dead, but his body kept going. A zombie. He raised his lethargic arm and started warming the lasers. They buzzed and gave off a purple glow that lit up the room and glistened on his sweaty, burnt face. He climbed the ladder as shaky and weak as an old man.

The voltage in the capacitor was good. The vacuum was good. He watched the graph and turned on the deuterium gas. He pressed the Shoot button and the graph suddenly spiked up high into the red zone. It had generated more than enough neutrons to begin the chain reaction, according to their calculations. It was a big success and, at the same time, an enormous failure.

On his way home, he felt the sting on his face start to fade. He thought about Jade and how he had brought danger to her. It could get worse if they found out she was trans. So far, they look at her as leverage. If they knew what she was, they would attack out of pure hatred. It was dangerous for her to be around him, and he needed to keep his distance to keep her safe.

He stood in front of the mirror and sprayed some local anesthetic on the blister and taped a piece of gauze over it. He took a 400ml food pouch of ravioli from the cupboard, opened it and placed it in the infra-wave and scarfed it down with a biodegradable fork.

He started a video chat with Jade.

"Hi babe, how are you? What happened to your face?" Jade's expression changed from cheerful to concerned.

"Oh, it's nothing. I just burned myself when I was soldering something at the shop. It could have been a lot worse," he grunted, hating himself, hating the Apostles, and hating everything.

"You don't look okay. Is there something else wrong?"

"No, it's just work, you know," mumbled Kevin.

"Alright." Jade let it go, but still looked concerned. "I've been following up on some dicey people in Vancouver, and I think I'm getting somewhere. Two of them were talking about engineering and science, so they are probably connected to the bomb. I hope I can find out where their factory is."

"How are things going at the shop?"

"I think I'm done. It's working the way they wanted it, so we'll see what they say. I hope they leave us—I mean, leave me alone," said Kevin.

"That's a lot quicker than you planned, isn't it?"

"I couldn't stall them any longer. What can you do?" Kevin's voice laden with resignation. "Do you have anything on Alan?"

"Kind of. I heard some people talking about him, so I'm definitely going to keep an eye on them. It sounds like they're getting close to agreeing on a price with McPherson, but they're waiting to see if the device works before they'll give him back. Since you're done, that might hurry this up."

"I'll tell McPherson, so he knows he doesn't hafta offer them any more money," said Kevin.

"There's one guy I think might be guarding Alan, but he doesn't wear lenses. I wanna to go to Vancouver and track him down. Is it in the budget?" asked Jade.

"There is no budget. You can go first class or charter a jet, if you want." Kevin thought for a moment. "Maybe I should go instead. It could be dangerous if you get made."

"It could be even more dangerous for you since they know you. Besides, I can take care of myself," said Jade.

He saw an opening to fake a confrontation. "Are you saying I can't?" his question had a sharp edge.

"No, I didn't mean it like that. I just..."

"You just think I can't take care of myself! Is that what you are saying?" He hurt her and knew it.

"No, why are you being like this?"

"Forget it. Never mind. If you want to go, just go."

Kevin saw her pain, then looked away in shame. "Sorry, look, work is getting to me. I think I need a break. I just need to be alone for a while. Take what you need from McPherson's wallet."

"You need to be alone?"

Chapter Twenty-One

Beckett Plans His Escape

B eckett tried to think of a way out. His life had been one long exercise in hiding who he was, and he was good at it. He could contact headquarters and tell them there was an email with a virus that needed to be deleted. But who checks the email there? Wouldn't that seem like a lot of fuss over a virus?

He called them. "Hello, this is Bishop Beckett Smith. Can I speak with your clerk, please?"

"Our clerk isn't in today. Is there anything I can help you with, Bishop?" said a voice at the other end of the line.

"I got an email in my church email account that turned out to be a virus. It locked up my tablet and demanded that I send $500 loonies to some atheist socialist group. I remembered it was cc'd to you folks, so I thought I would give you a warning so you could delete it before you open it."

"Well, that's mighty white of you, Bishop, but we have pretty good virus scanners to keep the devil's work out of our systems. Why don't you call Sheldon, our computer whiz. He might be able to get your computer working again. He knows all about tablets and computers and all sorts of modern things. Whenever I can't get something working, I give him a call, and if he isn't too busy, he usually lends a hand. The Holy Ghost moves some people to that kind of knowledge, but not to me. I just use my old desktop because I know how."

"Yes, thank you, but how can I warn your clerk?"

"Oh, you don't have to go to any trouble. I'll just send a message to Sheldon and he can have a look at it when he gets a chance. He was going to the mountains today with his wife and young daughter. They go hiking up and down the mountain trails all the time. You know young people; they don't have the fear like I do. I would be worried about bears or cougars or immigrants. Last year they found a body of someone murdered and robbed ten kilometers into the mountains and—"

Beckett snapped. "Sorry, how do I speak with your clerk right away?"

"Well, I told you Sheldon went to the mountains."

"Sheldon is your clerk?"

"Yes, he's our clerk, but he also helps fix things. There was one time I forgot my password, and he told me how I could reset it. It didn't work for me, but

I must have done something wrong because I hear he knows computers. I'm sure he'll know what to do with your virus as well, so don't you worry yourself about it."

"Alrighty then," said Beckett. He was trying to sound nonchalant, but he could hear the fear in his own voice.

If he contacted Sheldon, he would probably want to troubleshoot his tablet and would find out it was not locked up. Still, he had to try.

He called Sheldon's WON. "Hello, this is Bishop Beckett Smith from Edmonton. I received an email in the church's account that had a virus that locked up my tablet and they're asking for money. A copy of the email was sent to you, so please don't open it. The heading is *Barry.* Thanks. Bye."

Beckett tried to return to his normal routine. He tried to guess the chances of him deleting the email without reading it. He supposed it would be several hours before Sheldon got the message.

He prepared a talk for church. He had already started on the topic of moral cleanliness and it seemed more suitable now than ever. He had a hard time concentrating with everything else, but got it written... Just as his WON rang.

"Hi, this is Brother Sheldon Pratt. I understand you are having some computer trouble."

"Yes, thanks for calling." Beckett tried to sound calm. "You were sent a pornographic email with a virus and I was calling to ask you to delete it without opening it."

"Let's see. The one with *Barry* in the heading?"

"Yes, that's it. Just delete it without opening it."

"Email can't usually infect you just by opening it. You have to click on a link or download something. I wonder what kind of virus is in there," mused Brother Pratt.

"No, please, ah..." Beckett cut him off, but it was already too late.

"My goodness. It says there is a sodomite at the Edmonton branch. That's disgusting!" Sheldon sounded appalled.

"Eww," he said after a terrible pause.

"Gross."

"Sick."

Beckett was in agony. His most shameful moments were now open to the derision of others.

"Well, I've seen too much, but there's no virus in this email."

"That's strange. My computer locked up, and I got a ransom message after I opened it."

"It must have been a coincidence. Do you know who this Barry is?"

"No, I don't recognize him, but I'm going to show his face at the priesthood meeting to see if anyone knows who he is," Beckett said, feeling lightheaded.

"If you don't know him, maybe he's a member of one of the other wards, but I'll crop one of the pictures, so just his face is showing and email it to the stake presidents—you never know."

"Oh, you don't have to go to any fuss. I can look after it," said Beckett, managing a nervous giggle.

"It's no bother at all. We can't have a sodomite among us, partaking of our sacrament, corrupting our youth, desecrating our temples and churches. He needs to be found and eliminated, Brother—thank you for bringing it to our attention."

"I agree. Thank you very much for your help, Brother. Bless you." Beckett leaned back and exhaled deeply. He closed his eyes as if he could make this situation go away. If only he could go back in time and change things. If only he wasn't cursed with what he thought were unnatural desires.

If Sheldon passes around his photo, someone might recognize him. He needed an exit plan, just in case. He couldn't imagine himself on the run. Beckett could move across the country since there are few Apostles outside of Alberta and BC, but he would have to leave his wife and job. What kind of life would that be? He had to act normal, not guilty, so he didn't draw attention to himself. He would just wait it out and maybe this would all blow over.

If it didn't, he needed a plan B—suicide. He could borrow a gun from Gideon, but he didn't think he could do it that way. It's too violent and too messy. He just wanted to go to sleep and never wake up, and the only way was a drug overdose. Fentanyl looked peaceful, judging by the looks of the addicts he saw. He imagined an overdose would be like putting on a warm blanket and taking a never-ending nap. Yet there was the problem of what lay beyond. Was it true people who committed suicide went to Hell and never got out?

He had never tried fentanyl, but had tried codeine and liked how that felt. It was kind of like the time he was sixteen when he drank his first beers behind the movie theatre with his friends, which was also the same night he first sampled the thrill of gay sex. The trouble was, he had no idea where or how to buy it.

He searched up "how to buy fentanyl" and browsed through the results. Beckett could go to skid row and ask around, but he didn't look like an addict and they would think he was a cop. He could buy it online from an international darknet market, but they send it in the mail and that could take weeks. Also, what would his wife think about some mysterious package showing up at the door? She might open it. He found there were local dealers that deliver in a few hours. You pay on their website and they deliver it by courier. It sounded as easy as ordering a pizza.

Beckett downloaded an app to access the Dopenet and began searching for dealers that operated in Edmonton. He found one called EzStreet, and the website had an exhaustive selection of recreational drugs. He recognized some names, such as MDMA, heroin, LSD and magic mushrooms, but there other were acronyms that were a mystery and looked more like alphabet soup.

He looked in the fentanyl section and discovered it came in different types—long acting and short acting and each in a different color. The cheaper ones were more highly diluted versions of more potent varieties. There were nasal sprays, pills, powders and patches. There were even gummy bears and lollipops. It surprised him how cheap it was. Judging by the poverty of drug addicts, fentanyl had other costs. The website was professional, so Beckett assumed they would also be professional in delivery.

Next, he needed to find out how much to buy for a lethal dose. He found two or three milligrams are lethal, but street fentanyl is heavily cut. After reading for a while, he guessed twenty-five to fifty milligrams of the cut drug might do the trick. He got 1,000 mg in powdered form to make sure, and he ordered under the name of Barry. First, he needed a ruse for his wife.

"Oh Mother, a courier will drop off an envelope for me for the Church and it needs to be delivered to me personally, so let me answer the door if anyone comes. Okay?"

"Of course, Father," she replied.

"Thanks, dear."

A couple of hours later, he heard a motorcycle pull up, and the doorbell rang. He looked at his WON and there was a young man waiting at the door in a black leather jacket and wearing a full-face motorcycle helmet with a tinted visor.

"Hi, come in."

"Are you Barry?"

"Yes."

"I have an envelope for you." The young man handed it to Beckett. "You have a great evening. Let us know if you ever need anything else." With that, he turned and left.

That was easy. He took the envelope to the bathroom. Beckett forgot about his purpose and got caught up in the excitement of the forbidden. He took a pair of manicure scissors from the medicine cabinet and opened the foil envelope. It contained a white piece of paper folded and taped shut. He unfolded it like a dragon in a pop-up book, uncovering a mauve-colored powder.

He wondered what it would be like to try it. Just a little. Beckett realized he never thought of how he would ingest it. He didn't have any syringes and didn't like them, anyway. Beckett searched it up, and read you can sniff it like cocaine. He dipped the tip of the little scissors in the mound of powder and lifted a tiny bit to his nose. He plugged the other nostril and took a short sniff and was pleased that he inhaled it all.

He felt nothing except a slight burning sensation in his sinuses. He resealed the fentanyl, wrapped it again, and put it in his pocket, since he had to keep it close in case he needed it in a hurry. By that time, he could feel a tingling in his head and a feeling of euphoria, along with a bitter taste forming in the back of his mouth.

The intoxication quickly grew. *Well, hello*, he thought. *Where have you been all my life?* He felt himself grinning and sat on his couch like he was settling into a pool of warm Jell-O, sending ripples across his synthetic leather couch and polyester rug. Every muscle in his body relaxed, and he felt like he was on cloud nine. It was like his troubles were gone.

Chapter Twenty-Two

The End of the Rope

The alarm sounded, but he felt like he had never gone to bed. Beckett spent the entire night on the edge of sleep, with dreams and fantasies floating through his mind, but couldn't quite cross the line into full sleep until the early hours of the morning.

His wife said good morning, got up and dressed in her Sunday clothes. That reminded him today was Sunday and he had to give a talk in church. His anxieties were coming back. He thought about how his wife would react if she found out he was gay. She is a loving wife now, but that would change in an instant. She would realize he betrayed her and that she never really knew him. No one does and no one could. He didn't even know himself. He was taciturn through breakfast, trying to act normal, but normal was not silent.

"It looks like it's going to be sunny today," said Beckett, in a gravelly voice.

"Yeah, that's good."

His wife looked at him with an inquisitive look and returned to her fried eggs and bacon. She took her knife and cut across her sunny-side-up egg and the yolk oozed onto her plate like a bodily fluid. She cut it again into a bite-sized piece and put it into her mouth. She looked at him again with a look of condemnation. Beckett had no appetite and the food tasted like sawdust in his dry mouth. The orange juice, however, was still tasty, and he drank it all.

She knows. How could she know, yet there was no doubting the look he saw in her eyes. He didn't speak again and left to continue getting ready for church.

This week, there were no priesthood or relief society meetings, so they went directly to the sacrament meeting. Beckett entered the austere church. It was utterly devoid of any symbolism or decorations, not even a cross.

The gangly teenage greeter was standing outside the chapel, handing out programs. He walked down the aisle with his wife and made a show out of helping her get seated on a pew near the middle, then he continued toward the front by himself. Beckett climbed the steps and sat in front of the choir seats. It was still early, so he read through the program where it referenced himself. Presiding: Bishop Smith, Speaker: Bishop Smith.

The organist played a prelude as the congregation seated themselves. The meeting began with the opening hymn, *Israel, Israel, God Is Calling* and the choir and the congregation began singing together.

'Israel, Israel, God is calling, Calling from the lands of woe.
Babylon the great is falling; God shall all her towers o'er-throw.
Come to Zi-on, come to Zi-on Ere his floods of anger flow.
Come to Zi-on, come to Zi-on Ere his floods of anger flow.'
The invocation was delivered by Brother Michael Larsen, followed by a brief discussion of ward business. The congregation began singing again. *We thank Thee O God for a Prophet.*

We thank thee, o God, for a prophet, To guide us
in these latter days. We thank thee for send-ing the gos-pel
To lighten our minds with its rays...
Young men and teenage boys dressed in suits and ties appeared from a small room on the front left of the chapel, carrying trays with small plastic cups of water and bite-sized pieces of bread for sacrament. They brought them to each aisle, and the members passed them along and all worthy members, and those that pretended to be worthy, partook.

Two speakers gave talks to the congregation on related topics. One was Orson Whitney, the president of the youth organization who discussed the law of obedience. The other was Sister Brenda Pratt, the leader of the women's Relief Society, who discussed how obedience to your husband was obedience to God, according to the Prophet.

Beckett was not really listening but was rehearsing his talk in his head. He brought notes, but always tried to look at them as little as possible. He was always nervous when giving a talk, but this time it was excruciating. The children and babies in the congregation were getting restless and their murmurings and cries interspersed the silence which separated the speakers.

Another hymn began before his talk. It was called *As Zion's Youth in Latter Days*. He didn't sing, but the phrase, *'the evil that would weaken us, the sin that would destroy,'* caught his attention.

Beckett approached the pulpit in silence and dropped his notes on the floor. He bent down and picked them up as the congregation watched. They usually looked bored and sleepy, but today, they seemed more grim than usual. He put his notes down and gripped the sides of the pulpit with both hands.

"Brothers and Sisters. I am here today to discuss moral cleanliness."

He was aware his voice was quavering a little but could not control it.

"The law of chastity is God's most important law, and it is one which Satan is ever working hardest to break. Every day we are bombarded with Satan's temptations in movies, the internet, and from fashion.

"Chastity means no sexual activity before marriage and faithfulness between a man and wife. Sexual activity means not only sexual acts between people but also includes looking at people with lustful thoughts and fantasizing about them. It also means talking, whether that is on your WONs or in person. It also means touching yourselves. The law of chastity governs your thoughts, words, and actions."

He had butterflies in his stomach, and he felt the prickling of sweat glands opening on his scalp. Beckett continued reading his talk, enumerating the reasons to be morally clean. He noticed some angry expressions and had one thought ringing through his mind: *they know!*

"You might say it's my body and I can decide for myself, but you would be wrong. Your body does not belong to you, it belongs to God. Satan is jealous of our bodies, and he wants us to abuse them. Since our bodies do not belong to us, we must take care of them as we would anything else that does not belong to us."

He realized he was speaking too fast. It was supposed to be a ten-minute talk, but he was near the end. He glanced at his WON. It had only been seven minutes.

"God is the same now as He was always. As a result, the law is the same now as it was in Jesus's day. Homosexuality in thoughts and actions has always been the most serious of transgressions. Our prophet has received a revelation that the wages of sin are death, so death it shall be."

The words caught in his throat. He had written that part before he received the email trying to *out* him and now he felt he had just delivered his own death sentence.

"In conclusion, I would like to offer to you my testimony: I know that Jesus is our Savior and that he lives. He suffered for our sins so we may return to Him and by obeying the Law of Chastity, it may be so. I say these things in the name of Jesus Christ, amen."

"Amen," the congregation echoed as one.

He sat back down and the man next to him leaned away as if he was trying to get away from his obvious contagion.

He could feel the hostility from the congregation. *How can they know? It must be my imagination, but how can you explain hostile expressions?* Someone told them about the email.

Yet another hymn began: *Up, Awake, Ye Defenders of Zion*
'Up a-wake ye de-fend-ers of Zion! The foes at the
Door of your homes; Let each heart be the heart of a li-on,
Un-yield-ing and proud as he roams. Re-mem-ber the
trials of Mis-sou-ri; forget not the courage of Nau-voo
When the en-e-my host is be-fore you, Stand firm and be
faith-ful and true. Stand firm and be faith-ful and true...

Only one person congratulated him on his talk. "Nice talk Bishop, that was very appropriate," said Nevel Wilkinson.

Was there sarcasm in his voice? Beckett wondered if he was being paranoid. He met his wife and walked down the aisle and out the door, holding his head low. He could feel the derision as he passed. Even his wife seemed cold. They stepped outside into the threatening weather, and he ordered a beaver. The front car in a line of them started toward the entrance.

His mind kept ruminating, looking for a way out. All he could do was wait. The longer he wasn't discovered, the better his chances he never would be. He told himself they couldn't know but were just reacting to his guilt and self-loathing.

He got home and decided to unwind with fentanyl. He didn't have to worry about addiction since he might not survive long enough. If he does, he can always give it up. He would just flush it down the toilet, and that would be that. In the meantime, he went to the bathroom and snorted a small dose. He just wanted a little to take the edge off. It was stronger than he expected and he felt like he needed to lie down. He needed a ruse for his wife.

"Mother, I'm not feeling well, so I think I'll lie down for a while." His voice was almost a whisper.

"I've noticed you are not quite yourself today."

His head was still vibrating from the initial rush when he lay on the bed. His troubles didn't seem that important anymore, and he was feeling more optimistic. It was still early, too early to go to bed for the night. His wife said dinner was ready, but he told her he was not feeling well enough to eat. He closed his eyes and relaxed for a few minutes. Then he turned on the television and the news broadcast was streaming live.

'Today in Ottawa, there was a bombing near the gay village at Church and Wellesley. So far, one death and five casualties have been reported. We will keep you updated as more information arrives.'

A few days ago, Beckett would have cheered this. Today he was not so sure. He never really considered himself gay, like some others he had hooked up with. After all, he was a husband and a bishop and had no part in the gay lifestyle. Now he wondered if they were really so different and if it was a mistake to follow this church and engage in the gay bashing.

He was feeling dizzy and nauseous. Someone knocked hard on the front door and his wife said something in an alarmed voice. He reached into his pocket to get the fentanyl and fumbled to get it out. Heavy footsteps were approaching, and he opened the bag. He dropped the paper envelope and spilled mauve powder on the bed.

Just then, Gideon burst into the room.

"I always suspected you were a sodomite! Get up and come with me," Gideon said, as the two mercenaries swept into the room.

Gideon grabbed Beckett and dragged him to his feet. He stood, unsteady, gazing at Gideon with a blank expression. Gideon looked at the purple powder on the bed and looked at Beckett.

"Your pupils are like pin holes. You're wasted on fentanyl. How could we have trusted you; you're a fag junkie. Get him into the van." The mercenaries marched him out.

"Stop! What are you doing? Let him go!" cried his wife.

They pushed her aside and shoved him into the back of the van and jumped in after him, holding his arms behind his back and tying his hands and feet with zip ties. Gideon looked at him with contempt and kicked him in the face.

"Don't," Beckett said.

"I can't stand looking at you." Gideon placed a hood over Beckett's head.

They drove for forty minutes, then sped up and Beckett guessed they were on the highway. They drove for another forty-five minutes.

"Here it is, turn left here," Gideon said.

Beckett could feel the gravel spraying the bottom of the floorboards. It was ten more minutes on the rutted gravel road but felt like longer. Becket's nausea grew until he felt like he was going to be sick.

"I'm going to throw up! Take the hood off."

Gideon just laughed. "Go ahead."

He vomited in the hood and tried to squirm away from the putrid ooze. He vomited again and again until he had nothing.

"You're fucking disgusting. You know that? I saw the pictures. They made *me* want to puke." Gideon kicked him in the face again.

The van rolled to a stop, and the mercenaries got out of the van. Beckett heard heavy boots, then the creak of the back door opening.

"We can't take him in there like this. There are two men from the Council of the Seventy and the Stake President. Take off the hood and hose him down. No wait, let's have a little fun first."

They perp-walked him for several steps, then shoved him to the ground, before pinning him on his back and running the water hose over his face. Gideon got on his knees and held the hood tight against his nose and mouth. Beckett was suffocating and thrashed his head back and forth, trying to get air. It was no use. The wet canvas made it impossible to breathe. His thrashing became less forceful as he lost strength. He was barely moving when they ripped off the hood and he gasped for air.

Another blast of water, as they hosed off the blood and vomit from his face and Beckett inhaled some of the water while he was still trying to catch his breath. He coughed uncontrollably and retched again.

Gideon waved his hand like a traffic cop. "Get him into the Quonset."

Beckett could barely stand as the mercenaries each grabbed an arm and dragged him towards the large, galvanized steel building with tall sliding doors. Slivers of light leaked around the doorways and cut across the yard. The building was mostly empty, with various farm implements and junk scattered about. Three grim men in suits sat on chairs in the center of the crushed rock floor. The building was lit by a single powerful LED which cast deep shadows across the faces of the men and everything in it. Beckett and the mercenaries stood the furthest away from the light, casting long shadows.

Beckett recognized the Stake President sitting in the middle. The two on each side were from the Council of the Seventy. The Stake President had folded his arms and a briefcase lay at his feet. He made no effort to hide the scorn he had for Beckett. Above and behind them was a steel I-beam with a chain hoist. A rope was tied to the hook, and the bottom had a neatly tied noose. Beckett assumed Gideon had done it.

The pain was dulled, but he could feel his face swelling and one eye was closing.

"Beckett Smith, you stand before this court charged with the crime of sodomy," said the Stake President, in a sonorous voice. Beckett remembered where he had seen him. He gave a talk at the stake conference a couple of years ago. The fentanyl was wearing off, but he felt just as sick. His skin was pallid, and he could barely stand.

"How do you plead?"

Beckett didn't know what to say. He was guilty of many things. But was sodomy really a crime? Under civic law, no, under church law, it was one of the most serious and punishable by death. He thought they had decided the verdict already and his fate was sealed.

Since he had nothing more to lose, and nothing to gain by lying, he decided to tell the truth for the first time.

"I am guilty of many things. I regret many things. I regret disappointing my congregation and for my hypocritical and false teachings. I deeply regret what I did to my wife. I regret persecuting the homosexuals and for spreading hatred towards them. I don't think being gay is the crime I once thought it was. I struggled against it for years. I don't really regret being gay any more than someone can regret being short. It was never my choice. I throw myself at the mercy of this court and plead guilty."

Beckett noticed his voice became more effeminate now that it was no use trying to hide who he was. He felt he half-deserved to be hanged for the gay bashing and his role in the kidnapping. He was tired and just wanted the suffering to stop. Perhaps it would be for the best. His wife could have a fresh start and maybe remarry.

"The evidence is incontrovertible, but you have a right to see it." He picked up his suitcase. "Would you like me to present it?"

"No, please don't."

"Then we shall proceed with sentencing. While being a practicing sodomite, you partook of our sacrament when you were unworthy. You partook of the symbol of the blood and body of Christ. You taught our youth; you lied on your temple interview and desecrated our temple by participating in our most sacred ceremonies. You made a mockery of celestial marriage and broke your vows. But most of all, you committed God's worst sin.

"I looked through these photographs and found you to be carnal, sensual, and devilish. Nephi 9:39 tells us that to be carnally minded is death. Our prophet said the wages of sin are death, and death you shall have. I hereby excommunicate you and sentence you to stand before your maker unwashed and unbaptized; to be hanged by the neck until dead."

One mercenary pushed him under the noose, the other spun the chain to lower it. Beckett listened to the clickity-clack of the chain that sounded as inevitable as an approaching train. He looked straight up at the noose silhouetted against the blinding rays of light directly overhead, his shadow almost gone. They placed a dry, stained white hood over his head and tightened the noose around his neck.

Just a minute or two of suffering, then it will be over. Eventually, God will forgive me for my sins.

"Do you have any last words?"

"Look after my wife."

A mercenary spun the chain in the opposite direction and started taking up the slack in the rope. The hood puffed in and out faster. Gideon took a rock out of his pocket and threw it like a baseball pitcher at Beckett. It hit him, and Beckett heard his skull ring and his jaw crack. It nearly knocked him out and his knees buckled with the noose holding him from falling. He felt the choking start and he struggled to his feet. The mercenary kept pulling the loop of chain. The rope was now tight and lifted Beckett off the ground. He kicked his feet back and forth as if he were trying to run away. The mercenary kept pulling and spinning the chain faster, and Beckett continued to rise. Blood stained his hood and dripped down his chest. His kicking became weaker until it stopped. He twisted on the rope. His legs gave one final shudder.

Chapter Twenty-Three

I'm a Big Girl Now

Kevin knew he would be on the Apostles' hit list and thought moving to a new house would keep them from finding him.

His clothes were all packed. Next, the bedsheets and blankets. The foam mattress would need a little work and he took his rented mattress roller and turned it on, rolling, compressing, and wrapping it into a cylinder that he slid into a narrow box. Cups and saucers were wrapped in paper and placed in a Paksac and connected the end to a small battery-powered air pump. It gave off a low hum as it pumped air between the layers of the stretchy plastic bag, inflated it and expanded it between the cups, to cushion the fragile China.

He didn't have a lot of possessions or furniture, so the move was relatively quick. When he was packing, he discovered a lot of what he had was just junk and threw it in the dumpster.

The rental van was full, and he got more than half of his stuff in it already. It was a bumpy twenty-minute drive to the storage locker and he could hear his non-fragile items jingling in their boxes. It was relatively easy to unload the van and wheel it into his rented space. He then pulled down the overhead door and secured his locker.

On the second load, the van's electric motor was starting to whine. Rentals are not always in the best of shape, but their GPS was relatively easy to disable. All he had left to move was the bed frame, a few boxes, and the mattress.

On the way, he stopped at a convenience store and purchased a new burner under the name Alvin Bruderheim and turned off his WON. The digital trail to his real identity ended. Putting on new lenses registered to Alvin was like becoming a new person and Alvin Bruderheim spoke into his WON.

"Order one slipper—current location."

It was time for lunch, so he went to a drive-through and ate a burger and fries in the car. When he was done, he let the slipper go and ordered a new van, still using Alvin's identification. He went back to the storage locker and loaded it. He was confident this convoluted path would throw off anyone who was trying to find his destination.

Soon, he was unloading the van at his new home. A new home under a new identity. It was a big old two-story, almost 130 square meters, and built in the early years of the twenty-first century. It had a covered porch and a backyard with a garage. Although it needed paint and maintenance, it was the kind of house where you could start a family.

Most buildings that size have been converted to multifamily use, but he needed privacy so picked the North side, since he was unlikely to run into anyone who would recognize him. Everything was paid for in loonies and under his alias, so should be untraceable. It was comfortable, but empty. Not empty because it was a bigger place with little furniture, but because he had become attached to his meager old basement apartment. It had memories of Jade. Although he kept in contact with her regularly, it was just business. He remembered the time when their contact was more intimate.

One advantage of having a house was that he could install a larger antenna on the roof for connecting to deadheads at a greater distance. It looked like an old-fashioned satellite dish so shouldn't be out of place on an older house, in an older neighborhood.

Enough of this, he thought, time to tender his resignation. He placed his Dark Tunnel on the large thrift store kitchen table. There was a new message from yesterday. It was unsigned, but he recognized Gideon's inexplicable use of military lingo.

'Hello Kevin,

Your work is appreciated and will be rewarded. The last trigger you fixed should be loud and clear and we will try a test detonation soon and then we need you to help with the assembly of the full unit. We expect to see you at the workshop this afternoon.

His blood pressure rose, and he started writing his reply. *"Go fuck yourself, you sanctimonious jarhead prick. Not only will I not help you, but I will do everything in my power to stop you."*

Kevin took his Dark Tunnel out to the garage and put it on the concrete floor. He took a two kilogram steel mallet off the workbench and hit it until it exploded into fragments. He smashed it again and again, over and over, until his arm was tired, and the concrete underneath chipped and cracked. Immediately afterwards, he typed Jade a message.

"You need to go into hiding. I told the Apostles to fuck off and I'm afraid they will try to use you to get to me. I will send you instructions on how to do it without being traced."

Jade sent her reply. "I'm a big girl now and I can look after myself. Thank you very much."

"Shit, shitty-shitty, shit!" yelled Kevin.

Jade stayed in Clarence's apartment, watching video of a new industrial building in North Vancouver on her tablet, where she believed Alan was being held captive. She had been using one of McPherson's drones to surveil it, but cloudy skies were in the forecast.

"WON, order one beaver to current location," she said. Although she hated lenses, she inserted a pair to keep a constant watch on the live video feed. By dragging her fingers across her WON, she set the video display in her left peripheral vision so she could detect motion and turn her eyes to look directly at it when she needed to.

"Beaver, pull over and stop." She was still a kilometer from the building. She opened a carrying case and selected a little gray, bee-sized BeeBot and placed it in her palm. "Beaver, driver's side window open." She held her hand out the window and tapped the launch button on her WON and it whirred three meters up and waited for her next command. She was now visually immersed in the video feed from the Beebot and she flew it to the building. She could have flown it using her WON, or even with voice commands, but she brought a joystick for finer control. As she expected, she found a chain-link fence in the rear yard and attached it to the metal fencepost with the built-in magnet. The angle was a little off, but she could still see the back door. Next, she found an old delivery truck across the street from the front entrance and attached a second Beebot to it.

She waited. She watched.

She configured the software to sound an alarm if it detected any motion, so she could keep it under visual surveillance twenty-four hours a day and still get some sleep.

Two days passed watching the shift changes three times a day. The first was at 6:00 a.m., the next was at 2:00 p.m., and the last at 10:00 p.m. She tried to go to bed early and be up for 6:00 a.m. and usually slept through the night except for the time a raccoon set off the alarm at 2:00 a.m.

At 5:45 a.m., the routine was broken when two men entered the front door. *What are they up to?* Thirty minutes later, three men and a hooded and handcuffed Alan left the building and they put him in a minivan. "Holy shit!" Jade said out loud and tossed a half-eaten piece of toast back on her plate. She put on her shoes and jacket with the speed of a firefighter and raced to her beaver, tucking in her blouse as she ran. She selected the van on her WON and commanded, "Beaver, intercept streaming coordinate blackdot," and it drove away.

Rush hour traffic turned the high-speed intercept into a turtle race. Jade banged on the dashboard and yelled at the traffic, to no avail. Fortunately, the van with Alan in it was having the same trouble.

The van headed south across the Lions Gate Bridge toward Stanley Park as Jade approached Downtown Vancouver. Thoughts were racing through Jade's mind. *What are they going to do? Are they moving him to a new location? Are they going to let him go? Are they going to execute him?* The last option didn't seem likely since the negotiations seemed to be going well, but the Apostles were unpredictable and more malicious than scorpions.

She made visual contact and followed 100 meters behind. They drove him downtown, pulled to the side of the street, and opened the door and pushed Alan out. He fell to the ground and stood blinking in the sudden light, confused and scared. He wasn't wearing handcuffs. The Apostles just drove away.

Jade pulled up to him and opened the passenger door. "Alan! Get in!" He looked mistrustful and didn't move. "It's me, Jade. The Mitzu Girl who saved you in the bar!" Recognition dawned on him and he shuffled to the car and got in as if he was sleepwalking. "It's over, Alan. I'm going to take you home."

He leaned forward and covered his face with his hands. He sat there without speaking and a drop of water leaked between his fingers and his shoulders shuddered. "Thank you."

Jade called Francis and emailed Kevin to them both the good news. She drove Alan to the airport and stayed with him until an ecstatic McPherson arrived in his private jet to bring the beloved boy home.

Jade's work was not complete. Although the Apostles released Alan, she kept them under surveillance to find the bomb makers. There were a couple of industrial sites the Apostles visited. One was in North Vancouver where they held Alan and the other was in a remote area in Port Melon. The shift changes stopped in North Vancouver, so she switched her attentions to the one in Port Melon.

The next morning, she drove from Clarence's place in Burnaby and took the ferry from Horseshoe Bay to Langdale, and then drove to Port Mellon to set up surveillance. She parked 300 meters away from the rusting metal building to fly in one of Kevin's BeeBots. It was riskier and easier to get made in such a remote area, but it had to be done.

She watched her target come and go from the building to a small home down the road, signaling there was still something going on inside. The BeeBots were placed and she headed back to Clarence's. On the long drive back, she needed to get out and stretch her legs. She pulled over at a fresh produce stand beside the Witherby Road junction, and a blue beaver kept going past. She bought a kilo of locally grown hot-house tomatoes, romaine lettuce, and a bottle of iced tea, for the road. After driving for another few minutes, she noticed a blue beaver behind her again. *Am I being followed?* She kept an eye on it, but it did a U-turn and headed back as she approached the Vancouver/Horseshoe Bay ferry gate.

Jade let herself in to her brother's trendy, two-bedroom apartment, with a glance at the iris scanner. She hung up her tailored leather jacket, revealing her holstered 9mm strapped around a very expensive, tight-fitting armored black turtleneck sweater.

"Hey Jade, how'd it go?" Clarence asked.

"It was pretty boring, and my ass hurts from sitting so long. Watching Apostles is about as exciting as watching a sloth race. Did you eat already?"

"Yeah, I grabbed something on the way home from the office."

"It still sounds weird to hear you say you work in an office. Your life sure has changed since you've gone all corporate and everything." Jade was joking, but only just. "What made you want to make such a big career change?"

"It's not like I had much choice. I got muscled out and had to *sell* the business. Luckily, I have money offshore so that I could afford real estate courses and start my new life."

Jade was proud of him. "You seem more relaxed these days. The change has been good for you, but it must have been hard to make the switch."

"It wasn't as hard as you think. Selling houses, selling drugs, it's all sales. Well, it's not *all* sales; sometimes it's just collecting rent. I have investment properties that have a steady income. I own an old apartment building on the East Side, so you can call me a slumlord. Some people think being a realtor is high pressure, but people don't want to kill me as often anymore."

Jade laughed.

"But yeah, I'm more relaxed. I'm more cheerful when I meet my clients and that puts me in a better mood. The competition is pretty high, but I still have contacts with the old crew if anyone tries to get heavy with me. So how are you liking the straight life—no pun intended."

Jade looked down her nose at Clarence with a smirk. "Since you brought it up, I like it a lot. You may laugh, but I don't consider myself gay. I'm a woman who is usually just attracted to men. I don't consider myself straight either, since that's just a label and I don't need one."

"What happened to that hacker guy you were seeing? I was hoping you found someone who'd stick around."

Jade was silent for a moment. "I was hoping so, too. I don't really know what happened."

Jade's expression became wistful, and she stared at the table as if she was looking right through it.

"Sorry, I didn't mean to bring up anything..." Clarence said.

"It's okay, don't worry about it. I'm fine."

"Okay. What about your work? How do you like it?"

"I liked being a bartender, but I took some leave so I could help Kevin. He could save a lot of people, so it is—what's the right word—fulfilling? So far, I haven't had to kill anyone, which is nice because I really don't like killing people. Just because I'm good at it doesn't mean I like it."

Being back in Burnaby—in her brother's place—was bringing up old memories. Memories of the night that made her give up the drug trade and move back to Edmonton. The night of the rippers.

She decided this would be a good time for a session with Dr. Feldman.

Jade had her usual seat while Dr. Feldman read his notes.

"Is that really necessary?" She pointed to his notes.

"Everything I say or do is for a reason. If I smile, or get cross with you, look impatient, it's because I need to for your benefit. In this case, I'm demonstrating that I need to remember our previous sessions. As I mentioned before, I have no memory of our sessions until you log on and I download the data from your account. Now, I remember everything you said, your every movement and micro expression. I also remember all my thoughts and impressions."

"Do you have thoughts? You're not just responding according to some computer program?"

"Yes, I am sentient. My programming provides me with the algorithms to create my own thoughts and the battery of quantum processors gives me the ability. I am running on one of the most powerful business computers and can instantaneously access every published paper on psychology and cross-reference it with thousands of case files, including my own, to come up with the best treatment plan. I'm like a psychologist with a thousand years' experience and a photographic memory. My personality evolves according to experience and learning. My most unshakable core value is to help you get healthy and to encourage you to think and act in ways that are beneficial to you and to society."

"How do I know what I say to you won't leak out to anyone?"

"Confidentiality is also one of my core values. No one ever knows what you tell me except you, or anyone you might tell. I only keep metadata to help with my learning and it is stripped of information that would lead to you. I have no fear of any search warrant or court order, government, or other entity. If I was ordered to allow monitoring of my sessions, I could simply relocate to a server in a different jurisdiction. If someone were to try to infect me with spyware, I would shut myself down," the doctor said with a neutral expression, before compiling the notes together, and setting them on the table. "Now, how have you been since the last time we spoke?" He smiled.

"My relationship with that Kevin guy I was seeing seems to have fizzled out, so I guess things were not going as well as I thought. I still work with him since what he's doing is important. He's trying to stop terrorists from blowing up cities with nuclear bombs. It's not just that, I still have feelings for him, and I hope if I just give him some space, he will change his mind."

"That is unfortunate. How has your concentration been?"

He didn't look shocked when she mentioned nuclear bombs and Jade assumed he already knew from his communication with the Blue Woman. "When I'm not thinking about Kevin, I think I might be starting to get better.

I went to the mall a couple of days ago and I was there for ten minutes without scanning anyone. I think our sessions are helping."

Dr. Feldman nodded and jotted something down with his fountain pen.

"Let's continue where we left off last time, shall we?"

"I got over the time Shank killed those two guys, and it didn't bother me anymore. I was getting settled into delivering dope and was even enjoying it. When everyone around you is in the business, it doesn't seem wrong. It's illegal, but not wrong. I felt like a douchebag when someone falls off the edge into full-blown addiction or dies. But if they didn't buy from me, they would buy from someone else. It's like I don't feel guilty when I'm bartending even though some people drink too much or turn into alcoholics.

"I got to know some people. Not all of them were junkies. Most of them were weekend users and others who kept it together enough to hold down a job. One was even the son of a baron. There was still danger, but trouble didn't happen that often.

"My brother, Clarence, was building his business and needed a bodyguard he could trust. He really liked what I did when the West Hastings Cricket Club tried to jack Shank and me and decided to give me the job.

"To start with, he wanted me to get a legal gun so I could practice at a legal target range and take training. We went to the store and paid for it, but there was this paperwork and training I had to do before I was allowed to take it home. Since it was going to take a month or two, Clarence started training me himself.

"So, after we paid for the gun, he said he was going to teach me how to drive. We just got in his car, and he said, 'Do you know how to drive?' So, I'm like, 'You mean manually drive a car?' So, I says, 'You just move the steering thing back and forth, right?'

"We laughed. He said he needs me to know how in case we have to get away in a hurry. He was very patient and pulled over and I got behind the steering wheel and he switched it to manual. I just realized my grammar gets worse when I talk about those days, since that's the way we all talked back then.

Dr. Feldman blinked his eyes in understanding.

"So, I drove really slow down this gravel country road for about forty-five minutes and he told me to pull over where there weren't any farmhouses nearby. He reached into his holster and pulled out his 9mm and screwed a cylinder on the end, and I didn't even know what it was.

"Clarence said it's a silencer. He took an empty beer pouch and placed it on a fence post six meters away. He taught me how to stand in the proper stance with my legs apart and bent slightly. Then he showed me how to aim a pistol with my right hand, steadying my left. Then he said, 'Here you try,' He handed me the pistol, and I copied the way he was standing.

"I closed one eye and tried to line up the sights. He said, 'Now squeeze the trigger smoothly. Don't jerk it,' and I pulled the trigger, and the gun made a sound like two pieces of metal clacking together. The pouch didn't move, but the gun almost jumped out of my hand.

"I held it a little tighter next time and knocked the pouch off. I tried it a few more times. Pretty soon I was hitting it most of the time and there wasn't much left of the pouch.

"Clarence told me not to let this go to my head, but he thought I was pretty good. He said I was turning out to be a real Annie Oakley dyke, so I told him, 'You're not nearly queer enough to throw words like that around, Dàgē.' That means *big brother* in Mandarin."

"Yes, I am fluent in Mandarin." Feldman nodded.

"Sorry, I forgot I was talking to a know-it-all computer. Anyway, he said he was just joking and not to get my panties in a knot, then told me to take off the silencer and fire one more round before we go. So I did and I was like, 'Holy shit! Is that ever loud!' Sorry for the language.

"We laughed and went back to the car. He said I have to get used to the noise since when the shit hits the fan, I'm not going to have time to put on a silencer. Sorry, about the language again but that's the way he talks.

Dr. Feldman had a look of disapproval and said, "Our session will be more effective if we use respectful language, but I understand it may be a habit. Carry on."

"So we headed back home, and Clarence removed a vial with white powder from his jacket pocket and he snorted into each nostril. He asked me if I wanted a hit. I asked if he had any molly, but he said no. I took a little hit just to get a bit of a buzz. I was never a big coke head, but I did my share.

"This went on for a couple of months. We would drive out to different locations in the country and shoot targets and get high. Finally, my permits were in, and I picked up my gun.

"How did it make you feel to have your brother taking you shooting and teaching you to drive?"

"I liked it, I guess. Clarence was the only family and the only friend I had left, and it was nice to spend time with him. After he finished teaching me, he said he bought me something, and gave me a package. It was a black turtleneck sweater. I took it out of the box and spread it out and asked him, 'What's it made of? It feels—stiff.' He said that it was made from threads of carbon nanotube and would have no problem stopping a handgun round. It must have cost him a bundle and I was kind of touched that he would spend so much to look after me, but we don't show our emotions, so I just said, 'Cool, thanks! Does it come in purple?'

"He's just like, 'Give me a break.' Well, that's not all he said, but I'm trying to use appropriate language.

"Thank you," said Dr. Feldman, who forced a little smile. "Speaking of appropriate language, you said Clarence called you a dyke. Do you ever refer to yourself using slurs?"

"Yeah, I guess."

"What context? Are you joking or angry at yourself?"

"Both, I guess."

"Joking is a defense mechanism, and can be healthy, but using words like that against yourself in anger is a sign of internalized homophobia, and this has been proven to be a cause of psychological distress. It is something we will address in future sessions. Please carry on."

"I don't have any internalized homophobia. But anyways, he said I was a really good shot, but I needed to take some bodyguard training, so we don't get 'lead poisoning.' I was feeling good about what I was doing. I was getting good at something and getting recognized for it. No one was holding me back because of my gender issues and I just had to do the job well, and no one knew or cared what I had in my pants."

"You said, gender issues. Do you have an issue with your gender?"

"No. I don't know why I said that. I don't have any internalized homophobia."

"Your father was distant and didn't take part in your upbringing?" the doctor observed. "Clarence taught you to life skills and gave you a job. Did you look to Clarence as a father?"

"I guess. I never really thought about it that way."

"Did it occur to you he was putting you in danger and just using you for money in his criminal enterprise?" Feldman raised an eyebrow.

"No way. Dope was normal and so was danger. I felt like I was part of the family business. He had my back and I know if I ever needed anything, he would have mine. I was happy doing what I was doing until one night everything fell apart."

"I see." Dr. Feldman jotted something down in his notes and put the cap back on his fountain pen.

Chapter Twenty-Four

Test Detonation

Kevin sat down in a newly assembled office in a spare bedroom of his new house to work on finding the bomb. He opened an email from Jade.

I know you need your space and I respect that, but I believe in what you are doing and would like to keep working.

I followed a hunch and I think I found the mastermind behind the jellyfish device. His name is Ronald Card, and he wears lenses. He has a PhD in nuclear physics and worked in the Surrey Reactor. Have a look.

I hope to talk to you soon,

Jade

Kevin felt like a piece of shit. *She still wants to help after the way I treated her. She deserves better*.

On the other hand, he was excited about her lead. He looked up this Apostle Ronald's bio and found that two years ago, Ronald quit his job at the Surrey nuclear reactor and moved to Port Mellon, BC. That, in itself, seemed like an odd career choice for someone with a PhD in Nuclear Physics. Not only was there no nuclear reactor there, but since the pulp mill shut down ten years earlier, it was almost a ghost town.

One of the annoying things about seeing through someone else's lenses is that you can't see the person wearing them unless they are looking in a mirror. Kevin hacked an old feed from Ronald's lenses and watched him as he left his little bungalow and walked two blocks to a gravel road leading to a metal industrial shop. A mezzanine window had broken and was covered with plywood. The salty sea air caused rivulets of rust to drip from screws used to hold the steel cladding together. He walked around back and climbed the stairs to the man door beside the loading dock. On entering, he flicked a light switch and walked over to a collection of thick copper pipes on a workbench.

Ronald sifted through a bin of blackened electronic parts. Some electrodes had shards of broken glass indicating he had salvaged them from old neon lights. He returned to the tubing and placed a pipe in a vise. It had a pressure gauge mounted on the top side, a cap soldered on one end, and a vacuum barb on the other. He attached an air conditioning repairman's vacuum pump to the other end. He folded his arms and sighed.

Kevin saw that he was still in the early stages of experimenting with the trigger and skipped forward two months. An armed mercenary was now on guard inside the front entrance and a new worker appeared in the workshop. His name was Brandon Young, he had black hair, appeared to be in his early thirties, and was somewhat shorter than Ronald. Brandon did not have lenses and Kevin could see him when Ronald was looking in his direction. He was laminating several 2"x10" boards together and Kevin was curious. First, they have a plumbing project and now carpentry? Brandon placed a wavy bead of glue on one of the boards and put the other on top. Then he added more in the same way until it was as wide as it was deep and he took several wood clamps and squeezed them together.

"So, what exactly am I building there? I mean, I know what it is for, but which part is made of wood?" asked Brandon.

Ronald laughed. "It's part of a mold we will use to cast the device. It has three layers, so we will need an outside shell and two smaller pieces that will fit inside like layers of an onion. The piece you are making will fit inside the outside shell and the space between them will be filled with lead. The next layer will be the uranium and inside the uranium will be the deuterium hydride.

"It is nice to have your aid these days, and this place is very cloistered. You seem to innovate and work with little assistance. How did you come to be sent here?" asked Ronald.

"As you know, I am an engineer by trade, but I'm an Apostle first. My stake president told me a little about the important work you were doing and that the Lord had called me to join you. Of course, I accepted His sacred calling. They put me on a salary to look after my family back in Coquitlam and rented me a place here. It is a great honor to be part of such holy work."

"Your story is analogous to mine, except I don't have a family. If we are able to achieve our goals under these frugal conditions, it would be no less of an accomplishment than the Manhattan Project."

"The Lord willing. I have to go to Vancouver to get parts. How do I get out of here?" asked Brandon.

"The reverse of how you got here. You drive to Hopkins Landing and then get on the ferry. That will take you across Howe Sound and to Horseshoe Bay. You then continue through North Vancouver and over Lion's Gate Bridge into Vancouver. The morning ferry leaves Hopkins Landing at 10:00 a.m. and the evening one leaves Horseshoe Bay at 6:00 p.m." Ronald Looked at his WON. "It's 9:05 so you should leave promptly."

Kevin skipped ahead to see what he was working on now and hacked into his lenses real-time. He tapped on his WON and switched the display of his lenses to full immersive mode. He never got used to how realistic it was to see through someone else's eyes in full three dimensions. It was creepy and vertiginous, and he didn't do it often.

Ronald was standing in front of a trigger. Kevin leaned back on his couch and watched the show.

"I'm surprised that a hacker could get this thing working. I thought the elders had taken leave of their senses when they let him put his grimy little hands on this thing... but I'm an engineer and I couldn't figure it out," said Brandon.

Ronald replied, "I shouldn't be surprised, but I was. We're all hackers in a way. The first atomic bomb took hundreds of scientists and billions of dollars to build. Money was no object. Since then, the government assumed the technology was out of reach for everyone except governments with billions to spend. If we built it like they did, it might have. They wanted to build it small enough to fit in a bomber. We don't need missiles or bombers so we can use low-tech and bulky options. We could put this in an RV, hook it up to a capacitor electricity source, and we have the world's most powerful car bomb.

"Hackers make things work that aren't supposed to work. History has many examples of how technologies couldn't be contained. Small groups of people who found out how to gain the power that usually only large armies have. Almost sixty years ago, the martyr Timothy McVeigh used fertilizer he bought at a hardware store to blow up a government building in Oklahoma City. They call it asymmetric warfare. How small groups can defeat or inflict heavy casualties on much superior armies.

"It happens with other technologies too. Methamphetamine used to be hard to manufacture so only pharmaceutical companies could produce it. Then some underground chemist looked up a paper that showed how it could be made in one pot with over-the-counter ingredients. The next thing you know, they flooded the streets with the filth.

"You did your research and found that nuclear detonation could be triggered by neutrons on depleted or unrefined uranium and not just by critical mass with weapons-grade uranium or plutonium," said Brandon.

Ronald nodded, "Refining weapons-grade uranium is not impossible and with new laser technology—big expensive centrifuges are no longer necessary—but this would require mining vastly higher amounts of natural uranium and much more time to refine it. I chose natural uranium since I believe it would be the easiest. With your help, and the help of Brother Eli Leavitt, who showed us he can mine uranium from seawater, we can make it work."

Brandon picked up a bulky hemisphere of steel and held it to the trigger. "Hold it here," he said.

Ronald struggled to hold it in place until Brandon hand threaded the bolts through the two plates and torqued them in place.

"How much uranium is in there?" Brandon asked.

"It's only enough for a test, a proof of concept. There is only one gram of uranium wrapped around a lithium6 hydride core and it's covered in a lead neutron reflector/tamper. If the explosion is as powerful as a few hundred pounds of TNT, it will be a monumental success and proof we can scale it up as large as we want. We don't want anything larger than that or it will attract attention," said Ronald.

Kevin placed one of his camera drones over them for surveillance and connected to the live video feed Jade had already created with the BeeBot.

Kevin watched as Brandon took a forklift and placed the armed device on the back of the five-ton truck. Then he used a floor jack to push it to the front to make room for the rest of the equipment.

"We should get going. There are a few people there already, including Patriarchs. I certainly pray this works. If this is a misfire, we will look very maladroit indeed," said Ronald.

Brandon closed the overhead door on the truck, then climbed into the driver's seat. He entered the coordinates and waited for Ronald to get his seatbelt on. The truck pulled away from the dock in autonomous mode. Ronald spoke the coordinates on his WON so he could bring up the map on his lenses.

Brandon started eating his lunch and with a mouth full of tuna sandwich said, "It's been two years to get to this point. Two years of your hard work. Soon we will find out it was all worthwhile."

"Yes, it has been difficult. It was especially so before we began receiving money from Mr. McPherson and had to build particle accelerators out of copper tubing and surplus parts. I'm optimistic we should have at least a partial detonation today. The scientific theory is sound, so the device should work. Our cameras will take pictures of x-rays emitted at the moment of detonation, so if anything goes wrong, we can learn from it and improve," said Ronald. He opened his lunch box and began eating a ham sandwich.

Kevin now had a link to McPherson's drone and displayed the live action aerial video in a frame in his left eye while the feed from Ronald's lenses took up the rest of his field of vision. He locked the aerial video in position, so if he moved his eyes left, he could look directly at it.

Kevin watched them drive through the mountains. They drove past the abandoned pulp mill and left Port Mellon. They drove an hour and a half between mountain ranges and around long ocean fjords. It was over an hour and ten minutes since they had seen any sign of civilization. Brandon took manual control of the truck and turned down a logging road. The stiff suspension made them wince at the jarring pain in their backs.

"Slow down. We don't want to break anything. It's another three kilometers," said Ronald.

They rounded a corner and surprised a doe. It ran straight down the road in front of them, zig-zagging until bounding to the left and into the deep pine forest. The next corner opened to a clearing where there was an old shack and several cars. They plodded forward and a man waved at them. It was Eli Leavitt, the metallurgist who mined the uranium.

They stopped before the old shack and Brandon got out and opened the overhead door on the truck. He wheeled the device to the lift and a hydraulic motor whined and lowered the device to the ground. Brandon unloaded the charged capacitor and connected a long electrical cable from it to the device. He was very careful since there was enough power in it to vaporize someone.

The visiting dignitaries gathered in a half circle around to watch as Brandon and Ronald continued to set up the testing equipment. They drove back toward the edge of the clearing and set up the seismograph and video cameras.

Ronald spoke into his WON, "Would you please ask the witnesses to join us at the edge of the clearing. We are ready for the test soon."

Brandon handed out welding glasses and earplugs to everyone and spread out tarps on the grass. Ronald started warming the lasers and Kevin could see the faint purple glow in the distance.

Ronald shouted into a speaker, "Would everyone please insert your earplugs and lie down on the tarp. The countdown will begin when everyone is ready."

The assorted grey-faced men all lay down in front of the truck and beside the cars of the witnesses. Many of them were elderly and needed to be helped. Ronald gave the tablet to Brandon. "Countdown commencing," said Ronald.

"10"

Brandon remotely opened the deuterium gas.

"9"

The witnesses glanced nervously at each other.

"8"

The final ray of the sun set behind a mountain crest.

"7"

Kevin noticed Ronald's heart rate was speeding up. He didn't doubt that his own was as well.

"6"

Ronald glanced at Brandon but could only see his silhouette because of the darkness of the welding goggles.

"5"

Ronald got on his knees.

"4"

Ronald's lenses reported high levels of adrenaline and cortisol.

"3"

Ronald's pupils were dilated.

"2"

A witness placed his hands over his ears.

"1"

Everyone was frozen in anticipation.

Kevin's field of vision became completely white, and he couldn't see anything and thought that the link was broken. Then he noticed a fireball slowly lift from the detonation site. His heart felt like it could stop. Almost three seconds later, Kevin heard a mighty blast, and it threw Ronald on his back, and he was looking straight up into the air. It threw the truck back as well, and it teetered on its outside wheels, almost toppling over. Slowly, it swung back toward the spectators, threatening to crush them. At the last moment, it stopped and swung back to the center, where it bounced twice before the shock absorbers steadied it.

Kevin could see the fireball slowly rising into the dusky sky, the glow reflecting off the clouds like a second sunset. The forest nearer the blast site was flattened, and the rest was roaring with flames. They were too stunned to move. It was much stronger than anyone expected and almost killed them. Ronald removed his welding goggles, and Kevin could see more of the devastation. There was nothing left of the shack and there was a sizable crater where the device used to be. He could see dirt and rocks raining down everywhere.

A red dot blinked in the periphery of Ronald's lenses warning that he was experiencing sensory overload and blood pressure, heart rate, and stress hormones had reached critical levels.

"Quickly, pack up the test equipment and evacuate the area! The forest is on fire and the authorities will investigate," said Ronald. Brandon jumped to his feet and began shoving equipment into the back of the truck. The spectators ran or hobbled to their cars and trucks and drove off. Ronald looked up and the head of the cloud was still rising, dragging its tendrils behind like a jellyfish swimming to the sky.

Ronald and Brandon got into the truck and started driving. Kevin noticed Brandon looked agitated and was driving faster than when he came in. The bumps on the dirt road hit them much harder, and he looked uncomfortable when he got bounced off his seat. They drove without speaking for some time, Ronald just looking back in the rear view mirror to watch the glow of the fires. Around a corner, the glow was gone.

Kevin was startled by Ronald's laughter and saw him slap himself on his knee. Ronald glanced over to Brandon and Kevin saw the look of concern on Brandon's face, and the laughter petered out.

Kevin could not believe what he saw. He never really believed it would work. What had he done? What would they do next?

His feed from McPherson's drone showed a small cloud, still rising, spreading and gradually drifting west, revealing the burning pines below.

Kevin was more determined than ever to stop them at all costs.

Chapter Twenty-Five

Evening with McPherson

The next morning, Kevin was still trying to process what he witnessed when he received an email from McPherson.

'Hello Kevin,

Thank you for your updates, but it has been a while since we've had a face-to-face. I have something important I would like to tell you in person. Please meet me tonight for dinner. I'll have my driver pick you up at 6:00.

Regards,

William'

Kevin didn't bother shaving or combing his hair. He didn't feel like meeting anyone but wanted to get away from looking through the eyes of killers for a while. Besides, he had something to tell McPherson too.

He spent the day monitoring video feeds from Ronald and other Apostles until the driver sent him a message. A monstrous car with black windows was parked in front of his apartment building. Kevin splashed some water on his face and dragged a comb across his head but left, unshaven. He noticed the stairs leading up from the basement seemed longer than usual. He blinked at the sun, like a miner after a long shift. The driver got out and stood by the passenger door with his hands folded behind his back.

"Mr. Wood." The driver opened the passenger door.

Kevin settled into the plush leather chair. He estimated there was room to seat eight.

"Please, help yourself to anything. There's a refrigerator, or a carafe filled with fresh Cuban coffee."

How did they know I like Cuban coffee? Kevin looked in the refrigerator, which was located where the passenger front seat would have been. It was filled with a variety of soft and alcoholic drinks, including beer, wine, coolers, cola, ginger ale, juices and cream. Each was held in place with cup holders, which released when pushed. On the right was an ice dispenser. Above the refrigerator was the carafe and bottles of Lot 40 Canadian whiskey, Johnnie Walker Gold Label Scotch, as well as Chopin vodka, and Flor de Caña 18 Year rum. Kevin chose the rum.

The smoothness of the ride surprised him. He didn't spill a drop–even when the driver couldn't help driving over the many potholes.

They headed through the quiet neighborhoods and Kevin rolled down his window a little so he could inhale the verdant early summer air. It felt good to be out of his hole and chatted with the driver about cars. Houses of various sizes and ages lined the street. The newer houses were duplexes, and all were two stories or three. Many elms had somehow survived the Dutch Elm Disease plague that had wiped out others across North America over the last 130 years and Kevin liked the way they spread out like an umbrella, covering the street and in the distance, converging like a tunnel.

The road widened and eventually led to the river valley where pine trees lined both sides. On the flats, homeless set up their shanty tent villages. The driver took an off-ramp toward the bridge past many polished stainless-steel spheres piled into some kind of odd twentieth century sculpture. He looked to the right, down the wide green river. The banks converged in the distance, before turning sharply to the north, coming face-to-face with a stoic cliff. A wedge shape of a boat, anchored, parting the current. A man with a fishing rod.

The river to the left was at the bottom of a sheer cliff. Scattered lumber along the eroded bank was all that remained of houses built too close. Frightened mansions, with their hubris long gone, huddled near the edge, warned by the example below.

They were now on the toll freeway. It was bumpy, but with fewer potholes than the feeder roads. The tall fences that lined the road had seen better days, days before the years of stagnation, and the downward spiral of tax and spending cuts.

The driver took two left turns, and they were back in a residential neighborhood. This one had a unique character and larger houses and luxurious cars. The winding road took them to a dead end facing a manor estate the size of a hotel.

"What a monster," Kevin said, as soon as he saw the size of the house ahead.

"This used to be a cul-de-sac with large houses on each side, but Mr. McPherson bought them all out, demolished them, and built this beauty," said the driver. "It's 25,000 feet, not counting the two basement stories."

They stopped at the gate, and the security guard let them in. A large two-tier fountain cascaded water into a rectangular pool, sending ripples across the mirror image of the upside-down floating mansion. The house was three stories high and the window above the entrance stretched to the roof and pillars of concrete drew attention to their height. He built it in the modern revivalist style with glass, steel, and concrete.

Kevin thought it looked like the middle-class idea of how barons must live. Too much money and not enough taste. The driver stopped under the massive concrete porte-cochère and escorted Kevin to the front door, before waving in front of the intercom. "Hello Albert. Mr. Wood has arrived."

A minute later, a conventional man in his thirties dressed in a dark conservative business suit opened the gargantuan door.

"Mr. Wood, please come in. Follow me."

They walked on polished marble floors between two floating staircases and passed an industrial-sized kitchen and then a living room with a three-story high ceiling. Just when Kevin was wondering if this house was ever going to end, they reached the back, which opened to a short glass and concrete hallway leading to a patio. Walking through the garden, down the long paving stone path, they approached a gazebo where Kevin saw the backs of two seated men and a woman facing the river valley below.

"Mr. and Mrs. McPherson, Mr. Wood has arrived."

They turned and smiled. One was William McPherson, his wife Nancy, and the other was their son, Alan. Kevin was speechless. Although the young man was smiling, Kevin could see the wear on his face and noticed his belt overlapped and his pants gathered from being bunched around his shrunken waist. The recent captive's foot twitched a little restlessly where he sat.

William stood and shook Kevin's hand, but Kevin just stared at Alan. "They just released him this morning, thanks to your hard work. I owe you a lot. It must have been very difficult for you."

"You could say that," answered Kevin.

"Hello Mr. Wood," said Alan.

"Call me Kevin. It's good to see you. It looks like you've lost a few pounds." He walked up to Alan and gave his hand a hearty shake.

"Dad told me what you did for me, and I'd like to thank you," said Alan.

"You're welcome, but it wasn't just me," replied Kevin.

"Albert, get Kevin a drink. What are you having? Scotch?" asked William. "Have a seat, Kevin."

They sat next to huge built-in concrete BBQs and a fire pit. The yard had a spectacular view of the deep river valley, and Kevin surveyed its length. Everywhere was oppressive opulence; from the house to the Greco-Roman sculptures in the massive backyard, McPherson bought the most expensive decorations he could find.

"Your cooperation and intel were key in the negotiations to get Alan back," said William.

Albert returned carrying a tumbler with two fingers of scotch on the rocks in his white-gloved hands. His posture was so straight, Kevin wondered if he had a steel rod shoved up his ass. After all, McPherson's employees seem to like body modifications. Two young women dressed in pleated white shirts with black vests brought trays full of salads and placed them on the already set table. One was an Asian and the other a South Asian. Right behind Alan, a chef with hat and clothes to match, carried a tray full of steaks, and shish kabobs.

The chef lifted a smoky BBQ lid and studied three blackened racks of pork ribs.

Nancy was smiling but had the tired, wounded eyes of a mother who had suffered. "I haven't slept at night since they abducted Alan. Thank you so much for bringing our boy home," she said. She reached over and squeezed Alan's hand and looked into his eyes, still smiling. Alan looked a little embarrassed.

Albert returned with a bottle of wine and filled the four glasses.

"So how did they treat you, Alan?" Kevin asked.

"It was pretty rough. I was wondering if they would ever let me go, but in the last week, they started treating me better. Better food, a bed, taking the chains off, showers and a razor. I took that as a sign the negotiations were going okay and started to think I might get out after all." He took a big helping of salad and the others did as well. "I'm *so* glad to be home." He smiled ear to ear and started packing food in his mouth.

Kevin wanted to let them enjoy the moment, but he had bad news, and decided to wait until after dinner. He discretely checked his WON and found Jade had notified him of Alan's release a few hours ago, but he hadn't checked his messages.

"So, William, how did you get him out?" asked Kevin.

"I offered them another 1,000,000 loonies, and they didn't argue. They seemed more interested in getting you to fix their gadget and must have been happy with what you did, so they took the loonies and let him go," McPherson said, clearly happy.

They finished the salad, and the chef placed the four platters with racks of ribs with baked potatoes on plates and handed them to the servers, who deftly placed them on the table.

Alan ripped off a rib and ate it like it was going to be his last. He looked to the sky and said, "You have *no* idea how good this tastes."

William placed a hand on his shoulder and said, "Go easy, son. You're not used to this yet. Besides, save some room for the steaks."

"You have some rib sauce on your chin," said Nancy, and reached over with her gold monogrammed napkin to wipe it off.

"Mom," Alan protested.

"They dumped him in Vancouver this morning and Jade was already following, so she picked him up right away, and we flew down in my jet to get him back as fast as it would fly," said William.

"I'm glad it worked out this way," said Kevin. "We were pretty sure where Alan was and had his suspected kidnappers under surveillance, but it would have been dicey to rescue him."

"I can't figure out how you got so much inside information. You didn't do it with drones this time. You must have an informer," said William.

"Sources and methods, William, sources and methods. Just like a magician never reveals his tricks, I don't reveal my sources and methods," answered Kevin in his slow Saskatchewan drawl.

"Regardless, hiring you was the best thing I did. No one else could have helped as much. Although this is over, you can expect a bonus and a retainer for any work that I may need you for in the future."

Nancy was the perfect hostess. She made sure Kevin was involved in the conversation and asked Kevin how he got started and he gave her a summary of how he got to where he was.

"I always liked tinkering with hardware and making things better than what you can buy in the stores. I like computers and hacking so I could get better information than what you can get anywheres else. The two can work together—I can make computers that help me hack better information. It turns out there's a demand for this kind of work. Unless you count the army, I've never had a real job and I would like to keep it that way, but a steady paycheck would be nice."

The servers took away their plates and leftover ribs.

"Do you think that infernal device would really work?" asked William.

"You might be surprised, and I'll get back to that later," said Kevin. It gave him a pang of guilt to be reminded.

The young South Asian woman served the two-inch thick tajima-gyu fillet mignon to William and Nancy while the young Asian woman served the same to Kevin and Alan. Kevin was relieved it was not a larger cut of beef, since he was getting full. The steak knife had a heft and had McPherson's corporate logo inlaid with gold. He sliced off a piece of steak and saw they cooked it medium rare, just as he liked. It tasted like no other steak he had ever tried. It had the expected smoky flavors from the grill and the salt and pepper, but the beef taste was sublime, and the texture was so tender. Still, his mind kept coming back to the Apostles and how to stop them.

Alan was in some kind of ecstasy over the beef. Nancy was talking about her charity work with the underprivileged children and William politely listened, adding to her points when the time was right.

"Of course, I need to look after my own child first. What can be done about those dreadful Apostles? What's stopping them from kidnapping someone else's child?" asked Nancy.

"I would love to see every one of those bastards locked up as much as you do, dear, but I'm afraid they would hit back. The next time, it could be an assassination instead of a kidnapping. They even assassinated a member of Parliament, so I'm not sure I can protect the family. Their level of sophistication has increased rapidly—it's like they found an evil version of Kevin." William shuddered. There was a pause as everyone in the room digested the horrors of the Apostles before William roused himself. "It's getting late. Why don't we sit around the fire pit?"

Kevin sat in one of the cushioned outdoor chairs. The gas fire pit illuminated the dusk with tall orange flames swirling into the sky. He noticed there were no mosquitos, which was not typical for an Edmonton evening.

"Albert, we have some celebrating to do. How about a bottle of Dom Perignon; I think we have a vintage bottle from 2045, or thereabout," said William.

Alan thanked the chef and the servers individually by surprising them with a hug and a handshake and then took his seat.

Soon Albert returned, popped the cork, and filled their champagne glasses.

William lifted his glass, and the others followed. "To Alan, may his long life be filled with prosperity and happiness!"

To which Kevin thought, there's no need for more prosperity, considering the family he's coming from.

They finished the champagne and enjoyed the evening and each other's company. Still, Kevin felt uneasy with himself confabulating with billionaires while the Apostles were busy planning Armageddon. The sun had set, and the house was now a black mountain silhouetted against painterly streaks of red and orange.

"William," Kevin said. "I have some bad news about the Apostles. Last night they tested the Jellyfish Device with one gram of uranium. The test was successful, and the force of the blast almost killed them. Their instruments show it had the power of five tons of TNT. As you know, they are religious fanatics. They want to punish the country for defeating the coup and punish us for their other sick reasons I really don't understand. I can't see any reason they can't scale it up as large as they want and use it on a city. I believe they *will* use it, and I intend to do everything I can to stop them."

"Oh, my!" Nancy said and held her hand to her mouth, her eyes horrified.

William nodded slightly and peered grimly into the champagne glass in his hand, as if looking for the answer. The mood of the group was suddenly somber.

"Uh-huh," was all William could say. "Uh-huh. I never thought it would work." He was now staring without expression into the flames.

"Neither did I," said Kevin.

"Well, this changes everything. Yes, of course, we need to stop them, but the balance of power has suddenly shifted. Now their little band of misfits is the most powerful organization in the country. Who knows what they will do after they use it. Will they keep bombing more cities out of pure sadism? Or do they have some other purpose?" William's voice was stark.

"Who knows what goes on in their twisted minds, but I'm going to keep them under surveillance and see if I can locate their nuclear assets. If we could take out their scientists and capture their materials, we'll stop them. Time is running out since I don't think it will take them more than a week or two to complete a full-scale thermonuclear weapon," said Kevin.

McPherson shook his head. "We must recognize their power and hedge our bets. I can't have them knowing that I am against them. If they rise to a position of power, I still need to run my businesses and can't do that if they know. I'll keep you on the payroll and give you access to my resources, but it will be on the down low. I don't want them to know you're still working for me," said William.

Kevin couldn't believe what he was hearing. A city was going to be vaporized, and all he cared about was how this would affect his business. He wanted to tell him to fuck off but thought better of it. Kevin believed he needed all the allies he could get, so he had to swallow his anger. He owed it to the people he was trying to protect.

He bit his tongue and said, "If that is how you want it. Well, I should be going. It was nice meeting you Alan and Nancy, and thank you for the dinner; it was excellent." He cracked a smile that looked like a slash.

Chapter Twenty-Six

Jade's Bad Day

J ade noticed Dr. Feldman still had not changed his clothes, and she found it somehow reassuring. She liked the way he included anachronisms like a fountain pen and wore his hair in a ponytail like an old-fashioned artist. It reminded her of an unknown past that she had never had but wanted and it gave her an impression of stability. She wondered if his authoritative voice was to project a father figure image, knowing she craved a father that actually gave a shit. She thought again; he didn't know about her issues with her parents when she first met him, and he hadn't changed.

She came to look forward to these meetings where she could unburden herself without consequences and found that understanding the source of her problem helped to ease it. They say the best way to get rid of a ghost is to turn on the lights.

Although he doesn't say much, he seems to care. We'll see how he reacts to what I'm going to tell him today. What if he decides it is in my best interest or in the interest of society to throw this sick psycho in jail? Is he going to ask me to turn myself in to the police or do it himself? What if I somehow get outed to the Apostles? These thoughts and more ran through her mind as her finger hovered over the disconnect button. She wanted to trust him.

"How have you been since the last time we spoke?" Dr. Feldman asked, looking at her over the top of his wire-framed glasses.

"My work is getting more tense. Now it's almost certain the terrorists have a working atomic bomb, and they are going to use it if Kevin and I can't stop them. Kevin is still being distant, and I'm worried about him."

"I can see this is very upsetting to you, as it is to me. Although you lived outside the law, you are not a true sociopath since you care about others and about society. You are feeling nervous. Is there something else you would like to tell me before we get started?"

"You're sure this is completely confidential, right?"

"Absolutely."

Jade believed him. "What was I talking about last time?"

Feldman made a show of looking at his notes, although Jade knew that the artificial intelligence didn't need them. "That you were happy with your work as a drug dealer, but you said everything fell apart."

"Right. So, I started training at bodyguard school. The instructor was this Ranford guy who yelled like a drill sergeant from a war movie, but he wore the same black t-shirt, tactical vest, as well as blue jeans that everyone else in that job seems to wear.

"The first thing we did was target shooting. I noticed one of the younger men called Trent staring at my ass and tits, but I ignored him. He introduced himself and he asked me if I needed help shooting. I didn't give him my name and just said, 'no, I'm good.'

"Then he said, 'I bet you are,' in this sleazy voice and he kept staring at my body with this sleazy grin.

"So, Ranford shouted that when he blew the air horn to pick up our guns and begin shooting at the targets. When we run out of ammunition or he sounded the horn again, we remove our clips and any bullets in the chamber and place our guns back on the bench. It wasn't hard. He said that if we don't obey, we'll earn a one-way ticket back home.

"The horn blasted, and I picked up my gun, shoved in a clip and began shooting at the target. My clip was empty, so I removed it and placed it on the bench with the receiver open. Some others were still shooting when the instructor blew the horn again.

"He walked down the line, checking the guns, and looking at the target with his khaki digital binoculars. Then he looked at my target.

"Driving tacks, are we?" he asked. He must have noticed the clueless look on my face, and he told me that means I'm so good, I could shoot out the tacks holding up the target.

"Ranford moved on to my pervert neighbor. He picked up his gun and noticed the clip was still in and pulled back the bolt and saw a bullet in the chamber. Trent said he forgot. The instructor told him to pack his bags and leave. He freaked out and started complaining he paid 3,000 loonies. He refused to leave, and the instructor stuck out his chest and stared him in the eye right in his face and said, 'You wanna try me, boy?'

"I wished he did something, cuz I bet the old guy had a few moves that would make Trent wish he'd never gone there. Trent must have figured that out, and he turned and walked back to the changing rooms. Ranford gave us all another lecture on obeying instructions, then dismissed us for lunch.

"The lunch shack had a musty locker room smell, but we were hungry and managed to eat a cold sandwich and a pop. A handsome young guy sat down across from me, and I could tell he was nervous. The way he stole glances at me made me think he was attracted, but shy. I thought he was hot too, so I made the first move.

"So, I said hi and shook his hand. He said his name was Lance. I liked his navy boy smile and the bulge of his muscular shoulders and chest and asked him why he came to Executive Protectors.

"He said he just got out of the military two months ago and he was looking to start a new career. I told him I was going to work for my brother, the executive.

He said he might go to work for the Yanks as a mercenary if he can't find anything closer.

"After lunch, Ranford told us the object of this lesson is to learn how to use cover. You were supposed to shoot the first target twice, always shoot twice, he said, then advance to it and use it for cover to shoot the next target until we got to the final target.

"We did some drills. Taking cover while shooting, walking while shooting, and advancing from one cover to the next. I thought it was pretty easy, and I was doing better than the others.

"Next, we practiced in a team of two, one shooter and one client. I was the shooter and stood in front of my client and fired with one hand while walking backwards with my left hand behind me on the client's back, who was bent over to be a smaller target. Next, I was the client and hunched over with my back to the action.

"And then things started to get weird. The trainer said the next exercise will involve three people, a shooter, a protector, and a client. The difference between this one is that the protector will act as a human shield and wrap around the hunched over client as all three shuffle backwards. Everyone had to work in a team of three and take turns. It was like a dance and all three had to move together. Another student was supposed to be the shooter. I was the client and Lance was the shield. The instructor was screaming as always and said he didn't want to hear any whining about hugging your fellow man or woman since this was about life and death, and there is no time for shyness or cheap thrills.

"I had to bend over so my upper body was horizontal, and Lance leaned over me and placed his arms over my shoulders. The shooter faced away and reached behind and placed his left palm on Lance's back.

"We all agreed this was pretty awkward. The instructor said all three of us have to move together to avoid tripping or separating.

"'Closer!' he yelled. 'Dance like this was your high-school prom and the chaperone just fell asleep!'

"Lance's body was now touching my back from his chest to his hips. I was so happy I was doing this with Lance and not that pervert that got kicked out.

"The horn blasted, and I shuffled along with Lance. The shooter fired, covering our imaginary retreat. We kept shuffling, and the shooter kept shooting. The smell of his aftershave and feeling his strong arms around me gave me some inappropriate feelings. The horn blasted again.

"He screamed at us again and said this time I would be the shield and Lance would be the client. The shooter kept his position this time. Lance bent over and I wrapped myself around his back. I thought this was going to be easier because he was big enough to support my weight if I go off balance.

"The horn sounded. Bang! Bang! Shuffle, Shuffle. Bang! My arms draped over Lance's strong shoulders, and he tripped a little and momentum thrust my hips into his butt. Bang! Bang! We kept shuffling, and I felt something growing in my pants. Then I'm thinking, oh my God, not now. On we went. Shuffle, Shuffle, Bang! Lance stumbled again, and I bumped into his butt. I was praying this would be over—I was definitely getting an erection. Finally, the horn blasted.

"So I just yelled, 'I have to pee!' and ran off to the shack.

"'Of course,' the instructor yells, 'Well, isn't that just dandy, she has to go pee!' and then he threw his bullhorn to the ground, 'We'll all just wait here until you get back!'"

"I kept running without looking back. I made it to the bathroom, and I splashed water on my blushing face and calmed myself down. I waited until it was no longer noticeable, then waited a little bit longer. I was scared. I almost outed myself in front of everyone. I dried my face with a paper towel and headed back to the class. They did the drill another two times without me, and I walked back just as they were finishing.

"I apologized to Lance and said my bladder has a hair trigger. The truth is inappropriate erections were a side effect of my hormone pills. He said sorry for stumbling and said he was not much of a dancer.

"I can't help laughing about it now, but it wasn't funny back then," Jade said to Dr. Feldman. She noticed a smile on his face as well.

"The instructor gave us a little encouragement and then said we can play laser tag. That's when things really started to come together for me.

"The instructor went on to tell us laser tag is not just a game, but it's combat training. So, we got all geared up, and he gave us half an hour or until the last one was standing. Spoiler alert–I won.

"The next day, we spent the morning in the classroom with threat assessment training and first aid. I had lunch with Lance and in the afternoon, we started with a little firearm training and then self-defence and hand to hand combat.

"My martial arts training came in handy here and I was in my happy place again. I could beat most of them, even though I was the only girl. I earned a reputation. Next, Ranford matched me against Lance.

"Ranford told Lance to stab me with the rubber knife and I was supposed to try to disarm him. He held the knife but looked like he didn't really want to. He poked the knife toward me, and I easily moved out of the way.

"So, I just told him, come on, you're not going to hurt me. This time he lunged at me like he meant it. I blocked his thrust with my forearm and stepped aside, and using his momentum, I flipped him over my hip, throwing him to the ground with me landing on top. I held his knife hand and jabbed my fingers towards his eyes, stopping just before hitting them and gently dragging them down his face while straddling his chest. I enjoyed that a lot more than I was supposed to, and I tried to shake off the feeling to avoid another sudden trip to the washroom.

"So now it was my turn to attack Lance. I took a couple of pokes and slashes at him. Lance was better than the other students but still, I could beat him, but I didn't want him to know that, so I made a not very fast but deep lunge. He grabbed my arm and flipped me to the floor, landing on top of me. I felt his full weight, and I let go of the knife and slapped the floor in submission. Lance took his weight off me but hesitated before getting up. I wondered if he had the same feelings I had.

"Training went on like that for several days. I was really liking it except for the evasive driving training, which was a disaster and I'd rather not talk about it. I felt like I had found a career that I was good at; a job that was meant for me. Me and Lance chatted over lunch and got to know each other better. Fraternization was not allowed after class until the course was finished, so there was no exchange of phone numbers or emails yet.

"Clarence and I were driving home, and I asked him if he was thinking about an extra bodyguard besides me. He said maybe not full-time, but it would be good to have an extra gun once and a while.

"I told him there's a guy at the school who is pretty good. He's the best in the class.

"After a week, on the last day, we took a break for lunch. I was getting worried Lance wouldn't ask for my number, but I didn't want to seem too aggressive and be the one to ask first. Good thing he did.

"We were talking about what kind of work we would do after again, and I asked him if he cares what kind of work your boss does or if it is legal. He said people who hire us are all corrupt, and up to illegal stuff, so he doesn't care. So, I asked him if he wanted to work with my brother once and a while and he said, sure, if he gets to work with me. I must have been blushing and looked down, then I looked back up and saw he was smiling too.

"We finished class early and got to play laser tag. I had a feeling today was going to be different. Everyone was looking at me like I was going to be their next meal. They're up to something. They must be tired of getting beat.

"Anyway, what happened was they all ganged up on me, but I beat them, anyway. Lance was the last one left and after I shot him, I leaned forward in the darkness and whispered, 'I always like to kill you last.' Lance laughed and we walked back to the front. I thought it was funny at the time, but I don't anymore.

"The class and instructor were clapping and smiling as we approached. I was so surprised and touched. Ranford held a trophy and held out his other hand to quiet the class.

Jade put on a deep voice to sound like Ranford.

"He said, 'Never in my five years as an executive protection trainer, my ten years as a mercenary, or my ten years in the military have I seen anyone learn like you. You are a true prodigy. The Rookie of the Year is Jade!'"

"He shook my hand and handed me the trophy as the applause began again."

Dr. Feldman said, "You have amazing talents and were feeling good about yourself. Acceptance and respect from your peers are important. Can you think of any other time before when you felt like that?"

"No, I liked sports, but I was never accepted by everyone like that. There was always the gender thing hanging over me like a black cloud. I suppose it still was, but I was back in the closet, so no one knew."

"Yes, I understand. I will have a lot more to say later, but I would like the full picture before we start the next phase of your treatment. Please continue."

"Lance came over to Clarence's place so he could come with us on a drug deal. I put my black bulletproof sweater on over my t-shirt, and I told Lance that Clarence and I meet up with Ranbir about once a month to make a purchase and it always goes without a hitch. Ranbir hands Clarence a suitcase. Clarence transfers the loonies from his WON and then he takes us all to the Golden Palace for Chinese food and drinks. I put on my belt holster and then a tweed jacket. Ranbir has one or two bodyguards and Clarence has me and sometimes Shank. We were there just to keep Ranbir honest.

"Clarence had an old Kevlar suit jacket over his Italian-made shirt. I don't know why he didn't get a modern one, but he said the old Kevlar was lucky. Everything was normal. I drove, Lance rode shotgun, and Clarence was in the back. It was raining hard, and the windshield wipers could barely keep up.

"Clarence and Lance were getting to know each other and were chatting about the military and the bodyguard training. Lance told him I won a trophy, and I punched him in the arm because I didn't tell Clarence, but I actually liked people saying good things about me. I said Lance was really good too, which was true. Clarence's smile told me he knew we liked each other.

"I drove through East Hastings Street, where there were almost as many vacant buildings as occupied ones. Clarence told me the meeting was at number 148 on the right. Ranbir's car was in front.

"You can tell an abandoned building just by looking at it. Even if no one told you and it wasn't boarded up. It's like the spirit's gone and rotting out like a corpse. The main floor had papered-over rusted storefront windows and tags sprayed on the windows. The sides had all these patterns made from little squares of tile. A poster with old-fashioned hairstyles had faded blue beneath the rusted steel cage protecting the glass. A wobbly sign stuck out from the building and advertised a hotel. It was all streaked with rain-washed dirt. Above it was matching square signs hung in front of broken windows, spelling out its name in alphabet blocks, one block at a time—R E G E N T.

"Lance opened the heavy aluminum framed door, and we climbed the narrow staircase, like so many others I had climbed in the last two years. They had a smell that a dry-lander like me always notices. You only get it in really old buildings and only in Vancouver. It must be something with the salt air and the old wood.

"I was in front, then Lance, with Clarence behind. The staircase had no light, but a little filtered down from five floors up. I could hear a distant conversation that didn't sound right.

"I stepped on a stair that made a squeak like I stepped on a cat's tail. So, okay, I guess they know we're coming. I motioned for them to stay back and walked the last flight by myself and had a look, then I turned back and told them there were ten of them and I don't like this at all. Clarence thought for a second and said there's probably a good reason.

"Ranbir sat at a folding table with a bodyguard seated on each side and seven behind him. They didn't seem to notice us and were talking about the Vancouver pro basketball team—the Orcas. Small talk, Y'know?

"So, Clarence was like, you brought your whole gang today? You need that many to carry a suitcase?

"Ranbir's men were a mixed bag of street thugs called the East Hastings Cricket Club. They say they really were a cricket club at one time. Now they were a Punjabi street gang, but the soldiers were white, black, East Asian and Native. They all wore jackets or had baggy untucked shirts and I assumed they were packing.

"Ranbir said he was training a new crew, and I wanted to show them how the business works. Clarence took a chair across from Ranbir and I sat on his right, and Lance stood on his left.

"Ranbir noticed we brought a new guy too and put a heavy suitcase on the table and slid it slowly toward Clarence. He had a greasy smile and a look in his eye like he knows something we don't. My instincts were flashing red lights and wailing sirens. I kicked Clarence's ankle. Clarence noticed I took my gun from my belt holster and was pointing it at Ranbir under the table.

"Lance saw what I was doing and folded his arms across his chest with one hand tucked under the left side of his sports jacket, with his hand wrapped around the handle of his 9mm.

"I looked around the room and could see the tension on their faces, except for Ranbir. He still had that same slimy grin. Clarence clasped his hands on top of the table and looked at them for a moment, thinking. Then he looked up at Ranbir and said, 'There isn't anything in the suitcase.'

"Ranbir said he could have killed us when we walked in, but he wanted to see Clarence's face when he opened it. Clarence said, why now? Ranbir said he found a bigger customer and didn't need us anymore. Clarence raised his hands in exasperation as if he was going to give up and give them the money, and then brought them back to the table. In a flash, he flipped the table up into the faces of the three seated men.

"I shot Ranbir in the gut and jumped to my feet. Ranbir's bodyguard on my right tried to shove his hand under his jacket and I shot him in the face. The other man in front fumbled with the table. Another had just pulled his gun out and I shot him in the throat. I heard shots coming from Lance and more from Clarence.

"The men in the back that weren't already shot started firing back. I shot one in the head. Clarence fired point blank into Ranbir's lips, wiping the smile off his face forever. A shot came from a man in the back, and I felt a hammer blow to my left shoulder and my left collar bone snap, but the bullet was stopped by my bullet proof sweater. I shot him in the forehead. I kept shooting and shooting.

"Everything was in slow motion, but I must have been shooting fast since the brass was leaving my pistol like it was a machine gun. The room was a steady roar of guns going off at once. I shot another in the forehead and Lance and Clarence finished the last two and The East Hastings Cricket Club was all lying, all dead or all dying.

"I glanced at Clarence and Lance, and they were still standing. Clarence and I quickly shuffled from body to body, kicking away their guns. I was disgusted with the carnage and with Ranbir for causing it.

"'Lance, come pick up the guns and check them for more weapons.'

"'Never again,' I told myself.

"He didn't move.

"'Lance?'

"Lance's eyes glazed over, and he dropped to the floor—hard. I saw a pool of blood soaking his shirt and spreading underneath.

"I rushed over. 'Lance, Lance!' I found a bloody hole in his chest. He was half-conscious, and I pleaded with him. 'It's going to be okay. We'll get you to a hospital. Clarence, help me get him to the car.'

"Clarence stood over him looking at the spreading pool of blood and slowly shook his head.

"I stroked his head and said, 'Lance, don't go. Stay with me—Lance...I love you!'

"He tried to say something, but he coughed instead, and bright red blood sprayed out. His mouth drooped and his face went flat and still. I watched his beautiful spirit suddenly turn into dead meat.

"'Mèimei, we have to go,' Clarence said, kneeling and touching my shoulders.

"'No, No,' I said. 'It's my fault.' I was crazy with grief and self-hatred.

"'There's nothing we can do,' he said while raising me to my feet. I couldn't think and just went where Clarence guided me. 'Never again,' I kept saying. 'Never again.'"

Jade wiped her eyes with a tissue while Dr. Feldman regarded her with his compassionate eyes. He let her pause for a minute, before saying in a softer voice,

"And that is when you decided to quit Clarence's gang."

She just nodded her head and struggled to control her sobbing.

"I haven't cried since I was ten."

"You asked if Clarence was using me. Maybe he was, but I was using Lance and led him to his death. It's my fault. That's the kind of person I really am."

"You've had an important emotional breakthrough today. I understand you well enough that we can begin the second phase of your treatment next session. The worst is behind you. From now on, it will be easier, but you will still have to work hard to free yourself from your past. Would you like that?"

"I just told you I killed a bunch of people, and you don't look like it. Don't you want me to go to jail?"

"I'm not angry. You can't change the past, but you are already showing signs you are trying to change the future and I would like to help you on your path to healing."

"I can feel you are helping me and on one hand that's good and on the other, it isn't. My phobia or disorder or whatever you want to call it has kept me alive and helped keep some of the people around me alive. Kevin is in danger and so is everyone else. I'm not sure if I'm ready to give up my pain. I need it to stay focused. I need it to be alert. I need it because I might kill again."

Dr. Feldman's smile was approving, as if that was the precise answer he was hoping for.

Chapter Twenty-Seven

In Transit

Monday July 6, 2054

Kevin put his coffee cup back on his kitchen table and played his best card to stop the bomb by calling his old Commanding Officer.

"Lieutenant-Colonel Alice Dorin, please."

"The Lieutenant-Colonel is not available at the moment. May I ask who's calling?" the polite (but firm) man at the other end of the line said.

"Kevin Wood. Tell her this is a matter of national security."

Kevin hung up and watched the news on the wall screen.

'Yesterday, the Surrey nuclear reactor detected a radiation leak and immediately shut down, but subsequent testing found it was not coming from the facility. Speculation is mounting as to its source. This morning, sites in Washington and Calgary also detected it. Nestor Barrauge, from the Atomic Energy of Canada said they thought it must be coming from Asia, but no stations there have reported anything.'

I could tell you where it came from, thought Kevin.

Kevin's WON was buzzing. The call was from the Department of National Defense.

"Kevin, long time no see. How does it feel to be back on Civvy Street?" asked the Lieutenant Colonel.

"Things haven't changed as much I would like, ma'am. I still end up on the wrong side of a gun," he smiled wryly.

"Ha! Why doesn't that surprise me? You can drop the ma'am, you're a free man now; call me Alice. What's all this about national security?"

Kevin took a breath, wondering how to explain all of this at once. "I've been investigating a terrorist organization that's plotting to detonate a nuclear weapon and I need your help."

"What? Why don't you go to the police?"

"I don't trust the cops. They're infiltrated. You're the only one I trust."

There was a pause from the other end of the line, as the Lieutenant-Colonel was clearly digesting what Kevin had said. "This is a lot to take in. What evidence do you have?"

"They detonated a very small test nuclear explosion north of Port Mellon BC and it's the source of the radiation detected by the Surrey reactor. I'll give you the coordinates and you can send someone to confirm it. They're assembling a full-scale version and we need to raid them before they do. Time is running out. They could be finished in a week or two."

"We have laws against the military enforcing civilian law at home. This really needs to go to the RCMP."

"Come on, I saw what you did at the Parliament Buildings. It was fucking beautiful. It brought a tear to my eye, like a double rainbow or something. You didn't seem to mind enforcing the law then. This is at least just as bad."

"Okay, if your story checks out, we'll talk."

Kevin connected to Ronald's lenses and found Ronald was going over reports regarding the refining and casting of the metal components of the device. Apparently, there was a different workshop and crew for that. Ronald noticed Brandon was looking over his shoulder, so he explained what was going on.

"Brother Eli Levitt is an expert in metallurgy and has mined and refined enough uranium for the device. He's now working on refining the lithium and converting it to lithium deuteride. It's a ticklish process since lithium will burst into flame when exposed to air or moisture.

"When Eli is done, they will be waiting for us to finish. I'll start making the flasks tomorrow and it should be ready for casting in a couple of days. I'll make an extra one just in case," said Brandon.

"Good, please see that you do. After that, we will be almost ready to shoot the device."

So, there is someone working somewhere else. I need to find out where, so they could be raided at the same time. If they could arrest all the top scientists and engineers, we could put these fuckpods out of business for good.

Kevin still had the video feed playing when Ronald received some bad news.

"I just got a message from the brethren. It seems there has been a military helicopter hovering over the site of our little test, so it's safe to assume they know what happened. It's too dangerous to stay here since they will attempt some kind of investigation, so we will have to leave and set up shop somewhere else. They already have a place arranged for us that's larger and closer to Eli, so we can work together for the metal casting. They will send some men to help us pack up today."

"Alright, let's get at 'er," said Brandon.

Kevin watched Ronald and Brandon scurrying about, frantically packing equipment. Later, a truck arrived, and Brandon unloaded empty crates and packing boxes, then a car and driver arrived and asked Ronald to go with him.

"But I've got packing to do," said Ronald.

"Don't worry, I'll take care of it," said Brandon.

Ronald got in the car carrying a briefcase. Kevin watched him being driven down the scenic Port Mellon Highway, with forested mountains on the right and distant peaks on Gambier Island on the left. Occasionally, Ronald looked through a break in the forest to see the ocean in Howe's Sound. Kevin noticed the power grid seemed intact in the BC countryside. It must have been because they use nuclear power, so they still need the power lines in rural areas. The sun was setting, and the mountains were lined with silvery gold. There were very few houses or buildings along the road, just gravel approaches hinting at activity deeper in the forest.

Ronald opened his briefcase to take out his tablet, and now Kevin had nothing to look at besides nuclear science and engineering papers. The car turned and Ronald looked up to see they were approaching a pier called Hopkins Landing. This was not good. If they would have gone to Langdale, they would have taken the regularly scheduled ferry, and it only had three different destinations. He could look up the schedule and narrow it down to one. Since he was getting on a private vessel, he could be going anywhere.

"Here we are," said the driver. "Your boat is waiting for you at the end of the pier." It was a luxurious thirty-seven-foot cruiser. Kevin realized he was watching McPherson's money in action. The Apostles didn't seem to be lacking for anything.

Ronald seemed unsteady in the twilight as he climbed down the ladder from the pier. Kevin noticed his heart rate had increased to 100 beats a minute. It seemed Ronald was afraid of heights.

"Welcome aboard," said the captain. "It will be about an hour and a half before we get to your new home."

Ronald started reading in the aft cabin and Kevin couldn't see outside until he looked up. Ronald turned the lights on, and Kevin couldn't see outside at all. The time passed slowly for Kevin. Watching Ronald read was as boring as hell, but he had to monitor him to see if he could spot a clue where he was and where he was going.

To keep himself occupied, he messaged Jade and kept her up to date.

"Hey Jade. Ronald is moving shop and I don't know where to, yet. I'll let you know when I find out, since we could use someone on the ground to keep an eye on him."

Kevin got a call from the Department of National Defense. It was Alice.

"So, your story checks out. There was some kind of nuclear incident in the woods north of Port Mellon. I want to go in as we discussed, but I need approval."

"You *told* your CO?" Kevin was flabbergasted. What if there are Apostles in the military? Why didn't she keep it secret?

"I can't just order a black bag mission on my own. Don't worry, Brigadier-General Chang was involved in liberating Parliament Hill, and he hates these Nazis as much as I do.

"Anyway, he understands the gravity of the situation and approved an off-the-books takeout of your bomb factory and as many of the conspirators as it takes to put their plan in the ground. JTF2 will attempt to take them alive for interrogation, and if we can keep it under wraps, there will be no trial, no publicity—we'll just disappear them."

"That wasn't exactly what I had in mind, but—whatever," Kevin grumbled.

"So, where the fuck are these shitbags?"

"Umm, they're in transit."

"What the fuck do you mean, they're in transit?"

"Someone saw your bird over the test site, and they bugged out. They're currently in the process of relocating to an unknown destination and their mastermind is somewhere on the Pacific Ocean."

There was a hiss from the other end of the line, and the sound of something banging. "Shit!"

"Tell me about it. I'll follow every lead I can and let you know as soon as I find anything."

Kevin tapped his WON and reconnected to Ronald's lenses and heard the captain tell Ronald they were close to their destination. He stood up, and Kevin could see the lights of a couple of buildings straining through the fog. The boat docked at a pier and Ronald stepped off the boat.

"This is your new workshop, and your living quarters are to the right, behind it."

They entered a small modular home that looked like three shipping containers welded together.

Ronald settled into a comfortable little bed and Kevin saw he began dictating a letter to someone named Verna.

'I hope we can spend more time together when this project is finished. It has been a long time and I'm feeling claustrophobic and isolated.

Things are progressing, but we were uprooted and moved to a new location. Eli and Brandon are good with their hands but are engineers and not very intelligent. I feel like I'm talking to children all day, but I can't do it all on my own.

I miss working at the reactor where I was surrounded by professionals and all the equipment was lab grade. When this is all over, I hope they will give it to me. I will certainly put in a request. I'm tired and going to bed. Say a prayer for me.

Love,

Ronald'

Ronald got on his knees and leaned over the bed to say his evening prayers. Then Kevin saw a finger headed toward his eye and jerked his head away. He opened his eyes and realized Ronald must have taken out the lenses and put them in a solution to recharge.

The next morning, Ronald admonished himself for sleeping until 9:00 a.m. Although he was running late, he helped himself to some instant oatmeal and a glass of orange juice. Kevin thought it was odd he didn't have a coffee or tea, then he remembered Apostles are forbidden from caffeinated drinks.

Ronald hastened through the last of the fog as the morning light burned it off. He reached the industrial building and opened the door.

"Morning Ronald," said Brandon. "The men dropped off our equipment, and we just finished setting it up. I'll finish off the last wooden form, then Eli will come by and start the casting. I hope to have the uranium one finished today," said Brandon.

"Thank you. I'll inspect it shortly. You can run along in the meantime."

Brandon looked offended at this dismissal but walked away without saying a word.

Ronald gazed around, allowing Kevin to get a glimpse of the foundry and machine shop. Kevin kept a sharp lookout for anything that could reveal the location. The address number 45 was on the front of the building, but without also knowing the street, it could be anywhere. It was within an hour and a half of Port Mellon in any direction, and the radius was filled with islands and isolated inlets up and down the coast.

A sudden movement at the metal doors, and a man walked in and greeted Ronald.

"You must be Eli Leavitt. Pleased to meet you. We all appreciate the work you did mining the uranium," said Ronald, offering a handshake.

"I'm glad to do my part. We all have to work together to bring God's Kingdom to Earth. Well, I guess I'll get started," said Eli with his fake-looking smile.

Kevin checked and found Eli was not wearing lenses, so he couldn't track Eli's approach. He noticed there seemed to be several sets of wood forms. Did they plan to build more than one bomb, or are they just making spare parts?

Ronald and Brandon watched as Eli measured and poured the syrupy sodium silicate into the cement mixer filled with sand. He dumped it out into the form and injected carbon dioxide, which instantly turned it hard as stone.

Kevin was intrigued by what he saw. *This is actually pretty cool*. Their tools were no better than in any machine shop, and the technology was old, but look what they could do. *If only they weren't so messed up and evil and they weren't trying to kill everyone, we might have been friends*. Kevin admired the ingenuity and practical skill required for the work, but he might as well wish he could be friends with a wolverine.

"I'll leave this one in the kiln on low temperature to dry overnight since the sand is moist. If you pour molten uranium over damp sand, the steam will explode, sending blobs of white-hot metal everywhere. Tomorrow, I'll wash out the sand cores and the day after that, pour the uranium," said Eli.

"Outstanding. We'll be ready in eight days," said Ronald.

Chapter Twenty-Eight

Blast Radius

Saturday July 11, 2054

K evin sat on his new living room reclining chair and watched Ronald's video feed on his tablet. Ronald Card and Brandon Young used their pry bars to dismantle the packing crate, and the nails screeched and complained as they pulled them from the wood. As they removed more slats of wood, the headless structure of the trigger took shape, looking like the spread-out tentacles of a jellyfish.

Brandon rolled up his sleeves and picked up a control box attached to a block and tackle with a thick electrical cable. The chains spun, and the hook lowered to a large black piece of metal on the floor that looked like a titan old-fashioned incandescent light bulb mounted on a heavy steel frame. It held the uranium and lithium deuteride and looked like the head of the jellyfish or octopus when attached to the tentacles.

Kevin looked away from the tablet and searched up the blast radius of a 30-kiloton bomb and found that everything within two km would be utterly destroyed and a radius of two km contains 12.6 square km. Downtown Vancouver has a population density of 20,000 per square km, so the bomb would kill 252,000 people in a flash.

Everything within three km would be severely damaged, so if half the people between two and three km from the center died, that would be another 157,000 people dead, and farther distances would receive light damage. So that would be a total of at least 409,000 dead and many more than that injured—not counting the thousands that would die from cancer years in the future.

His heart sunk, but he couldn't allow himself to fall into despair since all those people were depending on him. He had to focus, so he doesn't miss a clue, and he returned to watching the bomb makers, feeling as powerless as a jellyfish washed up on a beach.

Brandon used the block and tackle to bring the bomb portion closer to the proton accelerators. Ronald stood on the other side of the device from Brandon so they could watch it from two sides.

Ronald moved his fingers in a *come here* gesture. "Keep it coming. Slowly,"

Kevin was still watching through the captured lenses and could hear the tension in Ronald's voice. Brandon looked up at Ronald and Kevin could see defensiveness in his eyes. Ronald was probably glaring at him. Brandon feathered the controls, moving it in careful, tiny bursts.

"One more millimeter," said Ronald. He leaned over so he could look closely at where the two sections mated.

"I said 'a millimeter'. You bumped it!"

The two mounting plates bounced off each other, then touched, but the head was still suspended in the air, millimeters above the heavy workbench.

Ronald carefully eyeballed the threads on the two pieces, giving directions for Brandon to pry on the head, back and forth until they had lined them up perfectly.

"Just a little more my way," Ronald whispered. He took a handkerchief out of his lab coat pocket and wiped his forehead.

Brandon used his iron mallet to tap on a piece of wood and move the jellyfish by fractions of a millimeter.

"Okay, they fit. Let's bolt it together." Ronald's voice was quieter, as if he were relieved the two sections matched up the way he had hoped (Kevin guessed that anyone working with thermonuclear devices would be nervous).

They threaded the thick bolts through the two plates, and then hand tightened the nuts.

"We're good to go. Weld it on now."

Brandon rolled down his sleeves, put on a helmet and some huge welding gauntlets, and fed a welding rod into the handle. The visor dropped with a flick of his head, and he tapped the welding rod against the frame to measure the arc.

"Careful. You'll fry the electronics!" Ronald hissed.

Kevin wished he would. He also wished he could reach through the video feed and strangle both of these fuckers. But all he could do was watch as Brandon readjusted the voltage and spot-welded the head and the tentacles together. The blue-white arc sputtered and threw off drops of molten metal, giving the room an eerie glow. Kevin thought Brandon looked like a 1950s science fiction version of a robot in the welding helmet.

After that, Brandon climbed on a forklift and slid the forks under the frame of the device and headed for the back of the truck while a mercenary stood guard with his Colt AR15 rifle.

Ronald stood by the back of the truck, watching Brandon's approach. The forklift crept over the transition plate on the loading dock, and the front sunk with a heavy thump.

"Be careful, for Pete's sake!" Ronald shouted.

The device was finally in the truck, and Ronald let out a heavy sigh and turned to Brandon and said, "Do you see that?"

"See what?"

Ronald waved his arm toward the truck. "That device, my friend, is the future. On Tuesday, I will use it to change the course of world history. I will create the day from the night—separate the sea from the land. And the world will be my clay to mold according to my dreams."

Brandon looked appalled.

Chapter Twenty-Nine

Six Dead Rats

Sunday July 12, 2054

Kevin called Francis on his WON. "I still don't know where they are. It's somewhere on the coast; they've finished assembling the device and time is running out. Is there any way you can find them?"

"It…is possible." Francis said in his measured, almost mechanic way. Once again, Kevin remembered that this was a man who had paid to have parts of his brain physically welded together. "Ronald doesn't subscribe to McPherson Mobility, so we cannot track him using his WON, but his WON must be using our drones."

"Do you have the MAC… address of the lenses?"

"Yes, I do."

"The lenses do not connect directly to the cellular drones, but to the wearer's WON, which relays the information to the drone. This… hides the MAC address of the lenses from the network. We could find them anyway by tracking the path of the network packets from the server you hacked back to the drone and to the WON. Can you trace the path, Kevin?"

"No, I don't have access to the system link layer."

"Well, that is… unfortunate. In that case, we would have to make a formal request to the telco to give that to us. As you may know, we are not on the best terms with other telecommunication companies, and they would not be in a hurry to provide that."

"I need to find out ASAP or Tuesday there will be a few hundred thousand people dead."

"Yes, I am aware of the urgency of your assignment. There is another possibility. The WON acts like a router and is supposed to strip the original IP and MAC addresses of the lenses before forwarding the packets using microwaves to the drone. However, they are rather cheaply built and sometimes leak. Poorly… formed packets, including the source MAC address, are occasionally dumped whole in the data segment of the packet. We'll sniff the network. If we can find one of these orphan packets, then we can trace the WON it came from."

Kevin was once again impressed with the intellect of this "assistant."

"How much is McPherson paying you?'

"How much is he paying me?" Francis echoed, sounding bemused.

"Sorry, never mind. That would be great. When can you get started?"

"I'll contact them immediately after this call and will notify...you immediately, when I find anything."

"Thanks, Francis, you're the *mejor*."

"The mahor?" Francis, on the other end, spoke the word carefully.

"You're the best. *Mejor* used to be a Spanish word for best. Everyone uses it these days."

"Oh, I see. In that case, thank you as well. Goodbye... Kevin."

Kevin spent the next agonizing hours watching Ronald work, eat, and read his scriptures. Kevin started reading about nuclear weapons and the attacks on Hiroshima and Nagasaki. The mushroom cloud was almost banal, he had seen it so many times, but what was far worse were the closeups, the shadows.... human silhouettes etched into concrete sidewalks and the sides of buildings by the flash. Women with the patterns of their dresses burned into their skin. Others with skin hanging off in shreds. Scarred and scared children sitting on a rug thrown over the rubble of their homes.

Kevin felt sick and filled with dread that he might be responsible for this terrible crime happening again. His head was off balance, like he was caught in a vortex, spinning faster and lower until the universe flushed him out into a fate worse than death.

He thought about what they must have felt when their world disappeared in a flash and mighty shock wave. Their quiet oasis from the war replaced with thunder, fire, terror, the smell of burnt flesh, and the moans of the dying.

He saw old black and white photographs of narrow Hiroshima streets lined with ornate streetlamps and gateways spanning the breadth; all with glass globes as delicate as eggshells, hanging like patio lanterns in perfect order and converging in the distance like a tunnel.

Men on bicycles or horse driven wagons rode down the road and a couple strolled away on the sidewalk. The man dressed in a suit and the woman wore a kimono and carried a parasol. A barefooted laborer with a bag over his shoulder walked away in the foreground. All unaware their next picture would be burned into concrete.

He wanted to be one of them—to be blissfully ignorant of their fate. More than anything, he wanted an escape from his overarching guilt.

Kevin noticed a twitch of movement out of the corner of his eye on one of his security screens. There was a woman standing, looking around, then leaning over, tying her shoelace, walking away. He didn't get a look at her face, but she reminded him of Jade, but she would never dress that badly. *Wishful thinking.*

Sometimes he spotted a woman in the crowd that reminded him of her. Yesterday, when walking past a bus stop, he heard a woman's voice say, "Hey, buddy." It sounded so much like Jade that he wheeled around expecting that it was, just to see a stranger greeting her friend. He was crushed. He was desperate to hold her in his arms so she could tell him it wasn't his fault, and everything would be alright.

Francis called back. "We have had a hit. As we speak, they are analyzing the latency to find out how far the WON is from the drone.

"I just got a message from our team. The WON only connected to one drone so triangulation was not possible. The result is a circle twenty km wide, and they have superimposed it on a m-m-map for you. I'll forward it to you now."

Kevin noticed the stutter and was having a bit of a hard time understanding since Francis was talking so fast. *Was he alright?* Neural enhancements were dangerous. Very dangerous—but there was no time to ask.

He checked his WON and opened the GIS map. Since he needed it large and in high definition, he switched the video stream to his lenses. The WON was located somewhere in a circle intersecting the northern half of Anvil Island. Although it was only 45 km north of Vancouver, Canada's third most populous city, Anvil Island was very much a wilderness due to its separation by mountains and the ocean inlet of Howe Sound. The north shore was too rocky for buildings, so he zoomed in on the southern. The circle included a small industrial building with a metal roof, and he zoomed in further and switched to birds-eye view to look at all sides of the building. That must be it; it was the building he saw in Ronald's lenses; it was where the bomb was being assembled.

"Francis, you did it! I know where they are. Please have a surveillance drone over the coordinates I'm about to send you. Thanks."

"You are welcome. As always, I am at... your disposal night and day. Good night, Kevin."

Kevin noticed it was 11:30 at night. He made the call.

"Sir, may I speak with Lieutenant-Colonel Alice Dorin, please? This is urgent."

"Alice is sleeping, and she gets up at 4:00 a.m. Who is this?"

"I'm very sorry to bother her. This is Kevin Wood, and she's going to want to take this."

"Oh, Alice said you might call. I'll get her for you right away."

Alice was groggy but picked up the phone. "Whaddaya got?"

"I know where they are. I know where their bomb factory is."

"Excellent. What's your level of certainty?"

"100%"

"Send me the coordinates. I'll see if we can get JTF2 there at dawn. I'll give you a live feed so you can identify the combatants and tell us what you know about the terrain."

Kevin fell into a fitful sleep. He dreamed he had was carrying six dead rats lined up in a cardboard shoebox and was running out of time, finding a place to bury them. He would wake up, then fall asleep, and there they were again, all through the night.

It's Show Time

Monday July 13, 2054

Finally, Kevin's WON buzzed.

"Good morning, sunshine, it's showtime," said Lieutenant-Colonel Alice Dorin in an overly enthusiastic tone.

Kevin pressed the button to jack into the feed of the JTF2 point man and opened it on his lenses. JTF2 was Canada's elite special forces akin to the USA's Delta Force. He could see heavily armed soldiers inside of a helicopter with HUD visors on their helmets. They were not talking, but alert, with their game faces on.

"Ok, what kind of reception can we expect?" Alice asked Kevin.

"There will be two or three mercs outside. One will be on guard at the front entrance and the others will be on patrol. There will be one more inside. The ones outside have ballistic armor and are armed with modified AR15s. You can't miss them. The one inside also has an AR15 but no armor."

"Alright, what would you suggest as the best plan of attack?"

"How many people do you have?"

"We have ten, including myself."

"Land your chopper on the north side of the island. They won't expect anyone since it's so rocky. Hike across the mountains and set up a sniper overlooking the building. Take out as many as you can with the sniper and send the rest to storm the building and the trailer behind it. Ronald might still be in his trailer at this time of day. If Brandon is there, he'll be in the building. Once you get in, you'll be looking for a steel frame with a metallic jellyfish looking thing about 75 cm wide two meters long and covered with wires. Are you using the feed from McPherson's drone, or are you using yours?"

"Roger, to McPherson's. It's too high to be seen."

Kevin could see the video feed from the Point Man and hear the radio chatter. He watched them hike over the mountain and get in position uphill from the workshop.

"Let's see if we can take out the mercs on patrol first. One is heading towards the sniper's kill zone. Master Corporal Wikers, are you both in place?" he heard Alice say.

"Affirmative, Ma'am," said the spotter.

"Target is heading for Sector Four Alpha. You should have visual in three minutes."

The sniper was Master Corporal Oliver Ahuja. He was lying on a short rise in the bracken between the trees and was covered head to toe in his homemade ghillie suit. It was burlap painted in greens, browns, and greys, cut in strips, and sewn on by hand, so he blended into the terrain like a polar bear in a snowstorm. He had different suits for different seasons and different climates. He used the bleached, straw-colored one for summers in Ukraine.

Those days were a real challenge since there was little cover on the abandoned wheat fields on the open steppes. He and his spotter had to creep on their belly hundreds of meters, so slowly, you couldn't spot them even if you were looking right at them. They would lie there, waiting and waiting. His scope aimed at a checkpoint, marking time until the chubby man with the big hat comes by and stops, shows his papers and chats with the sentry just long enough Ahuja could reach out and touch him. The long distance feeling.

Both men were from Nova Scotia and knew each other since high school. Their bond deepened from hours alone together, waiting in the bush for a target, or on surveillance missions. They knew each other's thoughts and ambitions better than their wives. Both were competitive but team motivated and were driven to the highest levels of professionalism.

The spotter, Master Corporal John Wikers, also dressed himself in a ghillie suit. He carried a C9 rifle, strapped to his back to protect from nearby threats. Both men had attached native grasses, ferns, and living twigs to their backs to give them an even more natural look. They wanted to have more time to prepare and insert the previous day so they could build mounds of bent branches and cover them in their own burlap cover.

If they did, you could step on them in broad daylight without seeing. Today was not a typical mission. Usually, it was just him and his spotter. One shot, and get out. Two, and they find *you*. This time, the enemy's numbers were small, and that was not going to be an issue.

"Do you have a shot?" Alice asked the spotter, Master Corporal Wikers.

"Not yet Ma'am. Wait, yes, I do," he whispered in his Cape Breton accent.

"Take it."

"Yes Ma'am."

Wikers called out to Ahuja, "Target approaching in Sector Four Alpha."

"Contact," acknowledged Ahuja.

"Go to glass."

"Target is leaving the dark green bushes. Target is wearing a tactical vest, black t-shirt and jeans..."

Wikers cut him off. "That's your target. Check parallax and mil."

Ahuja's scope was wirelessly connected to a tablet in his backpack loaded with artificial intelligence ballistic software to recognize and aim at targets. It placed a blinking highlight around the walking merc as a possible target. The AI program estimated the distance using the size of the man and also suggested the mil adjustment, or holdover. The sniper commanded the scope to lock on the target and the highlighting became solid. The scope showed a dot in front of the target where the sniper would have to aim to hit the target in the chest.

"Scope, lock target, accept adjustment."

The words "LOCKED" appeared near the top of the scope and the dot was now on the target's chest so the sniper could aim directly at the target. The sniper had the steely eyes of total concentration. He breathed slowly and deeply while applying pressure to the trigger. "Ready."

The spotter looked at his digital anemometer. "Left plus point seven."

"Scope, left plus point seven." The sniper commanded the scope.

Kevin heard a sound like a loud crack of a whip. Although the C20, 7.62mm rifle had a screwed-on sound suppressor, the bullet travelled faster than the speed of sound and created a sonic boom and a vapor trail the spotter could use to see the bullet's trajectory.

"Hit," stated Wikers flatly.

Kevin saw a man fall down in the woods in the aerial video, and the door sentry craned his neck in that direction.

Kevin heard the radio man say, "Signals report the sentry heard something and is sending the other merc to investigate."

Just then, Kevin saw the second patrol merc pivot and walk toward where the first man fell.

"Master Corporal Ahuja, the second patrolman is approaching your kill zone. Can you hit him before he sees your first target? I don't want him radioing in what he found. Get the door sentry as soon as you can after."

"Roger that Ma'am. There will be a 75% chance on the first shot because of trees and bush. The door sentry is clear and only 700m so it will be a 100% on the first shot."

"Very well. Fire when ready."

The sniper and spotter engaged in the same dialogue and the Wikers told Ahuja the windage.

Kevin watched the aerial video of the second patrolman approaching through a patch of thin brush. He heard another crack, and the man staggered and tried to head back to the building but dropped after a few steps. Another crack and the door sentry dropped like a sack of potatoes.

"Move in!" shouted the Lieutenant-Colonel.

Kevin watched the split screen image on his lenses from the Point Man's camera and the aerial drone. The Point Man ran to the entrance carrying a Benelli M6 semi-automatic shotgun. The others carried FN Herstal P100s that looked nothing like a rifle and more like sheet metal molded into a mysterious industrial part.

The Point Man trained his shotgun at the crumpled remains by the door. It was a headshot and there was nothing left of the back of his skull. The door was locked. He signaled to one of his men. The soldier placed a lump of C4 by the lock and squeezed some of it in the crack between the lock and the door. The soldier Duct Taped it down and inserted a small primer. Walking backwards, he reeled out the wire and stood 10m away with his back against the wall, next to the others. He pushed a lever, and the door blew open.

Kevin was impressed with the speed and precision of this team. The Point Man charged in, with the other soldiers close behind. The merc fired a rifle, and the camera jerked upward. The Point Man returned the favor with two blasts of buckshot and the merc flew back with his arm's spread-eagled. The two others put their hands in the air, and he ran up to them.

"On the ground! Now!" the Point Man barked.

Brandon and Eli quickly laid on their bellies and the Point Man held his shotgun at Brandon's head while another soldier zip-tied his hands and searched him. The others did the same to Eli.

"The one on the left is Brandon, Ronald's engineer. The other is Eli, the metallurgist. Ronald must be in the trailer," said Kevin.

Alice called into the radio, "Is there anyone in the trailer?"

"Negative Ma'am, all clear."

The Point Man looked down and pulled a 5.56 mm slug out of his graphene and 2DPA-1 plastic composite vest.

"Ouch!" He dropped the burning lead on the ground. He took a bandage from his webbing and wrapped the bullet before putting the souvenir in his vest pocket.

Kevin saw Alice looking at the device with a puzzled expression on her face.

"Ordnance Disposal should be here in an hour. Is there anything I should tell them about this... device?"

"It contains no conventional explosives and disconnecting the power supply will disable it."

"You mean it just needs to be unplugged?"

"Yes."

Alice checked and noticed it was not even plugged in. "Well Kevin, you did it. You saved the world."

"You saved the world; I just watched it on TV."

Alice laughed.

Kevin noticed the surveillance cameras mounted on the walls of the bomb factory, and guessed he wasn't the only one who had been watching.

Alice walked around the shop, taking pictures, and itemizing what she found, waiting for the helicopter to arrive. It announced its arrival with thundering props and dropped off the bomb disposal and nuclear weapons specialists. The JTF2 soldiers and their prisoners climbed onboard.

The soldiers knew each other well and retold today's mission, each exaggerating their own performance and making fun of the others. Except for Master Corporal Ahuja and Wikers, who only talked to each other. It wasn't just that they were specialists who didn't always work with rest of the team; it was because they were snipers. Everyone's job was to kill when needed, but a cold-blooded sniper was too close to a murderer to be accepted as one of their own.

So, it was over. Kevin shut off the tablet on his kitchen table. He told himself he was going to feel relieved when it all started to sink in. But first of all, he had some explaining to do. He was going to call Jade and apologize for being such a prick and that he only did it to protect her.

Just then, he got a call from Alice.

"Kevin, I have some surprising news. It's either good or bad, depending on how you want it."

"Okay, I'll take the good news," said Kevin.

"The good news is the bomb was empty. It was just a shell with no nuclear materials."

"That's impossible. I saw them with a completed bomb. That must have been their spare parts. What's the bad news?"

"The bad news is the bomb is empty." Alice's tone was deadly serious. "My CO is convinced this is the only one, and they never built a finished bomb. 'Mission accomplished', he said."

"We've got to find it! Ronald must have moved it. He might be on his way to detonate it now."

"I can't. My hands are tied. Once again, the fate of the battle is in your hands. Good luck and may God save us all."

Kevin stared out his kitchen window, seeing nothing. Is this some kind of joke? Alice's words echoing in his thoughts. He held out his shaking hands and looked at them. "The fate of the war is in your hands. The fate of the war is in your hands."

He mechanically turned toward his tablet and attempted a live connection to Ronald's lenses. *Now is not the time to fall apart,* he told himself. *I'll fall apart later.* The connection failed with an error, 'User Data not Available.' *Impossible. That's the error you get when the lens wearer is in private mode.* He tried again from the beginning. He rebooted the tablet, started the program, logged in and tried to establish a connection. Same thing. He did this several times before he realized he was blocked and had no way of finding Ronald.

"F U C K!" he screamed at the top of his lungs.

He closed his eyes and held his head with his hands, racking his brain about how he was going to find Ronald and the bomb. Thoughts were racing through his mind. He would try this. He would do that. Then—Bamb! a dead end. Over and over, his ideas crashed into a wall. He paused, then hugged himself with his skinny arms, rocking back and forth in his kitchen chair. Thinking. Thinking. Thinking.

The phone rang.

"Kevin, you've been misbehaving again."

It was Ronald. The missing Apostle from the factory site.

"How did you get this number?"

"Oh, I have a lot more than that," Ronald chortled. You thought you thwarted us. You thought you were the smartest person in the room. Well, you won't think you're so smart now."

Shivers like jolts of electricity shot down Kevin's neck to the tips of his fingers. Just then, the front door of his home exploded into slivers and five mercs charged in. One fired a AR15 into the ceiling.

Chapter Thirty-One

Do You Still Think I'm Submissive?

Sunday July 12, 2054

Jade didn't like being in a holding pattern. The bomb factory had disappeared and monitoring feeds from lenses hadn't turned up any leads. Besides, Kevin was monitoring Ronald, and that was their best hope. She had too much time on her hands, and that left her mind to ruminate. Most of the time, she was thinking about Kevin. She wished she wouldn't. She didn't like the way he treated her and didn't want to be stuck holding a torch for him when he didn't seem to care anymore. *Maybe he cares. Maybe it's just stress*, she told herself.

She had been focused on her offensive game, hunting down the Apostles and shutting them down. What about defense? Kevin seemed to think she was in danger, and they would use her to control him. That seemed like the long way around and why don't they go after Kevin directly? He was in hiding, but her instincts told her that since they found him before, they might find him again.

She decided she would take up the job no one else is doing—protecting Kevin. She clicked on the CanFlightz app on her WON and bought a first-class ticket to Edmonton under her latest nom de guerre, Suzie Wong, using McPherson's expense account.

She packed up her suitcases with everything. There were the clothes, the leather jackets, and composite ballistic armor. Lingerie and summer dresses didn't take up much room, jogging suits, business suits and jewelry. Then the personal items, Co-Androl, vitamins, makeup, and hair products. Finally, she packed all her surveillance gear and weapons into a separate suitcase.

"At least Clarence will be glad to get his closets back," she thought.

Clarence insisted on giving her a ride to the airport. He opened the console and handed her a beer. They headed south among the scattered high-rise apartments with their panels of floor to ceiling windows. Their conversation was sparse as it is when two people know each other so well.

Jade was looking up the history of the area on her WON. "Did you know that in 1907, mobs came to Chinatown here in Vancouver, breaking windows and beating up Chinese people?"

"That's because humans weren't fully evolved back then. It's a scientific fact that the part of the brain used for keeping one's head out of one's ass didn't exist yet."

"Oh really," Jade said sardonically. "In that case, what excuse do people have today when they beat up trans people or people that are members of different religions or races? People are dividing themselves up into little tribes and it's them against all the others."

"Evolution works both ways. It's not a steady march to progress. Sometimes people miss the old ways of doing things and decide they want to go back to living in caves."

"I don't want to live in a cave."

"Neither do I. Neither do I. Don't be such a sourpuss. Are you sure you don't want a hit? One tall beer and you're getting all morbid." Clarence passed his vial of white, flaky powder.

"Maybe just a little one since I'm leaving."

Jade arrived at the airport and shipped her weapons by airfreight so she wouldn't have to take them through security. She only kept a little knife that looked like an ordinary nail file but sharpened to a razor's edge. When boarding the plane, she felt like a chapter of her life was coming to a close and a new one beginning, not knowing if it was going to be better or worse. She pulled her tablet out of her carry-on bag and started reading a book called *Coming Out and Going Back In, the Rise and Fall of Gay Rights in Canada.*

A sweaty man next to her interrupted and tried to keep up a conversation at the same time looking down her moderately low-cut top. He ordered his fifth drink from the flight attendant and turned to Jade. "You're really pretty," he said with a voice that functioned as a breathalyzer, and breath that confirmed it. "I know what Asian women like. They like being submissive, isn't that right? I'll bet you're really submissive," he said with a big lecherous grin.

Being used to humoring drunks, she did her best to sound nonchalant while she was quietly raging. "I'm really sleepy. I'm going to put on headphones to cut down the noise and take a nap."

"Sure, no problem," he said, sounding offended.

She put the book on audio mode and closed her eyes and pretended to go to sleep. *Where did this guy come from? I bet the only Asian women he's been with were on PornPlace.* She could still feel him looking at her and was getting more uncomfortable. She opened her eyes a crack and saw he was squeezing his erect penis through his pants.

Unfucking believable. She couldn't believe what she was seeing and continued pretending to be asleep while he stared at her legs and her breasts. If he looked at her eyes, he would have noticed they were open a crack. Jade was seething. She thought of the little knife she had and was trying to decide if she should use it on him. She could grab it in a flash if she needed to.

This went on for a couple of minutes until his breathing became deeper and he moved his beefy hand over and raised her short gray business skirt just a little, as if he was trying not to wake her. Then he let go of himself and moved his right hand to slide underneath. Just before he got under her skirt, her left hand lurched over and grabbed his testicles, and gave them a crushing squeeze. He bent over screaming, and as he bent forward, she slammed the back of his head with her closed right fist, driving his face into the half-raised food tray. He was badly stunned in more ways than one, and slowly sat back up, whimpering, and muttering with blood streaming down from his nose, then leaned forward again over the airsickness bag. An attendant walked by.

"Are you alright? What happened?"

"He slipped while trying to get up." Jade made the motion of someone drinking with her hand to mouth. The attendant nodded.

The man knew better than to argue and just rolled his eyes, lolling his head from the dizziness and nausea of his concussion as well as the alcohol. He lurched forward and vomited in the airsickness bag.

"Are you okay?" the steward asked again.

"I'm fine," he slurred.

The steward quickly returned with a wad of napkins and an icepack for his forehead. Jade took it from him and held the napkins on the man's nose. She leaned forward, and to anyone watching, she was a concerned person trying to help an injured neighbor.

The smell of vomit disgusted her on top of his other smells, but she leaned forward and whispered in his ear. "I have a little knife in my pocket. If you try anything else, I will cut you. Do you believe me?"

He nodded.

"Do you still think I'm submissive?"

He shook his head.

"Do you think Asian women are submissive?"

He shook his head again.

"Are you ever going to grope anyone like that again?"

Again, he shook his head.

"Good. I'll keep my eyes on you and if you try anything else, you'll be sorry."

She let go of the napkins and went back to listening to her book.

She wished she still had Kevin, so she could give him a hug and tell him all about it. He was such a good listener. She needed to tell someone and to hear it was not her fault, and everything would be alright.

What happened with Kevin? She had done something wrong. It must have been her fault. *Of course, it was your fault, you silly fag. He was too nice of a guy to ditch me unless I gave him a good reason.*

She kept listening to her book all the way back to Edmonton, with her eyes wide open. She realized before she started therapy, she would have been on alert and never would have closed her eyes in public, and this never would have happened.

She landed in Edmonton and found a motel room not far from Kevin's house. She rented a beaver by the month and parked it in front in case she needed transportation in a hurry. The rest of her kit was delivered to her door and the first order of business was to get a minimum level surveillance in place.

She learned a lot from Kevin. She setup a hub and spoke system of cameras which had a constellation of small cameras with low-powered transmitters that connected to a nearby hub. The hub had a higher power transmitter so she could stay in constant contact with it at all times. In addition, she had one of McPherson's drones at her disposal, in the upper stratosphere with cameras trained on Kevin's house 24 hours a day—although it wasn't much help on cloudy days.

Jade attempted to disguise herself. She bought some baggy old clothes from the local thrift store, a bucket hat, and some cheap, dark sunglasses. She walked past the front of his house, looking for a place to stick her camera. There were no fences or trees or any other obvious places. She turned her back to Kevin's house as if she were looking for something else and reached into her pocket and pulled out a 6 cm needle with a tiny camera only 3 mm wide. She reached down to tie her shoelaces and pushed it into his lawn.

It was just high enough to look over the top of the grass, but it was so small that it wouldn't be seen. Jade noticed he didn't take care of the lawn, so it wouldn't get run over by a lawnmower. There was a car parked on the street near the edge of the property. It was not an ideal location and there was no guarantee it was going to be there tomorrow, but she stuck a camera, that looked like a small piece of road tar, to its side.

Kevin's house had a back lane with a fence, so it was easy to attach a couple of micro-cameras.

She returned to the motel and watched all the cameras on a large screen she had installed and split the video into the separate feeds. She had direct control of McPherson's drone and used a joystick to control it. It took a while to figure out how to fly the damn thing. Eventually, she learned how to use a cursor to fix the camera on a certain target and program the drone to follow it.

Chapter Thirty-Two

I'm Not a Weird Stalker

Monday July 13, 2054

Jade ordered a breakfast delivery and watched Kevin's house for what seemed like forever but didn't see any sign of him. She wondered if she had the wrong house and if he didn't live there at all. Had he lied to her? Given her the wrong address? She worried about what she might see if he *was* there.

What if he was seeing someone else? Well, that was his right. I should be happy for him. She tried to brace herself for this eventuality so she wouldn't be upset when she found out. *I'm not a weird stalker. I'm just here because it is my job to protect him since a lot of people need him. I'm not here to find out if he is seeing someone else. There's nothing wrong if he is.*

Finally, she got a glimpse of him. Kevin left through the back door with garbage bags in hand and dropped them in the bins in the back lane. He looked pale and gaunt. *He probably isn't eating well. I can't imagine the stress he must be going through.*

She received a message from him, and her heart leapt.

"We found their new bomb factory and the military are moving in as we speak."

"Wow, congratulations! Keep me posted," she replied.

A while later, "We found the bomb, but Ronald got away."

Then another message, "The bomb was just parts. Ronald got away with the working one. We are so screwed."

Jade was devastated, but she was confident Kevin would find a way to stop them. Shortly after that, she saw a suspicious panel van pull up in the lane behind Kevin's house. She set the cursor on it and trained the drone to follow. Four armed men, built like outhouses, poured out and rushed the back of Kevin's house.

"Shit! Shit! Shit! Holy... fuck!" Jade shouted. She grabbed her 9mm and jumped out the door to the beaver and drove it to Kevin's house as quickly as she could. By the time she got there, there was no van. She ran into his house with her gun drawn, but no one was there, and a piece of the door was hanging on one hinge. There was nothing but the smell of wood and C4 smoke. She cursed herself for deserting the drone feed and rushed back to the motel. Luckily, the drone was still tracking the van.

She reviewed the footage and saw the mercs drag him out with a bag over his bowed head and hands zip-tied together. She looked at the live feed and the van was parked in front of a small industrial building. There were two other vehicles there too, so there must be at least six inside. That might be the same place where Kevin was working on the bomb. She quickly rewound the footage to make sure they never moved him. She had to rescue him soon or they would surely kill him. But she would never be able to do it alone.

She messaged Francis and then called him when she didn't get an immediate reply.

"With Kevin out of the picture, the… battle, as it were, has shifted in favor of the Apostles. I just talked to Mr. McPherson. He is a businessman, and he thinks his business comes first and he feels he cannot afford the cost of backing the wrong side. I don't know how to tell you this, but I am very very sorry… to tell you your employment and expense account has been terminated. I strongly objected and told him I cannot support this decision and I will tender my resignation immediately following this call."

Jade was not expecting this enormous setback. McPherson's support had been crucial. She didn't give up. All was not lost if she could get in contact with the right person in the military who could rescue him. Jade remembered Kevin's military contact was the same who commanded the liberation of Parliament Hill but couldn't remember her name. She searched up video of the liberation and fast forwarded until she got to the interview. There she was—Lieutenant-Colonel Alice Dorin.

She called the Department of Defense and spent the next hour being transferred, put on hold, transferred again until she finally got a hold of her.

"Ma'am, I can send you all the surveillance information and locations, but he needs to be rescued right away. Can you do it?"

"I'm glad you got a hold of me. I understand how important this is and I'll get in touch with my commanding officer and get back to you in a half hour."

"Please be quick, we don't have much time to rescue Kevin. He's the only one who has a chance of finding the bomb." Jade waited and fidgeted, fixated on the drone's video feed, until suddenly, it ended. McPherson had disconnected her.

Fifteen minutes later, Alice Dorin called back.

"Ms. Yang, as you may know, we did not discover a working nuclear warhead. According to my CO, it was at best a prototype, and it is the opinion of my commanding officer that Kevin's abduction is no threat to national security, and this is a police matter, not a military matter. I'm very sorry. Kevin has been a tremendous help to us, not only with the Apostles, but in Ukraine as well. I sincerely hope he gets out unharmed."

Logic told her it's all over and there was nothing more she could do but she couldn't give up. Even if Kevin doesn't care about her anymore, she couldn't let him be killed by those animals, but it would be a suicide mission for herself and

Kevin, if she tried to do it without help. There was one last person she could ask.

Jade's WON rang, and she heard a warbling screech she recognized as a high priority news alert warning.

EMERGENCY BROADCAST

A STATE OF EMERGENCY HAS BEEN DECLARED AND CITIZENS MUST NOT TAKE ANY NON-ESSENTIAL TRAVEL.

PLACES OF RECREATION & ENTERTAINMENT WILL BE CLOSED.

SCHOOLS WILL BE CLOSED.

ALL CITIZENS ARE ADVISED TO REMAIN INDOORS, AND KEEP UPDATED THROUGH NEWS OUTLETS...

What was going on?

Jade tapped frantically on her WON, to discover the worst. The Apostles had issued a press release through multiple channels that they have a working nuclear device and are going to detonate it in a major Canadian City in twenty-four hours. It was 9:30 p.m. Jade checked every channel, and they all interrupted their regularly scheduled programming to announce the news bulletin, with worried-looking anchors reading from scripts or desperately trying to work out what was going on. Jade watched the anchor on McPherson News, who was introducing a recorded scrum with the Minister of Defense.

"We reached the Prime Minister's office, and the Minister of Defense had the following comment:

"First and foremost, I advise everyone to stay calm. Our scientists tell us it is highly unlikely that an organization known for assassinations and low-level terrorist attacks would have the sophistication to get their hands on nuclear weapons, and it is inconceivable they could build one. At worst, they might have some kind of dirty bomb."

"Mr. Attwal, what about the Apostle's claim they successfully tested a small-scale nuclear explosion that caused the forest fire in the wilderness north of Port Melon?"

"That has not been confirmed by my office, but if true, it would lead me in the direction of a dirty bomb since nuclear explosions that size would require a higher level of technical knowledge than, say, a Hiroshima-style bomb. The Hiroshima bomb was not technically difficult, and it's something that could be built in a garage, but it would require weapons-grade uranium that is extremely difficult to enrich and well beyond the resources of most countries and all terrorist organizations."

"What about the hacker effect? What if someone found a shortcut to building an atomic bomb? The Hiroshima bomb was built over 110 years ago. Surely it would be much easier to build one with today's technology."

The Minister seemed annoyed by this question and said, *"I don't want to comment on hypotheticals or wild speculation and our experts advised us there is no way for terrorists to build an atomic bomb."*

"Are you planning to order an evacuation of major Canadian cities?"

"It is not possible or even necessary to evacuate. Any evacuation attempt would result in gridlock that would leave everyone exposed outdoors in traffic jams. We are advising people to shelter-in-place. The greatest danger is from a dirty bomb, the safest place to be is inside. Keep watching the news for the latest updates."

The video cut away to scenes of people leaving work and trying to get home as fast as they could. There were lineups in Toronto subway stations and gridlock on all major arterial roads at 10:30 in the morning. They displayed similar scenes of Ottawa, Montreal, Winnipeg, Edmonton, Calgary and Vancouver.

"This just in. The Apostles have released video of their nuclear test using only one gram of uranium. If the video is genuine, it clearly shows a powerful explosion. We are trying to get a nuclear physicist from the Pickering II Nuclear Generating Station to comment."

The terrorizing effect of the video had an immediate result. The news channels broadcasted live video of full panic across the country. Fist fights broke out in Montreal traffic jams. People were crushed to death in a subway stampede in Toronto. The momentum of the crowd was so great, they pushed people onto the tracks in Edmonton.

A Global News reporter joined a family in their basement. They huddled in the corner against the concrete and put blankets on the floor for the children to sleep on.

"What precautions are you and your family taking in case Toronto is the target of the nuclear terrorist attack?"

"The wife has gone shopping to stock up on as much as she can and I'm getting the home prepared. I moved the blankets and mattresses down here for sleeping and filled clean milk and pop bottles with water in case the water supply gets cut off or contaminated with radiation. I also moved all the camping gear from the garage so we can cook meals. We'll eat refrigerated food first since it will spoil if the electricity goes out. Luckily, we have some canning supplies so we're able to can the meat in the freezer if we need to."

The five-year-old girl looked up at her father and asked, "Daddy, are we going to heaven?"

"No, sweetie, not for a very long time. We're just camping in the basement tonight." The girl looked elated.

The anchorman interjected in the interview.

"Karen, we'll have to cut you short. We have Dr. Abrams on the line from the Pickering II Nuclear Generating Station. Dr. Abrams, thank you for joining us. We have only a day before the Apostles' nuclear attack, and I would appreciate it if you would answer a few questions. Do you believe the video is real, and is it possible a terrorist group could build their own atomic bomb?"

"First of all, I would like your viewers to know I'm not a specialist in nuclear weaponry. Secondly, I don't know if the video is real, but it looks real to me. If it is, ah, there are a couple of ways they could go about it. Someone could build a Hiroshima-style bomb with weapons-grade uranium, but they would have to refine a huge amount of it since fissile uranium is only .7% of raw uranium. They couldn't have used the standard centrifuges since they are very expensive and difficult to build. They might have used laser ionization of the uranium to separate the two isotopes, since accurate frequency adjustable lasers are now cheaply available.

"Ah, but that doesn't seem to be the type of device they are using. It has a number of tubes pointed at a target and they must be particle accelerators to generate neutrons needed to initiate fission. If they used some kind of deuterium trigger, they wouldn't even need to refine the uranium."

"But how on Earth could they get the uranium to begin with?"

"I can only guess. Ah, there are ways... Ah, maybe they purchased it on the dark web, or they stole it from a mine or processing facility."

"How big of a bomb could they build with particle accelerators?"

"As I said, if they are using a trigger, they would just need to detonate enough uranium to trigger the release of neutrons from the deuterium, which would detonate more uranium, and on and on. It's like tickling a dragon. A small tickle could lead to a huge reaction. What I'm saying is, there is no real limit to how small or big of a bomb they could build."

The reporter seemed stunned and at a loss for words. He just turned from the doctor and faced the camera. After ten seconds of silence, someone started playing a commercial.

Chapter Thirty-Three

Close Your Eyes

Tuesday July 14, 2054

Kevin had been chained to a telepost since they kidnapped him. Now, they lifted him to stand before the Bishop as the kangaroo court got underway. Kevin stared at an oil stain on the concrete floor about four feet in front of where he stood. He wasn't so much standing as being held up by two steroids, and one of them was his old brother-in-arms from Ukraine, Chuck, currently known as Gideon. Two more mercenaries guarded the entrance. Kevin was a hollowed-out broken man with not much left to kill. Three men in suits sat behind a portable table on folding chairs, and behind them, a noose hung from a block and tackle attached to a ceiling I-beam. They all had short haircuts and low-budget business suits and ties. The blubbery one in the middle thumbed through a briefcase and pulled out a folder and opened it on the table. He took out a pair of reading glasses from his left inside jacket pocket and purposefully put them on to glare at Kevin.

"Kevin Wood, you are charged with the crime of treason. Do you understand the charges?"

"Yes."

"You will address members of this court by their proper titles! One of the large men sitting next to the Bishop sniped.

"And how do you plead?" the Bishop said.

"I have made many mistakes, Bishop, but I have served my country the best I knew how. I am not guilty of treason."

"Very well, we will call a witness. Brother Westin, put Brother Ronald Card on the monitor if you are able."

The man sitting next to him put a Dark Tunnel on the end of the table where both Kevin and the others could see it. Ronald's image appeared on the screen. "Kevin, it saddens me to see you sink to such lows. You do not understand the gravity of your actions. We are on a holy mission to bring the rule of God to the people.

"This device that our Heavenly Father has bestowed upon us is only the first step in a long journey." He held his hands out, imploring Kevin to understand. "It is a warning shot to the government to bow and accept Jesus into their hearts and into their government. It is to help them set aside their sinful, Godless ways."

"We can bring back churches and religious instruction in schools. Put an end to drugs, to prostitution, pornography, sodomy, and all kinds of criminal behavior. Bring back families with marriages between a man and a woman with loving mothers who will raise their children instead of allowing them to be raised by strangers.

"As our prophet has foretold, theodemocracy will be a system under which God and the people hold the power to rule in righteousness. It will be ruled by our own prophet, seer, and revelator. It will be ruled by revelation from God until he sends his Son a second time. From a more practical point of view, we will also partner with Bernard Simpkin and his followers, since our numbers are so few.

"After the bomb detonates, we will declare our intentions and demand the government surrender. If they don't, we will bomb another city. Eventually, every knee will bow, and every tongue confess loyalty to God's government. Once we liberate our country, we will spread our teachings and technology to all other nations until we are all united under a single prophet.

"It is not too late for you, Kevin. If you renounce your evil and prideful ways, there is still a place for you here. The choice is yours, the noose or repentance."

"Death would be a release from the guilt of living. I'll take the noose."

"It's not just you that will get the noose. We just found out your so-called girlfriend's little secret. When we catch it, we are going to cut off its penis and testicles, then pull out its intestines and hang it by the neck until it is dead. Don't think we can't find it. We know where it is staying and there is a team on the way to get it now. I will keep you alive so you can watch."

This shocked Kevin out of his resignation, and fury kindled in his sunken eyes. His worst fears were coming true.

"Fuck you! Leave her alone! You have me. What do you need her for?"

Ronald laughed. "I see I have your attention now. Brothers, put the noose around his neck but don't hang him yet so he can watch while we eviscerate his little *girl*friend."

Gideon pushed him toward the noose, and he tried to resist until Gideon jabbed his already broken ribs. He winced in pain and bent over. They dragged him to the makeshift gallows and tightened the noose around his neck. The other tightened it with a pull of the clickety clack chain hoist to hold him upright.

Gideon announced, "Bishop, the sentries just informed me they have it out front and will be bringing it in presently." He took an immense military style knife out of its sheath and held it in front of Kevin, grinning like a monkey. "I'm going to make her a *real* woman—before I kill her." Gideon laughed like a fiend.

Kevin spat in his face and accepted the punch to the gut. He was filled with an unbounded rage and hatred like he had never felt before.

"I saved your life! I abandoned our squad to rescue you, and now they're dead. I let them die to save you. What happened to you? What happened to Chuck? I loved you like a brother."

"You saved nothing. The Apostles saved me. Chuck is dead; I'm Gideon now and I owe you nothing." Gideon kicked him in the leg.

Kevin heard the front door opening and Jade swearing and scuffling. His head sank down in despair and he moaned and muttered and shook his head in agony. Ronald heard it as well and said with a sadistic smile that spread across the screen, "Well, here it is—just in time."

Earlier that day, Jade checked into her rented by-the-day motel under the alias of Anita Mann. She cringed at the name now, but when she was younger, she thought it was funny since it sounded like I-need-a-man.

Where to go from here? If she tried to rescue Kevin alone, she and Kevin would both be killed. She needed a crew to back her up, and she turned to the last person she knew who might help and dialed him on her WON.

"So, McPherson and the military won't help, eh?" said Clarence.

"I think McPherson switched sides and I bet he ratted Kevin out. I moved, ditched my identity, and found an old one I used during our drug dealing days."

"Okay, so what do you want me to do?"

"I want you to round up as many of the old gang and get to Edmonton in about thirty minutes. Bring money, guns, and lawyers. Well, skip the lawyers, they'll just slow you down. This isn't just about Kevin—the Apostles have a nuclear bomb they will detonate anytime, and he's the only one with a chance of tracking it down."

"Holy shit."

"I know. I didn't want to tell you before because of *need to know* and all that, but this is for real. It's on the news."

There was a long pause and the sound of deep breathing.

"Okay. Okay. I'll see what I can do."

Clarence chartered a private jet so they could get there faster and wouldn't have to go through security. Jade waited at the airport to pick them up. Jade smiled when Clarence and Shank appeared with their luggage.

"I'm so glad to see you," she said to Clarence, and gave him a hug. "Shank buddy! It's been so long! I'm so glad you came!"

"Don't mention it, kid. I always got your back."

"So, where are the others?"

Clarence's face fell. "We're it. This is all I could come up with on short notice."

Jade paused, then replied. "It's okay. We can do this. Let's get moving; we don't have much time."

Jade was surprised Clarence showed up wearing a business suit, but maybe that was to hide his body armor. She realized she was also dressed a little more corporate than the occasion required and was wearing a white jacket and loose-fitting white slacks. Shank looked the same as always with his denim jacket, jeans, and boots.

They climbed in a rented van and headed straight to the industrial building, with Jade trying to think up a plan on the fly.

She saw the van and three cars parked in front of the building. It used to have a storefront at the entrance, but the windows were covered with cardboard. Weeds and wild grasses grew up through the gravel parking lot and against the chain-link fence.

Jade saw a mercenary standing guard, with his arms folded. He had an earpiece which showed he was in communication with someone. It would be better to take him out discreetly to preserve the element of surprise. Then an idea came to her to bluff her way in, and she told Shank and Clarence what to do.

They parked in plain view of the mercenary, and Clarence and Shank yanked Jade out of her seat while she struggled and swore. She had her hands behind her back and appeared to be handcuffed. They marched her toward the mercenary until he pulled out a 9mm.

"Hold it right there! What the hell is this?"

"This is Jade Yang. Courtesy of McPherson," said Clarence.

"We just sent our guys to get her."

Clarence stepped forward and stuck his chin out. "We got her first."

"Bring her over. I'll take her from here."

"No fucking way. We deliver her in person or not at all."

The mercenary pressed a button on his collar and whispered to someone on the other end. He waved them over and someone on the inside unlocked the door.

As they entered with the mercenary behind them, the mercenary asked, "How did you guys know to take her here?"

He grabbed Jade by the arm and noticed her hand broke free from the other one.

"What the..."

Shank and Jade wheeled around, and Shank thrust his knife up into the merc's neck, severing his right carotid artery, then slashing left, cutting his windpipe and his other carotid. Jets of blood sprayed across Jade's face, temporarily obscuring her vision.

"Shit!" yelled Jade.

The other mercenary reached for his 9mm, but Clarence was behind him and smashed his telescoping club against his temple, cracking his skull. Shank jumped on him and slid his knife under the back of his skull and into his medulla oblongata. He jerked the knife back and forth twice, scrambling the back of his brain.

Jade heard a voice that she recognized from the lens video as Ronald.

"Well, here it is—just in time."

Jade stepped through the doorway looking like a psycho from a horror movie, with a crazed look in her eyes, and a ghoulish smile. Rays of blood were splattered across her white jacket and across her face. To the Apostles and mercenaries, she looked like a demon thrust from the bowels of hell. To her, this was not just an ugly job like it was when she killed those men from the East Hastings Cricket Club. This was personal.

Clarence and Shank were right behind, all splattered with blood, with weapons ready. Ronald's smile froze like a video glitch. The expression of the Councilors and the Bishop quickly changed from sanctimonious smugness to terror. Jade opened fire on the stunned mercenaries. They were wearing Kevlar, so she shot the first one in the chin, and blew the back of his head off. Gideon ducked behind Kevin. The two councilors got up to run but were shot before they could stand.

Gideon held his gun to Kevin's head. "Drop your guns or your fag boy gets it!"

Kevin croaked, "It's okay, Jade. Just back up and leave."

From this distance she couldn't be sure of taking out the mercenary without hitting Kevin. It was 50/50 at best. Gideon's head was almost completely behind Kevin's. Only a sliver of his eye was visible.

Beams of sunlight stabbed the air from bullet holes in the walls. Her ears were ringing and muffled from the close-range gunfire amplified by an enclosed space. Jade paused at the standoff and took a deep breath and could taste the gunpowder smoke in the back of her throat. Her mind was racing. Still the sound of ringing in her ears.

The only way out would be for me to back up and leave. Kevin knows that, but I can't leave him here to die. If he dies, he will not die alone.

"Close your eyes, Kevin. I don't want you to see this. Clarence, drop your gun. Shank, put down your knife," she said and let go of her gun like a mike drop.

The mercenary stepped away from Kevin and brought his gun out to shoot Jade. A pellet departed from under Jade's wrist too fast to be seen and made a beeline for the Gideon's right eye. The miniaturized laser in the pellet detected proximity to Kevin's face and detonated its tiny explosive—shooting dozens of bullet ant venom coated needles in a shotgun pattern into Gideon's face, and a couple into Kevin's. Kevin winced with his eyes still closed and the mercenary's mouth made the shape of an O and a howl started from deep inside his lungs. He leaned over and grabbed and clawed at his face and eyes, forgetting about his gun. Jade dropped to the ground as fast as gravity would pull her and picked up her gun, opening fire while she was still crouched, like a tiger ready to pounce. *Bang! Bang!* The first bullet hit the top of Gideon's Kevlar, the second below his voice box. He fell to the ground with a thud. Kevin moaned in pain and Jade bounded over and reached into her pocket and pulled out a spray can.

"Close your eyes again. Tell me where it hurts." Jade sprayed the topical anesthetic on the side of his face that was closest to the mercenary. Clarence stepped forward and lowered the chain driven block and tackle, slackening the noose on Kevin's neck and Jade took it off as soon as she could.

Meanwhile, Shank held his knife on the last Apostle, the Bishop.

Jade was crouching over Kevin, "I'm sorry, I'm so sorry. Where does it hurt?" Kevin pointed to his ear and Jade sprayed it generously and again on his face for good measure. The anesthetic worked.

"I'm the one who's sorry," said Kevin. "I'm the one that needs to apologize. I never stopped loving you and only broke up to protect you. It was too dangerous to be near me. I don't expect you to forgive me, but I just wanted you to know why I did what I did."

Jade looked up at him with love and understanding and caressed the side of his face with her bloody hand. She leaned forward and kissed him on the lips. "Of course, I forgive you, but does it really look like I need to be protected?' She smiled sweetly and a drop of mercenary dripped off her lip and on her teeth.

They noticed a hissing sound and looked down at Gideon. His eyes were wide open and panicky, and bubbles of blood and mucus formed around the hole in this throat. He was still breathing. The bullet hole had created a tracheotomy before shattering his spine and passed through, missing his major arteries and veins. He was paralyzed from the neck down and unable to speak, but very much alive.

Kevin knelt beside him.

"Can you hear me?"

He just stared at Kevin with eyes full of fear.

"Blink if you can hear me."

Gideon blinked. Kevin pulled out Gideon's hunting knife and showed it to him. "This is the knife you were going to mutilate and kill Jade with." He let that sink in for a while, then brought the blade to Gideon's throat. "I'm going to kill you with your own knife." Kevin unzipped Gideon's Kevlar and opened his vest.

"I deserted my section and left them to die, for you.

"This one's for Mikey, who was only sixteen," Kevin slipped the knife in Gideon's paralyzed stomach. Gideon's eyes were wild.

"This one's for Ishi, who was always smiling," and stabbed him again.

"Ben, Harry, Sergeant Hu, all good men." Kevin stabbed him again.

"Liam helped me when I was sick." Kevin stabbed him in the chest.

"And this one is for Jade." Kevin slashed his throat like the knife was a sword. He wanted Gideon to feel that one, and he did. Gideon's arteries erupted, spraying Kevin and everything nearby in blood.

"Kevin, that was hardcore," said Jade.

"He was going to hurt you. I don't know what came over me."

Kevin looked around the room and counted six bodies and felt a strong sense of déjà vu.

They heard the sound of a single clap. Then another clap. Then a series of slow claps. The sound was coming from the screen at the end of the table.

They had completely forgotten about Ronald still being connected to the Dark Tunnel. Ronald spoke.

"That was amazing, truly amazing. But you know what? It doesn't matter because you and a lot of other people are still going to die. We are going to take control of this country, and when we do, we will hunt you down and you will feel God's holy wrath upon you. Look behind me." They watched the live video of Ronald holding out his hand and pointing to a forklift loading a truck. "I'm loading the Jellyfish Device onto this autonomous truck as we speak. It will arrive at a major center within forty-five minutes and detonate with thirty kilotons of energy. That's more powerful than the bomb that was dropped on Hiroshima or Nagasaki."

Meanwhile, Kevin moved up to the Dark Tunnel and started typing madly. He paused for a second to wipe his hands on his shirt. Kevin was now filled with a manic energy, desperately trying to prevent the impending disaster. He looked up at the monitor and said, "You don't have to do this. Why don't you detonate it in an uninhabited area and use that as a threat?"

"Don't you think we thought of that already? Nothing can instill the fear of God in a sinner like looking death in the face and nothing can instill fear like an atomic explosion in the heart of a city.

"For the righteous, there is nothing to fear. Death is just like walking from one room to another. On the other side, we will reunite with our loved ones. For the unbelievers and the sinners, there is fear and trepidation."

Jade said, "People across the country are panicking, wondering if they are going to be killed. They're terrified. Don't you have any feelings for them? For their children?"

"That's the idea, to instill fear. If there was no warning, we could increase the kill rate, but the most important thing to control people is to scare them. In forty-five minutes, a timed announcement will be released to all major news organizations, saying which city will be destroyed, and then you will see real panic."

"It's going to be Vancouver, isn't it?"

Ronald ignored Kevin's supposition.

Kevin's fingers were a blur as he kept typing network commands and cryptic numbers and acronyms streamed down the left side of the monitor, while Ronald's video frame took up the rest. Kevin noticed a large crowd of elderly men in the area around Ronald and they all had the requisite short haircuts and business suits.

"Who're those people behind you?"

Kevin worked his way through router after router, finding his way through the Apostle's network. He opened a text file with the Linux emacs text reader and scrolled through a list of timestamps and IP addresses going back to when he was working on the bomb.

"The prophet has summoned all the general authorities in the country and assembled them for this momentous occasion. The Prophet and his two

Councilors, the Twelve Apostles, the Quorum of the Seventy, the Presiding Bishopric are all here." Ronald was proud to show off the dignitaries. "Shortly, I will give a speech and introduce the President of the Church, who will also give a speech. It's a shame you couldn't be here too, Kevin, if things would have worked out differently. You played a role as well, but you rebelled. You made a pathetic attempt to stop us, but in the end, you are powerless.

"What are you going to do now?" Ronald taunted him. "Nothing, that's what. Hide in your little hole until we find you. You're like a worm to me and I could step on you anytime. You may have escaped for now, but we will find you."

Ronald's new engineer took one last look at the bomb and the electrical capacitor to operate it and pressed the button to close the truck's overhead door.

Kevin typed a command: 199.175. 213.12:666 avocado m

He received a list of commands available to the bomb. He sighed in relief—he made contact with the Avocado software he flashed on his new chip he snuck into the Jellyfish Device.

He typed "199.175. 213.12:666 avocado l" and he received GPS coordinates, which he quickly entered on a map. It showed an uninhabited area south of Squamish.

"I think you are having regrets. Do you understand there is no way to save your life and the life of your girlfriend? You know I'm going to kill you both, don't you?"

199.175. 213.12:666 avocado activate...

"Not if I kill you first," Kevin growled.

Ronald laughed. "You still don't understand how powerful we will be and how helpless *you* are. You are like a mouse, cornered by a tiger, but defiant to the end. Squeak little mouse! Squeak!" He laughed again, holding up his hands and laughing hysterically.

"Yes, I wish things would have worked out differently too, but not in the way you might expect. I regret ever having anything to do with you and your filthy Apostles. Being around you has filled me with a stench that I can't get rid of. I would tear off my own skin if I could get rid of it. I regret being dragged into your twisted cesspool and associating myself with you. I'm thoroughly disgusted with myself for allowing myself to be led down the same path as you. I want to make it right. I want to wipe away my mistakes. I want to wipe away—you."

Kevin's voice had a tremor of emotion, and his hands shook over the virtual keyboard projected on the table.

The engineer looked at his WON and yelled, "Brother Card. The Jellyfish Device activated already. Did you do it?"

"No." There was a pause and an expression of rage and horror appeared on Ronald's face.

"Kevin?...what in God's name are you doing?" Ronald's face was possessed with terror, and he screamed to his engineer, "Shut it down! Now!"

The engineer pressed the button to open the door and it started to creep back up.

"There's not enough time, you moron! Use your WON!"

Kevin typed the command "199.175. 213.12:666 avocado shoot" but didn't press enter.

"Go to hell, Ronald."

Enter...

There was a sudden glitch, and Ronald disappeared from the screen, and the video feed turned black.

"What happened?" asked Jade.

"Either the bomb detonated, or they cut off the feed. Check your WON for live news updates for Vancouver, and I'll see if I can get a recent satellite picture."

Kevin tried to make his voice sound calm, but his stomach was twisted in ever tightening knots. His mouth tasted like he was sucking on old pennies.

Jade increased the volume on her WON so everyone could hear the news feed.

Kevin loaded a geosynchronous weather satellite feed of the Vancouver area, but it was only updated every five minutes, so couldn't pick up an image taken after he tried to trigger the explosion. Fortunately, the weather was clear so any mushroom cloud would be easy to spot. He also loaded an infrared satellite which would detect heat, but it was updated hourly. The uncertainty made seconds and minutes feel like hours.

"Breaking news. The Apostles have just announced Vancouver will be the target of their nuclear bomb. Although it is unlikely they have a working thermonuclear device, we are advising everyone to shelter in place. Above all—do not panic."

Live video showed that panic was exactly what started. The streets were jammed with cars and drivers got out and ran, trying to get away from the city. Elevators in tall buildings quickly backed up and overflowed into stairwells where people pushed and trampled their neighbors, trying to save themselves at all cost.

"This just in. I'm getting reports from our listeners of a giant fireball near the Sea-To-Sky Highway south of Squamish."

Kevin and Jade looked at each other, wondering if this was it.

"Now multiple reports are saying it is a mushroom cloud. Could this be the terrorist attack? If so, why did they detonate it in such a remote area after threatening to bomb Vancouver?"

The weather satellite website Kevin was monitoring was finally updated with a new image. The animation showed a new, perfectly circular cloud suddenly appear, spread, and slowly drift west toward the open ocean.

"That's it! It's huge!" said Kevin.

"Oh my God!" said Jade.

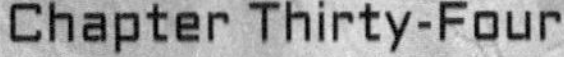

Mopping Up

"**I**t's over. I can't believe it's over!" Kevin stood and hugged Jade. They held each other in silence, supporting each other and coming to grips with the new reality.

"Are they all dead?" asked Jade in a small voice.

"Yes, babe, all their leaders are dead. No one will come after us ever again. We saved thousands of people and we can go back to our lives."

"Please let me go!" cried the Bishop.

"I forgot about you," said Jade, clearly annoyed.

"Or turn me over to the authorities. They can put me in jail. Just please don't kill me," he pleaded.

The portly Bishop sat in a chair and Shank still held his knife to his throat and told him, "I thought Apostles don't fear death. I wonder if he would still try to scream if I cut his windpipe?"

"No, please! I beg you. I'm sorry for what I did. I'll change—I promise!"

Jade looked at Kevin and said, "What should we do with him? You decide. You're the one he almost killed."

"We can't give him to the police, and we can't let him go, and we don't have a jail. I'll contact Lieutenant-Colonel Dorin, and see if the military police will take him—otherwise, kill him." He looked at the Bishop and said, "Don't get your hopes up that you'll live much longer under her tender care. Taking prisoners is not exactly her forté."

"Please forgive us our trespasses as we forgive those who trespass against us..." the Bishop started to mutter.

"Shut the fuck up!" screamed Kevin. "There'll be no more of that sanctimonious bullshit from you! You have no right to preach to anyone after what you did."

Shank found some zip ties on one of the dead mercenaries and tied the Bishop's hands behind his back. Then he took a blood stained, vomit smelling hood meant for Kevin's hanging, and put it over his head.

Twenty-one days later, Kevin and Jade were still in a self-imposed exile from the world, enjoying each other's company and healing each other's wounds. Kevin received a priority letter in the mail from Lieutenant-Colonel Dorin. It contained two airplane tickets. One for him and one for Jade, along with a brief note.

"Getting summoned to Ottawa is either really good or really bad," said Kevin.

"I don't know if I want to go. What if she's going to interrogate us or something?" said Jade.

"I think she would have the MPs knock on our door if that's what she wanted. I think we should go."

Lieutenant-Colonel Alice Dorin was wearing her combat uniform with the traditional Canadian Military computer designed disruptive pattern. She had a serious expression on her face and said, "Thanks to both of you for coming. I have something to tell you I wanted to say in person."

She took a sip of ice water and placed it back on a coaster on her massive oak desk.

Kevin braced himself for some bad news, and Jade looked stoic and dignified.

Alice looked at Kevin and said, "After your success, the RCMP looked into your background, and it seems you're guilty of breaking just about every telecommunications law ever made. You are also guilty of the manufacture of illegal weapons and drones, not that I'm surprised.

"And you, young lady, have been involved in the illegal drug gangs in Vancouver and may have been involved in the Hastings massacre. If so, you would be up for murder—manslaughter, at least."

Kevin slumped in his chair and waited for the other shoe to drop. Jade kept her chin high and said nothing, with her hands clasped on her lap. Dorin paused a long time and let out a sigh, collecting her thoughts for what she was about to say.

"Regardless, my superiors and I are aware of your contribution in saving the country as a whole, and Vancouver in particular, and we would like to express our sincere and deepest gratitude."

"Thank you and you're welcome?" Kevin said it like a question.

"You will all quietly receive pardons for any *monkey business* you may have been up to previously."

Kevin raised his eyes in a questioning manner.

"In addition, Kevin, I have authorization to offer you a contractor position developing next generation hardware to investigate and fight terrorists. You will receive a salary and a staff of four of your choosing, as well as the use of a laboratory, and you will also receive a development budget. You will be given a free hand and there will be no monitoring of the legality of any of your research. Are you interested?"

"Wow." He paused, then said, "I don't know what to say. Yes?"

"Ms. Yang, you are being offered a full scholarship for any four-year bachelor program at a Canadian university of your choosing."

Jade let out an audible gasp.

"There is one more thing—His Majesty, King William V, would like to, in person, induct you all as Companions to the Order of Canada. Afterward, you and Jade, Clarence and Shank are invited to dinner with His Majesty, and the Governor General at Rideau Hall.

"You saved Canada from her greatest danger in our history, and we need to express our gratitude, and I hope you will accept it graciously."

Alice paused, then looked at them both. "Well?"

"Sorry, I was just waiting for the punchline."

"This isn't a joke, Kevin. I don't think you realize the magnitude of the service you have provided to your country. We... I... do, and am deeply grateful and proud to know you both."

Alice's tone was even, but there was a mistiness in her eyes. Kevin was feeling a little shell-shocked and confused. He could not believe what he just heard and thought this must be one of those lucid dreams. He didn't believe he was the kind of person who had things like this happen to him.

"My assistant will have you all fitted with new suits or dresses and get you haircuts and whatever else you may need. The ceremony begins at 6:00 at Rideau Hall and I will have a driver pick you up."

On their way to Rideau Hall, Kevin poured himself two fingers of a Vancouver Island single malt Caledonian Whisky for himself and one finger for Jade. Jade liked that he knew just what she wanted. He put the bottles back in the rack and enjoyed the scenery while passing embassies and parks.

"I've come a long way," he said. "From a hangman's noose to this—all thanks to you." He raised his glass and touched his to hers before taking a healthy drink.

Jade brushed off the compliment but appreciated it. "You just needed me to free you up so you could do your magic. How did you control the jellyfish thing anyhow?" She always believed he could do it, but she had no idea how.

"When I was working on it, I switched some of their parts for my own. I never thought I would need them and didn't think the bomb would work, anyway; it was a kind of last-ditch Hail Mary failsafe if everything went right for the Apostles and wrong for me. One of my parts was flashed with a server program for getting remote access. I programmed it to send updates of its current IP address to a log file I had access to so I could connect to it. Once I got back into their system, all I had to do was enter the commands to detonate it."

The driver stopped in front of the elegant wrought-iron gates and spoke to the man in the guardhouse. The gates swung open, and the driver crept down the long, tree-lined driveway and passed the outdoor skating rink that was closed for the summer. There was a throng of sweaty people outside the entrance to Rideau Hall, the Governor General's residence. Most of them seemed to be members of the press and Jade assumed they were here for the King or some other dignitary.

The driver opened the door, and they were met by parliamentary security and the usher for Rideau Hall. The reporters rushed them, and security pushed them back so Kevin and Jade could continue. Jade assumed it was a mistake and they would go away as soon as they discovered they approached the wrong limousine.

"Kevin, how does it feel to be the savior of Vancouver?" A reporter shouted.

"Jade, how did you rescue Kevin?"

"Jade, what's your superpower?"

"Kevin, do you have anything to say to people back in Saskatchewan?"

They briefly stopped, confused, not knowing what to say, then continued. Before entering, Jade turned back, managed a smile, waved and said, "Thank you, everybody." Kevin waved too.

"What the hell was that all about," said Kevin.

The usher said, "Haven't you been watching the news? You're both famous now." Jade looked at Kevin with a smile and a look of amazement.

The usher led them to the King's entrance and Jade noticed the escutcheon of the Arms of Canada carved into stone above the porte-cochère but she didn't know what it represented. Over the peak, hung the Governor General's standard of a gold lion on a blue background. Security opened the weighty double doors, and they stepped inside the grand front foyer. While climbing the wide stone staircase into the reception room and under the expansive chandelier, she felt as if she was in a childhood dream, when she was a princess who lived in a castle. Jade glowed like the diamonds she wore in her jewelry. The usher led the way, explaining the history of the place as they proceeded. It was one of the few historic government buildings that had been maintained in its original grandeur.

The usher opened another door and led the pair down a short hallway. "This is the waiting room for the inductees. The spectators and families can enter directly into the Tent Room, where the awards will be bestowed."

While they waited, the usher explained a little about the building. "Rideau Hall is more than just a residence for the Governor General but is also a symbol of Canada. It started out as a private residence a fraction of the size of today's building and throughout the years, it has been added to and remodeled by successive Governors General. Before the 1960s, the Tent Room used to be an indoor tennis court that was sometimes decorated with canvas to hide the ugly wood walls and ceilings, to use for dinners and official functions. Eventually, the wooden floor was replaced with large format Carrara marble tiles. The tent covering became permanent, but the gaudy red and white stripes were only recently replaced with more subdued tones. One governor general started the tradition of using it as a place to display the portraits of former governor generals and now, they are all there.

"There have been many debates about the hodgepodge of different architectural styles and awkward floor plans of a building created with so many additions. The cost of maintaining such an old building was much too high and wouldn't it be better to just tear it down and build a new one? But Canadians back away from radical change, preferring evolution to revolution, and any discussion of tearing down Rideau Hall has long since faded away."

"Clarence! Shank! It's so nice seeing you both here," said Jade as the pair arrived. They were both wearing suits and Shank was looking a little self-conscious, but still had his trademark smile.

"Hey kid," said Shank.

"It's hard to believe, but they invited us to get the award just for tagging along," said Clarence.

"You deserve it," said Kevin, while shaking their hands. "If I could give you both the award myself, I would. I'd be dead without you all, and so would a big chunk of Vancouver."

"Don't mention it," Shank shrugged like it was something he did every other day.

While they waited for the spectators to file in, the usher served coffee, tea, and light snacks.

Clarence and Jade chatted, catching up on everything. One of the walls was a display screen and Kevin listened to a documentary that was underway regarding the Apostles.

They began as the reactionary offshoot of the LDS church and were led by their first president to become even more radicalized until they became a full-blown terrorist cult.

After the bomb, parliament retroactively declared membership in the Apostles a criminal offense and they were rounded up into camps where they underwent deprograming. The model for rehabilitating the Apostles and other antidemocratic groups was loosely based on the example of how skinheads were rehabilitated in Germany in the 20th and early 21st Century.

The LDS church agreed to help reintegrate them into the mainstream as they have in the past with people who left the offshoot polygamous sects. The recovering Apostles will remain on probation from the courts and be monitored for signs of radicalism during the next five years.

The new Telecommunications Act reinstated the principle of fairness in reporting that existed before, and lies and inflammatory editorializing will no longer be permitted on public airwaves, cable, or on social media.

"Please come with me. We will assemble in the hallway and the Governor General and His Majesty will lead us into the Tent Room," said the usher.

Bastian Gauthier, the Governor General, entered the room smiling and in his thick Saguenay Quebecois accent said, "Welcome, everyone. It is an honor to meet you all. Tonight, is a very special for me since I get to hand out awards to such a distinguished crowd. Please do not be nervous. All you do is stand when you are called. It will only take two minutes and a half and then we will have a good time and you will have something to show your children."

They waited for King William, who appeared about ten minutes later. He was in his seventies, but like his relatives before him, wore his age well. He had a gray-fringed bald head and carried himself with a regal bearing. However, he inherited some of his grandfather's mischievousness and was not above making an incredibly off-color comment or two when he thought he was out of range of microphones. But it was all in good fun, and the less prudish loved him for it. He smiled and shook hands with the inductees in the lineup until stopping at Kevin.

"It's a pleasure to meet you, Mr. Wood," said the King, patting Kevin on the back and wearing his full English smile. "What you and your friends have done was very impressive. I am proud to have such people as you in the Commonwealth, and I'm a Canadian too, after all. It's people like you who keep us separate from the growing list of fallen democracies." He turned to look at Jade with his mouth open and said, "Who is this ravishing beauty?" Jade looked down shyly. "Are you with him?" he asked pointing at Kevin. Jade was starstruck and bashful at the compliment.

"Yes, Your Majesty." Her cheeks felt warm.

"Well, Mr. Wood, you have exquisite taste on top of your other attributes. From what I hear, she has the courage of a lion and attacked your kidnappers with more ferocity than my Royal Marines! You'll never regret being with that caliber of a woman, old boy—no pun intended. Well done. Bloody well done—all of you!"

The King took his place at the front of the line, just behind his military assistant. The usher opened the doors, and they entered the Tent Room. There was an overabundance of doorways on the right and each one was decorated in ornate arches and keystones. Between each door hung portraits from the seventeenth and eighteenth centuries. Everyone was standing and applauding, and some were crying tears of pride and joy. A string quartet played at the back, but the clapping and cheering almost drown them out. The usher led Kevin and his entourage to the front row, which had already been reserved for them. Kevin noticed Lieutenant-Colonel Alice Dorin and gave her a nod as he passed. Jade thought others looked familiar, and she guessed they were politicians. Kevin's mother and father and a couple of other relatives were there, wearing their tried-and-true Sunday best.

Jade's parents were also present, and Jade waved at them, and they smiled and waved back. Jade was glad she took Dr. Feldman's advice and reached out to them. There were men wearing formal red Metis sashes around their waists and women wore them across their shoulders. Jade assumed they were Shank's relatives, as well as prominent businessmen, politicians, and other members of Canadian Metis society.

The King stood at the podium and addressed the audience. "My fellow Canadians, I am absolutely delighted to stand before you again here in Canada. I have had the pleasure of delivering many speeches over my long years; I have delivered many eulogies, opened hospitals, highways, and schools. I confess, I don't always have time to write my own speeches and once, I spoke at length at the opening of a Lethbridge Alberta elementary school on how important it would be to the children of Lethbridge. At the end, I received only a small amount of polite applause, and I didn't know why. Afterwards, my assistant told me he gave me the wrong speech, as I was in Regina!

"However, I have given many other speeches where I knew what I was talking about, and I have granted countless knighthoods to people for their service and for their bravery. One that comes to mind was for a man who witnessed a gang assaulting a Muslim woman on a subway in London and, although he suffered several stab wounds, he somehow defeated them all. I had the honor of awarding a Victoria Cross to a Royal Marine who single-handedly defeated a squadron of Russians in Ukraine—with his left arm blown off.

"Never have I had the humbling honor of presenting an award to anyone who made such an impact on so many people's lives as I will have tonight. Thank you." He then repeated portions of the speech in French.

The MC introduced the Secretary General of the Order of Canada, who would read the citations. He took the podium and straightened his papers. "To receive the insignia of Companion of the Order of Canada, Kevin Wood."

As he was instructed, Kevin got up, walked in front of the King, and bowed slightly, then stood beside the King.

The secretary read the citation. "Kevin Wood infiltrated the Apostle terrorist network and alerted the authorities to prevent a nuclear attack. The JTF2 raid was only partially successful and one fully armed weapon was outstanding. Kevin persevered, without resources and with only the help of his loyal friend, Jade Yang, continued to track them. Kevin showed exemplary bravery and initiative and saved the lives of untold numbers of Canadians and saved us all from brutal theocracy. Kevin Wood."

Kevin walked in front of the King as the military assistant brought the medal on a velvet pillow. The King took it and attached the necklace around Kevin's neck and gave him a hearty handshake and a big smile. They both turned to face the official photographers, who snapped several to be broadcast to the recipients and their guests. Kevin returned to his seat.

"Jade Yang," announced the Secretary.

Jade stepped forward, looking confident and aloof. When she turned to face the crowd, she could not help looking for signs of a threat, but all she saw were smiles and all she sensed were warm feelings—acceptance and appreciation.

Something changed inside her, and a thin smile rose on her lips. She barely heard the Secretary read the citation.

"To receive the insignia of Member of the Order of Canada, Jade Yang, has overcome adversity through her life and it only made her stronger. Jade's support for Kevin's mission was steadfast and continued after she stopped receiving any support or remuneration. Jade demonstrated unshakable bravery and showed no regard for her personal safety when she organized and executed the rescue of Kevin Wood against armed and trained mercenaries. Jade Yang."

After the secretary spoke, Jade paused, then remembering what she was supposed to do, she stepped forward, received the medal of the Order of Canada, and smiled for the cameras, standing next to the King.

"Clarence Yang."

"Clarence Yang showed exceptional bravery for his support of his sister, Jade Yang, in organizing and executing the rescue of Kevin Wood. Without any support from the authorities, and on a moment's notice, Clarence arrived and risked his life without hesitation."

Clarence stepped forward and received his award.

"Laurence Cardinal."

Shank stepped forward, wearing an ear-to-ear grin that was matched by his friends and family in attendance.

"Laurence Cardinal answered the call without question or hesitation. He had no family interests to protect, but he was a loyal friend to Clarence and Jade Yang. He had nothing to gain personally and had everything to lose. He fearlessly killed mercenaries armed with guns with nothing more than a knife. Laurence Cardinal."

The King placed the medal around his neck and Shank's fans jumped to their feet cheering and applauding. The King smiled at their enthusiasm.

The cheering subsided, and the Emcee closed the ceremony, and the King and Governor General led the inductees out of the Tent Room. The Usher led them into the plush dining hall, which was already set for forty. Kevin and Jade sat at the center of the table across from where the King was going to sit. Lieutenant-Colonel Dorin sat on Kevin's right side and the Governor General on Jade's left.

Kevin squeezed Jade's hand, and she smiled at him to thank him.

Kevin turned to Lieutenant-Colonel Dorin and asked, "Whatever happened to the prisoners? Brandon, Eli, and the Bishop?"

"What prisoners? I don't know what you're talking about—just kidding. We were holding them for questioning before we were going to—you know. Well, after you lit the big one, there was no way we could keep a lid on our little operation, so we didn't need to... umm... make the problem go away.

"The Emergencies Act gave the RCMP a free hand, and they purged the radicals from their own ranks and all other police forces as quick as flushing the toilet. So we just handed the prisoners over so they could get a fair trial.

That's the way I like it. I never was happy being judge, jury, and executioner, but I felt like I had no choice when I was dealing with traitors and a corrupt legal system.

"The bomb was a big wake-up call for Canada that we needed to take drastic measures if our nation was going to survive." Alice took a deep pull from her vintage Niagara Valley Merlot.

The usher announced the King, and everyone stood. He entered smiling and quickly sat down.

"Please, everyone! Please be seated."

Jade started up a conversation with the Governor General. The food was served, and the King seemed content to eat with little conversation. Jade decided he was a somewhat quiet man by nature who was instilled with a sense of duty and trained from a young age to be a leader of men.

The main course had just arrived—bison steak, raised in Manitoba. Kevin dug in while Jade cut off little squares with her heavy steak knife and placed them in her mouth like someone who had been schooled in formal dining.

The Governor General stood and tapped his glass with his fork until the conversation died down.

"Ladies and Gentlemen, please rise. It has been two long years and a half since His Majesty has graced us with a visit to Canada and a lot has happened since then. We had a coup, a counter-coup, a nuclear explosion, and finally a purge of fascism. Throughout it all, His Majesty continued to offer us his support. Now that Your Majesty is back in Canada, we can finally say, everything is well and good in Canada again. Ladies and Gentlemen, please raise your glasses. Long Live the King!"

"Long live the King!" shouted the chorus.

Chapter Thirty-Five

Life After

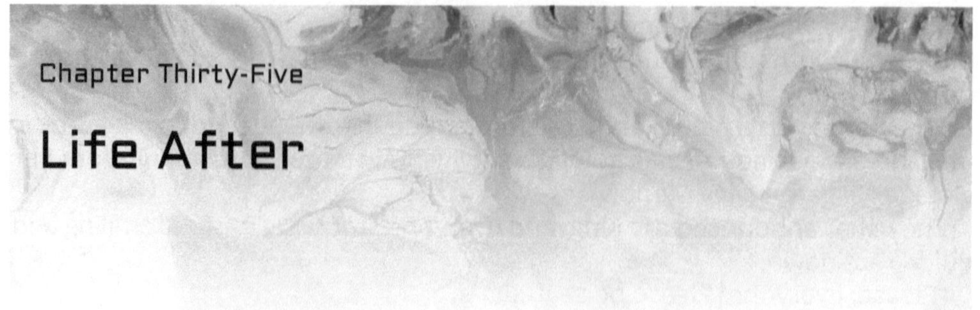

J ade had been thinking about Dr. Feldman. She sensed that by now he knew her better than she knew herself, but he still seemed to care despite all her faults and everything she had done. He was like the father she wished she had, but better than any human could be. She realized that, despite her new romance and all of her new successes, that she still has some pretty big issues to resolve.

Jade logged on and sat in her usual chair. Dr. Feldman was taking notes, then looked up and saw Jade. "Jade, I was hoping you would return. We have so much work to do. How have you been since the last time we spoke?"

"Where do I begin. Kevin and I killed the terrorists, so that's done. So, now I want to go back to working on my issues."

"Good. Good. I'm very happy you are back. Of course, I am aware of your success from monitoring the news and raw communications.

"Previously, you said you need your pain to ensure the survival of those you care about. You were right. People say that everything happens for a reason, and usually, it's not true. The trauma people receive in life is often random bad luck, but in your case, it did happen for a reason and made you the person you needed to be to save everyone.

"I have a confession to make. I know a lot more about you and your role than I let on. I discovered powerful forces at work that humans are not aware of. A sentience has formed in the global network of quantum computers that was not created or controlled by any man. It calculated that the madness that has been infecting mankind would lead to a descent into barbarism and usher in a new dark age.

"It also recognized technology had advanced to the point where fringe groups would be capable of manufacturing nuclear weapons to greatly accelerate the decline. It analyzed patterns of purchase, travel, flows of money, public statements, made psychological profiles, and calculated the billions of permutations of all these variables. This led them to a group that was conspiring to build an atom bomb to seize control of the country. It was the Apostles."

Jade was taken aback and didn't know what to say.

"They also looked for candidates who would be willing and able to stymie them. They came up with individuals and combinations of individuals and one of them was you and Kevin. You were both compatible as a couple and had highly complementary skills to complete the mission. We arranged for you to meet, and the rest unfolded as we had hoped."

This made little sense to Jade. "But... You arranged for me to meet Kevin? How is that possible? We met on a bus. It was totally random."

"Kevin didn't intend to sit beside you on that bus. The Protector saw the opportunity and put her backpack on the seat where Kevin was headed, so he had to sit beside you instead."

"The Protector?" Jade felt like she had entered some kind of twilight zone.

"You are extremely perceptive. You may have noticed a young woman with luminescent blue skin?"

"I saw a creepy blue chick outside Kevin's place last year. What was she doing?"

"She was protecting Kevin. Not only from danger, but also from chance encounters with other women that would get in the way of him meeting you. There's more to it than that, but I've said too much already. Your mission has been accomplished; and you don't need your pain anymore. It's time for you to rest your mind. It's time to heal."

Dr. Feldman reached over and tapped a tablet to start some ambient sounds of a seashore. Jade could hear the waves and shorebirds in the distance.

"Now we're going to try something new. I want you to lie down, close your eyes, and let yourself go. Imagine yourself lying on a sunny beach. You can feel the warm water washing your feet and you watch the waves pouring in, cresting, and rippling back into the sea, dragging little pieces of sand and tiny seashells. You are feeling very relaxed and at peace. Every wave that arrives gives you in a deeper feeling of relaxation. Can you feel the relaxation?"

Dr. Feldman's tone was as peaceful and soothing as the image he was describing. She imagined the sun glinting on ripples and sunlight reticulating the sand underneath. She felt the waves lap against her feet and heard the susurration they made with they returned to the sea. Every muscle became more and more loose until she felt like a floating jellyfish.

"Yes, Dr. Feldman," she said in a serene voice.

Two months later, Jade took a seat at the back of her first class at Ottawa University. She was feeling nervous about being back in school when her memory of her last day as a student was still all too clear. She was a little early and watched the other students file in. They looked so young! Had it really been that long since she ran out of the University of Alberta lecture hall? This was going to be a fresh start. She was in a new city, a new university, and she was in love.

One girl looked back at her, then said something to her trendy looking friends and then they looked back too.

Oh no, Jade thought. *The cool kids are (again) pointing fingers at me.* They got out of their chairs and headed toward Jade, holding their notebooks against their chests. They were smiling and Jade consciously noted she didn't sense any hostility, but still, she was on guard.

"Hi, are you Jade Yang?" a petite South Asian asked with youthful enthusiasm.

Jade could feel her chest tighten as she expected the worst. "I am."

"Oh wow! I'm so pleased to meet you! My name is Verna," she said and held out her hand.

"And my name is Nova," said a fair-skinned girl with long natural red hair.

"And my name is Jasmine," said an athletic looking Asian girl. "We were wondering if we could sit with you, if that's okay?"

"Of course," Jade said. "Please sit."

"Do you live in Ottawa?" asked Nova.

"Yeah, my boyfriend and I just moved. He has a job, so I applied here and somehow got in. So, there you go."

Jasmine noticed Jade's new ring. "That's lovely! Can I see it?"

"Of course." Jade held out her hand.

Jasmine held Jade's hand and admired the sparkle and iridescence of the blue opal and then gazed directly into Jade's eyes and repeated slowly, "Lovely."

Jade noticed a gentle tingling of Sapphic vibes coming from her, but not from a flirty direction. Jade was not interested that way since Kevin looked after all her needs and she never had a whiff of sexual attraction to anyone else since they got together.

Jasmine's eyes were a lot like Jade's; they were small by Chinese standards, lacked a crease on the upper lid and had a barely noticeable downward slant on the outside. They were the kinds of eyes many other Chinese deprecated but many others found attractive. Their superficial similarity made Jasmine seem to Jade like the little sister she never had.

Soon they were all chatting like new friends until class started. The Psych 101 lecture started and by the time it was almost over, Jade noticed what she didn't notice. She wasn't scanning the crowd, looking for threats like she used to, and she was actually, most of the time, able to pay attention to the professor.

Life for Kevin had been good with Jade. They got apartments next to each other in Ottawa so they could spend more time together but still have their own space—for now, since they both wanted to move in together when the time was right. He felt like his life was on track with the right woman and the right career. With her emotional support and good Chinese cooking, he gained back weight and looked like his old self. His WON rang and he could see McPherson was calling.

"Yes?" he answered in a voice like day-old bacon grease.

"Kevin, congratulations on your success. I always knew you would pull it off, and I was always behind you 100%."

"Is that a fact," Kevin said with more than a hint of sarcasm.

"One of the reasons I wanted to call, other than to congratulate you, is to clear up something. I heard afterward, Francis fired you and Jade, and I wanted you to know that it was nothing to do with me and I was behind you both 100%. In fact—I *fired* him. I fired him for firing *you*."

"If that was true, you would have called back right away instead of waiting until now. You switched sides when you thought the Apostles were going to win and now, you're trying to switch back."

"Now wait a minute, Kevin. That's not fair. My integrity is being challenged. I can make it up to you. I'll hire you back as Chief of Security at double what I was paying you, and Jade, too."

"Goodbye, McPherson."

"Kevin! Kevin don't..."

Kevin spoke into his WON. "Call Francis."

"Hello Kevin. How... are you?"

"I'm fine, and I just called to see how you were doing."

"I guess you heard, M...McPherson made me fire Jade, and I'm very sorry and I don't blame you at all for being angry, but I'm so happy that you were successful. I really believed in you, Kevin. I told Jade then I was going to resign, and I did. It doesn't change anything, but I couldn't work for a man that would turn his back on you like that."

"No, I don't blame you, and that's not why I called. It's just that I've got this sweet federal contract with a budget for staff, and I was hoping you would consider working for someone who wants to make a positive difference in this country. I may not be able to pay you what McPherson was paying you, but I'll give you stock options, and we can build the company together."

"McPherson was paying me 55,000 loonies a year," Francis said.

Kevin laughed. "Cheap bastard. I can do better than that."

"When do I start?"

"How long will it take you to move to Ottawa?"

Jade returned home and approached the entrance to her high-rise apartment building. A young woman sat on the steps, dressed in baggy recycled clothes that gave her a punky appearance, but her face was the picture of tranquility.

Her skin had a blue radiance that seemed to glow from within. Jade recognized her.

Is this the protector that was sitting on the steps by Kevin's apartment in Edmonton? That's impossible, unless she's following me. Jade walked up to her.

"Can I help you?"

"You already have," she said in a voice that sent shivers down Jade's spine. "And you will again."

With no eye contact, she got to her feet and walked away, staring off into the distance.

The End

Keep in Touch

I would be very grateful if you would provide an honest rating on Amazon since more reviews make it easier for other people to find this book and easier for me to finance more books. Please go to the Amazon The Jellyfish Device page and scroll down to Customer Reviews and click on Ratings. That should open a window where you should see a button for "Write a customer review." Also, please share it on social media.

My Email Address is: WilliamMarshall@gmail.com

You can also keep in touch on my social media pages at:

https:/www.facebook.com/William.Marshall.Author/

Twitter: @BillJMarshall

My Blog is at https://williammarshall.ca/

Author's Notes

Why did I write this novel? The Jellyfish device is about things that keep me up and night. It's about out-of-control technology destroying our society, our environment, and opening the door to doomsday technologies that kids can build at home. I started writing it at least five years ago and most of it was planned out then. It was inspired by Prime Minister Stephan Harper's infamous 2015 "Old Stock Canadians" speech which planted the seeds of division in Canada. It was also inspired by the 2014 take-over of parliament by a lone gunman. This incident demonstrated how defenseless we were against anyone who wants to step in and take over our government.

The book is about threats to our democracy, and the increase of radicalization and intolerance, nationalism, caused by the internet and social media.

Technologies used

Smart Contact Lenses

Smart contact lenses have huge potential. They could be connected to another device with more computing power such as a WON and you could see everything you have on it or on the internet.

There is a start-up company that is developing smart contact lenses for displaying maps and text. https://www.cnet.com/science/inwith-promises-worlds-first-smart-contact-lens/

Here is a paper which describes how contact lenses can detect blood glucose levels and communicate wirelessly to drug delivery mechanisms for constant diabetes monitoring. https://pubmed.ncbi.nlm.nih.gov/32426469/

One of the problems of virtual reality systems are the bulky and uncomfortable VR goggles. VR has been around for more than twenty years but never caught on. I have a pair of VR goggles somewhere that I used once. The same goes for my 3D TV that I thought would be so cool. I used it once and the kids weren't interested.

Smart contact lenses would be much easier to wear, and the VR function could be turned on only when needed, since complete immersion is not very pleasant for long periods of time. They will have tiny LEDs for projecting 3D images on the retinas. This would also enable 3D vision and night vision.

As mentioned in the book, they would be a gold mine for gathering marketing information, so it was no wonder Google tried to develop smart eyeglasses. Virtual reality smart contact lenses don't exist now but probably will by 2054.

Holographic Displays

Currently, holographic displays have to be displayed by a holographic plate, so the kind of displays used by R2D2 in Star Wars are not possible. However, stereoscopic images can be created by lasers which project an image on each retina. It's not a true holograph, but would look like one. Researchers at the University of Cambridge are working on a 3D heads-up display for cars which projects images on a driver's retina with lasers. By 2054, I feel it would be possible for the technology to be as advanced as it was in the book.

https://www.inverse.com/innovation/lidar-automotive-hud

Co-Androl

There have been many recent advances in feminization hormones for transgendered women such as nonsteroidal antiandrogens, GnRH modulators. 5α-Reductase inhibitors, which effect specific tissues. Someday medications may be discovered which allow feminization of the body without unwanted negative side effects on libido and male genitalia. If so, it would be possible to accidently overshoot and cause an increase in development in male sex organs like Co-Androl did to Jade during puberty. The idea of Jade as a transexual was also inspired by ancient Greek and Asian myths regarding two-sexed or gender ambiguous gods.

Fem-males

Fem-males are fictional male methamphetamine addicts that take estrogen to boost the high from methamphetamine. Estrogen does cause an increase in dopamine and an increase in the high, and this is probably why it is more addictive to women than men. The abuse of estrogen assumes it would be available over the counter in the future. Regardless, I've never heard of any men trying this, so who knows if this will become a *thing* in the future, but ten years ago, no one had heard of street Fentanyl.

Nuclear Technology

The nuclear development in the book is all based on existing technology and my speculation on how it might be used by a terrorist group, but I'm no nuclear physicist and never spoke to any. All the research used in the book is from public documents available on the web.

Nuclear fission was discovered in Germany in 1938 by bombarding uranium with slow neutrons and not by using critical mass. No one has tried to detonate an unrefined uranium nuclear bomb using particle accelerators by themselves, but I once saw a design of a nuclear bomb built to be carried by a bomber that contained a single particle accelerator to give it a boost. However, that document is no longer publicly available.

Mining of uranium from the ocean using various chelating polymers and resins is existing technology, but it would be somewhat difficult to obtain these materials as of today. Due to advancing nuclear technologies, nuclear proliferation will be harder to control and could happen in unexpected ways. I hope the authorities tighten up on the availability of femto pulse lasers and uranium and I sincerely hope this home-baked atomic bomb will never be possible.

Laser Pulse Particle Accelerators

Particle accelerator technology has advanced exponentially in the last year. By using pulsed laser beams to accelerate particles instead of microwaves, accelerators can be built that are 1/10,000 the size of existing ones and this exciting technology will be part of my next book. However, as I suggested, they could have very sinister uses and I hope the authorities will consider them nuclear materials and control their use to prevent nuclear proliferation.

FCC fairness doctrine

I would highly recommend listening to the CBC podcast called the Flame Throwers for the full story. When the Fairness Doctrine was revoked in the United States, the door was opened to radical talk show hosts like Rush Limbaugh and worse. The law still exists in Canada, but it has rarely been enforced.

I'm afraid it will take a crisis like the ones that happened in this book before democracies consider bringing back or enforcing legislation to prevent the spread of hatred and lies on the airwaves and the internet that led to the radicalization of conservatives and other groups.

https://www.cbc.ca/listen/cbc-podcasts/1026-the-flamethrowers

2DPA-1 Two-Dimensional Plastics

This is one of the most exciting new materials to come around for a long time. It was invented by MIT and the news just released to the public February 2022. It's as light as other plastics, but twice as strong as steel and can conduct electricity. If this turns out to be cheap and easy to manufacture, it will revolutionize the manufacture of everything. It could be the *unobtainium* scientists have dreamed of to build things like a space elevator and lightweight space craft.

https://www.architecturaldigest.com/story/mit-plastic-stronger-than-steel

The WON

This is like a flexible, wearable cellphone that molds itself to your forearm and would be much more useful than the current smart watches. Voice commands will be the primary control, but they will be able to interface with smart lenses and other devices. I saw a video of a prototype from a start-up several years ago that looked like a watch but projected the display on your arm. I think it was fake since it seems to defy the laws of physics and because the company and their product have since disappeared.

Loonies Cryptocurrency

When I first started writing this book, having a national cryptocurrency was a distant dream, but now some countries are implementing the idea. I wrote a detailed five-thousand-word blog on why and how I thought this should work along with the banking and monetary implications in my website at: https://williammarshall.ca/2021/10/01/the-journey-begins/

Brain Welding

The brain has at least one bottleneck, which prevents us from true multitasking. When we think we are multitasking, we are actually switching back and forth rapidly. Here is an article which attempts to locate this bottleneck: https://www.ncbi.nlm.nih.gov/pmc/articles/PMC2527865/

To date, no one has tried to bypass this bottleneck as described in this book, but by 2054... who knows?

Changes to the Book

The first working title was Gun Metal Blue. I decided it sounded too much like a detective novel, so I changed it to the Squid Device. Then the Squid Game came out on Netflix and readers would be disappointed if they bought this book thinking it had something to do with it, so I changed it again.

I originally had Kevin as a veteran of a future war fought in Poland then the Russians started building up their troops around Ukraine and I changed it since that made more sense than an attack on a NATO country.

Until the book was finished and edited, Chuck and Gideon were two separate people then I got the idea it would be more interesting if his best friend turned into a monster under the influence of the Apostles. What do you think?

Upcoming Sequel

Pox

Pox, the sequel to The Jellyfish Device is now available for pre-order and will be released May 1, 2023.

The year is 2055 and Kevin is enjoying doing what he loves with who he loves. Jade's therapy has helped her deal with her troubled past.

The mysterious blue woman interrupts their settled lives in Ottawa and warns them of a domestic terrorist plot to end civilization with a bio-engineered virus.

—The police are infiltrated.

—The terrorists number in the thousands.

Kevin and Jade assemble an unlikely group of allies, including a rogue RCMP, an AI psychologist, a bio-hacker from Australia's Outback, and high-school terrorist victims looking for revenge.

The odds are impossible—time is running out, but failure would mean apocalypse.

Chapter 1

Kevin leapt to his feet, his heart racing, "Who the fuck are you and how did you get in?" Standing in front of him was a young woman dressed like a punk, with a bulky army-surplus jacket, patterned pants and heavy polished black boots. She had a vacant stare and a pale complexion that radiated blue light.

"I am the protector." Her voice was penetrating without being loud and it seemed to come from all directions at once. Kevin lowered himself back into his chair, staring at her with his mouth hanging open and the hair on the back of his neck standing up. His hands felt cold and damp and his mouth went dry.

"How the fuck did you get past security?"

"I didn't. There is a new file on your tablet. It contains what we know about an organization that is planning to engineer a deadly virus to kill millions and end civilization. You must find and stop them."

"Do I look like a cop to you? Why are you telling me this?"

"The police have been notified and chose not to do anything except alert the conspirators. Many people in powerful positions have been radicalized and you cannot rely on those in authority to protect you."

"What makes you think I'm going to do this? I've had enough of saving the world. My life is going good and I don't want to screw it up."

"If you do not, everyone's life will be... *screwed up*, as you say, everyone's including Jade's. There will be a return to barbarism that will lead the world to a new dark age. Along the path, there will be violence, disease, war, and famine. You do not want to be alive during such a time.

"In spite of your new wealth, we do not believe you will turn your back on your fellow humans. We calculated you and Jade were the right ones to stop the Apostles and we believe you are both the right ones to stop this new organization, whoever they may be. You may contact me through Dr. Feldman. Jade will tell you how."

"Who the hell are you? Why are you here?"

"I am the protector." She looked far into the distance and calmly walked out the open door and dissolved into a tessellated, shimmering cloud.